Friedrich Nietzsche was born in 1844 in Röcken (Saxony), Germany. He studied classical philology at the universities of Bonn and Leipzig and in 1869 was appointed to the chair of classical philology at the University of Basel, Switzerland. Ill health led him to resign his professorship ten years later. His works include *The Birth of Tragedy, Beyond Good and Evil, On the Genealogy of Morals, The Case of Wagner, Twilight of the Idols, The Antichrist, Nietzsche contra Wagner* and *Ecce Homo*. *Thus Spake Zarathustra*, a work of philosophical fiction, was written in four parts and published in German between 1883 and 1885 as *Also sprach Zarathustra*. The work is incomplete, according to Nietzsche's original plan, but it is the first thorough statement of Nietzsche's mature philosophy and the masterpiece of his career. It received little attention during his lifetime, but its influence since his death has been considerable in the arts as well as philosophy. Nietzsche died in 1900.

Michael Hulse is a poet, translator and critic. He has won numerous awards for his poetry and his 2013 collection, *Half-Life*, was chosen as a Book of the Year in the *Australian Book Review*. He has translated many works from the German, including titles by Goethe, Rilke and W. G. Sebald. His translations have been shortlisted for every major translation award, including the PEN Translation Prize (US), the Aristeion Translation Prize and the Schlegel-Tieck Prize. A professor emeritus of Warwick University, he taught poetry and comparative literature there from 2002 until his retirement in 2020.

Joanna Kavenna is the author of several works of fiction and non-fiction including *The Ice Museum, Inglorious, The Birth of Love, A Field Guide to Reality* and *Zed*. Her short stories and essays have appeared in the *New Yorker*, the *LRB*, the *New Scientist*, the *Guardian* and the *New York Times*, amongst other publications. In 2008 she won the Orange Prize for New Writing, and in 2013 she was named as one of *Granta's* Best of Young British Novelists.

THUS SPAKE ZARATHUSTRA

A Book for All and None

–

Friedrich Nietzsche

Translated by
Michael Hulse

Introduction by
Joanna Kavenna

Notting Hill Editions

Published in 2022
by Notting Hill Editions Ltd
Mirefoot, Burneside, Kendal LA8 9AB

Series design by FLOK Design, Berlin, Germany
Cover design by Tom Etherington
Creative Advisor: Dennis PAPHITIS

Typeset by CB Editions, London
Printed and bound in the UK by Short Run Press Ltd

First published in German between 1883 and 1885 as *Also sprach Zarathustra*.

Translation copyright © 2022 by Michael Hulse
Introduction copyright © 2022 by Joanna Kavenna

A CIP record for this book is available from the British Library.

ISBN 978-1-910749-25-8

nottinghilleditions.com

Contents

JOANNA KAVENNA

– Introduction –

S ome years ago, Tom Kremer (the founder of Notting Hill
Editions) told me that he was going to commission a new translation of *Thus Spake Zarathustra*. He regarded it as the greatest work
of European literature. Tom was a truly extraordinary person. Born
in Transylvania, to a Hungarian-Jewish family, he survived the concentration camp of Bergen-Belsen. After the war, he lived in Israel,
South Africa and eventually the UK. He became a football coach, a
teacher, an inventor; he popularised the Rubik's Cube, wrote books,
set up his own publishing house. Tom was in his eighties when I first
met him but he was so robust and undaunted that it was genuinely a
surprise when he died in 2017.

Before he died, Tom commissioned Michael Hulse to be his
translator. This was an excellent idea because Hulse is such a distinguished poet as well as a renowned translator and critic. Readers may well know Hulse's work through his seminal translations of
W. G. Sebald, in which he brilliantly re-renders the elegiac atmosphere of the original German. He has also translated many other
authors, most notably Rilke and Goethe. The poetic atmosphere of
Thus Spake Zarathustra is also fundamental to the work. It's a wild
prose poem, a fantastical rhapsody. It was published between 1883
and 1885 in four parts. The subtitle is ironic: 'A Book for All and
None.' At the time, sales were poor and Nietzsche published the last
part at his own expense, having been dropped by his publisher.

Now, Nietzsche is a world-famous philosopher, though the met-
aphorical ambiguities of his style have often caused his work to be
misunderstood. He debunked the old religious and philosophical
traditions of binary thought – good/evil, God/devil. Despite this,
he has often been read in line with such binary traditions, as cat-
egorically one thing or another: good/evil, God/devil. He despised

monologic absolutes but his works were later appropriated by fascists in support of their own despicable monologic absolutes. He feared his work would one day be traduced yet he was opposed to clarity as a form of delusion. It is a further irony that any ostensibly factual claim about Nietzsche runs counter to his philosophical arguments against factual claims. His literary style is unbridled, provocative, contradictory, often humorous. He writes, possibly as a joke: 'I am no man. I am dynamite.' His work exceeds and explodes all traditional categories; it has also exploded across the world, influencing countless others including Georg Brandes, August Strindberg, Edvard Munch, W. B. Yeats, Martin Buber, Thomas Mann, André Gide, Sigmund Freud, Carl Jung, Rainer Maria Rilke, Karl Jaspers, Albert Camus, Jacques Derrida, Ralph Ellison, Allen Ginsberg, Gary Snyder, Luce Irigaray, Kelly Oliver, Marilyn Pearsall, Paul Tillich, Tamsin Lorraine and Maggie Nelson.

Nietzsche was born in 1844 in Röcken, Saxony, into a devout Lutheran family. His father was a pastor and died when Nietzsche was only four. After this, Nietzsche was raised by his mother and grandmother, along with his sister Elisabeth. At the age of twenty-five, he became a professor of classical philology at the University of Basel. He served as a medical orderly in the 1870 Franco-German War, and contracted diphtheria. He became friends with Wagner, wrote a highly Wagnerian book, *The Birth of Tragedy* (1872), but their friendship had cooled by the end of the 1870s. Around the same time, Nietzsche's poor health made it increasingly untenable for him to teach. In 1879, the University of Basel gave him a pension, and for the following decade he lived in Switzerland, Italy and France. He was constantly ill, partly blind and yet he wrote *Thus Spake Zarathustra* (1883–5), *Beyond Good and Evil* (1886) and *On the Geneaology of Morals* (1887). In 1888 he produced a final flurry of works including *Twilight of the Idols*, *The Antichrist* and *Ecce Homo*.

In 1889, Nietzsche broke down entirely. At the time, it was assumed that his madness was caused by syphilis, but there are other

theories including tumours and strokes. From Turin, he sent fren-
zied letters to his friends, signing off as Dionysus. In his last letter,
he wrote: 'I am just having all anti-Semites shot.' Finally he collapsed
in the street and was confined to an asylum; later his sister took him
under her care. He died, never having regained his sanity, in 1900.
After his death, *Thus Spake Zarathustra* became Nietzsche's
most famous work. By the First World War it was so popular that
every German soldier heading off to the trenches was given a copy,
to inspire them. This was an odd choice. Nietzsche wrote each part
swiftly; Part II was written in ten days. It contains many of the ideas
for which Nietzsche is most widely known: 'God is Dead,' eternal
recurrence, and the übermensch or superhuman. The protagonist,
Zarathustra, wanders through the world, encountering friends and
foes, trying to impart his ideas. People variously threaten, ignore or
worship him. The name is significant: Zarathustra is the pre-sixth
century BCE Iranian prophet regarded as the founder of the religion
of Zoroastrianism. The Greeks saw Zoroastrianism as the origin
point of the dualistic view of the world, in which reality is portioned
into opposites: God/devil, good/evil, soul/body, dark/light. In *Ecce
Homo*, Nietzsche explains 'what the name of Zarathustra precisely
meant in my mouth':

> Zarathustra was the first to see in the struggle between good and evil
> the essential wheel in the working of things. The translation of morality
> into the realm of metaphysics, as force, cause, end-in-itself, is his work.
> [Zarathustra] created this most portentous of all errors [...] he must be
> the first to expose it.

In *Thus Spake Zarathustra*, Nietzsche argues against all meta-
physical absolutes. Without God, they have no logic, because there is
no eternal referent: 'everlasting good and evil do not exist!' Equally
we should be suspicious of all absolute systems, not merely the
theological: we should not worship science without question, nor the
state, 'the coldest of all cold monsters.' Human life is not a journey
towards a goal – eternal life or the kingdom of heaven:

The human is a rope, fastened between the animal and the superhuman – a rope across an abyss. [...] What is great in the human is that it is a bridge and not an end in itself. What can be loved in the human is that it is both a crossing-over and a going-down.

The revised purpose of life is to become the superhuman. This is an idea that Nietzsche never clearly defines, typically enough, but it suggests a process of accepting mortal life as an end in itself, and living abundantly and without fear: 'All the gods are dead; now we want the superhuman to live.'

The work is ironic, mischievous and full of contradictions and paradoxes. Zarathustra tells his followers to listen to him, then he tells them not to trust him. Perhaps he is deceiving them! He is the 'laughing prophet,' the 'dancer,' who wants to 'kill the spirit of heaviness': the despair that threatens those who live without God. Just as 'all good things laugh' so 'all good things approach their goals obliquely.' Eternal recurrence is another oblique approach but, fittingly, it recurs throughout the book. Imagine, says Zarathustra, that 'we have already been here an infinite number of times, and all things with us.' The superhuman can contend with the idea of eternal recurrence, of experiencing the same life over and over again, because they have lived well.

There are caveats to all Nietzsche's arguments, and besides his meaning is never certain. Yet his dream of the laughing, dancing human – divested of heaviness, of cold eternal absolutes – remains radical even today. The path is fraught with danger; the rope is above an abyss, after all. In a letter, Nietzsche described *Thus Spake Zarathustra* as 'an explosion of forces that have been building up over decades.' The danger, he added, is that 'the originator of such explosions can often get blown up.' There are many interpretations, detonations, of Nietzsche's life and work; this short introduction can barely begin to invoke them. If you are interested and would like to read further, then Sue Prideaux's recent biography, *I Am Dynamite*, is a fascinating, nuanced portrait. Alexander Nehamas's equally compelling *Nietzsche: Life as Literature* proposes that the 'Nietzsche' of the works is a persona, a literary character and not the 'real' man at all. Each translation of Nietzsche is also an interpretation and occurs at a specific moment in time. Thomas Common emphasised the mock-devotional aspects of Nietzsche's style and based his 1909 translation on the King James Bible. Walter Kaufmann translated Nietzsche in the era of Camus and Sartre and presented Nietzsche as an early existentialist. There are also major translations by R. J. Hollingdale, Thomas Wayne, Graham Parkes, Clancy Martin and Adrian Del Caro, among others. Works of literature are not legal documents nor scientific papers. As the critic Eileen Battersby once wrote: 'no translation . . . is absolute; that honour belongs to the original book.'

As for this translation: I mentioned earlier that Michael Hulse is a distinguished poet. He is the first poet to translate *Thus Spake Zarathustra* into English. This is worth stating, though it doesn't mean that previous translations were unpoetic. Hulse was raised in both the UK and Germany; likewise, he has taught both in Germany and the UK. Until recently he was a professor of poetry and comparative literature at Warwick University. His collections include *Knowing and Forgetting* (1981), *Empires and Holy Lands: Poems 1976–2000* (2002) and *Half-Life* (2013). In 1978, he was the inaugural winner of the UK's National Poetry Competition, with 'Dole Queue'. This poem includes the phrase: 'I won't / pretend to understand the world. I don't.' These lines are indicative of Hulse's work, which is concerned with uncertainty, contradictory emotions, the mysterious bonds of love. He has won many further prizes, including the Eric Gregory and the Bridport. His translations have also been rightly lauded, most famously his translations of W. G. Sebald's works – *The Emigrants* (1996), *The Rings of Saturn* (1998) and *Vertigo* (1999). These brought Sebald's work to an international readership. He has also translated Elfriede Jelinek, Herta Müller, Alexander Kluge and Rainer Maria Rilke, among many others.

When Hulse first sent me this translation of *Thus Spake Zara-thustra*, he said it might be best if I read without any prior statements from him about methods or precepts. This is absolutely fair enough. With this in mind, I won't speculate here about Hulse's philosophy of translation. As a reader, I can say that Nietzsche was an early exponent of an exclamatory, aphoristic style, which later became characteristic of modernist writers such as T. S. Eliot, Wittgenstein and Beckett – as well as later writers of tribute modernism. The style of *Thus Spake Zarathustra* is quite mixed: at times clear and arresting, then mystical and hieratic. Sometimes it is all of the above, at once. Hulse beautifully conveys this paradoxical style: '. . . be wary of the good and just! They like to crucify those who devise their own virtue – they hate the solitary. Be wary of holy simple-mindedness as well! Everything that is not simple-minded is unholy in its eyes; and it likes to play with fire – and to burn at the stake.' These phrases are torrential; they draw us along like a fast-flowing river. Hulse is acutely sensitive to the spiralling metaphors of Nietzsche's writing, and always finds exciting ways to render them. For example:

> God is a thought that makes all straight things crooked and puts all standing things in a spin. What, are we to imagine time gone, and all transient things a mere lie? To think this is a whirling, dizzying experience for human bones, and sets the stomach heaving; truly, I call it the spinning sickness, to conjecture any such thing.

This passage escalates swiftly from a measured analogy of straight things becoming crooked to a series of whirling dizzying images that invoke whirling dizzying experience itself. *Thus Spake Zarathustra* always has this dynamic – explosive – energy. It depends on accumulation, irony, word play, dances with meaning. Hulse renders all these nuances, ambiguities and escalations in such wild, lovely poetry; his achievement is immense. He has crafted a bold, exhilarating translation of Nietzsche's revolutionary work.

PART ONE

– Zarathustra's Prologue –

1

When Zarathustra was thirty years old, he quit his home parts and the lake at his home and went up into the mountains. There he savoured the pleasures of his spirit and of his solitude, and for ten years they did not pall on him. At length, however, his heart underwent a change, and one morning he rose at dawn, stepped out before the sun, and addressed it in this way:

'Great star, what happiness would you have without those to whom you bring light?

'For ten years you have been coming up here to my cave. You would have wearied of your travails and of your own light, were it not for me, my eagle, and my serpent.

'But every morning we awaited you, took of your superabundance, and blessed you for it.

'Now, look, I have wearied of my wisdom, like the bee that has gathered too much honey. I am in need of hands outstretched.

'I should like to give and distribute, till that time come when the wise among humankind rejoice in their foolishness once again, and the poor rejoice in their riches.

'That that may be, I must go down into the depths, as you do in the evenings when you go down beyond the sea and, super-rich star, bring light to the underworld too.

'Like you, I must *go down*, to borrow the phrase of humankind, to whom I mean to descend.

'Bless me, then, steady eye that can gaze without envy on even the greatest of happiness.

'Bless the cup that is full to overflowing, that the water may flow golden from it and bear the reflection of your rapture everywhere.

'For the cup, you see, would be empty once more, and Zarathustra would be human again.'

So began the going-down of Zarathustra.

2

Zarathustra went down from the mountains alone, and no one came his way. When he entered the forest, however, he happened upon an old man who had left his holy cabin to look for roots in the woods. And the old man said to Zarathustra:

'This wayfarer is no stranger to me. He came by here years ago. His name was Zarathustra, but he has changed.

'Back then, you were taking your ashes up into the mountains. Are you bringing your fire to the valleys now? Are you not afraid to be punished as a fire-raiser?

'I'd know Zarathustra anywhere – his limpid eye, his mouth free of revulsion, his walk like a dancer's.

'But Zarathustra has been transformed. Zarathustra was become a child. Now Zarathustra is a man awoken. What, then, do you want among those who are asleep?

'You dwelt in solitude as in an ocean, and the ocean bore you up. Perish the thought, but do you mean to step ashore? – do you mean to haul your own body about once again, yourself?'

Zarathustra answered: 'I love humankind.'

'And why did I go into the forest and desert?' said the holy man. 'Was it not because of the-all-too great love I bore humanity?

'Now I love God: I do not love humanity. For me, humankind is too imperfect. To love humanity would be the end of me.'

Zarathustra answered: 'What was I thinking, to speak of love? I am bearing a gift to humanity.'

'Give them nothing,' said the holy man. 'You would do better to take something from them, and help them carry it. That will be of the greatest benefit to them. May it also be good for you!

'And if you really want to give them something, let it be no more than alms, and let them beg for it.'

'No,' answered Zarathustra, 'I am no alms-giver. I am not poor enough for that.'

The holy man laughed at Zarathustra, and said to him: 'Then see they accept your treasures. They are wary of hermits and do not believe that we come bearing gifts.

'Our footfall in the streets has too solitary a sound − and if at night in their beds they hear a man go by, long before the sun is up, you can be sure they think it's a thief and wonder where he's heading.

'Don't go among humanity. Stay in the forest. You would do better to go to the animals. Why not be like me, a bear among bears, a bird among birds?'

'And what does a holy man do in the forest?' asked Zarathustra.

The holy man answered: 'I make songs and sing them, and while I'm making up the songs I laugh and cry and rumble on in my way. That is how I praise God.

'Singing, laughing, crying and rumbling on is how I give praise to the God who is my God. But what gift is it you bring us?'

When Zarathustra heard these words, he saluted the holy man and said: 'Whatever could I give you? Let me go quickly, lest I take something from you.' And so they parted, the old man and the other, laughing as two boys laugh.

But once Zarathustra was alone, he spake to his heart in this way: 'Can it be possible? Can this old holy man in his forest really not have heard that *God is dead*?'

3

When Zarathustra reached the nearest town, on the edge of the forest, he found a crowd of people gathered in the marketplace there to watch a tightrope-walker who was due to perform. And Zarathustra spake thus to the people:

'My teaching to you is of the superhuman. The time has come to go beyond the human. What have you done to go beyond it?

'So far, every being has created something that went beyond itself. Do you mean to be the ebb of that great flood? Would you rather return to the condition of beasts than go beyond the human?

'What is an ape in the eyes of humanity? An occasion for laughter or smarting shame. And that is what the human will be for the superhuman: an occasion for laughter or smarting shame.

'The journey from worm to human lies behind you, and still there is much of the worm in you. At one time you were apes, and even now the human is more of an ape than any ape.

'The wisest among you is no more than a riving and twining of plant life and ghost. But am I urging you to become plants or ghosts?

'No – my teaching to you is of the superhuman!

'The superhuman is the meaning of the earth. May your will say: so be it – let the superhuman be the meaning of the earth!

'I call upon you, my brothers, to *remain true to the earth* and not believe those who would have you hope for things that lie beyond it. They are concocters of poisons, whether they do it knowingly or not.

'They hold life in contempt. They are a dying breed. They have been poisoned themselves, and the world is weary of them. Let them be gone.

'At one time, to sin against God was the gravest of sins. But God died, and with him the sinners of old. Now to sin against the earth is the most terrible of sins – and to prize the entrails of the inapprehensible more than the meaning of the earth.

'At one time, the soul regarded the body with contempt, and in those days that contempt counted higher than all else. The soul wanted the body skinny, grisly and famished, the better to give it the slip and escape the earth.

'But, oh, it was the soul itself that was skinny, grisly and famished, and what the soul delighted in was cruelty.

'What of you then, my brothers? Say to me: what does your body tell you of your soul? Is your soul not poverty and filth and miserable contentment?

'Humanity is truly a river of filth. It takes an ocean to absorb a river of filth without itself being defiled.

'So you see, my teaching to you is of the superhuman. That is the ocean. That is where your measureless contempt can go under.

'What is the greatest experience you could ever have? It is the hour of measureless contempt. The hour when you find even your own happiness, even your reason and virtue, revolting.

'The hour when you say: "What good is my happiness? It is poverty and filth and miserable contentment. But my happiness should justify existence itself."

'The hour when you say: "What good is my reason? Does it crave knowledge as the lion craves the next meal? It is poverty and filth and miserable contentment."

'The hour when you say: "What good is my virtue? It has not driven me to distraction yet. How weary I am of my good and my evil! All of that is poverty and filth and miserable contentment."

'The hour when you say: "What good is my justice? I do not see that I am fire and hot coals. But the just man is fire and hot coals."

'The hour when you say: "What good is my pity? Is pity not the cross on which the one who loves humanity is nailed? But my pity is no crucifixion."

'Have you ever uttered such words? Have you ever cried out in that way? Had I but heard you cry out in that way!

'It is not your sin but your sufficiency that cries out unto heaven. The meanness that is even in your sin cries out unto heaven.

'Where is the lightning, to lick you with its tongue? Where is the madness, to afford you protection?

'See, my teaching to you is of the superhuman. That is the lightning. That is the madness.' –

When Zarathustra had said this much, a man in the crowd shouted out: 'We've listened to the tightrope-walker long enough – now let's see what he can do.' And all the people laughed at Zarathustra. But the tightrope-walker himself, thinking the words were meant for him, began his performance.

4

But Zarathustra looked at the people and marvelled. Then he spake thus:

'The human is a rope, fastened between the animal and the superhuman – a rope across an abyss.

'A perilous crossing, a perilous transit, a perilous looking-back, a perilous shuddering and stopping.

'What is great in the human is that it is a bridge and not an end in itself. What can be loved in the human is that it is both a *crossing-over* and a *going-down*.

'I love those who cannot conceive of living except by going down, for they are the ones who cross over.

'I love those who are filled with a great contempt, for it is they who venerate greatly, they who are the arrows of longing for the other bank.

'I love those who do not first cast about beyond the stars for some reason to go down and be sacrificed, but who give themselves in sacrifice to the earth – that the earth, in the course of time, should be the province of the superhuman.

'I love the one who lives in order to know, the one who wants to know so that one day the superhuman shall live, and so wills his own downfall.

'I love the one who works and invents, that he may build a house for the superhuman and prepare the earth, animals and plants for him, for so he wills his own downfall.

'I love the one who loves his own virtue, for virtue is the will to downfall and an arrow of longing.

'I love the one who does not hold back a single drop of spirit for himself but wants to be unreservedly the spirit of his virtue, for so he strides as spirit across the bridge.

'I love the one who makes of his virtue both his taste and his doom, for so he determines to live or not live for his virtue's sake.

'I love the one who does not want too many virtues. One virtue is more virtue than two, because it is more of a knot for doom to tangle in.

'I love the one whose soul is spendthrift, who neither wants nor gives thanks, for he is always making gifts and has no intention of hoarding himself.

'I love the one who feels shame when the dice fall in his favour, and demands: Am I a cheat, then? – for he wills his own destruction.

'I love the one who casts golden words ahead of his deeds, and always delivers more than he promises, for he wills his own downfall.

'I love the one who justifies the people of the future and redeems the people of the past, for he means to perish through the people of the present.

'I love the one who chastises his god because he loves his god, for he must perish through the wrath of his god.

'I love the one whose soul is deep even its capacity to bear wounds, the one who can perish of any little thing, for he goes gladly across the bridge.

'I love the one whose soul is overfull, so that he forgets himself and all things are in him, for all things become his downfall.

'I love the one who has a free spirit and a free heart, for his head is no more than the bowels of his heart, while his heart drives him on to his downfall.

'I love all those who are heavy drops falling singly from the dark cloud that hangs over the human, for they prophesy the coming of the lightning, and as prophets they perish.

'See, I am a prophet of the lightning and a heavy drop from the cloud: but the name for this lightning is the superhuman.'

5

When Zarathustra had spoken these words, he looked once again at the people and was silent. 'There they stand,' he said to his heart, 'there they laugh: they do not understand me, I am not the mouth for these ears.

'Must one first smash their ears, that they might learn to hear with their eyes? Must one make a great noise like a drum or a hellfire preacher? Or do they believe the stammerer alone?

'They do have something they take pride in. But what do they call this thing they take pride in? Culture, they call it – it sets them apart from the goatherds.

'Because of this, they do not care to hear the word "contempt" used of them. That being so, I shall address myself to their pride.

'I shall speak to them of what is most contemptible: but that is *the last human.*'

And Zarathustra spake thus to the people:

'It is time for the human to set itself a goal. It is time for the human to sow the seed of its highest hope.

'His soil is still rich enough. But one day the soil will be poor and over-cultivated, and no tall tree will grow from it any more.

'Alas! The time is coming when the human will no longer shoot the arrow of his longing out beyond humankind, and the string of his bow will have lost its tensile whish.

'I tell you, one must still have chaos in oneself to give birth to a dancing star. I say to you, you still have chaos in you.

'Alas! The time is coming when humankind will no longer give birth to stars. The time of the most contemptible human is coming, the one who can no longer despise himself.

'See, I show you *the last human.*

'"What is love? What is creation? What is longing? What is a star?" asks the last human, and blinks.

'The earth has now grown small, and on it capers the last human, who makes everything small. His race is as ineradicable as the flea; the last human lives longest.

'"We have invented happiness," say the last humans, and blink.

'They have quit the regions where the living was hard: for one needs warmth. One still loves one's neighbour and rubs against him: for one needs warmth.

'To be sick and mistrusting count as sins with them, for they value paying attention, and the man who still stumbles over stones or men is a fool!

'A little poison now and then makes for pleasant dreams. A lot of poison, at the last, makes for a pleasant death.

'They still work, since work is a form of entertainment. But they make sure the entertainment doesn't wear them out.

'People no longer grow poor or rich, since either is too much trouble. Who would still rule? And who obey? Either is too much trouble.

'No herdsman and one herd! Everyone wants the same thing, everyone is the same: anyone who feels differently about it is entering the madhouse of his own free will.

' "In the old days, the whole world was mad," say the most discerning, and blink.

'They are clever and know everything that has happened: so there is no end to their mockery. They still squabble, but they soon make up – otherwise it ruins one's digestion.

'They have their little indulgence by day and their little indulgence by night: but they respect health.

' "We have invented happiness,' say the last humans, and they blink.

And here the first discourse of Zarathustra, also known as "The Prologue", ended; for at this point the crowd's shouting and jollity interrupted him. 'Give us this last human, oh Zarathustra' – so they cried – 'make us these last humans! You can keep the superman!' And all the people cheered and jeered. But Zarathustra was downcast, and said to his heart:

'They do not understand me: I am not the mouth for these ears.

'I must have lived in the mountains too long, and listened to the streams and trees too much: now I speak to them as if to goatherds.

'Unmoved is my soul, and bright as the mountains in the morning. But they think I am cold, and a mocker, making fearful jokes.

'And now they gaze upon me and laugh; and as they laugh they hate me still. There is ice in their laughter.'

6

But then something happened that left every mouth silent and every eye fixed. For the tightrope-walker had meanwhile begun his act, and, having emerged by a little door, was crossing the rope that was stretched between two towers above the marketplace and the crowd.

Just as he was halfway across, the little door opened again and a brightly dressed clown of a fellow leapt out and stepped lively after the first. 'Move along there, halt-foot,' he shouted in a fearsome voice – 'on with you, lazybones, sly-boots, paleface, or I'll tickle you with my heels! What are you up to between these towers? You belong inside the tower, locked up – you're getting in the way of a better man than you!' And with every word he came closer and closer. But when he was only a single step behind him, the dreadful thing happened that left every mouth silent and every eye fixed: he let out a shriek like a devil and jumped over the man who was in his way. But the latter, seeing his rival victorious, lost his head and the rope; he threw away his pole and, falling even faster than it did, plummeted in a whirl of arms and legs. The marketplace and the crowd were like a sea when a storm breaks, turbulently parting, especially where the body was about to hit the ground.

Zarathustra, however, did not move, and the body fell right next to him, mangled and broken but not yet dead. After a while the injured man regained consciousness and saw Zarathustra kneeling beside him. 'What are you doing?' he asked at length. 'I have long known that the devil would trip me up. Now he is dragging me off to hell. Are you trying to stop him?'

'On my honour, friend,' answered Zarathustra, 'the things you are talking of do not exist – there is no devil, and no hell. Your soul will be dead even sooner than your body. Do not be afraid of anything any longer!'

The man looked up mistrustfully. 'If what you say is true,' he then said, 'I am losing nothing if I lose my life. I am little more than an animal that has been taught to dance with blows and starvation rations.'

'No need to think like that,' said Zarathustra, – 'you took danger as your calling. There is nothing to be despised in that. Now your calling has been your undoing: I shall bury you with my own hands.'

When Zarathustra had said this, the dying man made no further reply; but he motioned with his hand, as if he were groping for Zarathustra's to thank him.

7

It had now grown evening, and the marketplace was mantled in darkness. The people went their ways, for even curiosity and terror tire. For his part, Zarathustra sat beside the dead man on the ground, lost in thought, oblivious to the time. At length, however, night fell and a cold wind blew about the lone figure – and Zarathustra arose and said to his heart:

'Truly, it has been a fine catch for Zarathustra today! He did not catch a human, but he did catch a corpse.

'Human existence is uncanny, and still it has no meaning; a clown of a fellow can spell doom to it.

'I mean to teach people the meaning of their existence – the superhuman, the lightning-bolt from the dark cloud of the human.

'Yet now I am still far from them, and my meaning does not speak to their minds. To humans, I am still the mean between a fool and a corpse.

'Dark is the night, dark are the ways of Zarathustra. Come, cold and stiff companion! I shall carry you to where I shall bury you with my own hands.'

8

When Zarathustra had said this to his heart, he took up the corpse upon his back and set off. He had not walked a hundred paces when a man stole up to him and whispered in his ear – and, see! it was the clown who had been on the tower. 'Get out of this town, oh Zarathustra,' he said; 'there are too many here who hate you. The good and the just hate you, and call you their enemy, who holds them in contempt; the faithful of the true faith hate you, and call you a public menace. It was fortunate for you that they laughed at you – and the truth is that you talked like a fool. It was fortunate for you that you gave company to that dead dog – for by abasing yourself in that way you survived for today. But get out of this town – or tomorrow it will be you I jump over, a living man over a dead one.' And when he had said this, the man vanished; Zarathustra, for his part, walked on through the dark streets.

At the town gate he was met by the gravediggers, who thrust their torch into his face and, recognizing Zarathustra by its light, heaped derision upon him. 'Zarathustra is carrying the dead dog away! Here's a fine thing – Zarathustra's turned gravedigger! Our hands are too dainty for this carcass, it seems. Is Zarathustra out to steal the devil's portion? Go to it, then! And good eating! Here's hoping the devil's not a better thief than Zarathustra, or he'll steal the two of them and eat up both!' And they all laughed with their heads together.

Zarathustra made not a word of reply and went his way. When he had walked for two hours past woods and marshes, the hungry howling of wolves began to be too much for him, and he felt hungry himself and stopped at a lonely house where a light was burning.

'Hunger is waylaying me like a robber,' said Zarathustra. 'My hunger is waylaying me in the woods and the marshes and in the deep of the night.

'My hunger is strangely capricious. Often it comes upon me only after a meal, and today it did not come at all: wherever was it?'

And with that Zarathustra knocked on the door of the house. An old man appeared, carrying a light, and asked: 'Who comes to me and my bad sleep?'

'A living man and a dead man,' said Zarathustra. 'Give me something to eat and drink – I forgot them during the day. He who feeds the hungry restores his own soul: thus speaks wisdom.'

The old man went away, but returned presently and offered Zarathustra bread and wine. 'These are bad parts for hungry people,' he said. 'That is why I live here as a hermit: animals and humans come to me. But tell your companion to eat and drink as well. He is wearier than you.' Zarathustra answered: 'My companion is dead. I don't see myself persuading him to join me.' 'That's none of my business,' said the old man morosely. 'Anyone who knocks at my door must take what I offer. Eat, both of you, and fare you well!'

After this, Zarathustra walked on for another two hours, trusting to the track and the light of the stars: for he was accustomed to walking at night, and loved to look upon the face of all that sleeps. At daybreak, however, Zarathustra found himself in a deep forest, and unable to make out a track any more. So he laid the dead man in a hollow tree at his head (wanting to protect him from wolves) and himself lay down on the mossy ground. And at once he fell asleep, his body tired but his soul free of turmoil.

9

Zarathustra slept for a long time, and not only the glow of dawn lit his face but also the whole of the morning. At length, however, his eyes opened; in wonder he gazed into the forest and the silence, in wonder he gazed within himself. Then he jumped up quickly, like a seafarer who suddenly sees land, and rejoiced; for he saw a new truth. And then he spake thus to his heart:

'A light has dawned on me. I need companions, living not dead, not corpses I carry with me wherever I go.

'It is living companions I need, who follow me because they want to follow themselves – wherever I want to go.

'A light has dawned on me. Zarathustra should speak not to the people but to companions. Zarathustra should not be the herdsman and dog to the flock.

'To lure away many from the flock – that is why I have come. Let the people and the flock be angry with me; Zarathustra says the herdsmen are robbers.

'I say herdsmen, yet they call themselves the good and the just. I say herdsmen, yet they call themselves the faithful of the true faith.

'See them, the good and the just! Whom do they most hate? – him who breaks their tablets of values, the breaker, the law-breaker. But he is the creator.

'See them, the faithful of all faiths! Whom do they most hate? – him who breaks their tablets of values, the breaker, the law-breaker. But he is the creator.

'The creator seeks companions, not corpses, nor flocks, nor the faithful. The creator seeks fellow-creators, those who inscribe new values on new tablets.

'The creator seeks companions, and fellow-harvesters; for all that he sees is ripe for harvesting. But he lacks the hundred sickles; so he plucks off ears of corn and is vexed.

'The creator seeks companions, such as know how to whet their sickles. They will be called destroyers who hold good and evil in contempt – but it is they who bring in the harvest, they who celebrate.

'Zarathustra seeks fellow-creators, fellow-harvesters, fellow-celebrators! What use are flocks and herdsmen and corpses to him?

'And you, my first companion, fare you well! I have buried you well in your hollow tree, hidden you well from the wolves.

'But I am leaving you. Our time is up. Between one dawn and the next a new truth came to me.

'Neither a herdsman nor a gravedigger shall I be. I shall not even talk again with the people; I have spoken to a dead man for the last time.

'My company shall be with the creators, the harvesters, the celebrators; I shall show them the rainbow and all the steps to the superhuman.

'To the hermits I shall sing my song, and to pairs in solitude; and those who have ears to hear the unheard-of I shall make heavy-hearted with my happiness.

'I shall go to my destination. I shall walk my way. I shall leap over those who hesitate and procrastinate. May my going be their going-down!'

10

Zarathustra had said this to his heart when the sun stood at midday. Then he looked askance into the sky, hearing above him the sharp call of a bird. And see, an eagle was flying wide circles through the air, and from it hung a serpent, not as prey but as a friend, coiled about the eagle's neck.

'Those are my animals!' said Zarathustra, and rejoiced in his heart.

'The proudest animal under the sun and the wisest animal under the sun are reconnoitring.

'They want to know whether Zarathustra is still alive. Am I still alive, indeed?

'I found it more dangerous among humans than among animals; Zarathustra walks a dangerous path. May my animals lead me!'

When Zarathustra had said this, he recalled the words of the holy man in the forest, sighed, and spoke thus to his heart:

'Would that I were wiser! Would that I were wise in the very ground of me, like my serpent!

'But I am asking for the impossible: so I ask my pride always to keep step with my wisdom.

'And if one day my wisdom should desert me – ah, how she loves to fly away – may my pride fly together with my wisdom.'

– So began the going-down of Zarathustra.

– Zarathustra's Discourses –

Of the Three Metamorphoses

There are three metamorphoses of the spirit. I shall name them for you: how the spirit becomes a camel, how the camel becomes a lion, and finally how the lion becomes a child.

There is much that is heavy for the spirit, for the strong spirit that bears burdens and is reverent; its strength demands what is heavy, and heaviest.

What is heavy? asks the spirit that bears burdens, and it kneels down like a camel, to be fully loaded.

What is heaviest, you heroes? asks the spirit that bears burdens – let me take it upon me and rejoice in my strength.

Is it not to abase oneself, that one's pride be mortified? To let one's foolishness shine forth, in mockery of one's own wisdom?

Or is it to abandon our cause at the moment of its victory? To climb high mountains in order to tempt the tempter?

Or is it to feed on the acorns and grass of knowledge, and for the sake of truth to suffer hunger of the soul?

Or is it to be ill and send away those who give comfort, and befriend the deaf, who never hear what you want?

Or is it to wade into dirty water, if it is the water of truth, and not to shoo cold frogs and hot toads away?

Or is it to love those who hold us in contempt, and offer our hand to the ghost when it wants to frighten us?

The spirit that bears burdens takes up all of these heaviest of things, and, like a laden camel hastening into the desert, it hastens into its desert.

But in the loneliest desert the second metamorphosis occurs: there the spirit becomes a lion, determined to take freedom as its prey and be master of its own desert.

There it seeks its ultimate master; it will be an enemy to him and to his ultimate god, and it will struggle for victory with the great dragon.

What is this great dragon that the spirit declines to regard as its master and god any longer? The name of the great dragon is 'Thou shalt'. But the spirit of the lion says, 'I will'.

'Thou shalt' lies in its path, glistening with gold, a scaly beast, and every scale bears the glittering golden words 'Thou shalt'.

The values of thousands of years glitter on those scales, and thus speaks the mightiest of all dragons: 'All the value that things possess glitters on me.

'All value has already been created, and all the value that has been created – is me. Truly, there shall be no more "I will"!' Thus speaks the dragon.

My brothers, why is the lion needed in the spirit? Why is the beast of burden, which goes without and is reverent, not sufficient?

To create new values – even the lion is unable to do that. But to create its own freedom, for new creation – that the lion has the power to do.

To create one's own freedom, and deliver a sacred 'no' even to duty: that, my brothers, is what the lion is needed for.

To assert the right to new values – that is the most fearful appropriation to make for a spirit that bears burdens and is reverent. Truly, to this spirit that is theft, and the business of a predator.

At one time it loved 'Thou shalt' as its holiest of holies; now it must discover delusion and caprice even in that holiest of holies, if it is to steal freedom from its love; the lion is needed for that theft.

But tell me, my brothers, what the child can do that even the lion could not? Whyever must the preying lion become a child?

The child is innocence and forgetting, a fresh start, a game, a wheel that rolls of itself, a prime movement, a holy saying of 'yes'.

Yes, my brothers, a holy saying of 'yes' is required for the game of creation; the spirit now wills *its own* will, and the one who is lost to the world gains *his own* world.

I named three metamorphoses of the spirit to you: how the spirit became a camel, how the camel became a lion, and finally how the lion became a child.

Thus spake Zarathustra. And at that time he was staying in the town known as The Cow of Many Colours.

Of the Professorial Chairs of Virtue

A wise man was praised to Zarathustra for his fine discourse on sleep and virtue. He was greatly revered and rewarded for it, and all the young men sat before his chair. Zarathustra went to him and sat before his chair with all the young men. And thus spake the wise man:

Honour to sleep and shame in the face of it! That is the first thing! And one must avoid all who sleep badly and lie awake at night!

Even the thief feels shame in the face of sleep: he always goes softly by night. But the night watchman is shameless, and shamelessly he bears his horn.

Sleeping is no paltry art. You have to stay awake all day to do it.

Ten times a day you have to exercise self-discipline; this makes for a goodly weariness and is opium for the soul.

Ten times you must be reconciled with yourself; for self-discipline is bitterness, and you sleep badly if you are unreconciled.

You must discover ten truths a day; otherwise you will be seeking truth at night as well, and your soul will still be hungry.

You must laugh and be cheerful ten times a day; otherwise your stomach, the father of sorrows, will give you trouble in the night.

Few know it, but one must possess all the virtues if one is to sleep well. Shall I bear false witness? Shall I commit adultery?

Shall I covet my neighbour's maidservant? None of these would be conducive to sound sleep.

And even if one possesses all the virtues, one must still bear one thing in mind: even these virtues should be sent to sleep at the proper time.

So that they do not squabble among themselves, those prim little misses! Nor about you, unhappy man!

Peace with God and the neighbour: thus good sleep would have it. And peace with the neighbour's devil, too! Or else he will haunt you by night.

Honour the powers that be, and show them obedience, even the crooked powers! Thus good sleep would have it. How can I help it if power likes to walk on crooked legs?

To my mind, the best herdsman will always be the one who leads his sheep to the greenest pastures; that goes well with good sleep.

I do not want numerous honours, nor great treasures; they only inflame the spleen. But one sleeps badly if one has no good name and a tiny treasure.

The company of a few is more welcome to me than bad company; but they must come and go at the proper time. That goes well with good sleep.

The poor in spirit also please me greatly; they help one sleep. Blessèd are they, especially if one always agrees with them.

This is how the day goes by for the virtuous man. When night comes, I am wary of calling out for sleep. Sleep, the lord of the virtues, does not care to be called.

Instead I think over what I have done and thought that day. Ruminating, I ask myself, patient as a cow: in which ten ways did you exercise self-discipline?

And which were the ten reconciliations and the ten truths and the ten bouts of laughter that succoured my heart?

Weighing matters such as these, and cradled by forty thoughts, I presently yield as sleep, the lord of the virtues, takes me unbidden.

Sleep knocks on my eyes, and they grow heavy. Sleep touches my mouth, and it hangs open.

Truly, he comes to me on soft soles, the dearest of thieves, and steals my thoughts away; there I stand, as witless as this chair.

But I do not stand for much longer; already I am lying down.

When Zarathustra heard the wise man speak in this way, he laughed in his heart; for, as he listened, a light had dawned on him. And he spoke thus to his heart:

This wise man with his forty thoughts strikes me as a fool – though I do believe that he is an expert in sleeping.

Any neighbour of this wise man is fortunate indeed – for sleep such as this is contagious, even through a thick wall.

There is magic even in his professorial chair. And the young men have not sat in vain before the preacher of virtue.

His wisdom is: stay awake so that you sleep well. And truly, if life had no meaning and I had to choose nonsense, this would be the nonsense I too would be most inclined to choose.

Now I understand clearly what people were chiefly seeking in olden times when they sought out the teachers of virtue. They were after sound sleep and opium virtues!

To all of these lauded wise men with their professorial chairs, wisdom was a dreamless sleep: they were unacquainted with any better meaning in life.

To this day there are still some, such as this preacher of virtue, and not all are as honest; but their time is up. And they shall not be standing for much longer – soon they will be lying down.

Blessèd are these sleepy ones – soon they'll be nodding off.

Thus spake Zarathustra.

Of the Afterworlders

Once Zarathustra too projected his delusions beyond humankind, as all afterworlders do. In those days the world seemed to me the work of a suffering and tormented god.

In those days the world seemed to me a dream, a fiction made up by a god; colourful smoke before the eyes of a divine malcontent.

Good and evil and pleasure and sorrow and I and you – it all seemed colourful smoke to me, before creative eyes. The creator wanted to look away from himself – so he created the world.

For the sufferer, looking away from his suffering and losing himself is sheer rapture. Rapture and loss of self were what I once believed the world was.

This world, forever imperfect, the image of an everlasting contradiction, and an imperfect image too – rapture, to its imperfect creator; that was what I once believed the world was.

So I too once projected my delusions beyond humankind, as all afterworlders do. Was it genuinely beyond humankind?

Ah, my brothers, this god I created was a human product and human madness, like all gods!

He was human, a mere miserable morsel of humanity and ego. It came to me from my very own fire and ashes, this phantom. The plain truth is that it did not come to me from the beyond!

What happened, my brothers? I, the sufferer, took myself in hand. I carried my own ashes up into the mountains, and made a brighter flame for myself. And see, the phantom *fled* before me.

For me now in my convalescence it would be torment and suffering to believe in such phantoms; it would be both suffering and humiliation. And so I speak to the afterworlders.

It was suffering and impotence that created all afterworlds; and that brief insanity of happiness that only the greatest of sufferers experiences.

Weariness, which aims to attain the ultimate in a single leap, in a death-leap – a wretched, ignorant weariness which no longer even intends any aim – this it was that created all the gods and afterworlds.

Believe me, my brothers, it was the body that despaired of the body – that felt after the last of all walls with the fingers of its deluded spirit.

Believe me, my brothers, it was the body that despaired of the earth – that heard the belly of being speak to it.

And then it tried to bang its head right through the last of all walls, and not only its head, and break through to the 'other world'.

But that 'other world', that inhuman, dehumanized world that is a heavenly nothingness, is well concealed from humans; and the belly of being does not speak to humans at all, except as a human.

In truth, all being is hard to prove, and it is hard to make it speak. Tell me, my brothers, has not the strangest of all things been given the best proof?

Yes, this ego and the ego's contradiction and confusion give the most honest account of its being – this creating, willing, evaluating ego, which is the measure and value of things.

And this most honest being, the ego – it speaks of the body, and it still wants the body, even when it fabulates and rhapsodizes and flaps its broken wings.

It learns to speak ever more honestly, the ego, and the more it learns, the more it finds words and honours for the body and the earth.

My ego taught me a new pride, and I teach it to humans – not to bury their head in the sand of heavenly matters any longer, but to hold it up freely, a head of the earth which creates meaning for the earth.

I teach humans a new will – to want to take this path that humans have followed blindly, and to find it good, and not slip away to one side as the sick and the dying do.

It was the sick and the dying who held the body and the earth in contempt and invented heaven and the redeeming drops of blood; but even these sweet and doleful poisons they took from the body and the earth!

They wanted to escape their misery, and the stars were too far for them. And they sighed: 'If only there were heavenly ways to sneak into another state of being and happiness!' And so they came up with their sneaky ways and their drinking of blood.

They now imagined themselves transported far from their bodies and this earth, these ingrates. Yet to what did they owe the pains and joys of their transport? To their bodies, and to this earth.

Zarathustra is gentle with the sick. In truth, he is not wroth at their sorts of comfort and ingratitude. May they be convalescents, practising self-discipline and creating a higher body for themselves!

Nor is Zarathustra wroth at the convalescent stealing a wistful look at his delusion and creeping about the grave of his god at midnight; but I still see even his tears as evidence of sickness and a sick body.

There have always been a great many sickly people among those who fabulate and are habituated to gods; they hate the man of understanding with a fury, as they hate that youngest of the virtues: honesty.

Their gaze is invariably backwards, to dark ages. At that time, indeed, delusion and faith were a different matter; ravings against reason showed likeness unto God, and doubt was sin.

I know these godlike people all too well: they want people to believe in them, and want doubt to be thought sinful. I also know all too well what they themselves most firmly believe in.

It is not in afterworlds, in truth, nor in redeeming drops of blood. What they too most firmly believe in is the body, and their own body is their thing-in-itself.

But it is a sickly thing to them; and they would be glad to get out of their own skins. That is why they hearken to preachers of death, and themselves preach of afterworlds.

My brothers, I advise you rather to listen to the voice of the healthy body, for it is more honest and more pure.

The healthy body, complete and four-square, is more honest and more pure of speech; and it speaks of the meaning of the earth.

Thus spake Zarathustra.

Of Those Who Hold the Body in Contempt

I will say my piece to those who hold the body in contempt. It is not that I wish them to rethink their learning and teaching. I would have them bid farewell to their own bodies – and become dumb.

'I am a body and a soul' – so says the child. And why should one not speak like children?

But the awakened man of understanding says: I am wholly a body, and nothing else; and soul is only a word for something about the body.

The body is a great reasoning intelligence, a multiplicity with a single sense, a war and a peace, a flock and a herdsman.

Your little reasoning intelligence, my brother, which you call 'spirit', is an instrument of your body too, a little instrument and plaything of your greater reasoning intelligence.

You say 'I' and are proud of the word. But greater, though you do not want to believe it, is your body and its great reasoning intelligence – which does not say 'I' but does I.

What the senses feel, what the spirit perceives, is never completed within itself. But the senses and spirit are out to persuade you that they are the end of all things. That is how vain they are.

The senses and spirit are instruments and playthings; beyond them there is still the self. The self seeks with the eyes of the senses too, and listens with the ears of the spirit too.

The self is always listening and seeking. It compares, subdues, conquers, destroys. It rules and is also the I's ruler.

Beyond your thoughts and feelings, my brother, stands a mighty commander, an unknown wise man – his name is self. He lives in your body, he is your body.

There is more reason in your body than in the best of your wisdom. And who knows, anyway, why your body needs the best of your wisdom?

Your self laughs at your I and its proud leaps. 'What do these leaps and flights of thought mean to me?' it wonders. 'They are a needlessly long way of achieving my purpose. I help the I learn to walk, and I inspire its conceptions.'

The self says to the I: 'Feel pain – here!' Whereupon it suffers, and thinks about how to avoid suffering – and that is what it is *meant* to think about.

The self says to the I: 'Feel pleasure – here!' Whereupon it rejoices, and thinks about how to experience pleasure often – and that is what it is *meant* to think about.

I will say a word to those who hold the body in contempt. It is their respect that leads them to contempt. What is it that created respect and contempt and value and will?

The creative self created respect and contempt for itself. It created pleasure and woe for itself. The creative body created the spirit for itself, as a hand of its will.

Even in your foolishness and scorn, you who hold the body in contempt, you are still serving your self. I say to you: your very self wants to die, and is turning away from life.

No longer is it able to do what it most wants to do – to create something beyond itself. That is what it most wants to do. All of its energy lies in that.

But it has grown too late for that – and so, you who hold the body in contempt, your self wants to go under.

Your self wants to go under, and that is why you came to hold the body in contempt! For you are no longer able to create anything beyond yourselves.

And for that reason you are now angry with life and the earth. An envy of which you are unaware is in the sidelong gaze of your contempt.

I am not taking your path, you who hold the body in contempt! To me, you are not bridges to the superhuman!

Thus spake Zarathustra.

Of Pleasures and Passions

My brother, if you possess a virtue, and that virtue is your own, you share it with no one.

You want to call it by its name, indeed, and embrace it. You want to tug at its ears and have fun with it.

And see, now you do share its name with the people. You and your virtue together have become both people and flock!

You would do better to say: 'Unutterable and nameless is that which is torture and sweetness to my soul, that which my bowels hunger for.'

Your virtue should be too exalted for the familiarity of names; and, if you must speak of it, do not be ashamed to stammer.

Speak and stammer like this: 'This is *my* good thing, this is what I love, this is exactly how I like it, I want the good be like this and nothing else.

'I do not want it as the law of a god, I do not want it as a human statute and necessity. To me, it shall not be the signpost to realms beyond the earth and paradises.

'Earthly virtue is what I love: there is little cleverness in it, and least of all is there common reason.

'But this bird has built its nest in my home, and so I love and cherish it. Now it sits in my home on its golden eggs.'

This is how you should stammer and praise your virtue.

At one time you had passions and called them evil. But now you have only your virtues, which grew out of your passions.

You urged your loftiest goal upon those passions, and they became your virtues and pleasures.

And regardless of whether you were of the hot-tempered breed or the sensual or the fanatical or the vengeful:

In the end, all of your passions became virtues and all your devils angels.

At one time you had wild dogs in your cellar; but in the end they were transformed into birds and delightful singers.

From your poisons you brewed your own balm. You milked your cow of melancholy and now you drink the sweet milk of its udder.

And no evil grows from you any more, unless it be the evil that comes from the conflict between your virtues.

My brother, if you are fortunate you will possess one virtue and no more; that way, you will cross the bridge more easily.

To possess many virtues is a sign of distinction, but it is a hard lot; many a one has gone into the desert and killed himself because he was exhausted by being the battlefield where virtues battled.

My brother, are war and battle evil? But this is a necessary evil. Envy is necessary, and mistrust and slander among your virtues.

See how each of your virtues covets the highest place. Each wants the whole of your spirit, to be *its* herald. Each wants the whole of your strength in anger, hatred and love.

Each virtue is jealous of the others, and jealousy is a terrible thing. Even virtues can be destroyed by jealousy.

He who is encircled by the flames of jealousy will finally, like the scorpion, turn the venomous sting against himself.

Ah, my brother, have you never seen a virtue turn on itself and stab itself?

The human is something that must be overcome; and for that reason you shall love your virtues, for they will be your downfall.

Thus spake Zarathustra.

Of the Pale Criminal

You do not wish to kill, you judges and sacrificers, before the beast has bowed its head? See, the pale criminal has bowed his head; his eye is expressive of immense contempt.

'My I is something that has to be overcome; for me, my I is immense contempt of the human' – that is what this eye expresses.

His highest moment was judging himself; do not let this sublime man lapse back into his lowliness!

There is no redemption for the one who suffers from himself in this way, unless it be a quick death.

When you kill, you judges, you should do so in sympathy and not as revenge. And in killing, see that you yourselves justify life!

It is not enough that you make your peace with the one you kill. Your sorrow should be love of the superhuman; in that way you can justify staying alive!

You should say 'enemy' but not 'wrongdoer'; you should say 'sick man' but not 'rogue'; you should say 'fool' but not 'sinner'.

And you, scarlet judge, if you were to say aloud all you have done in your thoughts, everyone would cry: 'Away with this scum, this poisonous worm!'

But the thought is one thing and the deed another, and the image of the deed is yet another. The wheel of causal connection does not roll between them.

An image made this pale man pale. He was equal to his deed when he did it; but he could not bear the image of it after it was done.

From now on he always saw himself as the perpetrator of that one deed. I see that as madness: what was an exception became, for him, the one essential thing.

A hen will be transfixed by a line drawn with chalk; and his one misdeed transfixed his poor wits – this I call madness *after* the deed.

Listen, you judges! There is another sort of madness as well, and it comes *before* the deed. Ah, you have not crawled deep enough into this soul!

Thus speaks the scarlet judge: 'Why on earth did this criminal commit murder? He intended to steal.' But I tell you, his soul wanted blood, not the wages of theft – he thirsted for the happiness of the knife!

But his poor wits did not understand the madness, and persuaded him otherwise. 'What is the good of blood?' it demanded. 'Don't you at least want to steal something as well? Or take revenge?'

And he heeded his poor wits. What they said lay like lead upon him – and he stole when he committed his murder. He did not want to be ashamed of his madness.

And now the lead of his guilt lies upon him once again, and once again his poor wits are so stiff, so paralysed, so heavy.

If only he could shake his head, his burden would roll off; but who can shake that head?

What is this man? A heap of illnesses that reach out into the world by means of the spirit, intending to catch their prey there.

What is this man? A tangle of wild snakes that are rarely at rest among themselves – so they go out one by one to seek their prey in the world.

See this poor body! This poor soul came to its own understanding of what the body suffered and what it craved – and took it to be a lust for murder and hunger for the happiness of the knife.

He who now falls sick will be laid low by evil that is now become evil; he wants to do hurt with the very thing that hurts him. But there have been other ages and another evil and good.

At one time doubt and the will to self were evil. In those days the sick became heretics and witches; as heretics and witches they suffered and wanted to inflict suffering.

But this is not something you are prepared to listen to; you tell me it harms the good among you. But what do I care about the good among you?

Much in the good among you disgusts me, and it is not their evil. How I wish they had a madness that would be their downfall, like this pale criminal!

Truly, I wish their madness were called truth or loyalty or justice; but they have their virtue, to live a long life in wretched comfort.

I am a railing beside a torrent – take hold of me who can! But I am not your crutch. –

Thus spake Zarathustra.

Of Reading and Writing

Of all that is written, I love only what a man writes in his own blood. Write in blood and you will realize that blood is spirit.

It is not easily possible to understand the blood of another; I hate indolent readers.

Anyone who is familiar with readers will not do anything more for them. Another century of readers – and the spirit itself will stink.

The fact that everyone may now learn to read will in time blight not only writing but also thinking.

Once spirit was God, then it became humanity, and now it is even becoming the mob.

He who writes in blood and sayings wants not to be read but to be learnt by heart.

In the mountains the shortest distance is from peak to peak, but you need long legs for it. Sayings should be peaks, and those to whom they are addressed should be big and tall.

The air thin and pure, danger near, and the spirit filled with merry malignance: these are things that go together well.

I want imps about me, for I am courageous. Courage that frightens off ghosts creates its own imps – courage wants to laugh.

I no longer feel as you all do; this cloud I see below me, this blackness and heaviness at which I laugh – it is your storm-cloud.

You gaze upwards when you wish to be exalted. And I gaze down because I am exalted.

Which of you can laugh and be exalted at one and the same time?

He who climbs the highest mountains laughs at all tragedies, earnest or jesting.

Courageous, untroubled, scornful, violent – that is how wisdom wants us to be. She is a woman and loves none but a warrior.

You tell me: 'Life is hard to bear.' But tell me why you have your pride in the morning and your resignation in the evening?

Life is hard to bear; come off it. Don't be so dainty! All of us are fine asses and she-asses and can bear our burdens.

What do we have in common with the rosebud that trembles if a drop of dew lies on it?

It is true; we love life, not because we are accustomed to living but because we are accustomed to loving.

There is always a grain of madness in love. But there is also a grain of reason in madness.

And to me too, who am fond of life, butterflies and soap-bubbles and humans who resemble these things seem to know the most about happiness.

To see these light, foolish, delicate, affecting little souls fluttering about moves Zarathustra to tears and songs.

The only god I would believe in would be one who could dance.

And when I saw my devil, I found him serious, thorough, profound, solemn; he was the spirit of heaviness, by which all things fall.

One kills not by anger but by laughter. Come, let us kill the spirit of heaviness!

I learnt to walk, and ever since I have let myself run. I learnt to fly, and ever since I have not needed a push to start moving.

Now I am light, now I am flying, now I see myself below myself, now a god is dancing through me.

Thus spake Zarathustra.

Of the Tree on the Mountain

Zarathustra's eye had seen that a youth was avoiding him. And as he was walking alone one evening in the mountains that enclose the town called The Cow of Many Colours, see: there as he walked was this youth, sitting leaning against a tree and gazing wearily into the valley. Zarathustra grasped the tree the youth was sitting beside and spake thus:

'If I wanted to shake this tree with my hands I should not be able to.

'But the wind, which we do not see, torments and bends it whichever way it wishes. It is invisible hands that bend and torment us the worst.'

At this the youth started up in confusion and said: 'I hear Zarathustra, and I have just been thinking of him.' Zarathustra replied:

'Why does that startle you? – But with humans it is the same as with the tree.

'The more it strives to grow high up where it is light, the more its roots drive down into the earth, stronger and stronger, into the dark, into the depths – into evil.'

'Yes, into evil!' exclaimed the youth. 'How can you possibly have discovered what is in my soul?'

Zarathustra smiled and spake: 'There are souls one will never lay bare, unless one has first invented them.'

'Yes, into evil!' exclaimed the youth once more. 'What you said is true, Zarathustra. Ever since I have striven to go high, I no longer trust myself, and no one else trusts me any more. How can this be?

'I am changing too quickly: my today refutes my yesterday. Often when I am climbing I skip steps – none of the steps forgives me.

'Once I am at the top I am always alone. No one talks to me. The frost of solitude makes me shiver. Whatever am I after up there?

'My contempt and my longing grow together; the higher I climb, the more I hold the climber in contempt. Whatever is he after up there?

'How ashamed I am of my climbing and stumbling! How I deride my heavy puffing! How I hate the one who can fly! How weary I am up on high!'

Here the youth fell silent. And Zarathustra contemplated the tree beside which they were standing, and spake thus:

'This tree stands alone here in the mountains. It has grown taller than humans or animals.

'And if it wanted to speak, it would have no one who understood it, so tall has it grown.

'Now it waits and waits – but what is it waiting for? It lives too near the seat of the clouds; it may well be waiting for the first lightning.'

When Zarathustra had said this, the youth gestured vigorously, exclaiming: 'Yes, Zarathustra, what you say is true. When I wanted to go high up, I was out for my own destruction, and you are the lightning I was waiting for! See, what have I been since you appeared among us? It is *envy* of you that has destroyed me!' So said the youth, and he wept bitterly. But Zarathustra took him in his arm and led him along with him.

And when they had walked together for a while, Zarathustra began to speak thus:

'It tears my heart apart. Better than your words can say it, your eye tells me all of your danger.

'You are not yet free – you are still *searching* for freedom. Your search has left you bleary with lack of sleep, and too wide-awake.

'You want to go up high where one is free, your soul is thirsting for the stars. But your bad instincts are thirsting for freedom too.

'Your wild dogs want their freedom; they bark for joy in their cellar when your spirit strives to open up all the prisons.

'To me you are still a prisoner picturing his freedom to himself; ah, the souls of such prisoners become resourceful, but cunning and baleful too.

'The man whose spirit has been set free must still purify himself. There is a great deal of the prison and of rottenness still in him, and his eye has yet to become pure.

'Yes, I know your danger. But by my love and hope I beseech you: do not throw your love and hope away!

'You still feel yourself to be noble, and others who are ill-disposed and cast an evil eye on you still feel you to be noble too. Know that a noble man is in everybody's way.

'Even for the good a noble man is in the way; and even if they call him a good man, it is only to push him aside.

'The noble man wants to create new things and a new virtue. The good man wants old things and the preservation of old things.

'But the risk facing the noble man is that he become not a good man but an insolent, scornful, destructive man.

'Ah, I have known noble men who lost their loftiest hope, whereupon they denigrated all lofty hopes.

'From then on they led insolent lives of short-lived desires, and they scarcely had aims that looked to tomorrow.

'"The spirit is a sensual pleasure too," they said. And the wings of their spirit broke; since then it has crept around, dirtying whatever it gnaws at.

'At one time they intended to be heroes: now they are creatures of lust. To them, the hero spells grief and horror.

'But by my love and hope I beseech you: do not throw the hero in your soul away! Hold on to your loftiest hope as something sacred!'

Thus spake Zarathustra.

Of the Preachers of Death

There are preachers of death; and the earth is full of those to whom the renunciation of life must be preached.

The earth is full of the useless, and life has been spoilt by those of whom there are far too many. They should be lured out of this life by 'eternal life'!

'The yellow ones', the preachers of death are called, or 'the black ones'. But I want to show you them in other colours.

There are the terrible ones who bear a beast of prey within them, and whose only choice is between sensual pleasures and self-torture. And even their pleasures are torture.

These terrible ones have not even become human. Let them preach renunciation of life and get out of it themselves!

There are the consumptives of the soul, who are barely born but they begin to die and to long for doctrines of weariness and abnegation.

They would gladly be dead, and we should approve their wish. Let us be wary of waking these dead and damaging these living coffins!

They have only to meet a sick man or an old man or a corpse and promptly they say, 'Life has been refuted!'

But it is only they who are refuted, and their eye, which sees only one face of existence.

Thickly wrapped up in melancholy, and eager for those little chance events that bring death, they wait, grinding their teeth.

Or else they reach for sweets and mock their own childishness in doing so; they clutch at the straw of life and mock the fact that they are clutching at a straw.

Their wisdom declares, 'Those who stay alive are fools, but that is how foolish we are! And that very thing is the greatest folly in life!'

'Life is only suffering' – so say others, and they do not lie. Then see to it that *you* cease to be! See to it that life which is only suffering ceases!

And may the doctrine of your virtue declare, 'Thou shalt kill thyself! Thou shalt slink away!'

'Lust is a sin' – so say some who preach death – 'let us withdraw and beget no children!'

'Giving birth is arduous' – say others – 'why go on giving birth? One is only bringing forth unfortunates!' And they too are preachers of death.

'Compassion is necessary' – so say yet others. 'Take what I have! Take what I am! Life will bind me so much the less.'

If they were fundamentally compassionate, they would make life a misery for their neighbours. To be evil – that would be genuine goodness in them.

But they want to be rid of life. What does it matter to them if their chains and gifts tie others even more tightly to it?

And you too, for whom life is a turmoil of work and anxiety; are you not very tired of life? Are you not very ripe for the sermon of death?

All you who are fond of the turmoil of work and of what is fast, new, unfamiliar – you are not good at enduring yourselves, and your industry is flight and the will to forget yourselves.

If you had greater faith in life, you would not cast yourselves upon the moment so much. But there is not enough in you for you to wait – nor even for idleness!

Everywhere the voice of those who preach death resounds; and the earth is full of those to whom death must be preached.

Or 'eternal life'; it is all the same to me − as long as they depart this life quickly!

Thus spake Zarathustra.

Of War and Warriors

We do not want to be spared by our best enemies, nor by those for whom we have a fundamental love. So let me tell you the truth.

My brothers in war! I bear you a fundamental love. I am and always have been of your kind. And I am also your best enemy. So let me tell you the truth.

I know the hatred and envy that is in your hearts. You are not great enough to be without hatred and envy. So at least be great enough not to be ashamed of them.

And if you cannot be saints of knowledge, at least be its warriors. They are the companions and precursors of such sainthood.

I see many soldiers − I wish I could see many warriors! What they wear is called 'uniform'; may what they conceal under it not be uniform too!

You should be men whose eye is always looking for an enemy − *your* enemy. And with some of you there is hatred at first sight.

You should look for your enemy, you should wage your war, a war for your way of thinking! And if your thinking is defeated, your honesty should still proclaim triumph.

You should love peace as a means to new wars, and a short peace more than a long one.

I do not counsel work for you, but battle. I do not counsel peace for you, but victory. May your work be a battle, may your peace be a victory!

One can be silent and sit still only when one has a bow and arrow; otherwise one chatters and squabbles. May your peace be a victory!

You say it is the good cause that hallows even war? I say unto you: it is the good war that hallows any cause.

War and courage have accomplished more great things than love of one's neighbour. It was not your compassion but your valour that has hitherto saved those who have suffered misfortune.

'What is good?' you ask. To be brave is good. Let the little girls say, 'To be good is to be what is both pretty and touching.'

They call you heartless; but your heart is true, and I love the modesty of your heartiness. You are ashamed of your flow, and others are ashamed of their ebb.

You are ugly? Very well, my brothers! Pull the sublime close about you, the mantle of ugliness!

And when your soul grows great, it grows imperious, and in your sublimity there is wickedness. I know you.

In wickedness the imperious man and the weakling meet. But they misunderstand each other. I know you.

You may only have enemies who are to be hated, not enemies to be held in contempt. You must be proud of your enemy; then the successes of your enemy are your successes too.

Rebellion – that is the nobility of the slave. But your nobility should be obedience! Even when you give orders, it should be a way of obeying!

To a good warrior, 'Thou shalt' sounds more pleasing than 'I want'. And all that is dear to you should first be commanded of you.

May your love of life be love of your loftiest hope; and may your loftiest hope be the highest thought of life!

But you should receive your highest thought from me, as an order, to this effect: the human is something that must be overcome.

So live your lives of obedience and war! What use is long life? What warrior wants to be spared?

I do not spare you. I bear you a fundamental love, my brothers in war!

Thus spake Zarathustra.

Of the New Idol

Somewhere there are still peoples and flocks, but not among us, my brothers; here there are states.

The state? What is that? Very well! Now open your ears to what I say, for now I shall speak my piece on the death of peoples.

The state is the coldest of all cold monsters. Coldly it lies, too; and this lie crawls from its mouth: 'I, the state, am the people.'

It is a lie. It was creators who created peoples and hung a faith and a love over them; in this way they served life.

It is destroyers who set traps for the many and call them the state; they hang a sword and a hundred desires over them.

Where a people still exists, it does not understand the state and hates it as the evil eye and a sin against customs and rights.

I give you this sign: every people speaks its own language of good and evil, which the neighbour does not understand. It devised its own language of customs and rights.

But the state lies in all the languages of good and evil, and whatever it says is a lie – and whatever it has, it stole.

Everything about it is false. It likes to bite, and bites with stolen teeth. Even its entrails are false.

Confusion of the language of good and evil – I give you this sign as a sign of the state. Truly, this sign means the will to death. Truly, it is a signal to the preachers of death!

Far too many are born; the state was invented for the superfluous!

Just see how it lures them to it, the far too many! How it gobbles them and chews them and chews them over and over!

'On earth there is nothing greater than I, the ordering finger of God' – thus the monster bellows. And it is not only those with long ears or short sight that fall to their knees!

Ah, even within you it whispers its dark lies, you great souls! Ah, it discerns the wealthy hearts that gladly squander themselves!

Yes, it discerns you as well, you who have conquered the old god. You grew weary in the battle, and now your weariness serves the new idol!

The new idol would like to set heroes and honourable men about it. It likes to sun itself in the sunshine of clear consciences – this cold monster!

It will give *you* everything if *you* worship it, the new idol; so it buys itself the lustre of your virtue and the gaze of your proud eyes.

It means to use you to lure the far too many. Yes, it is an infernal trick that it's come up with, a horse of death jingling with the trappings of divine honours!

Yes, death has been devised for many, and it commends itself as life: truly, a service to gladden the hearts of all preachers of death!

I call it the state where everyone, good and bad, drinks poison; the state where everyone, good and bad, lose himself; the state where the gradual suicide of all is called – 'life'.

Just look at these useless people! They steal the works of inventors for themselves, and the treasures of the wise, and call their theft culture – and they turn everything to sickness and woe.

Just look at these useless people! They are always ill, they puke up their bile and call it a newspaper. They gobble each other up and cannot even digest themselves.

Just look at these useless people! They acquire riches and grow poorer in the process. They want power, and primarily they want the crowbar of power, lots of money – these impotent creatures!

See them clamber, these quick-footed apes! They clamber over one another and in doing so drag each other down into the mud and the depths.

They all want to get to the throne; that is their madness – as if happiness sat on the throne! Often it is mud that sits on the throne – and often the throne sits on mud, too.

They are all madmen in my eyes, and clambering apes, overheated. Their idol, the cold monster, is a stench in my nose; the whole lot of these idolaters stink.

My brothers, do you really want to suffocate in the fug of their mouths and desires? Rather smash the windows and jump out into the open!

Get away from that stench! Leave the idolatry of the useless behind!

Get away from that stench! Leave the fumes from these human sacrifices behind!

Even now, the earth remains free for great souls. Many places are still free for the solitary ones and two about whom the scent of tranquil seas blows.

A free life still remains for great souls. Truly, whoever possesses little will be the less possessed; praised be a moderate poverty!

It is only where the state ends that the human who is not useless begins; there the song of what is necessary begins, that unique and irreplaceable melody.

Where the state *ends* – just look, my brothers! Do you not see it, the rainbow and the bridges of the superhuman?

Thus spake Zarathustra.

Of the Flies of the Marketplace

Flee, my friend, into your solitude! I see you deafened by the noise of great men and pricked by the barbs of the lowly.

The forests and cliffs know how to keep a dignified silence with you. Be once more like the tree you love, that tree with the broad branches; quiet and listening, it hangs over the sea.

Where solitude ends, the marketplace begins; and where the marketplace begins, the noise of the great actors begins too, and the buzzing of noxious flies.

In the world even the best things are worthless without one who will first present them; these presenters are known as great men by the people.

The people have little understanding of greatness, that is to say: creativity. But they do have a sense for all showmen and actors of what is great.

The world revolves about the inventor of new values; imperceptibly it turns. But the people and the fame revolve about the actors; that is the way of the world.

The actor has spirit, but little of the spirit's conscience. He always believes in whatever most powerfully makes others believe – believe in *him*!

Tomorrow he will have a new faith, and the day after a newer one. He has swift senses, like the people, and changes in his weather.

Knocking over is tantamount to proving, for him. Driving crazy is tantamount to convincing, for him. And blood is the best of all reasons, for him.

A truth that merely slips into the ears of the refined he calls a lie, and nothing. Truly, he believes only in gods who make a big noise in the world!

The marketplace is full of solemn clowns – and the people boast of their great men! That is how the men of the hour appear to them.

But the hour presses them; and so they press you. And from you too they want a yes or a no. Woe, if you want to set down your chair between pro and contra.

Do not be jealous, lover of truth, on account of these unconditional and urgent ones. Truth has never yet taken the arm of an unconditional man.

Because of these abrupt ones, return to your security; only in the marketplace is one beset with 'yes?' or 'no?'

The experience of all deep wells is slow; they have to wait a long time till they know *what* has fallen into their depths.

All greatness is to be found away from the marketplace and fame; since time immemorial, the inventors of new values have always lived away from the marketplace and fame.

Flee, my friend, into your solitude; I see you stung by noxious flies. Flee to where the rough, bracing breezes blow!

Flee into your solitude! You have lived too near to the lowly and wretched. Flee from their covert revenge! Towards you they are nothing but vengeance.

Do not raise your arm against them any more. They are innumerable, and it is not your lot to be a fly-swatter.

Innumerable are these lowly and wretched creatures; and proud edifices have been brought down by raindrops and weeds.

You are not a stone, but already you have been hollowed out by many drops. You will yet break and burst asunder from those many drops.

I see you wearied by noxious flies, see you bloodily scratched in a hundred places; and your pride declines to be angry.

They want blood from you, in all innocence, their bloodless souls crave blood – and so they sting, in all innocence.

But you, profound man, you suffer too deeply even from small wounds; and before you could even heal, the selfsame poisonous worm was crawling over your hand again.

You are too proud to kill these little nibblers. But beware that it does not become your fate to endure all their poisonous injustice!

They buzz around you even with their praises; and their praise is importunity. They want your skin and your blood near.

They flatter you as they might a god or devil; they whine before you as they might before a god or devil. What of it! They are flatterers and whiners, and nothing more.

And often they affect to be amiable towards you. But that has always been the resourcefulness of cowards. Yes, cowards are resourceful!

They think about you a good deal, with their attenuated souls – you are always an object of suspicion for them! Anything that is thought about a good deal becomes suspicious.

They punish you for all your virtues. Fundamentally they forgive you only your errors.

Because you are gentle and have a sense of justice, you say: 'It is not their fault that their existence is petty.' But their attenuated soul thinks: 'All great existence is guilty.'

Even when you are gentle towards them, they still feel you hold them in contempt; and secretly they answer your kindness with hurtfulness.

Your wordless pride always runs counter to their taste; they rejoice if for once you are modest enough to be vain.

When we perceive a quality in a human being, we also set it alight in him. So beware of the lowly!

In your presence they feel lowly, and their baseness glimmers and smoulders against you in covert revenge.

Did you not notice how often they fell silent when you joined them, and how their strength deserted them like smoke from a dying fire?

Yes, my friend, you are a bad conscience to your neighbours; for they are unworthy of you. So they hate you and would gladly suck your blood.

Your neighbours will always be noxious flies. What is great in you must make them more poisonous and more fly-like.

Flee, my friend, into your solitude, to where a rough, strong wind blows. It is not your lot to be a fly-swatter.

Thus spake Zarathustra.

Of Chastity

I love the forest. It is bad to live in towns; too many who are in heat live there.

Is it not better to fall into the hands of a murderer than into the dreams of a woman in heat?

And just look at these men; their eye says it – they know nothing better on earth than to lie with a woman.

There is mud at the bottom of their souls; and woe, if their mud has spirit to it, too!

If only you were at least perfect as animals! But to be an animal requires innocence.

Do I counsel you to kill your senses? I counsel you to innocence of the senses.

Do I counsel you to chastity? In some, chastity is a virtue, but in many it verges on a vice.

These people certainly abstain; but the bitch, sensuality, gazes out enviously from everything they do.

This strife-ridden beast goes with them even to the heights of their virtue and into the coldness of the spirit.

And how cutely the bitch, sensuality, begs for a scrap of spirit if a scrap of flesh is refused her!

You love tragedies and anything that is heartbreaking? But I mistrust your bitch.

Your eyes are too cruel for my liking, and you look upon those who suffer with a lustful gaze. Is your sensual appetite not wearing false clothing, pretending to be compassion?

And I give you this parable too: not a mere few of those who wanted to drive out their devils entered into the swine themselves.

Those for whom chastity is difficult should be counselled against it, that it be not their road to hell – that is, to the mud and lechery of the soul.

Am I speaking of dirty things? To my mind, that is not the worst of it.

It is not when the truth is dirty but when it is shallow that the man of understanding is reluctant to enter its water.

In truth, there are those who are fundamentally chaste; they are gentler of heart and laugh more often and more merrily than you.

They even laugh at chastity, and ask: 'What is chastity?

'Is chastity not folly? But this folly came to us and not we to it.

'We offered this guest shelter and affection; now it lives with us – let it stay as long as it wants!'

Thus spake Zarathustra.

Of the Friend

'There is always one too many around me' – so thinks the hermit. 'Always one times one – in the long run that will make two!'

I and me are always holding too-animated conversations; how could one stand it without a friend?

For the hermit, the friend is always the third person; the third is the cork that prevents the conversation of the other two from sinking into the depths.

Ah, there are too many depths for all the hermits. That is why they long so much for a friend and for his height.

Our faith in others betrays what it is in ourselves that we should like to believe in. Our longing for a friend betrays us.

And often with love we merely want to vault our envy. And often we attack and make an enemy in order to conceal that we are vulnerable to attack.

'At least be my enemy!' – so speaks true reverence, which does not dare ask for friendship.

If you want a friend, you must be prepared to go to war for him; and to go to war you must be *capable* of being an enemy.

You should still honour the enemy in your friend. Can you go up close to your friend without going over to him?

In your friend you should have your best enemy. In your heart you should be closest to him when you are at odds with him.

You want to go unclothed before your friend? You would have your friend think it an honour that you show yourself as you are? But he curses you to the devil for it!

He who is completely open about himself prompts outrage; that is how much reason you have to fear nakedness! Yes, if you were gods you could be ashamed of your clothes!

You cannot be too well turned out for your friend, for you should be an arrow for him, and a longing for the superhuman.

Have you ever watched your friend asleep, to learn what he looks like? What else is there to see in your friend's face? It is your own face, in a rough and imperfect mirror.

Have you ever watched your friend asleep? Were you not startled to see what your friend looked like? Oh my friend, the human is something that must be overcome.

Your friend should be a master at divining and at keeping silent; you must not want to see everything. Your dream should reveal to you what your friend does when awake.

Your compassion should be an act of divining, that you might first know whether your friend wants compassion. Perhaps what he loves in you is the unbroken gaze and the eye of eternity.

Your compassion for your friend should be concealed beneath a hard shell, so that you break a tooth biting through to it. That way it has its delicacy and sweetness.

Are you pure air and solitude and bread and medicine for your friend? There are those who cannot loose their own chains and yet they can deliver their friends.

Are you a slave? If you are, you cannot be a friend. Are you a tyrant? If you are, you cannot have friends.

All too long a slave and a tyrant were concealed within woman. For that reason, woman is not yet capable of friendship she knows only love.

In woman's love there are injustice and blindness towards everything that she does not love. And even when woman's love is enlightened, there is still ambush and lightning and night along with the light in it.

Woman is not capable of friendship yet; women are still cats, and birds. Or, at best, cows.

Woman is not capable of friendship yet. But tell me, you men, which of you is capable of friendship?

Oh, your poverty, you men, and your meanness of soul! What you give to your friend I will even give to my enemy, and I shall not be any the poorer for it.

There is comradeship; let there be friendship!

Thus spake Zarathustra.

Of the Thousand and One Goals

Zarathustra has seen many lands and many peoples, and has discovered the good and the evil of many peoples. No greater power has Zarathustra found on earth than good and evil.

No people could live without first assessing values; if it wishes to endure, it must not make the same assessment as its neighbours.

Much that one people deemed good meant derision and humiliation in the eyes of another; this was what I found. Much I found designated evil in one place and decked in purple honours in another.

No neighbour ever understood the other; always his soul was astounded by his neighbour's madness and malevolence.

A table of things that are good hangs over every people. See, it is the table of all it has overcome; see, it is the voice of its will to power.

What it considers hard it declares praiseworthy; what it considers indispensable and hard it declares good; and what affords deliverance from the worst of affliction, that rare and hardest of things, it extols as holy.

Whatever enables it to rule and conquer and shine, to the horror and envy of its neighbour, it deems the exalted, the foremost, the measure and meaning of all things.

Truly, my brother, if only you have recognized a people's need and land and sky and neighbour, you will divine the law by which it overcomes, and why it is on this ladder that it climbs to what it hopes for.

'Thou shalt always be the first and rise over the rest; your jealous soul shall love no one except your friend' – this made the soul of a Greek tremble; in following it, he followed his path to greatness.

'Speak the truth and handle bow and arrow well' – this seemed both dear and hard to that people from whom I have my name, the name that is both dear and hard to me.

'To honour one's father and mother, and do their will from the very roots of one's soul' – another people hung this table of overcoming over itself, and grew mighty and eternal by following it.

'To be loyal and to risk one's honour and blood even in evil and dangerous causes for the sake of loyalty' – another people mastered itself with this teaching, and in so mastering itself became pregnant and heavy with great hopes.

Truly, humans have given all their good and evil to themselves. Truly, they did not take it, they did not find it, it did not come down to them as a voice from heaven.

Humans first assigned value to things in the course of self-preservation – they created the meaning of things, a human meaning! That is why they call themselves 'human', that is, the one who evaluates.

Evaluation is creation; hear it, creative people! Evaluating is itself the treasure and jewel of all valued things.

Only through evaluation is there value; and without evaluation the nut of existence would be hollow. Hear it, creative people!

Change in values means change in the creative people. Those who must be creators invariably destroy.

At first, the creators were peoples. It was only at a late date that they were individuals. In truth, the individual is himself the latest creation.

At one time the peoples hung a table of what was good over themselves. Love that wants to rule and love that wants to obey made these tables together.

Pleasure taken in the flock is older than pleasure taken in the I; and as long as the good conscience is called flock, it is only the bad conscience that says: 'I'.

Truly, the cunning, loveless I that seeks its own advantage in what benefits the many – that is not the origin of the flock but its downfall.

It has always been loving and creative people who created good and evil. The fire of love and the fire of wrath glow in the names of all the virtues.

Zarathustra has seen many lands and many peoples; no greater power has Zarathustra found on earth than the works of loving people: 'good' and 'evil' are their names.

Truly, the power of this praising and blaming is a monster. Tell me, brothers, who will subdue it for me? Tell me, who will throw the fetter on the beast's thousand necks?

Hitherto there have been a thousand goals, for there have been a thousand peoples. All that is lacking is the fetter for the thousand necks. That one goal is lacking. Humanity still lacks a goal.

But tell me, my brothers: if humanity still lacks a goal, is not humanity itself also lacking?

Thus spake Zarathustra.

Of Love of One's Neighbour

You throng about your neighbour, and have fine words for what you are doing. But I say unto you: your love of your neighbour is your bad love of yourselves.

You flee to your neighbour, from yourselves, and would like to make a virtue of this; but I see through your 'selflessness'.

The 'thou' is older than the 'I'; the 'thou' has been canonized, but not yet the 'I'; so humans throng to their neighbour.

Do I counsel you to love your neighbour? Rather, I counsel you to flee your neighbour, and love those furthest from you!

Higher than love of one's neighbour is love of the furthest and the future; higher still than love of one's neighbour is love of causes and phantoms.

This phantom that goes before you, my brother, is lovelier than you; why do you not give it your flesh and bones? But you are afraid and run to your neighbour.

You cannot stand your own company and do not love yourselves enough; now you want to beguile your neighbour into love and gild yourselves with his mistake.

I wish you could not stand the company of neighbours of all

kinds, and the neighbours' neighbours; then you would have to create your friend and his overflowing heart out of yourselves.

You invite a witness in when you want to speak well of yourselves; and when you have beguiled him into thinking well of you, you too think well of yourselves.

The liar is not only the one who speaks contrary to what he knows, but still more the one who speaks contrary to what he does not know. And so you speak of yourselves in your dealings with others, and use yourselves to lie to your neighbour.

Thus speaks the fool: 'Having dealings with people ruins the character, especially if one has none.'

One person goes to his neighbour because he is looking for himself, and the other because he wants to lose himself. Your bad love of yourselves makes solitude a prison for you.

It is those who are further away who pay for your love of your neighbours; and the moment five of you are together, a sixth always has to die.

I do not love your festivals, either: I have found too many actors there, and the onlookers frequently behaved like actors too.

I teach you not the neighbour but the friend. May the friend be a festival of the earth to you, and a foretaste of the superhuman.

I teach you the friend and his overfull heart. But one must have the ability to be a sponge if one wants to be loved by overfull hearts.

I teach you the friend in whom the world is complete, a shell of goodness – the creative friend, who always has a complete world to give away.

And as the world rolled asunder for him, so it rolls back together for him in rings, as the evolution of good through evil, as the evolution of purposes from chance.

May the future and the furthest be the principle of your today; in your friend you shall love the superhuman as your principle.

My brothers, I do not counsel you to love your neighbours; I counsel you to love those furthest from you.

Thus spake Zarathustra.

Of the Way of the Creator

My brother, do you want to begin the path of solitude? Do you want to seek the way to yourself? Pause a little longer and listen to me.

'He who seeks easily gets lost himself. Seeking solitude is a fault'; thus speaks the flock. And you were long one of the flock.

The voice of the flock will still sound in you too. And if you say, 'I no longer share one conscience with you all,' it will be both lament and pain.

See, this pain was itself born of that one conscience; and the last glimmer of that conscience still glows upon your affliction.

But you want to go the way of your affliction, which is the way to yourself? Then show me your right to do so, and your strength for it!

Are you a new strength and a new right? A prime movement? A wheel that rolls of itself? Can you compel even the stars to revolve around you?

Ah, there is so much lust for pre-eminence! There is so much strenuous effort by the ambitious! Show me that you are not a person of lust and ambitions!

Ah, there are so many grand ideas that do no more than a bellows; they inflate and make emptier.

You call yourself free? I want to hear your ruling idea, and not that you have escaped a yoke.

Are you such a one as *ought* to escape a yoke? There are people who cast off the last of their value when they cast off their servitude.

Free from what? What is that to Zarathustra! But your eye should clearly declare to me: free *for* what?

Can you lay down your own good and evil, and hang up your own will above you as a law? Can you be your own judge, and avenger of your law?

It is terrible to be alone with the judge and avenger of one's own law. It is in such a way that a star is thrown out into the wastes of space and into the icy breath of solitude.

Today, you one, you still suffer from the many; today you still possess your courage entire, and your hopes.

But one day solitude will tire you out, one day your pride will bend and your courage creak. One day you will cry out, 'I am alone!'

One day you will no longer see what is exalted in you, and you will see your lowliness all too closely; your very sublimity will fill you with fear, like a phantom. One day you will cry out, 'Everything is false!'

There are feelings that are out to kill the solitary; if they do not succeed, well, they must die themselves! But do you have it in you to be a murderer?

My brother, are you familiar with the word 'contempt'? And with the anguish of justice in being just towards those who hold you in contempt?

You compel many to revise what they think of you; they hold that very much against you. You were close to them and yet you passed them by; that they will never forgive you.

You go higher beyond them; but the higher you climb, the smaller you appear to the eye of envy. He who is detested most of all, however, is the one who can fly.

'How could you possibly be just towards me?' – you must say – 'I choose your injustice as my portion.'

They throw injustice and dirt at the solitary; but, my brother, if you want to be a star you must shine no less brightly for them on that account!

And be wary of the good and just! They like to crucify those who devise their own virtue – they hate the solitary.

Be wary of holy simple-mindedness as well! Everything that is not simple-minded is unholy in its eyes; and it likes to play with fire – and to burn at the stake.

And be wary of being attacked by your own love, too! The solitary offers his hand too readily to anyone he meets.

There are those you should offer not your hand but your paw – and I wish your paw had claws, too.

But the worst enemy you can encounter will always be you yourself; you lie in wait for yourself in caves and forests.

Solitary man, you are taking the path to yourself! And your way leads past yourself and your seven devils!

You will be a heretic to yourself, and a witch and soothsayer and fool and doubter and an unholy man and an evil-doer.

You must wish to burn yourself in your own flame; how could you become new if you have not first become ashes!

Solitary man, you are taking the path of the creator; you mean to create your own god out of your seven devils!

Solitary man, you are taking the path of the lover: you love yourself and for that reason hold yourself in contempt, as only lovers can.

The lover wants to create because he despises! What does he know of love who has not had to hold the very object of his love in contempt!

Go with your love into your solitary and creative state, my brother; and justice will come limping tardily after.

Go with my tears into your solitary state, my brother. I love the one who aims to create something beyond himself, and perishes in the process.

Thus spake Zarathustra.

Of Old and Young Women

'Why do you creep about so shyly in the twilight, Zarathustra? And what are you carefully concealing under your cloak?

'Is it some treasure you have been given? Or a child that has been born to you? Or are you yourself now going the ways of thieves, you friend of the wicked?'

Truly, my brother, spake Zarathustra, it is a treasure that has been given to me: what I am carrying is a little truth.

But it is as unruly as a little child; and if I do not shut its mouth it will cry too loudly.

Today as I was going my way alone, at the hour when the sun is sinking, a little old woman came my way and said this to my soul:

'Zarathustra has spoken much to us women, too, but he has never spoken to us about woman.'

And I answered her: 'One should talk about woman only to men.'

'Talk to me about woman too,' she said; 'I am old enough to forget what you say right away.'

And I did as the little old woman wished and spake to her thus:

Everything about woman is a riddle, and everything about woman has one solution: pregnancy.

For woman, man is a means: the end is always the child. But what is woman for man?

The true man wants two things: danger and play. That is why he wants woman, the most dangerous plaything.

Man should be trained for war and woman for the recreation of the warrior; all else is folly.

Fruits that are all too sweet are not to the warrior's taste. That is why he likes woman; even the sweetest woman is still bitter.

Woman understands children better than a man, but man is more childlike than woman.

Within a true man a child is concealed; it wants to play. Come on, women, discover the child in man!

Let woman be a plaything, pure and fine, like a precious stone lit up by the virtues of a world that does not yet exist.

Let the ray of a star gleam in your love! Let your hope be: 'May I give birth to the superhuman!'

Let there be bravery in your love! With your love you should attack whoever instils fear in you.

Let your honour be in your love! Woman has little understanding of honour in other respects. But let it be your honour always to love more than you are loved, and never to be in second place.

Let man fear woman when she loves; then she makes every sacrifice, and everything else she regards as worthless.

Let man fear woman when she hates; for man is merely bad at the bottom of his soul, but woman is vile there.

What does woman hate most? Thus spake the iron to the magnet: 'I hate you most because you attract me but are not strong enough to draw me to you.'

Man's happiness is: I want. Woman's happiness is: he wants.

'See, the world has just been made perfect!' – so thinks every woman when she obeys out of complete love.

And woman has to obey and find a depth for her surface. The nature of woman is all surface, a changing, tempestuous film upon shallow waters.

But man's nature is deep, his current pours through underground caverns; woman senses its power but does not understand it.

To this the little old woman rejoined: 'Zarathustra has said many nice things, especially for those who are young enough for them.

'It is strange that Zarathustra knows little of women and yet he is right about them! Is that because, with woman, nothing is impossible?

'Now take as thanks a little truth! I am old enough for it, after all!

'Wrap it up and keep its mouth shut or it will cry too loudly, this little truth.'

'Give me your little truth, woman,' I said. And thus spake the little old woman:

'If you are going to women, don't forget your whip!'

Thus spake Zarathustra.

Of the Adder's Bite

One day Zarathustra had fallen asleep under a fig tree, since it was hot, and had laid his arms across his face. An adder came and bit him in the neck, so that Zarathustra cried out in pain. When he had taken his arm from his face he looked at the snake; it recognized Zarathustra's eyes, turned awkwardly, and attempted to get away.

'Don't go,' said Zarathustra; 'you have not accepted my thanks yet. You woke me at the right time, I still have a long way to go.' 'Your way is a short one,' said the adder sadly, 'my venom is deadly.' Zarathustra smiled. 'When did a dragon ever die of a snake's venom?' he said. 'But take your venom back! You are not rich enough to give it to me.' At this the adder fell upon his neck once again and licked his wound.

On one occasion, when Zarathustra told this to his disciples, they asked: 'And what, oh Zarathustra, is the moral of your story?' Zarathustra answered thus:

The good and just call me the destroyer of morals; my story is immoral.

But if you have an enemy, do not repay him with good for evil, for that would be shaming; instead, prove that he has done you a good turn.

Rather be angry than put to shame! And if you are cursed, I do not like it if you wish to bless. Better to join in and curse a little too!

And if you have been done a great wrong, quickly do five little wrongs in return! It is dreadful to behold the man who is oppressed by wrong alone.

Did you know this yet? A wrong shared is half a right. Let the one who can bear a wrong take it upon himself.

A little revenge is more human than no revenge at all. And if the punishment is not also a right and an honour for the transgressor, I do not care for your punishment.

It is more distinguished to own that one is wrong than to insist on being right, especially if one is in fact right. One must only be rich enough.

I do not care for your cold justice; and from the eye of your judges gazes always the executioner and his cold steel.

Say, where is the justice to be found that is love with eyes that see?

Devise a love that will bear not only every punishment but also every guilt!

Devise a justice that will acquit everyone except the judges!

Do you want to hear one more thing? The man who would be just from the very foundations transforms even a lie into a philanthropic deed.

But how could I be just from the very foundations? How can I render unto everyone what is his? Let this suffice me: I give everyone what is mine.

Finally, my brothers, beware of doing wrong to any hermit! How could a hermit forget? How could he requite?

A hermit is like a deep well. It is easy to throw a stone into it, but tell me: once it has sunk to the bottom, who will offer to fetch it out again?

Beware of offending the hermit! But if you have done so, kill him too!

Thus spake Zarathustra.

Of Children and Marriage

I have a question for you alone, my brother; I throw this question like a plummet into your soul, to know how deep it is.

You are young and wish for a child and marriage. But I ask you: are you a person who *ought* to wish for a child?

Are you the victor, the conqueror of the self, the ruler of the senses, the master of your virtues? That is my question to you.

Or is it the animal and sheer need that your wish tells of? Or isolation? Or a failure to be at peace with yourself?

I want it to be your victory and your freedom that long for a child. You should build living memorials to your victory and your liberation.

You should build beyond yourself. But first, I say, you must be built yourself, four-square in body and soul.

You should propagate yourself not only onwards but upwards! May the garden of marriage help you in this!

Thou shalt create a higher body, a prime movement, a wheel that rolls of itself – thou shalt create a creator.

Marriage: I give the name to the will of two to create the one that is more than those who created it. Reverence for each other, as for those who hold such a will, is what I call marriage.

Let this be the meaning and the truth of your marriage. But what the far too many, the superfluous, call marriage – ah, what shall I call that?

Ah, that poverty of soul in a twosome! Ah, that filth of soul in a twosome! Ah, that wretched contentment in a twosome!

All of that they call marriage; and they say their marriages are made in heaven.

Well, I do not care for it, this heaven of the superfluous! No, I do not care for them, these animals entangled in the heavenly net!

And let the god who limps over to bless what he did not join together stay far from me!

Do not laugh at such marriages. Where is the child who has no reason to weep over its parents?

This man seemed worthy to me, and ripe for the meaning of the earth; but when I saw his wife, the earth seemed to me a house for people bereft of their senses.

Yes, I would that the earth shook with convulsions when a saint and a goose mate with each other.

This man set out like a hero in quest of truths and at length bagged a pretty little lie. He calls it his marriage.

That man was stand-offish in his conduct and selective in his choices. But at a stroke he spoilt his company once and for all; he calls it his marriage.

That man was looking for a handmaid with the virtues of an angel. But at a stroke he became the handmaid of a woman, and now he needs to become an angel on top of it.

I have found all buyers to be cautious, and all of them have canny eyes. But even the canniest of them still buys his wife in a poke.

A great many short-lived follies – that is what you call love. And your marriage puts an end to a great many short-lived follies with one long-lasting stupidity.

Your love for woman and woman's love for man; ah, if only it were compassion for suffering and disguised gods! But two animals mostly sense one another.

But even your best love is merely a rapturous simulacrum and a red-hot pain. It is a torch that should light your way to higher paths.

One day you shall love beyond yourselves! So first *learn* to love! It is to that end that you have had to drink the bitter cup of your love.

Bitterness is in the cup of even the best love; thus it prompts longing for the superhuman, thus it makes you, the creator, thirsty!

The thirst of the creator, an arrow and longing for the superhuman: tell me, my brother, is this your will to marriage?

Such a will and such a marriage I call holy.

Thus spake Zarathustra.

Of Free Death

Many die too late, and some die too early. The doctrine still sounds strange: 'Die at the right time.'

Die at the right time: that is what Zarathustra teaches.

Of course, if a man never lives at the right time, how is he ever to die at the right time? Would that he had never been born! – That is my counsel to the superfluous.

But even the superfluous make a big thing of their dying, and even the hollowest nut wants to be cracked.

Everyone takes death to be important; but death is not yet a festival. Humankind has not yet learnt how to consecrate the fairest of festivals.

I show you consummating death, which shall be a spur and a promise to the living.

The man who consummates his life dies his own death, victorious, surrounded by the hopeful making vows.

That is the manner of dying one should learn; and there should be no festival where a man dying in this way does not consecrate the oaths of the living!

To die in this way is the best death; but the second best is to die in battle and squander a great soul.

But hateful to fighter and victor alike is your grinning death that sidles up like a thief – and yet comes as the lord.

I commend my kind of death to you – free death, that comes to me because *I* want it.

And when shall I want it? He who has a goal and an heir wants death at the right time for his goal and heir.

And out of reverence for his goal and heir he will hang no more withered wreaths in the sanctuary of life.

Truly, I do not want to be like the rope-makers; they pull out their strand to full length and are forever going backwards themselves in the process.

Many a one grows too old even for his truths and victories; a toothless mouth no longer has the right to every truth.

And everyone who wants glory must take his leave of honour in good time and practise the difficult art of – going at the right time.

One must stop letting oneself be eaten when one tastes best; those who want to be loved long know this.

There are of course sour apples whose lot is to wait until the last day of autumn – whereupon they become ripe, yellow and shrivelled.

In others the heart ages first, and in others still the spirit. And some are ancients in their youth; but if one is late to grow young, one stays young longer.

There are those for whom life goes awry: a poisonous worm eats its way into their hearts. All the more reason to see that their dying is a success.

There are those who never grow sweet, and already rot in the summer. It is cowardice that holds him on to their branches.

Far too many live and hang on their branches far too long. Would that a storm would come and shake all these rotten and worm-eaten ones from the tree!

Would that preachers of a *swift* death would come! They would be the right storms and shakers of the trees of life, to my mind. But I hear only slow death preached, and patience with all 'earthly things'.

Ah, so you preach patience with earthly things? It is those earthly things that have too much patience with you, you blasphemers!

Truly, that Hebrew honoured by the preachers of slow death died too early; and the fact that he died too early has proved fateful for many ever since.

He knew as yet only the tears and melancholy of the Hebrew, and the hatred of the good and just – the Hebrew Jesus; but then he was overcome by a longing for death.

If only he had remained in the wilderness, far from the good and just! Perhaps he would have learnt to live and learnt to love the earth – and to laugh, too!

Believe me, my brothers! He died too early; he himself would have recanted his teaching if he had lived to my age! He was noble enough to recant.

But he was still immature. A youth loves immaturely, and he hates humankind and the earth immaturely as well. His nature and the wings of his spirit are still bound and heavy.

But there is more of the child in a man than in a youth, and less melancholy; he has a better understanding of death and life.

Free for death and free in death, a holy naysayer when the time for yes has passed: that is his understanding of death and life.

That your dying be not a blasphemy against humankind and the earth, my friends: that is what I beseech from the honey of your souls.

In your dying, your spirit and your virtue should still glow like a sunset upon the earth; otherwise, your dying has turned out badly.

I myself would die in such a way that you my friends love the earth the more for my sake; and I want to become earth once more, that I may have peace in her who bore me.

Truly, Zarathustra had a goal, he threw his ball; now you my friends are the heirs of my goal, I throw the golden ball to you.

More than anything else I like to see you, my friends, throwing the golden ball. And so I shall linger a little longer on earth; forgive me for that!

Thus spake Zarathustra.

Of the Giving Virtue

1

When Zarathustra had bid farewell to the town his heart was attached to, which was called The Cow of Many Colours, many who called themselves his disciples followed and accompanied him. So they came to a crossroads, where Zarathustra told them that he wanted to go on alone; for he was fond of walking alone. But his disciples gave him a staff in farewell, on the golden haft of which a serpent was coiled about the sun. Zarathustra was pleased with the staff and leant on it; then he spake thus to his disciples.

Tell me: how did gold come to have the highest value? Because it is uncommon and useless and gleaming and mellow in its glister; it is forever giving itself.

Only as an image of the highest virtue did gold come to have the highest value. The gaze of the giver gleams like gold. The glister of gold makes peace between the moon and the sun.

The highest virtue is uncommon and useless, it is gleaming and mellow in its glister; a giving virtue is the highest virtue.

Truly, I divine you well, my disciples: you aspire as I do to the giving virtue. What could you have in common with cats and wolves?

You thirst to become sacrifices and gifts yourselves; and that is why you thirst to heap up all riches in your soul.

Your soul aspires insatiably to treasures and jewels, because your virtue is insatiable in wanting to give.

You compel all things to come to you and into you, that they may flow back from your wellspring as the gifts of your love.

Truly, a giving love of this kind must become a thief of all values; nonetheless, I call this self-centredness hale and holy.

There is another self-centredness, all too poor, and hungry, that always wants to steal – the self-centredness of the sick, the sick self-centredness.

With the eye of a thief it looks upon everything that glitters; with the greed of hunger it assesses the one who has plenty to eat; and it is always slinking about the table of givers.

Sickness speaks from craving of this kind, and invisible degeneracy; the thieving greed of this self-centredness bespeaks a sickly body.

Tell me, my brothers: what do we consider bad, and the worst? Is it not *degeneracy*? – and we always suspect degeneracy where the giving soul is absent.

Our path leads upwards, from the species over to the super-species. But the degenerate way of thinking, which says 'everything for me', is a horror to us.

Our thinking flies upwards; in this it is an image of our bodies, an image of rising. The names of the virtues are images of rising of this kind.

So the body moves through history, evolving and fighting. And the spirit – what is it to the body? The herald, comrade and echo of its battles and victories.

All names of good and evil are images: they do not state, they merely hint. It is a fool who seeks knowledge from them.

Give your attention to any hour when your spirit would speak in images, my brothers, for that is the origin of your virtue.

At that time your body is risen on high and resurrected; it delights the spirit with its joy, so becoming the creator and evaluator and lover and benefactor of all things.

When your heart surges broad and full like a river, a blessing and a danger to those who live near: that is the origin of your virtue.

When you are exalted above praise and blame, and your will wants to command all things, as the will of a lover: that is the origin of your virtue.

When you despise pleasant things and a soft bed, and cannot make your bed far enough away from the pampered: that is the origin of your virtue.

When you together will a single will, and this turning-point of exigency is necessity to you: that is the origin of your virtue.

Truly, it is a new good and evil! Truly, a new rushing deep below, and the voice of a new spring!

It is power, this new virtue; it is a ruling idea, and around it a resourceful soul: a golden sun and around it the serpent of knowledge.

2

Here Zarathustra was silent for a while and gazed lovingly upon his disciples. Then he continued speaking, in a changed voice.

Stay loyal to the earth, my brothers, with the power of your virtue! May your giving love and your knowledge serve the meaning of the earth! Thus I beseech and adjure you.

Do not let your virtue fly away from earthly things and beat its wings against eternal walls! Ah, there has always been so much virtue that has flown away!

Lead the flown-away virtue back to the earth, as I do – yes, back to body and life; that it give the earth its meaning, a human meaning.

In a hundred ways the spirit, as well as virtue, has hitherto flown away and erred. Ah, all that delusion and error still dwell in our bodies; they have become body and will.

In a hundred ways the spirit, as well as virtue, has experimented and gone astray. Yes, humankind was an experiment. Ah, a great deal of ignorance and error has become body in us!

Not only the reason of millennia – the madness of millennia breaks out in us too. It is dangerous to be an heir.

We are still struggling step by step with the giant, chance, and all of humanity is still ruled by nonsense, by no-sense.

May your spirit and your virtue serve the meaning of the earth, my brothers; and may the value of all things be newly assessed by you. To that end you shall be fighters. To that end you shall be creators.

By knowing, the body purifies itself; by experimenting with what it knows, it exalts itself; to the man of understanding, all drives are holy; the soul of the exalted man grows joyful.

Physician, heal thyself; then you can heal your patient too. Let the best help for the patient be to see with his own eyes the one who heals himself.

There are a thousand paths that have never been taken, a thousand ways of being healthy, hidden islands of life. Humankind and humanity's earth remain unexhausted and undiscovered.

Awake and listen, you solitaries! From the future come winds on a stealthy wing-beat; and good tidings go out to delicate ears.

You solitaries of today, you who withdraw, the time will come when you shall be a people; from you, who have chosen yourselves, a chosen people shall arise – and from among them the superhuman.

Truly, the earth shall yet become a place of convalescence! And already a new odour lies about it, bringing haleness – and new hope!

3

When Zarathustra had said these words, he was silent, like one who has not spoken his final word; for a long time he weighed the staff dubiously in his hand. At length he spake thus, in a changed voice.

I shall now go on my way alone, my disciples! Go you your own ways, and alone. I will have it thus.

Truly, I counsel you: leave me, and be on your guard against Zarathustra! And better still: be ashamed of him! Perhaps he has been deceiving you.

The man of understanding must be able not only to love his enemies but also to hate his friends.

It is poor recompense for a teacher if one always remains a mere pupil. And why should you not want to pluck at my laurel wreath?

You venerate me; but what if your veneration should one day come tumbling down? Beware of being killed by a falling statue!

You say you believe in Zarathustra? But what does Zarathustra matter? You are my believers; but what do any believers matter?

You had not yet sought yourselves; then you found me. All believers do the same; that is why all belief is worth so little.

Now I bid you lose me and find yourselves; and only when you have all denied me will I return to you.

Truly, my brothers, I shall then seek my lost ones with other eyes, and with another love I shall then love you.

And at that time you shall have become my friends once again, and children of one hope; then I shall be with you for the third time, to celebrate the great noon with you.

The great noon is when humankind stands at the midpoint of its way from animal to superhuman, and celebrates its path to evening as its highest hope; for it is the path to a new morrow.

Then the man who goes under will bless himself, as one who is going over; and the sun of his understanding will stand at noonday for him.

'All the gods are dead: now we want the superhuman to live' – may that be our last will when one day the great noon comes!

Thus spake Zarathustra.

PART TWO

'. . . and only when you have all denied me will I return to you.

'Truly, my brothers, I shall then seek my lost ones with other eyes, and with another love I shall then love you.'

Zarathustra, 'Of the Giving Virtue'

The Child with the Mirror

Then Zarathustra went back into the mountains and into the solitude of his cave and withdrew from humankind, waiting like a sower who has scattered his seed. But his soul filled with impatience, and desire for those he loved, for he still had a great deal to give them. That is indeed the most difficult thing: to close one's open hand out of love, and to preserve one's modesty as a giver.

In this way months and years passed for the solitary; his wisdom grew, however, and its fullness caused him pain.

One morning, though, he awoke before dawn, lay on his bed reflecting for a long time, and at length spake to his heart:

Why was I so scared in my dream that I awoke? Didn't a child come to me, carrying a mirror?

'O Zarathustra,' the child said to me, 'look at yourself in the mirror!'

But when I looked in the mirror I cried out and my heart was shaken; for I saw not myself but a mocking, grimacing devil.

Truly, I understand the dream's sign and warning all too well: my teaching is at risk, the weeds are pretending to be wheat!

My enemies have grown powerful and have distorted the image of my teaching, so that those dearest to me must needs be ashamed of the gifts I gave them.

My friends have been lost to me; the hour has come for me to seek my lost ones!

With these words Zarathustra leapt up, not like a fearful man gasping for air but like a seer and singer moved by the spirit. His eagle and his serpent gazed at him in astonishment; for a happiness that was to come lay on his countenance like the light of dawn.

What has happened to me, my animals? – said Zarathustra. Have I not changed? Has bliss not come to me like a storm wind?

My happiness is foolish and it will say foolish things; it is still too young, so have patience with it!

I have been wounded by my happiness; all who suffer from it

shall be my physicians!

Now I may go down to my friends once again, and to my enemies too! Once again Zarathustra may speak and give and show love to those he loves.

My impatient love overflows in torrents, downwards, towards the rising and the setting. My soul rushes into the valleys from silent mountains and storms of pain.

For too long I have been filled with longing, gazing into the distance. For too long I have belonged to solitude, and in that state I forgot how to be silent.

I have become wholly a mouth, and the tumbling of a stream from high crags; I want to hurl what I have to say down into the valleys.

And may the river of my love plunge into impassable places! How should a river not find its way to the sea in the end!

Surely there is a lake within me, a hermit lake, sufficient unto itself; but my river of love draws it down with it – to the sea!

I go new ways, a new way of speaking is come upon me; like all creators, I have wearied of the old tongues. My spirit no longer wants to walk on worn-out soles.

All talk goes too slowly for me – I leap into your chariot, storm! And even you I shall whip on with my malevolence!

Like a shout of jubilation I shall voyage across vast oceans till I find the Fortunate Isles where my friends tarry.

And my enemies among them! How I now love everyone I may so much as talk to! Even my enemies are a part of my bliss.

And when I want to mount my wildest horse, my spear is invariably the best help up; it is the ever-ready servant of my foot. –

The spear which I throw at my enemies! How I thank my enemies, that at last I may throw it!

The tension in my cloud has been too great; amid the lightning's cracks of laughter I shall hurl hail-showers into the depths.

My breast will heave mightily then, and mightily it will blow its storm upon the mountains; that brings it relief.

Truly, my happiness and my freedom come like a storm! But my enemies must suppose it is *the Evil One* raging over their heads.

Yes, my friends, you will be frightened by my wild wisdom as well; and perhaps you will flee from it together with my enemies.

Ah, if only I knew how to charm you back with shepherds' pipes! Ah, if only my lioness wisdom would learn to roar gently! After all, we have already learnt a great deal together.

My wild wisdom became pregnant on lonely mountains; on rough rocks she gave birth to her young, her youngest.

Now she runs foolishly about the harsh desert, searching and searching for soft grasses – my old wild wisdom!

On the soft grasses of your hearts, my friends! – on your love she would like to bed her dearest one down!

Thus spake Zarathustra.

Of the Fortunate Isles

The figs are falling from the trees, they are good and sweet; and as they fall their red skins split. I am a north wind to ripe figs.

These teachings fall to you, my friends, like figs; now drink their juice and their sweet flesh! It is autumn all around, and clear sky and afternoon.

See what abundance is around us! And it is a fine thing to gaze out from this plenty at far oceans.

At one time people said 'God' when they gazed at far oceans; but now I have taught you to say: superhuman.

God is a conjecture; but I want you to conjecture no further than the reach of your creative will.

Could you create a god? – Then spare me your talk of all these gods! But you could create the superhuman.

Perhaps not you yourselves, my brothers! But you can remake yourselves into the fathers and ancestors of the superhuman: and that should be your finest act of creation! –

God is a conjecture; but I want you to conjecture within the bounds of what is conceivable.

Could you *conceive* a god? – But the will to truth should mean this to you: that everything be transformed into the humanly conceivable, the humanly visible, the humanly palpable! You should think your own senses through, to the end.

And you yourselves should be the ones who create what you have called the world: it should come into being as your reason, your image, your will, your love! And in truth it will be for your happiness, you enlightened ones.

And how would you mean to endure life without that hope, you enlightened ones? You could not have been born into either the incomprehensible or the irrational.

But to reveal my heart fully to you, friends: *if* there were gods, how could I bear not to be a god? *Therefore* there are no gods.

I did draw that conclusion, yes, but now it draws me.

God is a conjecture; but who could drain the anguish of this conjecture to the lees without dying? Shall the creator be stripped of his faith, and the eagle of his soaring at remote heights?

God is a thought that makes all straight things crooked and puts all standing things in a spin. What, are we to imagine time gone, and all transient things a mere lie?

To think this is a whirling, dizzying experience for human bones, and sets the stomach heaving; truly, I call it the spinning sickness, to conjecture any such thing.

I call it evil and misanthropic: all this teaching of the one and perfect and unmoved and entire-unto-itself and everlasting!

Anything everlasting is no more than an image! And the poets tell too many lies.

The best images and parables should indeed be about time and evolution, though; they should be praise, and a vindication of transience.

Creation – that is the great deliverance from suffering, and the relief of life. But that the creator may exist entails in itself suffering and much transformation.

Yes, there must be a great deal of bitter dying in your lives, you creators! And so you are the advocates and vindicators of all transience.

If the creator is himself to be the child that is newly born, he must also want to be the mother and endure the mother's pain.

Truly, I have made my way through a hundred souls and through a hundred cradles and labour pains. I have taken leave many a time, and know those heartbreaking final hours.

But my creative will, my fate, wishes it so. Or, to put it more honestly to you: that is precisely the fate that my will wishes.

All feeling suffers through me and is in prison; but my wanting always comes to me as my liberator and bringer of joy.

The act of wanting is liberating; that is the true doctrine of will and freedom – thus Zarathustra teaches you.

No longer to want, no longer to value, no longer to create! – ah, may that great weariness remain forever far from me!

In the act of understanding, too, I feel only my will's relish of begetting and becoming; and if there is innocence in my understanding, that is because the will to beget is in it.

This will enticed me away from God and gods; what would there be to create if gods – existed!

But again and again it drives me to humankind, my ardent creative will – just as the hammer is driven to the stone.

Ah, you humans, an image slumbers within the stone, the image of my images! Ah, that it must slumber in the hardest, ugliest stone!

Now my hammer rages cruelly against its prison. Pieces break off the stone – what is that to me?

I want to bring it to completion; for a shadow came to me – once, the stillest and lightest of all things came to me!

The beauty of the superhuman came to me as a shadow. Ah, my brothers! What concern of mine are the gods now!

Thus spake Zarathustra.

Of the Compassionate

My friends, this mockery has reached your friend: 'Look at Zara-thustra! He moves in our midst as if among animals, does he not?'

But it would be better put like this: 'The man of understanding moves amid humans *as* among animals.'

To the man of understanding, the human is known as the animal with red cheeks.

How did this happen to humans? Is it not because they have too often had to be ashamed?

Oh my friends! Thus speaks the man of understanding: shame, shame, shame – that is the history of humanity!

And for that reason the noble man does not permit himself to make others ashamed; he commands himself to feel shame before all that suffers.

Truly, I do not like them, the merciful, who are blissful in their compassion; they are too lacking in shame.

If I must be compassionate, I do not want to be described in that way; and, if I am compassionate, then gladly, from a distance.

I should be glad to cover my head, too, and flee before I am rec-ognized; and that is what I bid you do, my friends!

May my fate always lead across my path those who, like your-selves, do not suffer, and such as I *may* have hope and repast and honey in common with!

Truly, I did do this and that for the afflicted; but I always seemed to do better things when I learnt to enjoy myself better.

As long as humankind has existed, people have enjoyed them-selves too little; that alone, my brothers, is our original sin!

And if we learn to enjoy ourselves better, we are best able to unlearn how to harm others and how to devise harm.

For this reason I wash my hand whenever it has helped a suf-ferer, and for this reason I wipe my soul clean as well.

For, having seen the sufferer suffer, I was ashamed because I had seen him, on account of his shame; and, when I helped him, I grievously wounded his pride.

Great obligations engender not gratitude but the desire for revenge; and if a small act of kindness is not forgotten it becomes a gnawing worm.

'Be aloof when you accept! The fact that you accept should confer distinction!' – that is my counsel to those who have nothing to give.

I, however, am a giver: I give gladly, as a friend to friends. But strangers and the poor may pick the fruit from my tree themselves; that way, it is not so shaming.

Beggars, however, should be entirely done away with! Truly, it is annoying to give to them and annoying not to give to them.

And it is the same with sinners and bad consciences! Believe me, my friends: when your conscience bites you, it makes you want to bite others.

But worst of all are petty thoughts. Truly, it is better to have acted wickedly than to have thought pettily!

You will say, 'Pleasure in petty malice saves us from many a great evil deed.' But this is the wrong place to save.

An evil deed is like a boil: it itches and irritates and bursts out – it declares itself honestly.

'See, I am an illness' – that is what an evil deed says; that is its honesty.

But the petty thought is like mould; it creeps and crawls and its aim is to seem to be nowhere – till the whole body is rotten and limp with petty mould.

But to him who is possessed by the devil I offer this advice, in his ear: 'It would be better for you to raise your devil! Even for you there is still a pathway of greatness!'

Ah, my brothers! One knows a little too much about everyone. And there are those who become transparent to us, yet that does not by any means signify that we can get right through them.

It is hard to live with humankind because remaining silent is so hard.

And we are most unjust not towards the one we detest but towards the one who prompts no feelings in us at all.

But if you have a friend who is suffering, be a place for his suffering to rest, but be as it were a hard bed, a camp-bed; in that way you will serve him best.

And if a friend should do you wrong, say: 'I forgive you what you did to me; but that you did it to *yourself* – how could I forgive that?'

All great love speaks thus. It overcomes even forgiveness and compassion.

One should hold on tight to one's heart; for if one lets go of it, how soon one loses one's head as well!

Ah, where in the world have greater follies been done than by the compassionate? And what in the world has caused more suffering than the follies of the compassionate?

Woe to all lovers who do not still command a height that is above their compassion!

Once the devil said to me: 'Even God has his hell: it is his love of humanity.'

And recently I heard him say this: 'God is dead; God has died of his pity for humanity.'

So be warned against compassion: a heavy cloud will yet come to humanity *from that source*! Truly, I can read the signs of the weather!

But mark this too: all great love is superior to any compassion it feels – for it still wants to create what is loved!

'I give myself as an offering to my love, and my neighbour as myself' – that is what all creators say.

All creators, however, are hard. –

Thus spake Zarathustra.

Of Priests

And at one time Zarathustra made a sign to his disciples, and spake these words to them:

'There are priests here; and even though they are my enemies, pass them by quietly and with a sleeping sword!

'Even among them there are heroes; many of them have suffered too much, so they want to make others suffer.

'They are evil enemies; nothing is more vindictive than their humility. And anyone who attacks them is easily sullied.

'But my blood is related to theirs; and I will have my blood honoured even in theirs.'

And when they had walked by, Zarathustra was struck by pain; and when he had been fighting his pain for only a short time he began to speak thus:

'I am sorry for these priests. They strike me as contrary to taste, too; but that is the least of my concerns, now that I am among humankind.

'But I suffer with them, and have suffered. I see them as prisoners and marked men. The one they call their redeemer has put the fetters on them.

'Fetters of false values and words of delusion! Ah, if only someone would redeem them from their redeemer!

'Once, when the sea was tossing them about, they supposed they had landed on an island; but see, it was a sleeping monster!

'False values and words of delusion: these are the worst of monsters for mortals – their undoing slumbers within them, waiting.

'At length, though, it comes; it awakens, and eats and devours all who have built their shacks on it.

'Oh, just look at the shacks that these priests have built for themselves! Churches they call their sweet-smelling caves!

'Oh, that falsified light, that boggy air! Here, where the soul is not allowed to fly up to its heights!

'Quite the contrary. Their faith commands: "Up the steps on your knees, you sinners!"

'Truly, I would rather see the shameless man than their eyes twisted with shame and devotion!

'Who created these caves and penitential steps for themselves?

Was it not those who wanted to conceal themselves, and were ashamed before the clear sky?

'And only when the clear sky again gazes down through broken roofs, at the grass and red poppies on broken walls, shall I turn my heart once more towards the places of this god.

'They gave the name of God to whatever gainsaid and hurt them; and truly, there was much that was heroic in their worship.

'And they could conceive of no other way of loving their god than nailing the man to a cross!

'They thought to live as corpses, and decked out their corpse in black; even their speech reeks to me of the foul spices of death chambers.

'And anyone who lives near them lives near to black pools from which the toad sings its song with sweet profundity.

'They would have to sing songs that were more to my taste, if I were to learn to have faith in their redeemer; his disciples would have to appear more redeemed!

'I should like to see them naked; for beauty alone should preach penitence. Whoever would be persuaded by this covered-up gloom?

'Truly, their redeemers did not come from freedom and the seventh heaven of freedom themselves! Truly, they themselves never walked on the carpets of understanding.

'The spirit of their redeemers was all holes; but into every hole they had put their delusion, their stop-gap, to which they gave the name of God.

'Their spirit had drowned in their compassion, and when they became swollen and bloated with compassion, immense folly always floated on the surface.

'Zealously and clamorously they drove their flocks across their bridge; as if there were only one bridge to the future! Truly, these herdsmen too still belonged with the sheep!

'These herdsmen had small spirits and capacious souls; but, my brothers, what little countries even the most capacious of souls have hitherto been!

'They wrote signs in blood along the path they took, and their folly taught that the truth is proved by blood.

'But blood is the worst witness to truth; blood poisons the purest of doctrines, making of it the delusion and hatred of hearts.

'And if a man should go through fire for his teaching – what does that prove? It means more, in truth, when one's own doctrine comes from one's own burning!

'A sultry heart and a cold head: when these two come together, they produce that thunderous wind, the "redeemer".

'Truly, there have been greater men, and higher-born, than those the people call redeemers – those overpowering, thunderous winds!

'And you, my brothers, must be redeemed by still greater men than any redeemers were, if you want to find the way to freedom.

'Never yet has there been a superhuman. I have seen both of them naked, the greatest and the lowliest human.

'They are still all too similar to each other. Truly, I found even the greatest – all too human!'

Thus spake Zarathustra.

Of the Virtuous

In addressing slack and dormant senses, one must speak with thunder and heavenly fireworks.

But the voice of beauty speaks softly; it steals into only the most wide-awake souls.

Today my shield softly trembled and laughed; that is the sacred laughter and trembling of beauty.

Today my beauty laughed at you, you people of virtue. And this is what its voice said to me: 'On top of everything, they want to be – paid!'

You want to be paid on top of everything, you people of virtue! You want a reward for your virtue, and heaven for the earth, and eternity for your today?

And now you are angry with me for teaching that there is no one to give rewards, no paymaster? And truly, I do not even teach that virtue is its own reward.

Ah, that is my sorrow; they have mendaciously introduced rewards and punishments into the foundation of things – and now, even into the foundation of your souls, you people of virtue!

But my word, like the boar's snout, will turn up the ground of your souls. You shall call me a ploughshare.

All the secrets of your ground shall be brought to light; and when you lie turned up and broken in the sun, your lies shall also be separated from your truth.

For this is your truth: you are *too cleanly* for the dirt of words: revenge, punishment, reward, retribution.

You love your virtue as the mother her child; but whenever did one hear of a mother wanting to be paid for her love?

Your virtue is your dearest self. The desire of the ring to return upon itself is in you; that is what every ring struggles and turns for.

And every work of your virtue is like a star that goes out; its light moves on and travels forever – when will it cease to travel?

Thus the light of your virtue is still travelling even when the work is done. Though it may be forgotten and dead, its beam of light still lives and goes on.

That your virtue is your own self and not something other than you, a skin, a cloak: that is the truth from the foundation of your souls, you people of virtue!

But assuredly there are those for whom virtue means straining beneath a whip; and you have paid too much attention to their clamour!

And there are others who call the slackening of their vices virtue, and if for once their hatred and jealousy stretch their limbs, then their 'justice' perks up and rubs its sleepy eyes.

And there are others who are dragged down: their devils pull them. But the further they sink, the more brightly glows their eye and the desire for their god.

Ah, their clamour too came to your ears, you people of virtue; what I am *not* is god and virtue to me!

And there are others who come along laden and creaking, like carts carrying stones downhill; they talk a good deal about dignity and virtue – and call their brakes a virtue!

And there are others who are like clocks that are wound up every day; they go tick-tock and expect that tick-tock to be considered virtue.

The truth is that these amuse me. Wherever I come across these clocks I shall wind them up with my mockery; and I'll have them purr for me as I do it!

And others are proud of their handful of justice and for its sake commit all manner of outrages, so that the world is drowned in their injustice.

Ah, how unpleasant the word 'virtue' sounds from their mouths! And when they say, 'I am just', it always sounds like 'I am avenged'!

They want to scratch out their enemies' eyes with their virtue; and they raise themselves only in order to bring down others.

And then there are those who sit in their bog and talk like this from the reeds: 'Virtue means sitting quietly in the bog.

'We don't bite anyone and we avoid the ones who bite; and in all things we hold the opinion that is handed to us.'

And then there are those who love attitudes and think virtue is a kind of attitude.

Their knees are forever worshipping, and their hands praise virtue, but their hearts know nothing of it.

And then there are those who consider it a virtue to say: 'Virtue is necessary'; but at bottom they only believe that the police are necessary.

And many who cannot see what is high in humanity call it virtue if they see what is low all too closely; in this way the evil eye is designated a virtue.

And some want to be edified and propped up, and call that virtue – while others want to be knocked over, and call that virtue too.

And in this way almost everyone believes he has a part in virtue; and everyone at least supposes himself an expert on 'good' and 'evil'.

But Zarathustra has not come to tell all these liars and fools: 'What do *you* know about virtue? What *could* you know about virtue?'

Rather, my friends, he has come that you might tire of the old words you have learnt from fools and liars.

That you might tire of the words 'reward', 'retribution', 'punishment', 'just vengeance'.

That you might tire of saying: 'An action is good if it is selfless.'

Ah, my friends! That *your* own self be in the action as the mother is in the child; let that be *your* watchword on virtue!

Truly, I must have taken a hundred words away from you, and the favourite playthings of your virtue, and now you are cross with me as children are cross.

They were playing beside the sea – when a wave came and swept their toys into the deep; now they are crying.

But the same wave shall bring them new toys, and spread out new, brightly coloured shells before them!

So they will be consoled; and, just like them, you too shall have your consolations, my friends – and new, brightly coloured shells!

Thus spake Zarathustra.

Of the Rabble

Life is a wellspring of pleasure; but where the rabble drink too, all the wells are poisoned.

I am well disposed towards all that is cleanly; but I do not care to see the grinning mouths and the thirst of the unclean.

They cast their eye down into the well; now their odious smiles gleam up at me out of the well.

They have poisoned the holy water with their lasciviousness; and what is more, when they called their dirty dreams pleasure, they poisoned words as well.

The flame is reluctant to burn when they crowd their damp hearts to the fire; even the spirit bubbles and smokes when the rabble approaches the fire.

Fruit becomes sickly-sweet and over-ripe in their hands; their gaze leaves the fruit tree liable to be toppled by the wind, and withered at the top.

And many a one who turned away from life was only turning away from the rabble; he did not want to share the well and the flame and the fruit with the rabble.

And many a one who went into the desert, and was thirsty with the beasts of prey, was simply averse to sitting around the cistern with dirty camel-drivers.

And many a one who appeared to be a destroyer, like a hailstorm in the orchards, merely wanted to jam his foot on the rabble's throat and so stop its maw.

And that was not the mouthful I struggled hardest to swallow – the knowledge that life itself needs enmity and dying and the crosses of martyrdom –

Rather, I once asked, almost choking on my question: can it be that life *needs* the rabble too?

Are poisoned wells necessary, and stinking fires, and dirty dreams, and maggots in the bread of life?

Not my hatred but my disgust hungrily gobbled my life! Ah, often I tired of the spirit, when I found that the rabble had spirit too!

And I turned my back on the rulers when I saw what they now call ruling: haggling and bargaining for power – with the rabble!

Among peoples who spoke foreign tongues I dwelt, with my ears stopped; that the tongue of their haggling, and their bargaining for power, might remain foreign to me.

And, holding my nose, I passed among all that is yesterday and today, out of temper; truly, all that is yesterday and today bears the bad odour of the scribbling rabble!

Like a cripple who has gone deaf and blind and dumb I lived for a long time, in order not to dwell among the power rabble and the scribbling rabble and the pleasure rabble.

My spirit mounted steps laboriously and warily; alms of pleasure gave it refreshment; the life of the blind man crept along on a staff.

But what happened to me? How did I gain deliverance from disgust? Who gave youth back to my eye? How did I fly up to the heights where there is no rabble sitting by the well any more?

Did my disgust create wings for me itself, and water-divining powers? Truly, I had to fly up to the highest heights to find the wellspring of pleasure once again!

Oh, I have found it, my brothers! Here at the highest height the wellspring of pleasure rises for me! And there is a life at which no rabble drinks alongside me!

You pour forth almost too vehemently, wellspring of pleasure! And often, in wanting to fill the cup, you empty it again!

And I have yet to learn to approach you more discreetly; my heart still surges towards you all too vehemently –

My heart, on which my summer burns, that short, hot, melancholy, over-blissful summer; how my summer heart longs for your coolness!

Gone is the irresolute wretchedness of my spring! Past is the malevolence of my snowflakes in June! I have become summer entirely, a summer noontide!

A summer at the highest height, with cold springs and blessèd stillness; oh come, my friends, that the stillness become more blessèd yet!

For this is our height and our home; we live too nobly and boldly here for the unclean and their thirst.

Just cast your pure eye at the wellspring of my pleasure, friends! How should that muddy it? It shall laugh back at you with *its* purity.

In the tree, future, we build our nest; eagles shall bring food in their beaks to us lone ones.

Truly, not a food that the unclean might share! They would imagine they were eating fire, and would burn their mouths!

Truly, we are not keeping homes in readiness for the unclean here! For their bodies and spirits, our happiness would be a cave of ice.

And we shall live above them like strong winds, neighbours to the eagles, neighbours to the snow, neighbours to the sun; that is how strong winds live.

And one day I shall blow among them like a wind, and with my spirit I shall take their spirit's breath away; my future will have it so.

Truly, Zarathustra is a strong wind to all lowlands; and he offers this advice to his enemies and to all that spits and spews: 'Beware not to spit *into* the wind!'

Thus spake Zarathustra.

Of the Tarantulas

See, that is the tarantula's cave! Do you want to see the tarantula itself? Here is its web; touch it, so that it trembles.

Here it comes, of its own accord: welcome, tarantula! Your triangle and distinguishing mark sit black on your back; and I know too what sits within your soul.

Revenge sits within your soul; a black scab grows wherever you bite; your venom makes the soul giddy with revenge!

So I speak to you in a parable, you who make the soul giddy, you preachers of *equality*! I consider you tarantulas, hiding your craving for revenge!

But I mean to bring your hiding-places to light; that is why I laugh my laughter of the height in your faces.

That is why I pull at your web: so that your fury will tempt you out of your cave of lies, and your vengefulness leap out from behind your word 'justice'.

For *that humankind might be redeemed from vengeance* – that, for me, is the bridge to the highest hope, and a rainbow after long-lasting storms.

Of course the tarantulas would have it differently. 'What we call justice shall be precisely this: that the world shall be filled with the storms of our revenge' – that is how they talk among themselves.

'We shall practise revenge and abuse against any who are not as we are' – that is what the tarantula-hearts pledge to each other.

'And the "will to equality" shall henceforth be the name of virtue; and we shall raise our outcry against any that have power!'

You preachers of equality, that is how the tyrant-madness of impotence cries out of you for 'equality': your most secret tyrant-cravings disguise themselves in words of virtue.

Soured arrogance, repressed envy, perhaps the arrogance and envy of your fathers; they shoot out of you as a flame, as the madness of vengeance.

Where the father was silent, the son speaks; and often I have found the son to be the father's secret revealed.

They resemble enthusiasts; yet it is not the heart that inspires them, but revenge. And when they grow refined and cold it is not the spirit but envy that makes them refined and cold.

Their jealousy even takes them on to the paths of the thinkers; and this is the hallmark of their jealousy – they always go too far; so that in the end their weariness has to lie down to sleep, even on snow.

Vengefulness sounds from every one of their complaints, and all of their praise is hurtful; and to be judges seems a blessèd thing to them.

But this is my advice to you, my friends: mistrust all in whom the urge to punish is strong!

They are people of poor breed and stock; the executioner and the bloodhound gaze out of their faces.

Mistrust all those who talk a great deal about their justice! Truly, it is not only honey that their souls are lacking.

And when they call themselves 'the good and the just', do not forget that the only thing they lack to become Pharisees is – power!

My friends, I do not want to be confused with others or mistaken for what I am not.

There are those who preach my doctrine of life; and yet at the same time they are preachers of equality, and tarantulas.

That they speak well of life even though they sit in their caves with their backs to life, these poisonous spiders, means that they do so in order to hurt.

They want to hurt those who now possess power; for it is among these that preaching death is still most at home.

If it were otherwise, the teaching of the tarantulas would be different; and they themselves were at one time best at vilifying the world and burning heretics.

I do not want to be confused with these preachers of equality, or taken for one of them. What justice says *to me* is this: 'Human beings are not equal.'

And neither should they become equal! What would my love for the superhuman be if I said anything else?

They should press forward to the future across a thousand bridges and footbridges, and there should be ever more war and inequality between them; this is what my great love bids me say!

In their enmity they should become inventors of images and phantoms, and then with their images and phantoms they should fight the most exalted of battles with each other!

Good and evil, and rich and poor, and noble and lowly, and all the names that mean values: let them be weapons, and clashing signs that life must be overcoming itself ever and ever anew!

Life itself wants to build its way to the heights with pillars and steps; it wants to gaze into the far distances, and out towards blissful beauty – *that* is why it needs height!

And because it needs height, it needs steps, and conflict between the steps and those who climb them. Life wants to climb and, in climbing, to overcome itself.

And just see, my friends – here, where the tarantula's cave is, tower the ruins of an ancient temple – just see, with the eyes of understanding!

Truly, whoever once stacked up his thoughts in stone here knew the secret of all life just as well as the wisest!

That there are struggle and inequality even in beauty, and war for power and dominance: that is what he teaches us here, in the clearest of parables.

Just as vault and arch are divinely opposed here in struggle, just as these divine strivers contend with light and shadow against each other –

Let us be enemies with a like assurance and beauty, my friends! Let us strive *against* each other divinely!

Woe! Now the tarantula, my old enemy, has bitten me! Divinely assured and beautiful, it bit me on the finger!

'There must be punishment and justice,' it thinks; 'he shall not sing songs in praise of enmity here with impunity!'

Yes, the tarantula has taken revenge! And woe, now it will make my soul giddy with revenge too!

But to prevent my spinning round, my friends, tie me fast to this pillar! I should rather be a saint on a pillar than a whirl of vengefulness!

Truly, Zarathustra is no whirlwind or cyclone; and, though he may be a dancer, he is never a dancer of the tarantella!

Thus spake Zarathustra.

Of the Famous Wise Men

You have served the people and the people's superstitions, you famous wise men, all of you! – and *not* the truth! And for that very reason people have paid you reverence.

And for that reason too they put up with your wrong-headed belief – because it was a joke, and a circuitous way to the people. In like manner the master indulges his slaves, and even relishes their cockiness.

But the one who is hated by the people, as a wolf is by dogs, is the free spirit, the enemy of fetters, the one who refuses to worship, the forest-dweller.

Hunting him out of his lair has always been known by the people as 'having a sense of what's right'; to this day, they set their sharpest-toothed hounds upon him.

'For the truth is here; after all, the people are here! Woe, woe to those who seek!' – that is what has been said since time immemorial.

You sought to show that the people were right in their reverence, and called it 'the will to truth', you wise men!

And your heart always said to itself: 'From the people I came; from there too the voice of God came to me.'

As the people's advocates, you have always been stubborn and canny, like an ass.

And many a powerful man, wanting to fare well with the people, harnessed in front of his horses – a little ass, a famous wise man.

And now, you famous wise men, I wish you would finally throw off the lion-skin entirely!

The skin of the predator, bright and mottled, and the matted mane of the inquirer, the seeker, the conqueror!

Ah, for me to learn to believe in your 'truthfulness', you would first have to break your reverential will.

Truthful – that is what I call the one who goes into the godless wildernesses, and has broken his reverential heart.

In the yellow sand, burnt by the sun, he doubtless keeps a thirsty watch for islands rich in springs where living beings rest beneath shady trees.

But his thirst does not persuade him to become like those creatures of comfort; for where there are oases there are also idols.

Hungering, violent, solitary, godless: that is how the lion-will wants itself to be.

Free from the happiness of serfs, delivered from gods and worship, fearless and fearsome, great and solitary: that is the will of the truthful man.

The truthful ones, the free spirits, have lived since time immemorial in the wilderness, as the masters of the wilderness; while the well-fed, famous wise men live in the cities – the draught animals.

For they, being asses, are forever drawing – the *people's* cart!

Not that I am angry with them on that account; but in my eyes they remain servants, and in harness, even if their golden harnesses gleam.

And they have often been good and praiseworthy servants. For this is what virtue says: 'If you must be a servant, seek out the one who will benefit most from your service!

'The spirit and the virtue of your master should thrive if you are his servant; if that is so, you too will thrive together with his spirit and his virtue!'

And in truth, you famous wise men, you servants of the people! – you yourselves throve together with the people's spirit and virtue, and the people have thriven through you! I say this in your honour!

But you remain of the people even in your virtues, the people with their stupid eyes – the people, who do not know what the *spirit* is!

The spirit is the life that cuts into its own life; by its own agony it augments its own knowledge – did you know that?

And this is the spirit's happiness: to be anointed, and consecrated with tears, as a sacrificial animal – did you know that?

And the blindness of the blind man, and his seeking and tapping, shall yet bear witness to the power of the sun he gazed into – did you know that?

And the man of understanding shall learn how to *build* with mountains! It is a paltry thing for the spirit to move mountains – did you know that?

You are familiar only with the spirit's sparks; but you do not see the anvil that the spirit is, nor the awfulness of its hammer!

Truly, you do not know the spirit's pride! But still less would you endure the spirit's modesty, if ever it should care to speak!

And you have never dared to cast your spirit into a snow-filled hollow; you are not hot enough for that! So you do not know the rapture of its coldness, either.

In every respect, however, I find your attitude to the spirit too familiar; and you have often made wisdom into a poorhouse and hospital for bad poets.

You are not eagles; so you do not know the spirit's exhilaration in terror, either. And those who are not birds should not make their homes over abysses.

I find you lukewarm; but all deep understanding flows cold. The inmost wellsprings of the spirit are ice-cold – refreshing to hot hands and to people of action.

I find you stand honourable, stiff and straight-backed, you famous wise men! – no strong wind or will drives you before it.

Have you never seen a sail crossing the sea, rounded-out and billowing, and trembling before the impetuousness of the wind?

Like a sail, trembling before the impetuousness of the spirit, my wisdom crosses the sea – my wild wisdom!

You servants of the people, though, you famous wise men – how *could* you accompany me?

Thus spake Zarathustra.

The Night Song

It is night; all the springing fountains speak more loudly now. And my soul is a springing fountain as well.

It is night; only now do all the lovers' songs awaken. And my soul is a lover's song as well.

Something unstilled, unstillable is in me; it wants to be loud. A desire for love is in me, and it speaks the language of love.

I am light; ah, that I were night! But this is my solitude, that I am girded round with light.

Ah, that I were dark and night-like! How I would suck at the breasts of light!

And I should bless you, little twinkling stars and glow-worms above! – and be blissful because of your gifts of light.

But I live in my own light, I drink back into myself the flames that flare out of me.

I do not know the happiness of the one who receives; and often I have dreamt that to steal must be a more blessèd thing than to receive.

It is my poverty, that my hand never rests from giving; it is my envy, that I see expectant eyes and the lighted nights of longing.

Oh wretchedness of all who give! Oh eclipse of my sun! Oh craving for desire! Oh ravenous hunger in satiety!

They take from me; but do I yet touch their souls? There is a gulf between giving and receiving; and the smallest gulf is the last to be bridged.

A hunger grows from my beauty: I should like to hurt those for whom I light the way, and rob those to whom I give – that is how I hunger for malevolence.

Withdrawing my hand when another hand is already stretching out to it; hesitating like a waterfall that hesitates even as it plunges – that is how I hunger for malevolence.

That is the kind of vengeance that my copiousness dreams up; that is the kind of spitefulness that wells up from my solitude.

My happiness to be giving died in giving, my virtue wearied of itself through its own abundance!

He who is always giving runs the risk of losing his shame; he who is forever handing out will have calluses on his hand and heart from all his handing-out.

My eye no longer brims over at the shame of supplicants; my hand has grown too hard for the trembling of hands that have been filled.

Where have the tear of my eye and the down of my heart gone? Oh the solitude of all who give! Oh the silence of all who light the way!

Many suns circle in the wastes of space; to all that is dark they speak with their light – to me they are silent.

Oh, this is the enmity of light towards what gives light; it makes its way mercilessly.

Unjust in its inmost heart towards whatever gives light; cold towards suns – that is how every sun goes on its way.

Like a storm the suns fly along their courses; that is how they go their ways. They follow their unrelenting will; that is their coldness.

Oh, it is you alone, you dark ones of the night, who create warmth out of the given light! Oh, it is you alone who drink milk and vigour from the udders of light!

Ah, ice is all about me, my hand is burnt by ice! Ah, thirst is in me, and it craves your thirst!

It is night: ah, that I must be light! And thirst for whatever is of the night! And solitude!

It is night; my longing flows from me like a wellspring now – I long for speech.

It is night; all the springing fountains speak more loudly now. And my soul is a springing fountain as well.

It is night; only now do all the lovers' songs awaken. And my soul is a lover's song as well.

Thus sang Zarathustra.

The Dance Song

One evening Zarathustra was walking through the forest with his disciples; and as he was looking for a spring, see, he came out upon a green meadow with trees and bushes about it in tranquillity, and on it girls were dancing together. The moment the girls recognized Zarathustra they broke off their dance, but Zarathustra went up to them with a friendly gesture, saying these words:

'Do not stop dancing, dear girls! This is no spoilsport with the evil eye who has come to you, no enemy to girls.

'I am God's advocate before the devil; the devil, though, is the spirit of gravity. You light-footed ones, how could I be an enemy of divine dancing? Or of girls' feet with beautiful ankles?

'I am a forest, it is true, and a night of dark trees; but he who is not afraid of my darkness will find rose bowers too beneath my cypresses.

'And doubtless he will find the little god as well, who is the girls' favourite; beside the spring he lies, still, with his eyes closed.

'Truly, he fell asleep in broad daylight, the idler! Had he been chasing butterflies too much?

'You lovely dancers, do not be angry with me if I chastise the little god a little! No doubt he will yell and cry – but even when he cries he is a sight for laughter!

'And with tears in his eyes he will ask you for a dance; and I myself shall sing a song to go with his dance.

'A dancing-song and a mocking-song about the spirit of gravity, my all-highest and most powerful devil, who they say is "the lord of the world".' –

And this is the song that Zarathustra sang as Cupid and the girls danced together.

'Of late I gazed into your eye, oh Life! And it seemed to me I was sinking into unfathomable depths.

'But you pulled me out with a golden rod; you laughed in derision when I called you unfathomable.

'"All fish talk like that," you said; "what they do not fathom is unfathomable.

'"But I am merely fickle and wild and in all things a woman, and no virtuous one:

'"Even though I am known among you men as 'the profound one' or 'the faithful one', 'the eternal', 'the mysterious' –

'"But you men always give to us your own virtues – ah, you virtuous ones!"

'At that she laughed, the incredible one; but I never believe her or her laughter if she speaks badly of herself.

'And when I spoke one to one with my wild Wisdom she told me angrily: "You want, you desire, you love, that is the only reason why you *praise* life."

'I was on the point of answering crossly, and telling the angry one the truth; and one cannot answer more crossly than when one "tells the truth" to one's wisdom.

'So that is how things stand between the three of us. At bottom I love only life – and, truly, most of all when I hate it!

'But that I am fond of wisdom, and often too fond: that is because she reminds me so much of life!

'She has her eyes, her laugh, and even her little golden rod; how can I help it if the two of them look so alike?

'And when Life once asked me, "Who is she, then, this Wisdom?" – I eagerly said, "Ah yes! Wisdom!

'"One thirsts for her but one is never satisfied, one gazes through veils, one snatches through nets.

'"Is she beautiful? I cannot tell! But the oldest carp are still caught with her bait.

'"She is fickle and defiant; I have often seen her bite her lip and comb her hair against the wave.

'"Perhaps she is bad and deceitful, and in everything a female; but when she speaks ill of herself she is at her most seductive."

'When I said this to Life, she laughed spitefully and closed its eyes. "Who are you talking about?" she asked – "it's me, isn't it?

'"And even if you were right – is *that* something to tell me to my face? But now speak of your wisdom, too!"

'Ah, and then you opened your eyes again, oh beloved Life! And it seemed to me once again that I was sinking into unfathomable depths.'

Thus sang Zarathustra. But when the dance was ended and the girls had gone, he grew sad.

'The sun has long since set,' he said at length; 'the meadow is damp, coolness comes from the woods.

'Something unfamiliar is all about me, gazing contemplatively.

What! Still alive, Zarathustra?

'Why? What for? Whereby? Where to? Where? How? Is it not folly to go on living? –

'Ah, my friends, it is the evening that raises these questions within me. Forgive me my sadness!

'Evening has fallen: forgive me, that evening has fallen!'

Thus spake Zarathustra.

The Grave Song

'Over there is the island of graves, the silent island. There lie the graves of my youth, too. Thither I shall bear an evergreen wreath of life.'

Making this resolution in my heart, I set forth across the ocean. –

Oh you visions and apparitions of my youth! Oh all you looks of love, you divine moments! How quickly you died! I remember you today as I remember my dead.

A sweet odour that eases the heart and tears reaches me from you, my dearest dead ones. Truly, it shakes and eases the solitary seafarer's heart.

Still I am the wealthiest and most enviable of men – I, the loneliest! For I *had* you, and you have me still; tell me, who has had such rosy apples fall from the tree as have fallen to me?

Still I am the heir and the soil of your love, flowering in your memory with wild-growing virtues of many colours, oh you most beloved!

Ah, we were made to remain close to one another, you fair and singular wonders! It was not as timid birds that you came to me and my desire, no, but with trust to one who also trusts.

Yes, made for faithfulness, like me, and for tender eternities; must I now name you according to your unfaithfulness, you divine looks and moments? I have not yet learnt any other name.

Truly, you died too quickly, you fly-aways. Yet you did not fly from me, nor did I fly from you; in our unfaithfulness we are innocent towards one another.

Songbirds of my hopes, they wrung your necks in order to kill *me*! Yes, wickedness always shot its arrows at you, my dearest ones – to hit my heart!

And it did hit it! You, after all, were always dearest to my heart, my possession and my being-possessed; *that* was why you had to die young and all too early!

The arrow was shot at the most vulnerable thing I possessed: that was you, whose skin is like down, and still more like the smile that is killed by a look!

But I will say this to my enemies: what is the slaughter of people compared with what you did to me?

You did something worse to me than any slaughter: you took from me something that can never be brought back – and for that reason I now speak to you, my enemies!

You killed the visions and dearest wonders of my youth! You took away my playmates, those blessèd spirits! It is in their memory that I lay down this wreath and this curse.

This curse upon you, my enemies! You have cut short my eternity, as a note breaks off on a cold night! It came to me as no more than the flash of divine eyes, barely that – as a moment!

At a goodly hour, my purity once spake thus to me: 'All beings shall be divine to me.'

But you assaulted me with filthy phantoms; ah, where has that goodly hour fled to now?

'Every day shall be holy to me' – so said the wisdom of my youth, at one time: truly the words of a merry wisdom!

But then you, my enemies, stole my nights and sold them off for sleepless torment; ah, where has that merry wisdom fled to now?

At one time I longed for good omens from birds; but you crossed my path with a monster of an owl, an ill-omened creature. Ah, where did my tender longing flee then?

At one time I vowed to put all revulsion from me; but you transformed those near and nearest to me into boils of pus. Ah, where did my noblest vow flee then?

At one time, as a blind man, I walked on blessèd paths; but you flung filth on the blind man's path, and now he is revolted by the old blind man's footpath.

And when I accomplished my most arduous task, and celebrated the triumph of my overcomings, you made those who loved me scream that I was hurting them the most.

Truly, that was invariably what you did: you spolit my best honey and the industry of my best bees.

You always sent the most insolent beggars to my charity, and thronged the incurably shameless about my pity. In this way you wounded my virtue in its faith.

And if I brought what was holiest to me to sacrifice, your 'piety' promptly placed its fatter offerings beside it, so that what was holiest to me choked in the smoke from your fat.

And at one time I wanted to dance as I had never danced before; I wanted to dance beyond all of the heavens. But then you lured my favourite singer away.

And then he sounded a grim, dismal tune; ah, he tooted in my ears like a doleful horn!

Murderous singer, instrument of wickedness, most innocent of men! I stood there ready for the best of dances, and with your notes you killed off my delight!

It is only through dance that I can tell the parable of the highest things; – and now my greatest parable remained unuttered in my limbs!

My highest hope remained unspoken and unrealized! And all the visions and consolations of my youth died!

However did I endure it? How did I recover from such wounds and overcome them? How did my soul rise again from these graves?

Yes, there is something invulnerable about me that resists burial and breaks rock asunder: it is *my will*. Silent and unchanged, it strides through the years.

It will go its way on my feet, my old will; its intent is hard of heart and invulnerable.

I am invulnerable only at my heel. Still you are alive there, and have remained true to yourself, most patient one! You have always broken through every grave!

In you there still lives on what was unrealized in my youth, too; and here you sit, as life and youth, hopeful upon the yellow ruins of graves.

Yes, for me you are still the one who demolishes every grave; hail to you, my will! And only where there are graves are there resurrections.

Thus sang Zarathustra.

Of Overcoming the Self

What is it that drives you and fires your passions, you wisest of men? – do you call it 'the will to truth'?

The will that all that exists should be conceivable – that is what *I* call your will!

You first want to *render* all that exists conceivable; for you doubt, with well-founded mistrust, whether it is indeed conceivable.

But you must have it submit to you and bend! That is what your will demands. It must be made smooth, and subordinate to the spirit, as its mirror and reflection.

That is the whole of your will, you wisest of men, and it is a will to power even when you talk of good and evil and of assessing values. You still want to create the world before which you can kneel; in that sense, it is your final hope and intoxication.

The unwise, of course, the people – they are like a river down which a boat drifts; and in that boat, solemn and disguised, sit the evaluations.

You floated your will and your values on the river of becoming; what the people believe to be good and evil betrays to me an ancient will to power.

It was you, the wisest of men, who placed such passengers in this boat and gave them pomp and proud names – you and your ruling will!

Now the river bears your boat onwards; it *must* bear it. If the broken wave foams and angrily resists the keel, it is of little consequence.

It is not the river that is your danger and the end of your good and evil, you wisest of men: rather, it is that will itself, the will to power – the unexhausted, procreating life-will.

In order that you shall understand what I say about good and evil, however, I shall tell you my understanding of life and of the nature of all living things.

I have followed the living, I have taken the broadest and the smallest of paths in order to understand the nature of life.

In a hundredfold mirror I caught its gaze when its mouth was shut, that its eye might speak to me. And its eye did speak to me.

But wherever I found living things, I heard the language of obedience. All living things are obedient.

And this is the second thing: if one cannot obey oneself, one will be at another's command. That is the way of all that lives.

But this is the third thing I heard: to command is more difficult than to obey. Not only because the commander bears the burden of all who obey, and that burden can easily crush him: –

Whenever someone gives orders, it seemed to me, experiment and risk are involved; and the living always risks its own self when it commands.

Yes, even when it is commanding itself; even then it must atone for its orders. It must be the judge and avenger and victim of its own law.

How can this be? I wondered. What persuades the living creature to obey and to command and to be obedient even when giving orders?

Listen now to what I say, you wisest of men! Give serious scrutiny to whether I have crept into the very heart of life, as far as the roots of the heart!

Wherever I have found a living creature I have found the will to power; and even in the will of the servant I have found the will to be master.

It is his will that persuades the weaker to serve the stronger, since it wants to be master over whatever is still weaker: that pleasure alone it is unwilling to go without.

And just as the smaller yields to the greater, that it may have pleasure and power over the smallest of all, so too the greatest yields itself up, staking its very life for the sake of power.

That is the devotion of the greatest: it is risk-taking, and danger, and dicing with death.

And even where there are sacrifice and service and loving looks, the will to be master exists too. The weaker creeps on secret paths into the castle and into the heart of the more powerful – and steals the power.

And Life herself told me this secret: 'See,' she said, 'I am that which must forever be overcoming itself.

'You indeed know this as the will to procreate or the drive towards a higher, remoter, more manifold goal; but all of that is one, and one secret.

'I should rather go under than renounce that one thing; and truly, where there is downfall and the falling of leaves, see – that is life sacrificing itself for power!

'That I must be a struggle and a becoming and a purpose and the conflict of purposes: ah, anyone who divines my will doubtless divines as well what *crooked* paths it must take!

'Whatever I create and however much I love it – before long I must be an opponent, to it and to my love; that is how my will would have it.

'And you too, man of understanding, are no more than a path and footstep of my will; truly, my will to power even walks on the feet of your will to truth!

'Whoever shot the phrase "will to existence" at the truth missed the mark – for that will does not exist!

'For what does not exist cannot exert a will; but how could what already exists wish to come into being?

'Only where there is life is there also a will: however, not the will to life, but – this is my teaching for you – the will to power!

'The living values many things above life itself – but out of that very valuation speaks the will to power!'

That was the teaching Life once gave me; and with it, you wisest of men, I shall yet solve the riddle of your heart.

Truly, I say to you: everlasting good and evil do not exist! By their own efforts they must overcome themselves again and again.

You exercise power with your values and your pronouncements on good and evil, you evaluators; and that is your hidden love, and the glittering, trembling and overflowing of your soul.

But a stronger force grows out of your values, and a new mastery; egg and egg-shell shatter against it.

And whosoever must be a creator in good and evil, truly, must first be a destroyer and smash values.

Thus the greatest evil belongs together with the greatest good; it is the latter, however, that is creative.

By all means let us *talk* about it, you wisest of men, even if it is bad. Remaining silent is worse; all truths that are kept in silence become toxic.

And let everything shatter that can be shattered against our truths! There is many a house still to build!

Thus spake Zarathustra.

Of Sublime Men

Still is the bottom of my ocean; whoever would guess that it harbours jesting monsters!

Imperturbable are my depths; but they glitter with swimming riddles and laughter.

Today I saw a sublime man, a solemn man, a penitent of the spirit; oh how my soul laughed at his ugliness!

With his chest forward, and like someone drawing a breath, he stood there, the sublime man in silence:

Hung about with ugly truths, the bag of his hunt, and rich in tatters; many thorns hung upon him, too – yet I saw no rose.

He has not yet learnt laughter or beauty. Sombrely this huntsman returned from the forest of understanding.

He returned home from fighting wild beasts; but a wild beast still gazes out from his earnestness, too – one that has not been overcome!

He stands there like a tiger about to spring; but I do not care for these tensed souls, my taste is averse to all these withdrawn men.

And you tell me, friends, that one cannot dispute taste and tasting? But all life is a dispute over taste and tasting!

Taste is at once weight and the scales and the weigher; and woe to all living beings that would live without dispute over weight and the scales and the weigher!

Only if he were to weary of his sublimity, this sublime man, would the beauty in him set in – and only then will I taste him, and find him to my taste.

And only if he turns away from himself will he jump over his own shadow – and, truly! into *his* sun.

All too long he sat in the shade; the penitent of the spirit's cheeks grew pale; with all his expectations he almost starved.

There is still contempt in his eye, and revulsion is in the set of his mouth. He is resting now, indeed, but his rest has not yet lain down in the sun.

He should behave like a bull, and his happiness should reek of the soil and not of contempt for the soil.

I should like to see him as a white bull, snorting and bellowing as he goes before the plough; and his bellowing should sound the praise of all earthly things!

His countenance is still dark; the shadow of his hand plays upon him. The sense of his eye is in shadow too.

His action itself is still the shadow upon him; the hand leaves the doer in darkness. He has not yet overcome his action.

Though I do love the bull's neck in him, I now want to see the angel's eye as well.

The hero's will he has learnt he must cast off too: I would have him an exalted man and not merely a sublime man – the ether itself should raise him up, this fellow without a will!

He has subdued monsters, he has solved riddles; but he should also deliver his monsters and riddles, transforming them into heavenly children.

His understanding has not yet learnt to smile and be free of jealousy; his torrential passion has not yet grown tranquil in beauty.

Truly, his desire should fall silent and vanish from sight, not in satiety but in beauty! Grace is a part of the magnanimous person's generosity.

With his arm laid across his head: that is how the hero should rest, and that his how he should go beyond resting.

But for the hero, of all people, it is *beauty* that is the most difficult thing of all. For all violent wills, beauty is unachievable.

A little more, a little less: in this case, that is a great deal; in this case, that is the most.

To stand with relaxed muscles and an unharnessed will: to all of you sublime men, that is the most difficult thing of all!

When power becomes gracious and descends to the visible: beauty is what I call such a descent.

And, man of power, there is no one I so much want to have beauty from as from you, of all people; may your goodness be your ultimate conquest of self.

I believe you capable of all evil; that is why I want good from you.

Truly, I have often laughed about weaklings who suppose themselves good because they have feeble paws!

You should emulate the virtue of the pillar: the higher it rises, the more beautiful and delicate it grows, yet within it is harder and able to bear more weight.

Yes, you sublime man, one day you too shall be beautiful and hold up the mirror to your own beauty.

Then your soul will shudder with divine longings; and even in your vanity there will be worship.

For this is the secret of the soul: only when the hero has deserted it is it approached in dreams by – the superhero.

Thus spake Zarathustra.

Of the Land of Culture

Too far I flew into the future; horror assailed me.

And when I looked around, see! time was my only contemporary.

Then I flew back, homewards, ever more hurriedly; and so I came to you, people of the present, and to the land of culture.

For the first time I brought with me an eye for you, and kindly desire; truly, I came with longing in my heart.

But how did things go with me? Fearful though I was, I had to laugh! Never had my eye beheld such a motley mess!

I laughed and laughed, while my foot still trembled and my heart as well: 'This must be the homeland of all paint-pots!' I said.

There you sat, to my astonishment, with fifty splotches daubed on your faces and limbs, you people of the present!

And with fifty mirrors about you, flattering and repeating your play of colours!

Truly, you people of the present, you could wear no better masks than your own faces! Whoever could *recognize* you?

Written up fully with the signs of the past, and with new signs overpainted on to those signs – you have hidden yourselves well from all interpreters of signs!

And even were one to examine the entrails – does anyone still believe that you have any guts? You seem fired in colours, with glued-on scraps of paper.

Every age and people gazes in many colours from your veils; every custom and belief speaks in many colours from your gestures.

If one were to tear off your veils and cloaks and colours and gestures, there would be just enough left to scare the birds.

Truly, I myself am the scared bird that once saw you naked and without paint; and I flew off when the skeleton beckoned me lewdly.

I would rather be a day-labourer in the underworld, among the shades of yesteryear! – even the inhabitants of the underworld are fuller and more robust than you!

This, yes, this is bitterness to my bowels, that I cannot bear you either naked or clothed, people of the present!

All that is uncanny about the future, and whatever has scared off flown-away birds, is truly more familiar and intimately known than your 'reality'.

For this is what you say: 'We are real people through and through, without belief or superstition': that is your boast, even though you have nothing to boast about!

Indeed, how should you be *able* to believe, you creatures of motley! – you who are paintings of all that has ever been believed!

You are walking refutations of belief itself, and you break the limbs of all thought. *Unworthy of credence*: that is what *I* call you, you real people!

All ages babble contra each other in your spirits; and the dreams and babble of all the ages were still more real than your waking is!

You are unfruitful; *therefore* you have no belief. But anyone who had to create always had prophetic dreams and astrological signs – and believed in belief!

You are gateways half open, at which gravediggers wait. And that is *your* reality: 'Everything is worthy of perishing.'

Ah, how you stand there, you unfruitful ones, how skinny-ribbed! And many a one of you has indeed noticed this for himself.

And he said: 'It must have been a god who secretly removed something from me while I slept. Truly, enough to make himself a little woman!

'The meagreness of my ribs is a wondrous thing!' Many a man of the present day has spoken to this effect.

Yes, I find you laughable, you people of the present! And particularly when you are amazed at yourselves!

And woe unto me if I were unable to laugh at your amazement, and had to drink down all that is repulsive in your bowls!

I shall make light of you, though, since I have something *heavy* to carry; what is it to me if beetles and flying bugs settle on to my bundle too!

Truly, I shall find it no heavier on that account! And it is not from you, people of the present, that the great weariness will come upon me. – Ah, where shall I climb to now with my longing? From every mountain I look out for fatherlands and mother countries.

But nowhere have I found a home: I am restless in every town, and at every gate I am departing.

The people of the present, to whom my heart impelled me not long since, are strange to me, and an object of ridicule; and I have been driven out of fatherlands and mother countries.

So now I love only the *land of my children*, the undiscovered, in the furthest ocean: for that I bid my sails seek and seek.

I shall make up to my children for being the child of my fathers; and to all the future – for *this* present!

Thus spake Zarathustra.

Of the Immaculate Perception

When the moon rose yesterday, I thought it was going to give birth to a sun, so fat and pregnant did it lie on the horizon.

But it was lying to me about its pregnancy; and I would rather believe in the man in the moon than in woman.

Granted, it is not much of a man either, this timid night owl. Truly, he moves across the rooftops with a bad conscience.

For he is lascivious and jealous, the monk in the moon, lusting after the earth and after all the pleasures of lovers.

No, I do not like him, this tomcat on the rooftops! I find any creature that slinks around half-closed windows repugnant!

Pious and silent, he moves across carpets of stars: – but I do not care for men's feet that tread softly, without so much as the jingle of a spur.

The step of any honest creature declares itself; but the cat slinks across the ground. See how the moon comes, catlike and dishonest.

I give this likeness to you hypocrites, you with your sensibility and your 'pure understanding'! *I* call you – lascivious!

You too love the earth and earthly things; I know you well! But shame and bad conscience are in your love – you are like the moon!

Your spirit has been persuaded to hold earthly things in contempt, but not your guts; *they*, however, are what is strongest in you!

And now your spirit is ashamed that it must do the bidding of your entrails, and in order to avoid its own shame it takes byways and the paths of falsehood.

'For me,' your lying spirit tells itself, 'the highest thing would be to look upon life without desire, and not like a dog with its tongue hanging out;

'To be happy in the looking, with an extinct will, without the grasping and greed of self-centredness – the whole body cold and ashen, but with drunken moon-eyes!

'That would be the best thing for me,' says the seduced one, seducing himself – 'to love the earth as the moon loves it, and to touch its beauty with my eyes only.

'And that, for me, shall be called the *immaculate* perception of all things: that I want nothing from things except that I may lie before them like a mirror with a hundred eyes.' –

Oh you hypocrites, you people of sensibility, you lascivious ones! There is no innocence in your desire; and now, for that reason, you traduce desire itself!

Truly, you do not love the earth as creators or procreators, as people who rejoice in making things new.

Where is innocence? Where there is the will to procreate. To my mind, the man who wants to create something beyond himself has the purest will.

Where is beauty? Where I am *obliged to want* something with all of my will; where I want to love and go under, in order that an image should be more than a mere simulacrum.

Loving and going under: since time immemorial they have gone together. The will to love means being prepared to die, too. This is how I speak to you cowards!

But now you would have your emasculated sidelong glances thought of as 'contemplation'. Anything that allows cowardly eyes to touch it, you would christen 'beautiful'! Oh, how you besmirch these noble terms!

But it will be your curse, you immaculate ones, you of pure understanding, that you will never give birth, even if you lie fat and pregnant on the horizon!

Truly, your mouths are full of noble words; do you really suppose we believe that your hearts are overflowing, you inveterate liars?

But *my* words are lowly, despised, bent words; I am glad to have whatever falls from your table at dinner.

Even with them, though, I can still – tell the truth to hypocrites! Yes, my fishbones, shells and prickly leaves shall – tickle hypocrites' noses!

Bad air always hangs about you and your dinners; your lecherous thoughts, your lies and secrets, are in the air!

Only dare to believe in yourselves – in yourselves and in your guts! Those who do not believe in themselves invariably lie.

You are wearing the mask of a god, you 'pure ones'; your revolting ringworm has hidden away behind the mask of a god.

Truly, you deceive, you 'contemplative' people! At one time, even Zarathustra was fooled by your godlike skins; he did not guess at the serpent coils with which they were stuffed.

At one time I imagined I saw the soul of a god at play in your games, you of the pure understanding! At one time I imagined there was no better art than your arts!

The filth of serpents and the dreadful stench were concealed from me by distance – and that a lizard's cunning was slinking lasciviously about.

But I came *close* to you; then day broke for me – and now it breaks for you – the moon's love affair has come to an end!

Just see! There he stands, pale, caught in the act – before the dawn!

For the glowing sun is already coming – *her* love of the earth is coming! All of the sun's love is innocence and the desire to create.

Just see how impatiently she moves over the ocean! Do you not feel the thirst and hot breath of her love?

She wants to suck at the ocean, and drink its depths up to her heights; now the ocean's desire quickens with a thousand breasts.

It *wants* to be kissed and sucked by the sun's thirst; it *wants* to become air and height and the footpath of light and light itself!

Truly, like the sun I love life and all deep oceans.

And this *I* call perception: all that is deep shall rise up – to my height!

Thus spake Zarathustra.

Of Scholars

While I lay sleeping, a sheep munched the ivy wreath on my head – and as it was munching it said: 'Zarathustra is no longer a scholar.'

Having said which, it went off stiff and proud. A child told me about it.

I like to lie here where the children play, by the crumbling wall, among thistles and red poppies.

To the children I am still a scholar, and to the thistles and red poppies. They are innocent, even when they are bad.

But to the sheep I am no longer a scholar; that is how my fate would have it – blessèd be my fate!

For this is the truth: I have quit the house of scholars, and even slammed the door behind me.

Too long my soul sat hungry at their table; unlike them, I am not focused on cracking understanding as one would crack nuts.

I love freedom and the air over fresh earth; I should rather sleep on ox-hides than on their honours and reverences.

I am too hot, and scorched by my own thoughts; often it almost stops my breath. At those times I have to get into the open air, away from any kind of dusty room.

But they sit cool in the cool shade; in all things they want to be mere onlookers, and they take good care not to sit where the sun burns on the steps.

Like those who stand in the street and gape at the passers-by, so they too wait and gape at thoughts that others have had.

If one grabs hold of them, they raise a cloud of dust like sacks of flour, unintentionally; but who would guess that their dust came from grain, and from the yellow joy of summer fields?

If they affect to be wise, their little maxims and truths give me the shivers: often their wisdom smells as if it came from the swamp; and truly, I have even heard a frog croaking in it!

They are dexterous, they have clever fingers; what is *my* simplicity to their diversity? Their fingers are expert at threading and knotting and weaving of every sort; that is why they are busy at the stockings of the spirit!

They are good clocks; one must only take care to wind them up properly! Then they tell the time without error, and make a modest noise as they do it.

They work like mills and pounders: just toss them some seed-corn – they know how to grind the grain fine and make white dust of it.

Each watches what the other is up to, and they have little trust in each other. Inventive in petty wiliness, they lie in wait for those whose knowledge walks on lame feet – they lie in wait like spiders.

I have seen them preparing their poisons, invariably with care; and they always wore glass gloves on their hands to do it.

They are also adept at playing with loaded dice; and I have found them playing with such concentration that they were sweating.

We are strangers to each other, and their virtues are even less to my taste than their falsehoods and loaded dice.

And when I lived among them, I lived above them. For that, they bore me ill-will.

They refused to hear that someone was moving about above their heads; and so they put wood and earth and rubbish between me and their heads.

Thus they muffled the sound of my steps; and to this day it has been the scholars who have heard me worst.

They put all the failings and weaknesses of humankind between themselves and me – they call this a 'false floor' in their houses.

Yet nonetheless I go about *above* their heads with my thoughts; and even if I were to move upon my own errors, I should still be above them and their heads.

For humans are *not* equal: that is what justice declares. And what I want, *they* may not want!

Thus spake Zarathustra.

Of the Poets

'Ever since I have known the body better,' Zarathustra told one of his disciples, 'I have thought of the spirit as merely figurative; and all that is "everlasting" is a mere likeness as well.'

'I heard you say as much once before,' replied the disciple; 'and on that occasion you added: "but the poets tell too many lies". Why did you say that the poets tell too many lies?'

'Why?' said Zarathustra. 'You ask why? I am not one of those of whom you ask their reason why.

'Does my experience date from yesterday? It is a long time since I experienced the reasons for my opinions.

'Would I not need to be a barrel of memory if I wanted to have my reasons with me, too?

'It is already too much to keep my opinions about me; and some birds have flown away.

'And there are times when I find some unfamiliar migrant creature in my dovecote, one that trembles when I lay my hand upon it.

'But what was it Zarathustra once said to you? That the poets tell too many lies? – Yet Zarathustra is a poet too.

'So do you now believe that he was telling the truth? Why do you believe it?'

The disciple replied: 'I believe in Zarathustra.' But Zarathustra shook his head and smiled.

'Belief does not make me blessèd,' he said, 'least of all belief in me.

'But supposing that someone has said in all seriousness that the poets tell too many lies: he is right – *we* do tell too many lies.

'We also know too little and are poor learners; so we have to tell lies.

'And which of us poets has not adulterated his wine? Many a poisonous mishmash has been concocted in our cellars, many an indescribable thing has been done there.

'And because we know little, the poor in spirit give us heartfelt pleasure, especially when they are young women!

'And we crave to know even those things that old women tell each other of an evening. We ourselves call it the eternal-womanly in us.

'And as though there were some special secret route to knowledge that is *closed* to those who have learnt anything, we put faith in the people and their "wisdom".

'But all poets believe this: that anyone who lies in the grass or on secluded hillsides and pricks up his ears will find out some of the things that are between heaven and earth.

'And if they have tender feelings, the poets invariably suppose that Nature herself is in love with them.

'And she steals up to their ears to tell them secrets and the flattering sweet nothings of love; and on that account they brag and swell up before all mortal kind!

'Ah, there are so many things between heaven and earth that only the poets have bothered to dream about!

'And particularly *above* heaven; for all gods are images made up by poets, fabricated by poets!

'Truly, something does draw us ever onwards – to the realm of the clouds; on those we sit our motley manikins and promptly call them gods or superhumans.

'Indeed, they are just lightweight enough for those seats! – all those gods and superhumans.

'Ah, how weary I am of all this insufficient stuff passed off as real events! Ah, how weary I am of the poets!'

When Zarathustra spoke in this way, his disciple was wroth with him, but he remained silent. And Zarathustra was silent too; and his eye had turned to gaze within, as if into the far distance. At length he sighed and drew a breath.

'I am of today and of bygone times,' he then said; 'but there is something in me that is of tomorrow and of the day after tomorrow and of some day.

'I have tired of the poets, old and new: they all seem superficial to me, and shallow seas.

'They have not thought deeply enough: that is why their feeling has not plumbed the depths.

'A little sensuality and a little tedium: that has been the full extent of their thinking.

'All the jangling of their harps is no more than the puffing and flitting of phantoms to me; what have they ever known of fervent tones!

'They are not clean enough for me, either: they all cloud their waters so that they seem deep.

'In doing it they like to pose as conciliators; but to my mind they remain mediators and meddlers, neither one thing nor the other, and unclean!

'Ah, I did indeed cast my net in their seas, and aimed to catch fine fish; but what I pulled up was always the head of an old god.

'So it was that the sea gave the hungry man a stone. And they themselves may well come originally from the sea.

'Granted, one does find pearls in them; they themselves are all the more like hard shellfish. And in them, instead of the soul, I have often found salty slime.

'From the sea they even learnt its vanity, too – for is the sea not the peacock of peacocks?

'Even before the ugliest of buffaloes it spreads out its tail. It never wearies of its lace fan of silver and silk.

'Defiantly the buffalo looks on, his soul like the sand, still more like a thicket, but most of all like the swamp.

'What are beauty and the sea and the finery of a peacock to him? I address this parable to the poets.

'Truly, their spirit is itself the peacock of peacocks and an ocean of vanity!

'The spirit of the poet wants an audience, even if only of buffaloes! –

'But I have grown weary of this spirit: and I see the time coming when it will weary of itself.

'I have already seen the poets transformed, their gazes turned upon themselves.

'I have seen penitents of the spirit coming; they have grown out of the poets.'

Thus spake Zarathustra.

Of Great Events

There is an island in the ocean – not far from Zarathustra's Fortunate Isles – on which a volcano smokes unceasingly; the people, and especially the old women among them, say that it is placed like a rock before the gateway to the underworld, but that the narrow path that leads down to this gateway to the underworld passes through the volcano itself.

Now at the time when Zarathustra was living on the Fortunate Isles, a ship anchored at the island on which the smoking mountain stands, and its crew went ashore to shoot rabbits. Towards noon, however, when the captain and his men had reassembled, they suddenly saw a man approaching them through the air, and a voice said clearly: 'It is time! It is high time!' But when the figure was closest to them – it flew quickly past like a shadow, however, in the direction of the volcano – they were most alarmed to recognize that it was Zarathustra; for all of them had seen him before, except the captain himself, and they loved him as the people love, with love and wariness in equal measure.

'How do you like that!' said the old helmsman – 'Zarathustra's going to hell!'

About the same time as these mariners landed on the volcanic island, it was rumoured that Zarathustra had disappeared; and, when his friends were questioned, they said he had boarded a ship at night without saying where he was voyaging to.

This was disquieting; but three days later the mariners' story was added to the disquiet – and now all the people said that the devil had taken Zarathustra. Though his disciples laughed at this talk, and one of them even said, 'I'd sooner believe that Zarathustra had taken the devil,' at the bottoms of their souls they were all filled with anxiety and longing; so their joy was great when, on the fifth day, Zarathustra appeared among them.

And this is the story of Zarathustra's parley with the hound of fire.

The earth, said he, has a skin; and this skin has diseases. One of those diseases, for instance, is called 'humankind'.

And another of the diseases is called 'hound of fire'; people have told and been told a good many lies about *him*.

To get to the bottom of this mystery, I crossed the ocean; and I have seen truth naked – truly! – barefoot up to its neck.

I now know all about the hound of fire, and also about all the devils that erupt, and the devils that revolt, which are feared not only by old women.

'Out with you, fire-hound, out from your depths!' I cried – 'and admit how deep those depths are! Where does that stuff you are snorting up come from?

'You drink deeply from the sea: the bitter saltiness of your eloquence gives that away. Indeed, for a dog of the deep you feed too much on the surface!

'At best I think of you as the earth's ventriloquist; and whenever I have heard the devils that revolt and the devils that erupt speaking, I have found them to be like you: salt, lying and superficial.

'You are good at bellowing, and casting darkness with ashes! You are the champion big-mouths, and have become expert in the art of making mud boil.

'Wherever you are, there must always be mud nearby, and a great deal that is mouldy, cave-like and confined, which wants its freedom.

'You all like to bellow "freedom" more than anything else; for my part, I have lost my faith in "great events" if there is too much noise and smoke about them.

'And believe me, friend Infernal Racket – the greatest events are not our noisiest but our quietest hours.

'It is not around the inventors of new noises but around the inventors of new values that the world revolves; and it revolves *inaudibly*.

'Own up! Whenever your noise and smoke had cleared, little had ever happened. What did it matter if a town was mummified and a statue lay in the mud?

'And I say this to those who topple statues: it is surely the greatest of follies, to throw salt into the sea and statues into the mud.

'The statue lay in the mud of your contempt; but its law lies precisely in the fact that new life, and living beauty, grow from that contempt!

'Now it rises again, with features more divine, and seductive in its suffering; and, truly! it will thank you yet for having toppled it, you topplers!

'But I give this counsel to kings and churches and all that is weak with age and virtue – let yourselves be toppled! That you may come back to life, and that virtue may be yours!' –

This was what I said to the hound of fire. At this point he interrupted me sullenly and demanded: 'Churches? What is a church?'

'A church?' I answered. 'It is a kind of state, the most mendacious kind. But be quiet, you hypocritical hound! You know your own kind best, I'll warrant!

'Like you, the state is a hypocritical hound; like you, it likes to speak with smoke and bellowing – so that, as with you, people believe it speaks from the belly of things.

'For the state claims to be the most important beast on earth, one way or another – and people fall for it, too!'

When I had said that, the hound of fire carried on as if beside himself with envy. 'What?' he yelled – 'the most important beast on earth? And people fall for it?' And so much steam and so many hideous voices came from his gorge that I thought he would suffocate with vexation and envy.

At last he calmed down and his panting eased off. As soon as he was quiet, though, I said with a laugh:

'You are angry, hound of fire – so I am right about you!

'And to show how right I am, hear now about another hound of fire, one that really speaks from the heart of the earth.

'He breathes out gold and golden rain; so his heart will have it. What are ashes and smoke and hot mud to him!

'Laughter flutters from him like many-coloured clouds; he does not care for your gurgling and your spewing and your griping in the bowels!

'Gold, however, and laughter – these he takes from the heart of the earth; for this you need to know – the heart of the earth is made of gold.'

When the hound of fire heard this, he could no longer bear to listen to me. Humiliated, he drew in his tail, said a pathetic 'Bow wow', and crawled down into its cave.

Thus was the story Zarathustra told. His disciples, however, were hardly listening to him, so great was their wish to tell him about the mariners, the rabbits and the flying man.

'What am I to make of that!' said Zarathustra. 'Do you take me for a ghost?

'But it will have been my shadow. No doubt you will have heard things about the wanderer and his shadow?

'But this much is certain: I must keep it under better control – or it will ruin my reputation.'

And Zarathustra shook his head once more and wondered. 'What am I to make of that!' he said again.

'Whyever did the apparition cry out, "It is time! It is high time!"

'What is it high time *for?*'

Thus spake Zarathustra.

The Prophet

– 'And I saw a great sadness come upon humankind. The best grew weary of their works.

'A doctrine was put out, and a faith accompanied it: "All things are empty, all things are the same, all things are over and done!"

'And from all the hills the echo answered: "All things are empty, all things are the same, all things are over and done!"

'We have brought in a good harvest; but why have all our fruits turned rotten and brown? What fell from the ill moon last night?

'All our labour has been in vain. Our wine has turned to poison. The evil eye seared our fields and hearts yellow.

'We have all dried out; if we were visited by fire, we should crumble to dust like ash – yes, we have wearied fire itself.

'All our wells have run dry, even the sea has receded. All of the earth wants to tear open, but the depths will not swallow up!

"Ah, where is there still a sea in which one could drown" – that is our lament, sounded out across the flat marshes.

'Truly, we have grown too weary even to die; now we keep watch and live on – in sepulchres!'

Thus Zarathustra heard a prophet speak; and his prophecy went to Zarathustra's heart and transformed him. He went about sad and weary; and he came to resemble those the prophet had spoken of.

'Truly,' he said to his disciples, 'in a short while this long twilight will be upon us. Ah, how am I to keep my light burning?

'May it not go out in this sadness! It ought to be a light to worlds further off, and to the furthermost of nights!'

Thus troubled in his heart, Zarathustra went his ways, and for three days took neither food nor drink, took no rest, and lost his speech. At length it came about that he fell into a deep sleep. His disciples sat about him in long night watches, though, and waited anxiously to see whether he would awaken and speak again and recover from his affliction.

This, however, is what Zarathustra said when he awoke, his voice reaching his disciples as if from a great distance.

'Listen to the dream I dreamt, friends, and help me work out its meaning!

'It is still a riddle to me, this dream; its meaning is hidden within it, and imprisoned, and does not fly above it yet with its wings freely outstretched.

'I dreamt that I had renounced all life. I had become a night and grave-watchman, over there at the lonely mountain fortress of death.

'Up there I guarded death's coffins. The musty vaults were stacked full of these tokens of death's victory. Vanquished life gazed out at me from glass coffins.

'I breathed the odour of dusty eternities; my soul lay sultry and dusty. And who could have aired his soul there?

'The brightness of midnight was constantly about me, with solitude crouching beside it, and, making a third, the death-rattle silence of death, the worst of my companions.

'I was carrying keys, the rustiest of keys; and with them I could open the most creaking gate of all.

'Like a bitter, evil cawing the sound ran down the long passages when the wings of the gate opened; this bird gave a fiendish cry, and did not want to be awoken.

'But it was still more frightful and heart-constricting when it was silent once more, and stillness returned all around, and I sat alone in that pernicious silence.

'So time passed for me, creeping by, if time still existed; what do I know! But at length the thing happened that woke me.

'Three blows pounded on the gate like claps of thunder. The vaults echoed and moaned three times in response, and I went to the gate.

'"Alpa!" I called out, "who is bearing his ashes up the mountain? Alpa! Alpa! Who is bearing his ashes up the mountain?"

'And I turned the key and pulled at the gate and gave it my all. But it did not open so much as a finger's breadth.

'Then a roaring wind tore the gate wings apart; whistling, shrilling and cutting, it flung a black coffin to me.

'And in the roaring and whistling and shrilling the coffin burst open and spat out a thousand gales of laughter.

'And from a thousand masks of children, angels, owls, jesters and child-sized butterflies the laughter and jeering and roaring fell upon me.

'That gave me a dreadful fright and threw me down. And I screamed with horror as I had never screamed before.

'But my own scream woke me – and I came to myself.'

Thus Zarathustra told his dream. Then he fell silent, for he did not yet know how to interpret his dream. But the disciple whom he loved most rose swiftly, grasped Zarathustra's hand, and said:

'Your life itself interprets this dream for us, oh Zarathustra!

'Are you not yourself the wind that whistles shrilly and tears open the gates of the fortress of death?

'Are you not yourself the coffin full of many-coloured wickedness and life's angelic masks?

'Truly, Zarathustra enters into every death-chamber like a thousand gales of children's laughter, laughing at these night and grave-watchmen and anyone else who rattles dismal keys.

'You will scare them and knock them over with your laughter; a faint and an awakening will show your power over them.

'And even when the long twilight comes, and weariness unto death, you will not set in our heaven, you advocate of life!

'You have shown us new stars and new glories of the night; truly, you have spanned laughter itself above us like a many-coloured tent.

'From now on, it will always be the laughter of children that issues from coffins; weariness unto death will always be overcome by a strong and victorious wind; you yourself are our guarantor and prophet of these things!

'Truly, *you dreamt them yourself*, your enemies: that was your gravest dream!

'But just as you awoke from them and came to yourself, so too they shall awake from themselves – and come to you!' –

So said the disciple; and all the others now thronged about Zarathustra and seized hold of his hands, wanting to persuade him to leave his bed and his sadness behind and return to them. But Zarathustra sat upright on his bed, with the look of one who was a stranger to all. He gazed upon his disciples like a man returning home from a long absence in strange lands, and scrutinized their faces; and still he did not recognize them. But when they raised him and set him on his feet, see: suddenly his eye was transformed;

he grasped everything that had happened, stroked his beard and said in a firm voice:

'Very well. This has had its time; but see to it, my disciples, that we have a good meal, and soon! That is the penance I propose for bad dreams!

'But the prophet shall eat and drink at my side; and truly, I will yet show him an ocean in which he can drown!'

Thus spake Zarathustra. But then he gazed long into the face of the disciple who had interpreted the dream, and shook his head as he gazed.

Of Redemption

As Zarathustra was crossing the big bridge one day, cripples and beggars surrounded him, and a hunchback addressed him with these words:

'See, Zarathustra! The people are learning from you too, and coming to believe in your teaching; but one thing remains to be done if the people are to believe in you fully – first you must convince us cripples as well! You have a fine assortment here, truly an opportunity with more than one head of hair! You can cure the blind and make the lame walk, and you could jolly well take a little off a chap who has too much on his back – that, in my opinion, would be the proper way to make cripples believe in Zarathustra!'

But Zarathustra made this reply to the man who had spoken: 'If you take away a hunchback's hump, you take away his spirit – that is what the people teach. And if you give the blind man his eyes, he sees too many bad things on earth – so that he curses the one who cured him. But the one who makes the lame man walk does him the greatest harm, for no sooner can he walk than his vices run away with him – that is what the people teach concerning cripples. And why should Zarathustra not learn from the people, if the people learn from Zarathustra?

'But ever since I have been among humankind, it has been of least concern to me to see that this one lacks an eye and that one an ear and a third a leg, and that there are others who have lost their tongue or nose or head.

'I see and have seen worse things, many so heinous that I should not care to speak of them all, nor even to remain silent about some: that is, people who are lacking in everything except for one thing which they possess to excess, people who are no more than a big eye or a big mouth or a big belly or some other big thing – I call people of this sort inverse cripples.

'And when I came out from my solitude, and crossed this bridge for the first time, I did not believe my eyes, and looked and looked again, and said at length: "That is an ear! An ear as big as a human!" I looked more closely still, and underneath the ear something else really was moving, something pitiably small and meagre and puny. And indeed the monstrous ear sat upon a thin little stalk – but the stalk was a human being! With a magnifying glass it was even possible to make out a tiny, envious face, too – and that it was a bloated little soul that dangled from the stalk. The people told me, however, that the big ear was not only a man but a great man, a genius. But I never believed the people when they talked of great men – and I held to my belief that it was an inverse cripple, who had too little of everything and too much of one thing.'

Once Zarathustra had said this to the hunchback and to those whose mouthpiece and advocate he was, he turned to his disciples in considerable displeasure and said:

'Truly, my friends, I go my ways amid humanity as if among fragments and limbs of humans!

'To my way of seeing, the terrible thing is to find human beings smashed into pieces and scattered, as if across a field of battle and slaughter.

'And no matter if my eye flees from the present to the past, it invariably finds the same thing: fragments and limbs and horrific mishaps – but no humans!

'The present and the past on earth – ah, my friends! – that is what *I* find most unbearable; and I should not be able to live, were I not also a seer of what must come.

'The man who sees and wills and creates, a future himself and a bridge to the future – and also, alas, something much like a cripple beside the bridge: Zarathustra is all of these.

'And even you have often wondered: "Who is Zarathustra to us? What shall we call him?" And like me you have answered with questions.

'Is he one who promises or one who fulfils? A conqueror or an inheritor? A harvest or a ploughshare? A doctor or a convalescent?

'Is he a poet or a man of truth? A liberator or a controller? A good or evil man?

'I go my ways among people as among fragments of the future: that future which I envisage.

'And it is all my art and endeavour, to compose into one and bring together whatever is a fragment and a riddle and an horrific mishap.

'And how could I bear to be human, if humankind were not also poets and solvers of riddles and redeemers of happenstance!

'To redeem those who belong to the past, and to re-envisage every "There was" into "That is how I wanted it!" – that alone would I call redemption!

'The will – that is the name of the liberator and bringer of joy: that is what I have taught you, my friends! And now learn this as well: the will itself is still a prisoner.

'Acts of will liberate; but what is it that chains even the liberator?

'"There was" – that is the name of the will's gnashing of teeth and loneliest affliction. Powerless in the face of all that has been done, it is a baleful onlooker on all that is past.

'The will cannot exert its intentions retroactively; that it cannot breach time and the desire of time – that is the will's loneliest affliction.

'Acts of will liberate; what does intentionality devise for itself, to be rid of its affliction and mock at its dungeon?

'Ah, every prisoner ends up a fool! The manner in which the imprisoned will achieves its redemption is foolish too.

'The fact that time does not run backwards sparks the will's wrath: "that which was" is the name of the stone it cannot roll away.

'And so, out of wrath and displeasure, it rolls stones, and exacts revenge on any who fail to feel wrath and displeasure as it does.

'In this way the will, a liberator, has become a source of hurt; and it takes revenge on all that can suffer, for its own inability to go back.

'This, yes, only this is *revenge* proper: the will's antipathy to time and its "There was".

'Truly, a great foolishness inhabits our will; and the acquisition of spirit by that foolishness has proven a curse to all humankind.

'The spirit of revenge: my friends, that has hitherto been humankind's foremost concern; and, wherever there was suffering, it was always thought that there must be punishment.

'For "punishment" is what vengefulness calls itself: with one lie it hypocritically awards itself a clear conscience.

'And because there is suffering in the one who exerts the will, since he cannot exert that will retroactively – in consequence the exertion of will itself, and all life, were perceived as a punishment!

'And then cloud upon cloud passed over the spirit; until at length madness preached: "Everything passes away, therefore everything deserves to pass away!

'"And that law of time by which time must devour its own children is itself justice": this was what madness preached.

'"Things are ordered morally according to justice and punishment. Oh, where is redemption from the flow of things and the punishment that is existence?" This was what madness preached.

'"Can there be redemption if there is eternal justice? Ah, the stone of 'There was' cannot be rolled away: all punishments must be everlasting too!" This was what madness preached.

'"No deed can be annihilated: how could it be undone through punishment? This, this is what is everlasting in the punishment that is existence: that existence too must be an eternal recurrence of deed and guilt.

'"Unless the will should redeem itself at last, and the exertion of the will become a non-exertion −": but you are familiar with this fable-song of madness, my brothers!

'I guided you away from these fable-songs when I taught you: "The will is a creator."

'Every "There was" is a fragment, a riddle, an horrific mishap − until the creative will tells it: "But that is how I wanted it!"

'Until the creative will tells it: "But that is how I want it! That is how I shall want it!"

'But has it ever spoken in this way? And when will this happen? Has the will already been uncoupled from its own folly?

'Has the will already become its own redeemer and bringer of joy? Has it put behind it the spirit of revenge and all gnashing of teeth?

'And who has taught it to be reconciled to time, who has taught things that are higher than any reconciliation?

'The will that is the will to power must want things higher than any reconciliation − but how is that to come about? Who taught it to exert the will retroactively?'

− At this point in his discourse, however, Zarathustra abruptly fell silent, with the appearance of one who is scared out of his wits. With fright in his eyes he gazed upon his disciples; as if with arrows, his eyes pierced their thoughts and what lay behind their thoughts. But after a little while he laughed again and said in a calmed tone:

'It is difficult to live among humankind because it is so difficult to remain silent. Especially for someone who likes to talk.'

Thus spake Zarathustra. The hunchback, however, had listened to the conversation and had covered his face; but when he heard Zarathustra laugh, he looked up inquisitively and said slowly:

'But why does Zarathustra speak differently to us than to his disciples?'

Zarathustra answered: 'What is surprising about that? One may talk in a hunchbacked way when one talks to hunchbacks!'

'Very well,' said the hunchback; 'and with students one may tell tales out of school.

'But why does Zarathustra speak differently to his students − than to himself?'

Of Human Cleverness

It is not the peak that is terrifying, but the precipice!

The precipice, where the gaze plunges *down* and the hand reaches *up*. There, the heart is dizzied by its twofold will.

Ah, friends, have you guessed at my heart's twofold will too?

This, this is *my* precipice and my danger − that my gaze plunges into the heights and my hand wants to hold fast and support itself − on the depths!

My will clings to humankind, I chain myself to people, because I am drawn up to the superhuman; that is where my other will wants to go.

And *the reason why* I live blindly among humankind, as if I did not know them for what they are, is so that my hand does not wholly lose its faith in what is firm.

I do not know you people; this darkness and consolation is often spread about me.

I am any rogue's as I sit by the road to the gate, wondering: who is out to cheat me?

That is my first principle of human canniness: to let myself be cheated, so that I need not be on the alert for cheats.

Ah, if I were on the alert for humankind, how might not people be an anchor for my ball! I would be torn upwards and away too easily!

My fate is under the provision that I must be without foresight.

And those who do not want to die of thirst among humankind must learn to drink from any kind of glass; those who would stay clean among humankind must be able to wash even in dirty water.

And for my own comfort I often said this: 'Very good! Onwards, old heart! You have come through a misfortune; savour that as your – good fortune!'

But this is my next principle of human canniness: I spare the *vain* more than the proud.

Is injured vanity not the mother of all tragedies? But where pride is injured, something better than pride will grow.

For life to be good to watch, the play must be well acted; but that requires good actors.

I have found all vain people to be good actors: they act, and want people to enjoy watching them – their entire spirit is in that desire.

They perform themselves, they invent themselves; I love watching life when they are around – it cures melancholy.

That is why I spare the vain: because they are physicians to my melancholy, and involve me in humankind as in a play.

And then, who can plumb the full depth of the vain man's modesty! I feel affection and sympathy for him on account of his modesty.

He wants to learn belief in himself from you; he feeds on your gaze, he eats up praise from your hands.

He even believes your lies when you tell good lies about him; for his heart sighs in its depths: 'What am *I*?'

And if true virtue is that which is unconscious of itself – well, the vain man is unconscious of his modesty! –

But this is my third principle of human canniness: that I do not let your fearfulness spoil the sight of the *wicked* for me.

I am blissfully happy to see the wonders hatched by the heat of the sun: tigers and palms and rattlesnakes.

Among humans, too, the heat of the sun produces a fine brood, and much that is wondrous in the wicked.

It is true that, just as the wisest men among you did not strike me as so very wise, human wickedness did not live up to its reputation either.

And often I shook my head and wondered: why go on rattling, you rattlesnakes?

Truly, there is still a future, even for evil! And humankind has not yet discovered the hottest south.

Many a thing is now called the worst of wickedness that is only twelve feet wide and three months long! But one day bigger dragons will come into the world.

For it will yet take a lot of hot sunshine burning upon the humid jungles if the superhuman is not to be without his dragon, the super-dragon worthy of him!

Your wildcats must first have become tigers, and your venomous toads crocodiles; for the good huntsman should have a good hunt!

And truly, you good and just people! There is a great deal in you that is risible, especially your fear of what used to be called 'the devil'!

You are so unfamiliar with greatness in your souls that the superhuman would *terrify* you with his goodness!

And you wise and understanding people, you would flee from the burning sun of wisdom in which the superhuman delights to bathe his nakedness!

You highest of people my eyes have beheld! – this is the doubt I have about you, and my secret laughter: my guess is that you would call my superhuman the devil!

Ah, I tired of these highest and best of men; I felt the urge to go up from their 'heights', out, away to the superhuman!

Horror beset me when I saw these best of men naked; promptly I grew wings, to fly off into distant futures.

Into yet more distant futures, more southerly souths, than any artist has ever dreamt of; away, where the gods are ashamed of all clothes!

But I want to see you disguised, you neighbours and fellow-beings, well dressed and vain and dignified, as 'the good and the just' –

And I myself shall sit among you in disguise, that I may *fail to know* you and myself. That, you see, is the last of my principles of human canniness.

Thus spake Zarathustra.

The Stillest Hour

What has happened to me, my friends? You see me troubled, driven out, unwillingly obedient, ready to leave – ah, to leave *you*!

Yes, Zarathustra must go into his solitude once more; but this time the bear is returning to his cave without any pleasure!

What has happened to me? Who has given this order? – Ah, it is my wrathful mistress who wants me to go. She has spoken to me. Did I ever tell you her name?

Yesterday, as evening approached, my stillest hour spoke to me: that is the name of my fearsome mistress.

And this is how it happened – for I must tell you everything, that your hearts may not harden against me for departing so suddenly!

Are you familiar with the terror a man feels when falling asleep? –

He is terrified to his very toes, fearing that the ground may crumble beneath him and the dream begin.

I tell you this by way of a likeness. Yesterday, at the stillest hour, the ground crumbled beneath me; the dream began.

The hand moved, the clock of my life drew breath – never had I heard such stillness about me; so that my heart was terrified.

Then something spoke to me without voice: 'You know it, Zarathustra?' –

And on hearing that whisper I cried out in terror, and the blood drained from my face; but I remained silent.

Again something spoke to me without voice: 'You know it, Zarathustra, but you do not say it!' –

And at last I answered, as if fractiously: 'Yes, I know it, but I don't want to say it!'

And again something spoke to me without voice: 'You *don't want to*, Zarathustra? Is that really true? Do not hide behind fractiousness!'

And I wept and trembled like a child, and said: 'Ah, I should like to, but how can I! Release me from it! It is beyond my strength!'

And again something spoke to me without voice: 'Of what consequence are you, Zarathustra! Say your piece and break apart!'

And I answered: 'Ah, is it *mine* to say? Who am I? I am waiting for one who is more worthy; I am not even worthy to be broken apart by him.'

And again something spoke to me without voice: 'Of what consequence are you? I do not find you sufficiently humble yet. Humility has the toughest hide.' –

And I answered: 'What has the hide of my humility not endured already! I live at the foot of my heights – how high are my peaks? No one has yet told me. But I know my valleys well.'

And again something spoke to me without voice: 'Oh Zarathustra, he who has to move mountains can move valleys and lowlands too.'

And I answered: 'My words have not moved mountains yet, nor has what I have spoken reached humankind. I did go among humankind, but I have not yet made an impression upon them.'

And again something spoke to me without voice: 'What do you know about *that*? The dew falls on the grass when the night is most silent.' –

And I answered: 'They mocked me when I found and went my own way; and, truth to tell, my feet did tremble then.

'And they said to me: You have forgotten the way you had learnt, and now you will even forget how to walk!'

And again something spoke to me without voice: 'Of what consequence is their mockery? You are one who has put aside the obedience he learnt; now you shall command!

'Do you not know who it is that all men have greatest need of? The one who commands great things.

'To do great things is hard; but to command great things is harder still.

'The most unpardonable thing about you is that you have the power but will not rule.' –

And I answered: 'I do not have the lion's voice to issue commands.'

And again something spoke to me like a whisper: 'It is the stillest words that usher in the storm. It is thoughts that go on the feet of doves that govern the world.

'Oh Zarathustra, you shall go as a shadow of what must come; thus you will command, and, commanding, lead the way.' –

And I answered: 'I am ashamed.'

And again something spoke to me without voice: 'You have yet to become a child, and without shame.

'The pride of youth is still upon you. You became young late. But anyone who wants to become a child must transcend his youth, too.' –

And I considered long, and trembled. But at length I said what I had said at first: 'I don't want to.'

At that there was laughter all around me. Woe, how that laughter tore my entrails and slashed open my heart!

And for the last time something spoke to me: 'Oh Zarathustra, your fruits are ripe but you are not ripe for your fruits!

'So you must go back to your solitude, for you need to be soft with ripeness.' –

And again something laughed, and was gone; and it grew still about me, as if with a twofold stillness. I, however, lay on the ground, and the sweat poured from my limbs.

– Now you have heard everything, and why I must go back to my solitude. I have kept nothing back from you, my friends.

But you have also heard from me *who* is still the most silent of men – and wants to be!

Ah, my friends! There is something more I should like to tell you, something more I should like to give you! Why do I not give it? Can it be that I am mean? –

When Zarathustra had spoken these words, however, the force of his pain and the nearness of the parting from his friends beset him, so that he wept aloud; and no one was able to console him. But that night he went away alone and left his friends.

PART THREE

You gaze upwards when you wish to be exalted. And I gaze down because I am exalted.

Which of you can laugh and be exalted at one and the same time?

He who climbs the highest mountains laughs at all tragedies, earnest or jesting.

Zarathustra, 'Of Reading and Writing'

The Wanderer

It was about midnight when Zarathustra crossed the spine of the island, intending to reach the shore on the other side by early morning and take ship. There was a good harbour there, where foreign ships liked to anchor too; they took many with them who wanted to leave the Fortunate Isles and cross the ocean. As Zarathustra was now climbing the mountain, his thoughts turned as he went on his way to the many solitary walks he had taken since his youth, and how many mountains and ridges and peaks he had already climbed. I am a wanderer and a mountain-climber, he said to his heart. I do not love the plains, and it seems I cannot sit still for long.

And whatever fate and experience may yet lie ahead of me, wandering and mountain-climbing will be part of it; in the end one experiences only oneself.

The time is gone when chance happenings could still befall me; and what *could* still fall to me that was not already my own?

It is returning, at last it is coming home to me – my own self, and whatever of myself was long abroad and scattered among all manner of thing and happenstance.

And one thing more I know: I now stand before my final summit, and before what was deferred for the longest time. Ah, I must now set out on my hardest path! Ah, I have begun my loneliest wandering!

But for a man of my kind there is no way around an hour such as this, the hour that says to him: 'Only now are you taking your path of greatness! The peak and the abyss – they are now one!

'You are taking your path of greatness; what was your ultimate danger until now has become your ultimate refuge!

'You are taking your path of greatness; now the fact that there is no path behind you any more must be the source of your finest courage!

'You are taking your path of greatness; no one shall come creeping after you here! It was your own foot that rubbed out the path behind you, and above the path is written: Impossibility.

'And when there are no ladders any more, you will have to know how to climb your own head; how else do you expect to climb upwards?

'Upon your own head and beyond your own heart! Now the gentlest part of you must become the hardest.

'Those who have always been greatly protective of themselves will end by ailing of that excessive protectiveness. Praise be to whatever hardens us! I do not praise the land where butter and honey – flow!

'If one is to see *a great deal*, one must learn to *look away* from oneself: – this hardness is a requisite in every mountain-climber.

'But how should those whose eyes are intrusive in their quest for understanding see any more of things than the foregrounds!

'You though, oh Zarathustra, have sought to see into the very ground and background of all things; so you must climb over yourself – onwards, upwards, till even your stars are *below* you!

'Yes! To look down on myself and even on my stars: that alone I would think of as my *summit*, that has remained for me as my *final* summit!'

Thus spake Zarathustra to himself as he climbed, comforting his heart with hard sayings; for he was sore at heart as never before. And when he had reached the top of the mountain ridge, see, the other ocean lay outspread before him; and he stood still and remained silent for a long time. But the night was cold at that height, and clear and bright with stars.

I recognize my fate, he said at last in sorrow. So be it. I am ready. My final solitude has just begun.

Ah, this black, sorrowful ocean below me! Ah, this pregnant night-time sombreness! Ah, fate and ocean! Now I must climb *down* to you!

Before my highest mountain I stand, and before my longest wandering; and so I must first descend deeper than I have ever done before:

– deeper into pain than I have ever descended, down into its blackest current! My fate demands it. So be it. I am ready.

Where do the highest mountains come from? I once asked. Then I learnt that they come from the ocean.

The evidence is inscribed in their rock and in the walls of their peaks. The highest must achieve its height from out of the greatest depths. –

Thus spake Zarathustra on the top of the mountain, where it was cold; but by the time he had come closer to the ocean, and at last stood solitary beneath the cliffs, he had grown weary on the way, and more filled with longing than ever before.

Everything is still asleep, he said; even the ocean is asleep. Its eye watches me sleepily and dispassionately.

But its breath is warm. That I feel. And I also feel that it is dreaming. It tosses and turns on its hard pillows, dreaming.

Listen! Listen! How it groans with bad memories! Or bad expectations?

Ah, I share your sadness, you dark monster, and for your sake am wroth even with myself.

Ah, that my hand has insufficient strength! Truly, I should gladly release you from bad dreams! –

And as Zarathustra was speaking thus, he laughed in melancholy and bitterness at himself. 'What is this, Zarathustra!' he said – 'do you intend to sing consolation to the very ocean?

'Ah, you fond fool, Zarathustra, so impetuously trusting! You have always been like that, approaching all things terrible in a spirit of trust.

'You would have stroked every monster. A little warm breath, a little soft fur on its paw – and you would have been ready to love and cajole it.

'Love is the danger for the loneliest man, the love of anything *if only it is alive*! Truly, my foolishness and my modesty in love are laughable!'

Thus spake Zarathustra, and he laughed once again; but then

143

he thought of the friends he had left, and, as if he had offended them with his thoughts, he was angry at himself for his thoughts. And presently the man who was laughing wept; – Zarathustra wept bitterly with anger and longing.

Of the Vision and the Riddle

1

When the rumour spread among the ship's crew that Zarathustra was on board – for another man who came from the Fortunate Isles had embarked at the same time as he – a great curiosity and expectancy filled them. Zarathustra, however, remained silent for two days, and was cold and deaf with sorrow, responding neither to looks nor to questions. But on the evening of the second day he opened his ears again, though still he was silent; for there were many strange and dangerous things to be heard on that ship, which came from far away and was bound even further. Zarathustra, though, was a friend to all who make long journeys and do not care to live without danger. And, see! at length his own tongue was loosened and he listened, and the ice in his heart broke up – and he began to speak in this way:

To you, the bold seekers, venturers, and anyone who has ever taken ship with cunning sails upon terrible oceans –

To you, who are drunken on riddles, who delight in twilight, whose souls are lured by pipes to every treacherous cleft –

For you do not want to feel for a thread with a cowardly hand, and where you can *guess* you hate to *deduce* –

To you alone I recount the riddle that I saw – the vision of the loneliest man.

Of late I walked sombrely in a twilight the shade of a corpse, sombrely and hard, with my lips pressed together. Not only one sun had gone down for me.

A path that mounted defiantly through scree, a wicked, solitary path that neither plant nor bush found amenable – a mountain path crunched beneath the defiance of my foot.

Striding out in silence over the derisive clatter of pebbles, treading down the stones that made it slip, my foot forced its way upwards.

Upwards, defying the spirit that was pulling it down, pulling it to the sheer drop – the spirit of heaviness, my devil and arch-enemy.

Upwards, although the spirit sat upon me, half-dwarf, half-mole; lame; laming; dripping lead into my ear, lead-drop thinking into my brain.

'Oh, Zarathustra,' it purled mockingly, syllable by syllable, 'you stone of wisdom! You have thrown yourself up high, but every stone that is thrown must – fall!

'Oh, Zarathustra, you stone of wisdom, you slingshot, you smasher of stars! It is you yourself that you have thrown up so high, but every stone that is thrown must – fall!

'Condemned to yourself and to your own stoning: oh, Zarathustra, you did throw the stone far – but it will fall back down on *you*!'

Here the dwarf fell silent, and remained so for a long time. His silence oppressed me, however; and to be in this state with another is truly lonelier than on one's own!

I climbed, I climbed, I dreamt, I thought – but everything oppressed me. I resembled a sick man tired out by his dreadful suffering and woken again, when he drifts into sleep, by a still more dreadful dream.

But there is something within me that I call courage; it has always put paid to any loathness in me. This courage at last bade me stop and speak out: 'Dwarf! You! Or I!' –

For courage is the best of killers – courage that *attacks*; for in every attack there is clashing play.

The human, however, is the most courageous animal; and with his courage he has overcome every animal. With that clashing play he has even overcome all manner of pain; human pain, though, is the profoundest pain.

Courage also kills dead the vertigo felt at the abyss – and where does humankind not stand at the abyss! Is seeing itself not – seeing abysses?

Courage is the best of killers; courage even kills compassion dead. But compassion is the deepest abyss: however deeply humankind looks into life, so deeply does it look into suffering.

Courage, however, is the best of killers – courage that *attacks*; even death it kills dead, for it says: 'Was *that* life? So be it! Once more!'

In such words, however, there is a great deal of clashing play. Let him hear who has ears to hear.

2

'Stop, dwarf!' I said. 'I! Or you! But I am the stronger of us two – you do not know the abysmal depth of my thinking! You could not endure *that*!' –

Then something happened that made me lighter; for the dwarf, all curiosity, jumped off my shoulder! And he crouched on a rock in front of me. But there was a gateway right where we had halted.

'Look at this gateway, dwarf!' I continued. 'It has two faces. Two roads meet here; no one has ever travelled them to the end.

'This long lane back goes on for an eternity. And that long lane heading out is another eternity.

'They are at odds with each other, these roads. They butt into each other head-on. And here at this gateway is where they meet. The name of the gateway is written above it: "Moment".

'But if one were to follow one of them further, and further still, and ever further; do you suppose, dwarf, that these roads would be at odds forever?'

'Everything straight lies,' muttered the dwarf contemptuously. 'All truth is crooked. Time itself is a circle.'

'You spirit of heaviness!' I said angrily – 'do not make too light of this! Or I shall leave you crouching where you are, Lamefoot – and I carried you *up*!

'See,' I went on, 'this Moment! From this gateway, the Moment, a long, everlasting lane runs *back*: behind us lies an eternity.

'Must not all things that *can* walk already have walked this lane? Must not all things that *can* happen already have happened, been done, gone by?

'And if everything has already been, what do you think, dwarf, of this Moment? Must not this gateway already have been as well?

'And are not all things knotted fast, in such a way that this moment draws after it *all* things that are yet to come? – and *therefore* itself as well?

'For all things that *can* walk *must* also at some time walk *out* along that long lane.

'And this slow spider that creeps in the moonlight, and this moonlight itself, and I and you at the gateway, whispering together, whispering of eternal things – must we not all have been here before?

– 'and must we not come again, and walk that other lane before us, out, down that long, dreadful lane – must we not keep coming back forever?' –

Thus I spoke, ever more softly; for I was afraid of my own thoughts, and of the thinking that lay behind them. Then suddenly I heard a dog *howling* nearby.

Had I ever heard a dog howl like that? My thoughts ran back. Yes! When I was a child, in my most distant childhood:

– back then I heard a dog howl like that. And I saw it too, bristling, head raised, trembling, in the dead of midnight when even dogs believe in ghosts;

– so that I was moved to pity. For the full moon was just passing over the house, silent as death, and was standing still, a burning circle, still upon the flat roof as if it were trespassing; –

that was what had scared the dog, back then; for dogs believe in thieves and ghosts. And when I heard the same kind of howling again, I was moved to pity once more.

Where had the dwarf gone now? And the gateway? And the spider? And all the whispering? Had I been dreaming? Was I now waking? All at once I stood between rugged cliffs, alone, desolate, in the most desolate of moonlight.

But there was a man lying there! And there! The dog, leaping, bristling, whining – now it saw me coming – and it howled again, then *cried out*; had I ever heard a dog cry for help like that?

And the truth is that I had never seen anything like what I then saw. I saw a young herdsman, writhing, choking, convulsed, his face distorted, a heavy black snake hanging out of his mouth.

Had I ever seen so much revulsion and pale horror on one face? Had he, I suppose, been asleep? The snake had slithered into his throat – and bitten itself fast.

My hand pulled at the snake, and pulled – in vain! It could not pull the snake out of his throat. Then I heard a cry within me: 'Bite! Bite!

'Bite the head off! Bite!' – from within me came the cry of my horror, my loathing, my revulsion, my pity, all that was good and bad within me cried out in a single cry. –

You bold ones around me! You seekers, venturers, and anyone who has ever taken ship with cunning sails upon uncharted oceans! You who delight in riddles!

Go on – solve for me the riddle I then beheld, interpret for me the vision of the loneliest man!

For a vision is what it was, and a premonition; – *what* did I see back then, in that likeness? And *who* is it who must one day come?

Who is the herdsman into whose throat the snake had slithered? *Who* is the person into whose throat all that is heaviest and blackest will slither in that way?

– The herdsman, however, bit as my cry had counselled him to; he bit with a good bite! He spat the snake's head far away – and leapt up.

No longer a herdsman, no longer a human – a transformed being, bathed in light, and *laughing*! Never till that day had anyone laughed on earth as *he* laughed!

Oh my brothers, I heard laughter that was no human laughter – and now a thirst eats away at me, a longing that is never still.

My longing for that laughter eats away at me; oh how do I bear to go on living! And how would I bear to die now! –

Thus spake Zarathustra.

Of Undesired Bliss

With such riddles and bitterness in his heart, Zarathustra set out across the ocean. Once he was four days' voyage from the Fortunate Isles and his friends, he had overcome all his pain – victorious, and with a firm footing, he stood once again upon his fate. And at that time Zarathustra addressed his jubilant conscience in this way:

Again I am alone, and want to be – alone with the clear heavens and the open seas; and again it is afternoon about me.

It was afternoon when I first found my friends, and afternoon the second time as well – at the hour when all light grows stiller.

For whatever happiness is still journeying between heaven and earth will now seek out a bright soul for its lodging; all light has now grown stiller *with happiness.*

Oh afternoon of my life! Once *my* happiness too descended into the valley to seek its lodging; there it found these open, hospitable souls.

Oh afternoon of my life! What would I not give to have one thing: this living planting of my thoughts, and this dawn of my highest hope!

At one time the creator sought companions and children of *his* hope; and see, it transpired that he could not find them, unless he first created them himself.

Thus I am in the midst of my work, going to my children and returning from them: for the sake of his children Zarathustra must perfect himself.

For one loves from one's very fundament only one's child and one's work; and where there is great love of oneself, that is the sign of pregnancy; so I have found.

My children are still greening in their first spring, standing close and shaken together by the winds, the children of my garden and of my best soil.

And, truly, where such trees stand together, there the fortunate isles *are*!

But one day I shall uproot them and position each one by itself, that it may learn solitude and defiance and caution.

It will stand by the ocean, gnarled and crooked and with pliant hardiness, a living lighthouse of invincible life.

Where the storms plunge down into the ocean, and the snout of the mountains drinks water, each one of them shall one day keep its day and night watches, that *it* be tested and identified.

It shall be identified and tested in order to tell whether it is of my kind and descent – whether it is master of a will of long duration, tacit even in speech, and yielding in such a way that in giving it *takes*: –

that it may one day be my companion and one of Zarathustra's fellow-creators and fellow-celebrants, such a one as inscribes my will on my tablets; for the greater perfection of all things.

And for its sake and others of its kind I must perfect *myself*; for that reason I now decline my own happiness and offer myself up to unhappiness of any sort – that *I* may be finally tested and identified.

And in truth it was time that I went; and the wanderer's shadow and the longest stay and the stillest hour all said to me – 'It is high time!'

The wind blew in at my keyhole and said: 'Come!' The door flew cunningly open and said: 'Go!'

But I lay chained to the love of my children; desire set this snare for me, the desire for love, that I might become my children's prey and lose myself to them.

To desire – this now means to me: to have lost myself. I have you, my children! This possession is conceived as containing all security and no desire.

But the sun of my love sat brooding upon me, and Zarathustra was cooking in his own juice – then shadows and doubts flew across me.

I hankered after frost and winter: 'Oh that frost and winter would make me crack and crunch again!' I sighed; – at that, icy mist rose up from within me.

My past broke open its graves, many a pain that had been buried alive awoke; it had merely been sleeping, concealed in winding sheets.

Thus everything called out to me in signs: 'It is time!' – But I – did not hear; until at length my abyss stirred and my thought bit me.

Ah, you thought as deep as an abyss, you who are *my* thought! When shall I find the strength to hear you digging and not tremble any longer?

My heart beats in my throat when I hear you digging! Your very silence will choke me, you who are silent and deep as an abyss!

Never yet have I dared to summon you *up*; it was quite enough that I bore you about with me! I have not yet been strong enough for the ultimate exuberance and perverseness of the lion.

Your heaviness has always been terrible enough for me; but the day will come when I shall find the strength and the lion's voice to summon you up!

Once I have overcome myself in that regard, I shall overcome myself in a respect that is greater still; and a *victory* will be the seal of my perfection! –

In the meantime, I am still drifting on uncertain seas; chance flatters me, with its smooth tongue; I gaze ahead and behind – but still I can make out no end.

The hour of my final struggle has not yet arrived – or is it perhaps arriving now? Truly, the ocean and life all about me look upon me with treacherous beauty!

Oh afternoon of my life! Oh happiness before the evening! Oh harbour out on the ocean! Oh peace in uncertainty! How I mistrust you all!

Truly, I do not trust your treacherous beauty! I resemble a lover who mistrusts smiles that are all too velvety.

Just as the jealous man thrusts from him the one he loves most, tender even in his hardness – so too I thrust this blessèd hour from me.

Away with you, you blessèd hour! With you there came to me an undesired bliss! Here I stand, willing to bear my deepest pain – you have come at the wrong time!

Away with you, you blessèd hour! Take up your lodging over there instead – with my children! Hurry! and bless them before evening with *my* happiness!

Now evening is approaching; the sun is setting. It is gone – my happiness!

Thus spake Zarathustra. And he waited all night for his unhappiness; but he waited in vain. The night continued clear and still, and happiness itself came closer and closer to him. Towards morning, however, Zarathustra laughed to his heart and said derisively: 'Happiness is chasing me. That is what comes of my not chasing women. Happiness, however, is a woman.'

Before Sunrise

Oh sky above me! – pure! deep! you abyss of light! Gazing at you, I quake with divine desires.

To cast myself into your heights – that is *my* depth! To find protection in your purity – that is *my* innocence!

The deity is veiled by his beauty: in that way you hide your stars. You do not speak: in *that* way you proclaim your wisdom to me.

Mutely over the raging seas you rose for me today. Your love and your modesty tell of revelation to my raging soul.

That you have come to me, beautiful, veiled in your beauty, that you have spoken to me mutely, revealed in your wisdom:

oh how should I not divine all that is modest in your soul! You came *before* the sun to me, the loneliest man.

We have been friends from the outset: we have sorrow and terror and the earth in common; the very sun we have in common.

We do not talk to each other, because we know too much – we keep silence together, smiling our knowledge to one another.

Are you not the light to my fire? Is yours not the sister soul to my insight?

Together we learnt everything; together we learnt how to climb above ourselves to ourselves and to smile cloudlessly –

to smile down cloudlessly from bright eyes and from leagues of distance, while below us compulsion and purpose and guilt steam like rain.

And when I wandered alone, *who* was it my soul hungered after during the nights and on the aimless pathways? And when I climbed mountains, *whom* was I always seeking on the mountains, if not you?

And whenever I went wandering and climbed mountains, that was exigency and nothing more, the helpless man's attempt to help himself; my entire will wants only to *fly*, to fly into *you*!

And whom have I loathed more than passing clouds and anything that besmirches you? And I have even loathed my own loathing, because it besmirched you!

I cannot abide the passing clouds, those slinking predatory cats: they take from you and me what we have in common – the vast and boundless saying of yes and amen.

We cannot abide those mediators and crossovers, the passing clouds; those half-and-half entities that have neither learnt to bless nor to deliver a fundamental curse.

I should rather sit in a barrel beneath an overcast sky, rather sit in the abyss without any sky, than see you, sky of brightness, besmirched by passing clouds!

And often I am tempted to tie them together with jagged golden wires of lightning, that I might drum upon their kettle-bellies as the thunder does –

a wrathful kettle-drummer, because they rob me of your yes! and amen! – you sky above me, you pure! bright! abyss of light! – because they rob you of *my* yes! and amen!

For I should rather have noise and thunder and storm-curses than this wary, dubious feline calm; and among humankind, too, I most of all detest all who are soft of foot and half-and-half, all doubting, hesitant, passing clouds.

And 'Those who cannot bless shall *learn* to curse!' – this clear teaching fell to me from a clear sky. Even in black nights, this star still stands in my sky.

I, however, am one who blesses and says yes, if only you are about me, you pure! bright! abyss of light! – And I will bear the blessing of my yes-saying into every abyss.

I have become one who blesses and one who says yes. To get there was a long struggle, and I struggled to have my hands free one day for blessing.

But this is my blessing: to stand over every thing as its own sky, as its round roof, its azure bell and eternal security; and blessèd is he who blesses thus!

For all things are baptized at the fount of eternity, and beyond good and evil; but good and evil themselves are mere shadows that come between, and damp afflictions, and passing clouds.

Truly, it is a blessing and not blasphemy if I teach this: 'Above all things stands the heaven of chance, the heaven of innocence, the heaven of happenstance, the heaven of exuberance.'

'Lord Happenstance' – that is the oldest noble line in the world. I have given it back to all things, releasing them from servitude to purpose.

I set this freedom and heavenly serenity, like an azure bell, above all things, when I taught that no 'eternal will' is expressing its will over and through them.

I set this exuberance and this folly in place of that will when I taught: 'With all things, one thing is impossible – rationality!'

A *little* reason, it is true, a seed of wisdom scattered from star to star – this leaven is mixed into all things: for folly's sake, wisdom is mixed into all things!

A little wisdom is indeed possible; but I have found this blessèd certainty in all things – that they would rather *dance* on the feet of chance.

Oh sky above me, you pure! lofty sky! This is what your purity now means to me: that there is no everlasting spider of reason, nor spider-webs of reason –

that for me you are a dance-floor for divine chance, that for me you are a divine table for divine dice and dice-players!

But are you blushing? Did I say something unutterable? Did I blaspheme when I meant to bless you?

Or is it shamefulness at our being together that has made you blush? – Are you telling me to go, and be silent, because now – the *day* is coming?

The world is deep – and deeper than ever the day supposed. Not everything may be put into words before the day. But the day is coming; so let us now part!

Oh sky above me, you modest! glowing sky! Oh you my happiness before sunrise! The day comes; so let us now part!

Thus spake Zarathustra.

Of Virtue that Makes Things Smaller

1

When Zarathustra was once more on solid ground, he did not go immediately back to his mountains and his cave, but instead took many paths and asked many questions, inquiring into this thing and that, to the point that he joked of himself: 'See, a river that flows back through many twists and turns to its source!' For he wanted to find out what had become *of humankind* in the meantime: whether humans had grown bigger or smaller. And one time, seeing a row of new houses, he was perplexed and said:

'What do these houses mean? Truly, no great soul put them up in its own likeness!

'Did some stupid child take them out of its toy-box? If only some other child would put them back in its box!

'And these rooms and parlours: can *men* go in and out there? They look to me as if they had been made for silk dolls; or for little ones who like their treats to eat, and let others nibble at them, too.'

And Zarathustra stood and pondered. At length he said sorrowfully:

'*Everything* has grown smaller!

'Everywhere I see lower gateways; anyone who is of *my* kind will still fit through, but – he will have to stoop!

'Oh, when shall I be back home once again, where I shall not have to stoop any longer – no longer have to stoop *before small people*!' – And Zarathustra sighed and gazed into the distance.

That same day, though, he delivered his discourse on virtue that makes things smaller.

2

I go among these people and keep my eyes open: they do not forgive me for not envying them their virtues.

They peck at me because I tell them: small people require small virtues – and because it is hard for me to accept that small people are *necessary*!

I still resemble a cockerel, here on an unfamiliar farmyard, pecked at even by the hens; I am no less well disposed towards the hens on that account, though.

I am polite to them, as I am to all petty nuisances; to be prickly towards petty things strikes me as the wisdom of hedgehogs.

They all talk about me when they sit around the fire in the evenings – they talk about me, but no one thinks – of me!

This is the new silence I have learnt: their noise about me spreads a cloak over my thoughts.

They make their noise together: 'What is that dark cloud

bringing us? Let us be sure that it does not have a plague in store for us!'

And recently a woman pulled her child back to herself when it wanted to come to me: 'Take the children away from here!' she yelled; 'eyes like that burn children's souls.'

They cough when I am speaking: they suppose coughing is an objection to strong winds – they do not divine the turbulence of my happiness!

'We do not have any time yet for Zarathustra' – that is their objection; but of what consequence is a time that 'has no time' for Zarathustra?

And even when they praise me; how could I sleep well on *their* praise? To me, their praise is a barbed belt; it scratches even when I take it off.

And this I have also learnt among them: those who praise adopt the posture of those who give something back, but in truth they want to be given more!

Ask my foot whether it likes their lauding and luring tunes! Truly, to such a beat and tick-tock it does not care to dance or to stand still.

They are out to lure and laud me towards petty virtue; they would like to persuade my foot to the tick-tock of small happiness.

I go among these people and keep my eyes open; they have grown *smaller* and are growing ever smaller – *because of their doctrine of happiness and virtue.*

For they are modest even in virtue – for they want their comfort. But only a modest virtue is compatible with comfort.

Granted, they too learn in their own way how to stride, and stride forward. I call it their *hobbling* – and it makes them a nuisance to anyone who is in a hurry.

And some of them go forward and look back at the same time, with a stiff neck; I like to bump into these.

The foot and the eyes ought not to lie, nor expose each other's lies. But there is a good deal of lying among the small people.

Some of them *will*, but most are merely *willed*. Some of them are authentic, but most are poor actors.

There are those among them who do not know they are acting, and others who are acting despite themselves – authentic people are always rare, especially authentic actors.

There is little manliness here: that is why their women are becoming mannish. For only he who is man enough will *release the woman* in woman.

And this hypocrisy I have found to be the worst among them: that even those who give the orders hypocritically affect the virtues of those who serve.

'I serve, you serve, we serve' – that is the prayer of ruling class hypocrisy here too – and woe, if the first lord is *only* the first servant!

Ah, the inquisitiveness of my eyes has even strayed into their hypocrisy, and I have readily made out all their fly-happiness and their buzzing at sunny window-panes.

So much kindness, so much weakness I see. So much justice and compassion, so much weakness.

They are blunt, honest and kind to each other, as grains of sand are blunt, honest and kind to other grains of sand.

To take a small happiness modestly in their embrace – that is what they call 'humility'! And at the selfsame time they are already casting about modestly for some new small happiness.

At bottom, they naively want one thing most of all: that no one should hurt them. For that reason they anticipate everyone and do them good.

That, however, is *cowardice* – even though it is known as 'virtue'.

And if they should speak roughly on occasion, *I* hear in it only their hoarseness – the fact is that every draught makes them hoarse.

They are clever; their virtues have clever fingers. But they have no fists; their fingers do not know how to hide behind fists.

For them, virtue is anything that makes a being modest and tame; with it, they have made the wolf a dog, and the human into humankind's best domestic animal.

'We have positioned our chair in the middle' – so their smirking tells me – 'as far away from dying warriors as from contented sows.'

But that is *mediocrity* – even if it is known as *moderation*.

3

I go among these people and the odd word escapes me; but they know neither how to take nor how to keep.

They are astonished that I have not come to inveigh against their lusts and vices; and truly, I have not come to warn against pickpockets, either!

They are astonished that I am not willing to lend wit and point to their cleverness; as if they did not already have enough wiseacres whose voices I find squeaky as slate pencils!

And if I cry out: 'Curse all the cowardly devils in you, who prefer to whine and clasp their hands and worship,' they declare: 'Zarathustra is godless.'

And those who especially declare this are their teachers of humility; but it is into their ears in particular that I love to shout: 'Yes! I *am* Zarathustra, the godless!'

These teachers of humility! They creep anywhere that is small and sickly and scabby, like lice; and only my revulsion keeps me from cracking them.

Very well! This is my sermon for *their* ears: I am Zarathustra the godless, who says: 'Who is more godless than I, that I may enjoy his instruction?'

I am Zarathustra the godless; where shall I find my equal? All who lay down their own will for themselves, and reject humility, are my equals.

I am Zarathustra the godless; I cook every chance in *my* pot. And only when it is quite cooked do I welcome it as *my* food.

And truly, many a chance has approached me with an imperious manner; but my will spoke to it still more imperiously, and promptly it was on its knees, begging –

begging me for lodging and affection, and urging me in flattering tones: 'Just see, oh Zarathustra, how one friend comes to another!'

But what is the point of speaking, where no one has *my* ears! And so I shall shout it out into the winds:

You are growing smaller and smaller, you small people! You are crumbling away, you people of comfort! You will perish yet –

of your many petty virtues, of your many petty omissions, of all your petty humility!

Too sparing and too appeasing: that is how your soil is! But for a tree to grow *mighty*, it wants to put down tough roots around hard rocks!

Even your omissions weave at the fabric of all humanity's future; even your nothing is a spider's web, and a spider that lives on the blood of the future.

And when you take, it is like stealing, you small people of virtue; but even among rogues the watchword of *honour* is: 'One shall steal only where one cannot rob.'

'It shall be given' – that too is a doctrine of humility. But I tell you, you people of comfort: *it shall be taken away*, and more and more shall be taken away from you!

Ah, if only you would put all your *half-held* intentions behind you, and were as resolute in your inertia as in your action!

Ah, if only you understood what I have said: 'By all means do what you will – but first be such as are *able to hold an intention*!'

'By all means love your neighbour as yourself – but first be such as *love themselves* –

– 'love with a great love, love with a great contempt!' Thus speaks Zarathustra the godless.

But what is the point of speaking, where no one has *my* ears! Here it is still an hour too early for me.

Among these people I am my own forerunner, my own cock-crow along the dark lanes.

But *their* hour is coming! And mine is coming too! Hour after hour they are growing smaller, poorer, more infertile – poor weeds! poor soil!

And *soon* I shall behold them standing there like dry grass and steppe, and truly! weary of themselves – and thirsting not for water but for *fire*!

Oh blessèd hour of lightning! Oh mystery before noon! – One day I shall turn them into running fires, and heralds with tongues of flame –

one day they shall yet proclaim with tongues of fire: it is coming, it is near, *the great noon*!

Thus spake Zarathustra.

On the Mount of Olives

Winter, a woeful guest, sits with me at home; my hands are blue from the handshake of his friendship.

I honour him, this woeful guest, but I am glad to leave him sitting on his own. I gladly run away from him; and, if one runs *well*, one can escape him!

With feet warm and thoughts warm, I run to where the wind is still – to the sunny corner of my mount of olives.

There I laugh about my severe guest, and still think well of him, for he catches the flies and disposes of them at home, and silences many a little noise.

For he cannot bear it if a gnat wants to sing, or even two; he even makes the lane lonely, so that the moonlight is afraid there at night.

He is a tough guest – but I honour him; and I do not pray to a fat-bellied fire idol, as weaklings do.

A little chattering of teeth is better than praying to an idol! – that is how my nature will have it. And in particular I dislike all rutting, steaming, dull-witted fire idols.

Whomever I love, I love better in winter than in summer; I mock my enemies better and more heartily now that winter is sitting in my home.

Truly, even when I *crawl* into bed, my happiness in its crawled-away hiding-place laughs heartily and is wilful; even my lying dream laughs.

I – a crawler? Never in my life have I crawled before the powerful; and, if ever I lied, I lied out of love. For that reason I am glad even in my winter bed.

A modest bed keeps me warmer than an opulent one, for I am jealous of my poverty. And in winter it is most faithful of all to me.

I begin each day by being naughty, mocking winter by taking a cold bath my severe house-guest grouches about that.

I like to tickle him, too, with a little wax candle; so that he will finally let down the sky to me from the ash-grey dawn.

In the mornings I am especially bad: at an early hour, when the bucket clatters at the well and the horses give their warm whinnies along the grey streets –

at that hour I wait impatiently, till at last the bright sky opens up for me, the snow-bearded winter sky, that white-haired ancient –

the silent winter sky, that often even keeps its sun hidden!

Was it from the sky that I learnt long, bright silence? Or did it learn it from me? Or did each of us devise it by himself?

The origin of all good things is thousandfold – all good, wilful things spring joyfully into existence; however should they do it – only once?

Long silence is a good, wilful thing too, and to gaze like the winter sky from a bright, round-eyed countenance –

like it, to keep one's sun hidden and one's unbending sun-will: truly, I have learnt this art and this winter wilfulness *well*!

It is my favourite wickedness and art, that my silence has learnt not to betray itself by silence.

Rattling words and dice, I outwit the solemn warders; my will and sense of purpose will elude all the severe guards.

In order that no one may see down into my fundamental reason and ultimate will, I have devised the long, bright silence for myself.

I have come across many a canny fellow who veiled his countenance and muddied his waters so that no one might see through him and to the bottom of him.

But it was to him, of all people, that the cannier distrusters and nutcrackers came; and from him, of all people, they fished out their best-hidden fish!

But those who are clear, upright, transparent – they strike me as the canniest of silent ones; for their bottom is so *deep* down that even the clearest of water does not – betray it.

You snow-bearded silent winter sky, round-eyed and white-haired above me! Oh you heavenly likeness of my soul and of its wilfulness!

And do I not *have* to conceal myself, like a man who has swallowed gold – so that they do not slit my soul open?

Do I not *have* to use stilts, so that they *do not notice* my long legs – all these envious people around me who are in love with their own misery?

These smoky, parlour-warm, used-up, withered, dismal souls – how *could* their envy endure my happiness?

So I show them only the ice and the winter on my peaks – and *not* that my mountain winds all the bands of sunlight around it, too!

They hear only the whistling of my winter storms – and *not* that I cross the warm oceans too, like hot south winds heavy with longing.

They presume to have pity when happenstance and accidents befall me – but *my* word on this is: 'Suffer chance to come to me: it is innocent, like a like child!'

How *could* they endure my happiness, if I did not pile up accidents and winter emergencies and polar-bear caps and wraps of snowy skies about my happiness!

– if I did not myself have pity on their *pity* – the pity of these envious people in love with their own misery!

– if I myself did not sigh before them, and chatter with cold, and patiently *permit* myself to be swaddled in their pity!

That is the wise wilfulness and goodwill of my soul: that it *does not conceal* its winter and its frosty storms; neither does it conceal its chilblains.

For one person, solitude is the flight of a sick man; for another, solitude is flight *from* the sick.

Let them hear me chattering and sighing with winter cold, all these wretched, envious scoundrels about me! This sighing and chattering is my way of fleeing their heated parlours.

Let them pity me and sigh with me on account of my chilblains: 'He will *freeze to death* on the ice of knowledge!' they lament.

Meanwhile I am walking hither and thither on my mount of olives, my feet warm; in the sunny corner of my mount of olives I sing, and mock all pity. –

Thus sang Zarathustra.

Of Passing By

So it was that Zarathustra, striding steadily among many people and through divers towns, returned by roundabout ways to his mountain and his cave. And see, on his way he happened unexpectedly upon the gate of the *great city*. There, however, a frothing fool with out-stretched hands leapt at him and stood in his way. But this was the selfsame fool the people dubbed 'Zarathustra's ape', because he had adopted something of his syntax and the rhythms of his language, and liked to borrow from his store of wisdom. The fool, however, addressed Zarathustra in this way:

'Oh Zarathustra, here is the great city; you have no business here, and risk losing everything.

'Why would you want to wade through this mud? Have mercy on your feet! Better to spit on the city gate and – turn round!

'This is hell for hermit thoughts. Here, great thoughts are boiled alive and cooked till they are small.

'Here, all great feelings rot. Here, only tiny skin-and-bone feel-ings are permitted to rattle!

'Do you not already smell the slaughterhouses and kitchens of the spirit? Does this city not reek of the fumes of slaughtered spirit?

'Do you not see the souls hanging like limp dirty rags? – and they even make newspapers from those rags!

'Have you not heard how the spirit has become a play on words here? It vomits up revolting verbal swill! – and they even make newspapers from this verbal swill.

'They jostle each other along and do not know where they're going. They get each other heated and do not know why. They tinkle their tins, they jingle their gold.

'They are cold and seek warmth in distilled liquors; they are heated and seek coolness in frozen spirits; all of them are ailing, and addicted to public opinion.

'Dissoluteness and vice of every kind is at home here; but there are virtuous people here too, and a good deal of proficient virtue in employment: –

'A good deal of proficient virtue with writing fingers and tough sit-upons hardened to waiting, blessed with little stars on the chest and with stuffed daughters with no behinds.

'There is also much piety here and a great deal of spittle-licking, toadying before the god of hosts.

'The star and the gracious spittle drip down "from on high"; every breast that lacks a star longs to move up "on high".

'The moon has its court, and the court has its moon-calves; and beggars and all proficient beggar-virtue pray to anything that comes from the court.

'"I serve, you serve, we serve" – that is the prayer offered up by all proficient virtue to the prince; so that the well-earned star might finally be pinned to that meagre breast!

'But the moon still revolves around all earthly things; so the prince, too, still revolves around the most earthly thing of all – which, however, is shopkeepers' gold.

'The god of hosts is not a god of gold ingots; the prince proposes, but the shopkeeper – disposes!

'By all that is bright and strong and good in you, oh Zarathustra! – spit on this city of shopkeepers and turn round!

'Here, all blood flows foul and tepid and frothy through everyone's veins; spit on the great city, which is the great rubbish heap
where all the scum froths together!

'Spit on the city of crushed souls and puny breasts, of sharp eyes,
of sticky fingers –

'on the city of the pushy, the shameless, the loudmouths in writing and speech, the overheated ambitious ones –

'where everything rotten, disreputable, dissolute, dismal, over-
ripe, ulcerous, conspiratorial festers together –

'spit on the great city and turn round!' –

At this point, however, Zarathustra interrupted the frothing fool
and clapped his hand over his mouth.

'Will you finally have done!' cried Zarathustra – 'what you say
and your manner have long disgusted me!

'Why did you dwell so long in the swamp, where you would
inevitably become a frog or toad yourself?

'Do you not now have foul, frothy swamp-blood flowing through
your own veins, that you have learnt to croak and fulminate like
this?

'Why did you not go into the forest? Or plough the earth? Is the
sea not full of green islands?

'I despise your contempt; and, if you warned me – why did you
not warn yourself?

'My contempt and my bird of warning shall fly up from love
alone, not from the swamp!

'They call you my ape, you frothing fool; but I call you my grunting pig – by grunting, you will even ruin my praise of folly.

'What was it that first started you grunting? That no one was
flattering you enough. And so you sat down in this muck, so that you
would have occasion to grunt a great deal –

'so that you would have occasion for much *revenge*! For revenge
is what all your frothing is, you vain fool. You don't fool me!

'But your foolish pronouncements are damaging *me*, even where
you are right! And even if Zarathustra's dicta *were* right a hundred

times over; *you* would invariably use my words to – *do* wrong!'

Thus spake Zarathustra; and he gazed upon the great city, sighed, and was silent for a long time. At length he said this:

'It is not only this fool but also this great city that disgusts me. In the one and in the other, there is nothing that can be made better, nothing that can be made worse.

'Woe to this great city! – And I would that I could already see the pillar of fire in which it will be consumed!

'For such pillars of fire must precede the great noon. That, though, has its own time and its own fate. –

'But I give you this teaching by way of farewell, fool: where one can no longer love, one should – *pass by*!' –

Thus spake Zarathustra, and passed by the fool and the great city.

Of Apostates

1

Ah, everything already lies wilted and grey that but lately was green and many-coloured in this meadow! And how much honey of hope have I carried from here to my beehives!

All these young hearts have already grown old – and not even old, but tired, mean, comfortable! – They say of this: 'We have grown pious once more.'

Not long ago I saw them running out early in the morning on valiant feet; but their feet of understanding grew weary, and now they even denigrate their morning valour!

Truly, many a one of them used to kick up his legs like a dancer, and the laughter in my wisdom beckoned to him; – then he thought better of it. Just now I saw him doubled over, creeping to the cross.

They used to flutter like gnats and young poets around light and freedom. A little older, a little colder; and already they are mystifiers and mutterers and sit beside the stove.

Did their hearts perhaps despair because solitude swallowed me like a whale? Did their ears perhaps listen long and longingly, *in vain*, for me and my trumpet and herald calls?

– Ah, there are always a mere few whose hearts have long-lasting courage and wilfulness; and in such the spirit continues to be patient, too. The rest, however, are *cowardly*.

The rest: that is invariably the majority, the everyday, the superfluity, the far too many – all of them are cowardly!

Anyone who is of my kind will also happen upon experiences of my kind; so that his first companions will needs be corpses and clowns.

His second companions, however, will call themselves his believers: a lively swarm, full of love, full of fatuity, full of beardless adoration.

Anyone among humans who is of my kind should not bind his heart to these believers; anyone who knows the fleeting and cowardly nature of humanity should not believe in these spring tides and many-coloured meadows!

If they were *able to do* otherwise, they would also *intend* otherwise. The half-and-halfers spoil anything that is whole. Leaves wither – what is there in that to lament over?

Let them fall and go, oh Zarathustra, and do not lament! Better still, blow rustling winds among them –

blow among those leaves, oh Zarathustra; so that all that has withered may run from you even faster! –

2

'We have grown pious once more' – so these apostates declare; and many of them are even too cowardly to declare it.

I look into their eyes, then I tell them to their faces and to their blushing cheeks: You are such as are *praying* once more!

But it is a disgrace to pray! Not for everyone, but for you and me and anyone else who has his conscience in his head. For *you* it is a disgrace to pray!

You know it well: that cowardly devil within you, who would be glad to clasp his hands, and lay his hands in his lap, and take things more comfortably – that cowardly devil is urging: 'God *does* exist.'

But *with that* you belong among those who are wary of the light, for whom the light never grants rest; now you must bury your head deeper every day in the night and the mist!

And truly, you have chosen the hour well; for the birds of night are once again taking wing even now. The hour has come for all people who are wary of the light, the evening hour of good cheer, when they show no 'good cheer'.

I hear and smell it; their hour for hunting and processions has come, not for any wild pursuit, true, but for a tame, lame, snuffling hunt, soft of tread and soft of prayer –

for a hunt in pursuit of soulful moral cowards; all the mousetraps of the heart have now been set again! And wherever I lift a curtain, a little moth comes fluttering out.

Was it huddled in there together with other little moths? For everywhere I smell little communities that have crept into hiding; and, wherever there are closets, there are more praying brethren inside, and the fug of praying brethren.

They spend long evenings sitting together, declaring: 'Let us become as little children again and say "Dear God"!' – their mouths and stomachs ruined by pious confectioners.

Or they spend long evenings watching a cunning, lurking cross-spider, which preaches cleverness to the spiders themselves and teaches: 'Below crosses is a good place to spin!'

Or they sit all day with fishing-rods beside swamps and suppose themselves *deep* on that account; but someone who goes fishing where there are no fish I do not consider so much as shallow!

Or they learn to play the harp in a pious, cheery fashion, under some *Lieder* poet who would dearly like to harp his way into young women's hearts – for he has tired of old women and their praises.

Or they learn to get the creeps with some learned half-madman who waits in dark rooms for spirits to come to him – and the spirit makes itself scarce!

Or they listen to some old frumpy, grumpy drifter, who whistles as he goes and has learnt the sorrowful tones from the sorrowful winds; now he whistles as the wind goes, and preaches sorrow in sorrowful tones.

And some of them have even become night watchmen; now they know how to blow horns and go about at night and waken old matters that have long since fallen asleep.

Last night by the garden wall I heard five things said about old matters, by this very sort of old, dismal, dried-up night watchmen.

'For a father, he does not look after his children well enough; human fathers do it better!' –

'He is too old! He does not look after his children at all any more' – so the other night watchman replied.

'*Has* he any children? No one else can prove it if he does not prove it himself! I have been wishing for a long time that he would settle the matter and prove it.'

'Prove it? As if *he* had ever proved anything! He finds it hard to prove anything; he sets great store on being *believed*.'

'Yes! Yes! Belief makes him contented, belief in him. That is what old people are like! We're like that too!' –

Thus the two old night watchmen and light-scarecrows talked together, and they tooted their horns dismally; that was how it happened last night by the garden wall.

My heart, however, was doubled up with laughter, fit to burst, and was beside itself, and sank into my midriff.

Truly, it will be the death of me, I shall laugh so hard that I shan't be able to breathe, to see asses drunk and night watchmen doubting God in this way.

For has not the moment for any such doubts *long* passed? Who will venture to rouse such old matters, wary of the light, that have fallen asleep?

The old gods have long since had their day – and in truth they came to a fine, jolly, divine end!

Their death was no twilight – that is a lie! Rather, a time came when they *laughed* themselves to death!

It happened when one of the gods himself came out with the most godless thing that can be said: 'There is one God! Thou shalt have no other gods before me!'

– an old wrath-bearded god, a jealous god, thus forgot himself:

And all the gods laughed, back then, and rocked about on their chairs and cried: 'Is that not what divinity means – that there are gods but no God?'

He that hath ears, let him hear. –

Thus spake Zarathustra in the town that he loved and which is known as The Cow of Many Colours. From there he had only two more days to go before he reached his cave and his animals once more; and his soul was unceasingly jubilant at the nearness of his homecoming. –

The Homecoming

Oh solitude! Solitude, my *home*! For too long I have lived wild, in wild and unfamiliar places, not to shed tears when I return home to you now!

Now, wag your finger at me, as mothers do when they threaten. No, smile at me, as mothers smile. Or merely say: 'Now who was it who stormed away from me then, like a storm-wind? –

'Who cried out as he left: Too long I have sat together with solitude, till I no longer knew how to remain silent! You have surely learnt *that* now?

'Oh Zarathustra, I know everything; and that you felt more *forsaken* among the many, you solitary one, than ever you did with me!

'To be forsaken is one thing, solitude another: *that* you have now learnt! And that you will always be wild and a stranger among humankind:

– 'wild and a stranger even when they love you; for above all they want to be spared!

'Here, however, you are in your own house and home. Here you can talk freely about everything, and pour out all the reasons. Nothing here is ashamed of concealed, congealed feelings.

'Here all things come with caresses to your discourse and flatter you; for they want to ride on your back. On every likeness you ride to every truth, here.

'Here you may speak to all things in a right and upright manner; and truly it sounds like praise in their ears, that someone should talk straight with all things!

'But to be forsaken is something else. For – do you recall it, oh Zarathustra? – when your bird called above you, back then when you stood in the forest, uncertain which way to go, unknowing, hard by a corpse: –

– 'when you said: may my animals lead me! I have found it more dangerous among humankind than among animals! – *That* was forsakenness!

'And do you recall, oh Zarathustra, sitting on your island, a wellspring of wine among empty buckets, giving and providing, offering gifts and drinks among the thirsty;

– 'till at last you sat alone, thirsty among the drunk, lamenting by night: "Is it not more blessèd to take than to give? And more blessèd to steal than to take?" – *That* was forsakenness!

'And do you recall, oh Zarathustra, when your stillest hour arrived, and drove you away from yourself, declaring in a wicked whisper: "Speak and break!" –

– 'when it made you rue all your waiting and silence, and discouraged your humble courage: *That* was forsakenness!

'Oh solitude! Solitude, my home! How blissfully and tenderly your voice speaks to me!

'We do not question one another, we do not complain to one another, we go openly together through open doors.

'For with you everything is open and clear; and even the hours run on lighter feet here. For time weighs more heavily upon one in the dark than in the light.

'Here, the words and word-hoards of all being spring open for me; here, all being wants to become words; here, all being wants to learn from me how to talk.

'Down there, however, whatever is said is in vain! There, forgetting and passing by are the highest wisdom. *That* is what I have now learnt!

'Anyone who aimed to understand all human affairs would need to take hold of everything. But my hands are too clean for that.

'I do not even care to inhale their breath; ah, that I lived so long amid their noise and bad breath!

'Oh, the blessèd stillness about me! Oh, the pure fragrances about me! Oh, how this stillness draws pure breath as if from a deep breast! Oh, how it listens, this blessèd stillness!

'Down there, however – everything is talk and everything goes unheard. One may peal in one's wisdom with bells – the stall-keepers in the marketplace will out-tinkle them with their pennies!

'Everything is talk in their world, no one has the wit to understand any more. Everything makes a splash in a teacup, nothing drops into a deep well any more.

'Everything is talk in their world, nothing develops and matures. Everything is cackling, but who will still sit quietly on the nest and hatch the eggs?

'Everything is talk in their world, everything is talked to pieces. And what was too hard for time itself and its teeth only yesterday, today hangs gnawed and picked from the mouths of today's people.

'Everything is talk in their world, everything is betrayed. And what used to be seen as secret, the privy matters of profound souls, is now the property of street-trumpeters and other butterflies.

'Oh, humankind, you wondrous creature! You noise in dark streets! Now you lie behind me once again – my greatest danger lies behind me!

'My greatest danger invariably lay in being sparing and compassionate; and all of humankind wants to be spared and to be felt for.

'Keeping truths back, with a fool's hand and a heart full of folly, and rich in the petty lies of compassion – that was how I always lived among humanity.

'I sat among them in disguise, prepared to misjudge *myself* in order to endure *them*, and eager to assure myself: "You fool, you do not understand humankind!"

'One ceases to know humanity when one lives among people: there is too much foreground in all humans – they have nothing to offer far-seeing, far-seeking eyes!

'And when they misjudged me, I, fool that I was, spared them more than myself; I was accustomed to being hard on myself, and often was even vengeful towards myself if I was sparing.

'Stung by poisonous flies, and hollowed out like a stone by many drops of wickedness, I sat among them, even telling myself: "Whatever is small is not to blame for being small!"

'Those especially who call themselves "good people" I found to be the most poisonous flies: they sting in all innocence, they lie in all innocence; how *could* they be just towards me!

'Anyone who lives among good people is taught by compassion to lie. Compassion makes the air fuggy for all free souls. For the stupidity of good people is unfathomable.

'To conceal myself and my riches – *that* was what I learnt down there; for I found everyone still poor in spirit. This was the lie of my compassion: that I knew, in everybody's case –

' – that I could see and smell in everybody how much spirit was *enough* for him and how much spirit was *too much*!

'Their stiff wise men: I called them wise, not stiff – in that way I learnt to swallow my words. Their gravediggers: I called them researchers and examiners – in that way I learnt to mince my words.

'The gravediggers dig up diseases for themselves. Evil vapours lie in wait below the ancient rubble. The morass is best left undisturbed. One should live on the mountains.

'My nostrils fill with bliss to breathe mountain freedom once more! At last my nose is delivered from the odour of all humankind!

'Tickled by keen breezes as if by sparkling wines, my soul *sneezes* – sneezes and cries jubilantly to itself: *Gesundheit!*'

Thus spake Zarathustra.

Of the Three Evil Things

1

In a dream, in the last dream of the morning, I was standing in the foothills today – beyond the world, I was holding scales and *weighing* the world.

Oh, the dawn came to me too soon; jealously she glowed me awake! She is always jealous of my morning dreams.

Measurable if one who has time, weighable if one is good at weighing, capable of being flown if one has strong wings, divinable for divine nutcrackers: that is how my dream found the world.

My dream, a bold mariner, half-ship, half-tempest, as silent as butterflies, as impatient as falcons; yet today it had the time and patience to weigh the world!

Doubtless my wisdom had a word with it in secret, my laughing, waking day-wisdom that mocks all 'infinite worlds'. For it says: 'Where there is power, *number* achieves mastery: it has more power.'

How confidently my dream gazed upon this finite world, greedy for neither the new nor the old, neither fearful nor beseeching;

– as if a whole apple presented itself to my hand, a ripe golden apple with a cool, soft, velvety skin: so the world presented itself to me:

– as if a tree waved to me, a broad-branched, strong-willed tree bent into a back-rest and also a foot-rest for the weary wanderer: so the world stood on my foothills:

– as if delicate hands bore a shrine to me, a shrine open for the delight of modest, reverent eyes: so the world presented itself to me today:

– not enough of a puzzle to scare human love away, nor enough of a solution to put human wisdom to sleep; today it was a humanly good thing to me, the world of which so many bad things are said!

How grateful I am to my morning dream, that I weighed up the world in this way, early today! It came to me as a humanly good thing, this dream and comforter of the heart!

And, in order that I may do the same as it has done, as the day goes on, and learn from it all that is best in it, I now propose to place on the scales the three most evil things, and weigh them humanly well.

He who taught how to bless also taught how to curse; which are the three most cursed things in the world? These I propose to place on the scales.

Sensuality, the lust for power, self-centredness: these three have hitherto been cursed the most, and held in the worst and most misrepresented repute. These three I propose to weigh humanly well.

Very well! Here are my foothills and there is the ocean; *it* rolls towards me, shaggy, fawning, the faithful old hundred-headed monster hound that I love.

Very well! This is where I shall hold the scales over the rolling seas; and I choose a witness to look on, too – you, hermit tree, richly scented and broadly arched, tree that I love!

By what bridge does the now cross over to the bygone? What compulsion brings the high down to the low? And what commands even the highest to grow – higher still? –

Now the scales are balanced and still. I have thrown in three weighty questions. The other pan holds three weighty answers.

2

Sensuality: a goad and stake for all the hair-shirted who hold the body in contempt, anathematized as 'the world' by all the afterworlders; for it scorns and makes fools of all teachers of the muddle-headed and wrong.

Sensuality: for the rabble, the slow fire over which they are roasted; for all worm-ridden wood and all stinking rags, it is the raging oven of lust, ever ready.

Sensuality: for the free of heart it is innocent and free, the garden happiness of the earth, all the future's overbrimming gratitude to the here-and-now.

Sensuality: a sickly-sweet poison only to those who have grown limp, but to the lion-willed the great restorative for the heart, and the reverently kept wine of wines.

Sensuality: the great symbolic happiness, of higher happiness and the highest hope. For many are promised marriage, and more than marriage –

many who are stranger to each other than man and woman; and who has fully grasped *how strange* man and woman are to each other!

Sensuality: – but I want a fence around my thoughts, and around my words, too; to keep the swine and hotheads from breaking into my garden! –

The lust for power: the glowing-hot scourge of the hardest of the hard-hearted; the cruel torture that keeps itself for the very cruellest; the dark flame of living pyres.

The lust for power: the spiteful gadfly that oppresses the vainest peoples, that scorns all wavering virtue, that rides on every steed and all pride.

The lust for power: the earthquake that breaks and tears apart all that is rotten and hollow; the rolling, moaning, punitive destroyer of whited sepulchres; the lightning-flash question-mark beside premature answers.

The lust for power: before its gaze, humans creep and cower and labour and become lower than snakes and swine – till at last the immense contempt cries out from within –

The lust for power: the terrible teacher of immense contempt, which preaches into the faces of cities and empires, 'Away with you!' – until at last they themselves cry out, 'Away with *me*!'

The lust for power: which is tempting even to the pure and the solitary, however, and rises to self-sufficient heights, glowing like a love that paints purple prospects of bliss enticingly on earthly heavens.

The lust for power: but who would call it *lust*, when whatever is high craves to descend to power! Truly, there is nothing infirm or addictive in such craving and descending!

That the lonesome height should not become solitary and sufficient unto itself for all eternity; that the mountain should go down to the valley, and the wind on high to the lowlands –

oh, who could properly name, by baptism or as a virtue, such a longing! The 'giving virtue' – this was the name Zarathustra once gave to the unnameable.

And at that time it also happened – and truly, it happened for the first time! – that he spoke in praise of self-centredness, that wholesome, healthy self-centredness that springs from a mighty soul; –

– from a mighty soul, which goes together with an exalted body, beautiful, victorious, invigorating, a body about which all things become mirrors;

– the supple, persuasive body, the dancer whose likeness and epitome is the soul that delights in itself. The self-delight of such bodies and souls calls itself: 'Virtue'.

Self-delight of this kind hides itself away with its teachings of good and evil, as if in sacred groves; with the names it gives its happiness it keeps all that is contemptible far from it.

It keeps all that is cowardly far from it; it says: Bad – *that* is cowardly! Those who are forever worrying, sighing, complaining, or on the lookout for even the tiniest of advantages, appear contemptible to it.

It also holds all doomful wisdom in contempt; for, truly, there is a wisdom that blossoms in the dark, a nightshade wisdom, forever sighing: 'All is vanity!'

It sees wary mistrust as low, and anyone too who wants oaths instead of looks and hands, and all-too-mistrustful wisdom as well, for such is the way of cowardly souls.

It sees as lower still anyone who is eager to please, like a dog that promptly lies on its back, the humble man; and there is also a wisdom that is humble and dog-like and pious and eager to please.

It sees as altogether hateful and repugnant anyone who will never defend himself, who swallows down bile and evil looks, the all-too-patient man who puts up with everything and is content with anything; for that is servility.

No matter whether a man is servile before gods and the kicks of the gods, or before humans and the stupid opinions of humans; it spits at *every* form of servility, this blessèd self-centredness!

Bad: that is what it calls all that is broken, and meanly servile, with unfree blinking eyes, oppressed hearts – that false, compliant sort of person who kisses with thick, cowardly lips.

And arse-wisdom: that is what it calls all the wit of the servile and ancient and weary; and especially all the unpleasant, wrong-headed, excessive wit in the folly of priests!

The arse-wise, however – all the priests, the world-weary, those with souls of a womanish or servile kind – oh, how their wicked tricks have ill-used self-centredness since time immemorial!

And that very ill-use of self-centredness was presented and identified as virtue. And 'selfless' was what these world-weary cowards and cross-spiders wished to be, with good reason!

But for all of them the day is now coming, the transformation, the sword of judgement, *the great noon*; then, many things shall be revealed!

And he who pronounces the I healthy and holy, and self-centredness blessèd, truly, he is a soothsayer speaking what he knows: '*See, it is coming, it is near, the great noon!*'

Thus spake Zarathustra.

Of the Spirit of Heaviness

1

My manner of speaking – is of the people; I talk in too coarse and heartfelt a way for silky rabbits. And what I say sounds even stranger to all ink-fish and quill-foxes.

My hand – is a fool's hand; woe to all tables and walls, and whatever else offers space for fools' frippery, fools' scribblery!

My foot – is a horse's foot; on it I tramp and trot over sticks and stones, criss-crossing the country, and take the devil's own delight in a fast gallop.

My stomach – is an eagle's stomach, I take it? For it loves lamb's meat best of all. But it is a bird's stomach, that is for certain.

Nourished on innocent things, and on little, ready and impatient to fly, to fly away – that is now my way; how should there not be something of a bird's nature in that!

And the fact that I am an enemy of the spirit of heaviness is especially bird-like; and, truly, a mortal enemy, an arch-enemy, an enemy since time began! Oh, where has my enmity not already flown, and flown away to!

I could sing a song about that – and I *will* sing it; even if I am alone in an empty house, and must sing it to my own ears.

Granted, there are other singers whose voices are softened, whose hands become eloquent, whose eyes become expressive, whose hearts awaken, only when the house is full; – I am not like them.

2

Whoever it is who one day teaches human beings to fly will have moved every boundary stone. The very boundary stones themselves will all fly up into the air for him. He will baptize the earth anew – as 'the lightweight'.

The ostrich runs faster than the fastest horse, but even it will stick its head heavily into the heavy earth; that is what the man who cannot yet fly is like.

Earth and life are known as heavy to him; and that is how the spirit of heaviness *wants* it! But whoever wants to become light and a bird must love himself – that is what *I* teach.

Not with the love of the infirm or addictive, of course; for in them even self-love stinks!

One must learn to love oneself – this is what I teach – with a wholesome and healthy love; so that one can bear one's own company, and not go off roaming.

Roaming of this kind has been baptismally named 'love of one's neighbour'; this phrase has hitherto licensed the most efficient lies and hypocrisy, notably from those who have lain most heavily upon the world.

And truly, to *learn* to love oneself is no commandment for today or tomorrow. Far more, this is the most delicate, subtle, far-reaching and patient of all the arts.

The fact is that all his possessions are well concealed from the man who owns them; and, of all treasure hoards, it is one's own that is the last to be dug up. That is the doing of the spirit of heaviness.

Well-nigh when we are still in the cradle we are given heavy words and values: 'good' and 'evil' – that is what this dowry is called. In the interest of these, we are forgiven for being alive.

And to that end they suffer the little children to come to them: to prevent them, from an early age, from loving themselves. That is the doing of the spirit of heaviness.

And we – we loyally shoulder the burden we have been given, and resiliently bear it across rugged mountains! And, if we perspire, we are told: 'Yes, life is a heavy burden!'

But it is only humanity itself that is a heavy burden! This is because a man carries too much that is not his own on his shoulders. Like a camel he kneels down and allows himself to be loaded up.

The strong, load-bearing man in particular, within whom dwells reverence, takes upon himself the burden of too many heavy words and values *that are not his own* – and thinks of life as a desert!

And truly, there are also things that *are one's own* that are heavy burdens to bear! And much that lies within a human being is like an oyster, disgusting and slippery and hard to get a grip on –

so that a noble shell must needs plead for attention with a nobly attractive appearance. But that art has to be learnt as well: to *possess* a shell and a beautiful semblance and an intelligent blindness!

Again, much in humankind is deceptive, and many a shell is of low value and wretched and too much shell. A great deal of hidden goodness and strength is never guessed at; the most delicious morsels remain untasted!

Women, the most exquisite of them, are aware of this; a little fatter, a little leaner – oh, how much fate there is in so little!

Humankind is hard to discover, and hardest of all to itself; often the spirit tells lies about the soul. That is the doing of the spirit of heaviness.

But he has discovered himself who says: This is *my* good and evil. With that, he has silenced the mole and dwarf who says: 'Good unto all, evil unto all.'

Truly, I do not care for those either who hail all things as good and this world as the best. People like this I call the universally satisfied.

Universal satisfaction, which is adept in sampling everything: that is not the best taste! I honour refractory, fastidious palates and stomachs that have learnt to say 'I' and 'yes and 'no'.

But to chew and digest everything – that is really swinish! Always to say yea-hah – only the ass and his kindred spirits have learnt that! –

Rich yellow and hot red: that is what *my* taste wants – it mixes blood into every colour. But anyone who whitewashes his house lays bare a whitewashed soul to me.

These are in love with mummies, those with ghosts, and both are equally foe to all that is flesh and blood – oh how both run counter to my taste! For I love blood.

Neither do I want to live and dwell where Everyman spits and spews; my taste, now, is *this* – I should rather live among thieves and perjurers. No one carries gold in his mouth.

But even more repellent, to my mind, are lickspittles of every sort; and the most repellent beast of a man I have come across, I have given the baptismal name of parasite: it refused to love, yet wanted to live on love.

Ill-starred I call all those who have only one choice: to become evil beasts, or evil tamers of beasts; I should not build my tabernacles among such.

Ill-starred I also call those who must forever be *waiting* – they run counter to my taste: all the tax collectors and shopkeepers and kings and other keepers of lands and stores.

Truly, I too have learnt to wait, and I have learnt it thoroughly – but only how to wait for *myself*. And above all I have learnt to stand and walk and run and jump and climb and dance.

But this is my teaching: he who one day intends to learn to fly must first learn to stand and walk and run and climb and dance – one cannot learn to fly by flying!

I learnt to climb to many a window using rope ladders, I climbed tall masts on nimble legs; to sit on tall masts of understanding seemed to me no small bliss –

to flicker on tall masts as little flames do: a little light, indeed, yet still a great consolation for mariners driven off their courses, and those who have been shipwrecked! –

I arrived at my truth by many and various routes and approaches; it was not on one single ladder that I climbed to the heights from which my eye surveys my distant prospects.

And it was only reluctantly that I would ask the way – it always ran counter to my taste! Rather, I interrogated and tried out the ways for myself.

Going forward along the way has always been a matter of trying out and interrogating – and truly, one even has to *learn* how to reply to such interrogation! That, however – is to my taste:

– it is not good, it is not bad, but it is *my* taste, and I no longer make a secret of it or am ashamed of it.

'So this is *my* way – where is yours?' I replied to those who inquired after 'the way'. The fact is – there is no such thing as *the* way!

Thus spake Zarathustra.

Of Old and New Tablets

1

Here I sit and wait, the old broken tablets about me, and new half-written tablets as well. When will my hour come?

– the hour of my down-going, my descent; for I want to go to humankind one more time.

I am now waiting for that; for the signs must first appear to me, that it is *my* hour – that is, the laughing lion with the flock of doves.

In the meantime I talk to myself, like one who has time. No one tells me anything new; so I tell myself about myself.

2

When I came among humankind, I found them sitting on an ancient wrong-headedness. All of them supposed they had long since known what was good and what was evil for humanity.

All talk of virtue appeared to them to be an old and tired affair; and those who wanted to sleep well would speak of 'good' and 'evil' before they turned in for the night.

I stirred up this doziness with my teaching that *no one yet knows* what is good and evil – except perhaps the creator!

– But he it is who creates a goal for humanity and gives the earth its meaning and its future; he alone *creates* the circumstance *that* things are good and evil.

And I told them to do away with their old professorial chairs, and anywhere that the old wrong-headedness had been sitting; I told them to laugh at their great masters of virtue and saints and poets and redeemers of the world.

I told them to laugh at their gloomy wise men, and anyone who had ever sat, a black scarecrow, on the tree of life uttering warnings.

I sat down by their great roadway of graves, even alongside the carrion and the vultures – and I laughed at their 'bygone age' and its crumbling, rotting glory.

Truly, I made a big angry noise, as preachers of repentance and fools do, about all they thought great and small – I laughed to think that their best was so very small! that their worst was so very small!

My wise longing burst out of me, crying out and laughing – truly a wild wisdom, born on the mountains! – my great longing, on sweeping wings.

And often it tore me away, and up and off, in the very midst of laughter; and then indeed I flew quivering, an arrow, through the sun-drunken rapture:

– out into distant futures never yet seen by any dream, to warmer souths than any artist has ever dreamt of; to where dancing gods are ashamed of clothes; –

– so that I might speak in likenesses, and limp and stammer like poets; and, truly, I am ashamed that I still have to be a poet! –

Where all becoming seemed to me a dance of the gods, and the wilfulness of gods, and the world was let go, and excluded, and was fleeing back to itself; –

– as an everlasting fleeing-from-themselves and seeking-themselves-once-again of many gods, as the blessèd self-contradiction, hearing oneself again, belonging to oneself again, of many gods; –

Where all time seemed to me a blessèd mockery of moments, where necessity was freedom itself, blissfully playing with the goad of freedom; –

Where I also encountered once again my old devil and arch-enemy, the spirit of heaviness, and everything that he created: compulsion, rules, necessity and consequence and purpose and will and good and evil;

For must not something exist that is danced *upon*, danced *across*? Must there not exist, for the sake of the light and the lightest, moles and heavy dwarfs? –

3

There it was too that I picked up the word 'superhuman' from the pathway, and that the human is something that must be gone beyond,

– that the human is a bridge and not an end in itself; counting itself blessèd on account of its noons and evenings, as a way to new dawns;

– Zarathustra's teaching of the great noon, and whatever else I have hung up over humanity like purple evening afterglows.

Truly, I have shown them new stars too, together with new nights; and over the clouds and day and night I spread out laughter like a many-coloured canopy.

I have taught them all that *I* was writing and devising; to compact into one thing, to gather together, whatever is fragmentary in humankind and puzzling and dreadfully subject to chance –

– as a poet, solver of puzzles, and redeemer of chance, I have taught them to work at making the future, and by creating to redeem – all that *was*.

To redeem what is past in humanity, and to re-envision every 'There once was' until the will avows: 'But that is how I wanted it! That is how I shall want it' –

– that I told them was redemption, that alone I taught them to see as redemption. –

Now I await *my* redemption – that I may go among them for the last time.

For I want to go to humankind one more time; I want my down-going to be *among* them, dying I want to give them my richest gift!

I learnt this from the sun when it sets, the super-wealthy sun; it scatters its gold into the ocean from its inexhaustible store of riches,

– in such a way that the poorest fisherman rows with *golden* oars! This I did once see, nor did I weary of shedding tears on seeing it.

Like the sun, Zarathustra too wants to go down; now he sits here and waits, old broken tablets about him, and new tablets as well, – half written.

4

See, here is a new tablet; but where are my brothers, to carry it with me into the valley and into hearts of flesh? –

This is what my great love demands of those who are furthest away: Do not spare your neighbour! The human is something that must be gone beyond.

There are many and various routes and approaches to going beyond – you, see how *you* deal with it! But only a clown of a fellow thinks: 'Humanity can also be *jumped over*.'

Go beyond yourself, even among your neighbours; and do not accept as a gift a right that you can steal!

What you do, no one can do back to you. See, there is no such thing as retaliation.

Those who cannot command themselves should obey. And there are those who *can* command themselves but are still a long way from obeying themselves!

5

This is the way that noble souls want it to be: they want to have nothing *gratis*, least of all life.

Those who are of the rabble want to live gratis; we others, however, to whom life has given itself – we are forever reflecting on *what* we may best *give in return*!

And truly, it is a mark of distinction to say: 'What life has promised *us*, *we* shall keep – for life!'

One should not wish to enjoy where one does not give enjoyment. And – one should not *wish* to enjoy!

For enjoyment and innocence are the most modest of things; neither wants to be sought. One should *have* them – but, if one seeks, it should rather be after guilt and pain! –

6

Oh my brothers, he who is first-born is invariably sacrificed. But now we are all first-born.

We all bleed at secret sacrificial tables, we all burn and roast in honour of the ancient idols.

The best of us are yet young; this piques old palates. Our flesh is tender, our skin is a mere lambskin – how should we not pique the old priests of the idols?

It is *in ourselves* that he lives on, the old priest of the idols, who roasts the best of us for his feast. Ah, my brothers, how should the first-born not be sacrifices!

But that is how our kind will have it; and I love those who do not aim to shield themselves. I love with the whole of my love those who embrace their down-going; for they go beyond. –

7

To be true – few are *capable* of that! And those who are do not yet want to be! The least capable of it are the good.

Oh, these good people! – *Good people never tell the truth*; being good in their sense is a sickness of the spirit.

They are yielding, these good people, they surrender, their hearts repeat the words, their inmost self obeys; but he who obeys *is not listening to himself!*

All that good people call evil must come together in order that one single truth be born; oh my brothers, are you really wicked enough for *that* truth?

Audacious daring, long-enduring mistrust, cruel nay-saying, antipathy, cutting into what is living – how rarely do *these* come together! Yet from such a seed – truth is brought into being.

Until now, all *knowledge* has grown *alongside* a bad conscience! Shatter, shatter the old tablets for me, you people of understanding!

8

When planks are laid across water, when footbridges and railings span the river; truly, no man is then believed if he says: 'Everything is in flux.'

Rather, even the boobies contradict him. 'What?' say the boobies. 'Everything is flowing? But the planks and railings are *above* the flow!

'*Above* the flow, everything is securely fixed, all the values of things, the footbridges, concepts, everything "good" and "evil": all of this is *securely fixed*!' –

If there is a hard winter, that animal-tamer of flux, even the wittiest learn mistrust; and, truly, it is not only the boobies who then say: 'Might not all things be – *unmoving*?'

'In essence, all things are unmoving' – that is a proper winter doctrine, a fine thing for an unfruitful time, a fine consolation for those who hibernate and love their firesides.

'In essence, all things are unmoving' – but the wind that brings a thaw preaches *against* it! –

the wind that brings a thaw, a bull that is no ploughing ox – a raging bull, a destroyer that breaks up ice with its angry horns! Ice, however – *breaks footbridges*!

Oh my brothers, is not everything *now in flux*? Have not all the railings and footbridges fallen into the water? Who would still *cling* to 'good' and 'evil'?

'Woe to us! Hail to us! The thaw wind is blowing!' – That is how you must preach for me, my brothers, in every street!

9

There is an old delusion that is called good and evil. Until now, the wheel of this delusion has revolved around soothsayers and astrologers.

At one time, people believed in soothsayers and astrologers; and *for that reason* people believed: 'Everything is fate: you should because you must!'

Then a time came when people mistrusted all soothsayers and astrologers; and *for that reason* people believed: 'Everything is freedom: you can because you want to!'

Oh my brothers, until now there have been only fanciful ideas concerning the stars and the future, not knowledge; and *for that reason* there have been only fanciful ideas concerning good and evil, not knowledge!

10

'Thou shalt not steal! Thou shalt not kill!' – Pronouncements such as these were once called holy; people bent their knees and bowed their heads and took off their shoes before them.

But I ask you: where have there ever been better thieves and killers in the world than holy words such as these?

Is there not, in all of life itself – stealing and killing? And in calling such pronouncements holy – did they not kill *truth* itself?

Or was it a sermon of death, that called something holy that contradicted and opposed all of life? – Oh my brothers, shatter, shatter the old tablets for me!

11

My pity for all that is past is this: I see that it has been abandoned – Abandoned to the favour, the spirit, the madness of every following generation that reinterprets all that has been as the bridge to itself!

A great despot could come, a canny monster, who might and would use his favour and disfavour to remake forcibly all of the past, till it served him as a bridge and omen and herald and cockcrow.

This, however, is the other danger, and my other pity: – those who are of the rabble have memories reaching back as far as their grandfathers – but with their grandfathers time stops.

In this way, all that is past is abandoned; for the rabble might one day be the masters, and drown all of time in shallow waters.

For this reason, oh my brothers, a *new nobility* is required, to oppose the rabble and despotism and to write anew, on new tablets, the word 'noble'.

For many nobles are required, and many kinds of nobles, *for nobility to exist*! Or, as I once said in a parable: 'That is what divinity means – that there are gods but no God!'

12

Oh my brothers, I dedicate and direct you to a new nobility: you shall be the begetters and cultivators and sowers of the future –

truly, not to a nobility that you could buy like shopkeepers, with shopkeepers' gold; for anything that has a price is of little value.

Not where you come from shall be the source of your honour from this day forth, but where you are going! Your will, and your foot, which wants to go beyond you – these shall be the source of your new honour!

Truly, not that you have served a prince – of what consequence are princes now! – or have become a bulwark to shore up the more securely whatever is standing!

Not that your family have acquired courtly ways at court, and you have learnt to stand for hours on end in shallow pools, many-coloured, like a flamingo –

for *being able* to stand is a merit among courtiers; and all courtiers believe that a part of bliss after death is – *being allowed* to sit!

Nor that a spirit they call holy led your ancestors into promised lands, which *I* do not praise; for in the land where the worst of all trees grew, the cross – there is nothing to praise! –

and truly, wherever that 'Holy Spirit' led its knights, goats and geese and the criss-and-cross-brained invariably *led* the procession! –

Oh my brothers, it is not back that your nobility should gaze, but *ahead*! You shall be exiles from all fatherlands and ancestral lands!

You shall love *the land of your children*; may this love be your new nobility – the undiscovered land in the furthest ocean! I bid your sails seek it and seek it!

You shall *make up* to your children for being the children of your fathers; *by so doing* you shall redeem all of the past! This new tablet I place above you!

13

'Why live? All is vanity! To live – is to thresh straw; to live – is to burn oneself and still not be any the warmer.' –

Antique blether of such a sort still counts as 'wisdom'; and it is the more highly revered *because* it is old and smells musty. Even mould is ennobling. –

Children have been permitted to talk like this; they are *wary* of fire because they have been burnt by it! There is a great deal of childishness in the old books of wisdom.

And how should those who 'thresh straw' be permitted to derogate threshing! Any fool of that sort would have to have his mouth stopped!

People like that sit down to dinner and bring nothing with them, not even a good appetite – and now they run everything down: 'All is vanity!'

But to eat and drink well, oh my brothers, is truly no vain art! Shatter, shatter for me the tablets of the eternally joyless!

14

'To the pure all things are pure' – so say the people. But I say to you: to the swine all things become swine!

That is why zealots, and those who hang their heads and their hearts too, preach: 'The world itself is a filthy monster.'

For all of these are unclean in spirit; especially those who know neither peace nor rest unless they see the world *from behind* – the afterworlders!

These I tell to their faces, even though it may sound indelicate: the world is like a human being in having a behind – *that much* is true!

There is a great deal of filth in the world: *that much* is true! But that does not make the world a filthy monster!

There is wisdom in observing that much in the world is foul-smelling; disgust itself lends wings and spring-diving powers!

Even in the best there is something to be disgusted by; and the best is something that must be gone beyond! –

Oh my brothers, there is much wisdom in observing that there is a great deal of filth in the world! –

15

Pronouncements such as these I heard pious afterworlders saying to their consciences; and, truly, without deceit or falseness – though there is nothing more false or deceitful in the world.

'Let the world be! Do not lift one single finger against it!'

'Let those who want to strangle and stab and slash and chop people get on with it. Do not lift one single finger against it! That way, they will yet learn to renounce the world.'

'And your own reason – you shall yourself choke and throttle it; for it is reason of this world. That way, you will yourself learn to renounce the world.' –

– Shatter, oh my brothers, shatter for me these old tablets of the pious! Shatter the sayings of those who vilify the world!

16

'He who learns a great deal will no longer have impetuous desires' – this is whispered nowadays in every dark side-street.

'Wisdom tires you out. Nothing is worthwhile. Thou shalt not desire!' – I have come across this new tablet hanging even in public marketplaces.

Shatter, oh my brothers, shatter for me this *new* tablet too! Those who are weary of the world hung it up, and the preachers of death, and the gaolers too; for, see, this too is a sermon on servitude! –

that they have learnt poorly, and not what is best, and all of it too early, and all of it too quickly; that they have eaten poorly, and that was what upset their stomachs –

for their spirit is an upset stomach: *that* is what counsels death! For truly, my brothers, the spirit *is* a stomach!

Life is a wellspring of pleasure; but every well is poisoned for those out of whom an upset stomach, the father of dejection, speaks.

Understanding: that is *pleasure* to the lion-willed! But he who has grown tired will himself be merely 'willed', the plaything of all the waves.

And so this is always the way with the weak: they lose themselves along their ways. And at length their weariness asks: 'Why did we ever go these ways? It is all one!'

To *their* ears it is pleasant when someone preaches this: "Nothing is worthwhile! Thou shalt not desire!' But that is a sermon on servitude.

Oh my brothers, Zarathustra is a breeze of fresh wind to all who are weary of the way; many a nose he will yet cause to sneeze!

My free breath blows even through walls and into prisons and imprisoned spirits!

The desiring will is liberating; for wanting is creating: that is what I teach. And you shall learn *only* in order to create!

And how to learn, too, you shall first learn from me – how to learn well! Let him hear who has ears to hear!

17

There is the barque. Over there may perhaps be the way into the great nothingness. – But who wants to embark on that 'perhaps'?

None of you wants to embark on the barque of death! How is it, then, that you claim to be weary of the world?

Weary of the world! And you have not yet separated from this earth! I have found you still with an appetite for the earth, still in love with your own weariness of the earth!

Not for nothing does your lip hang down – a little earthly wish is still sitting on it. And in your eye – is that not a little cloud of unforgotten earthly pleasure floating there?

There are many good inventions on earth, some of them useful, some of them pleasant; the earth is to be loved for their sake.

And there are things so well devised that they are like women's breasts: at once useful and pleasant.

But you who are weary of the world! – you indolent of the earth! – you should be caned! Your legs should be made sprightly again with strokes of the cane!

For, if you are not sick and worn-out wretches that the earth is weary of, then you are sly sloths or pleasuring-seeking cats that like to hide away with treats. And if you do not want to run about merrily once more, then you shall – pass away!

One should not want to be a physician to the incurable: that is Zarathustra's teaching. So away with you!

But it takes more *courage* to make an end than to make a new verse; every physician and poet knows that. –

18

Oh my brothers, there are tablets that were framed by exhaustion, and tablets that were framed by indolence, rotten indolence; although they may speak in the same way, they aim to be heard differently. –

See this man languishing here! He is a mere span away from his goal, but out of weariness he has lain down mulishly here in the dust; this brave man!

Out of weariness he yawns at the pathway and the earth and his goal and himself; he refuses to take another step – this brave man!

Now the sun burns down on him, and the dogs lick his sweat; but he lies there mulishly and would rather languish –

languish a span away from his goal! Truly, you will have to pull him up into his heaven by the hair – this hero!

Better still, leave him lying where he has lain down himself, so that sleep, the comforter, may come to him with a cooling down-rush of rain;

leave him lying till he wakes of his own accord, till he disavows all weariness of his own accord, and whatever weariness taught through him!

Just one thing, my brothers: shoo the dogs away from him, those skulking idlers, and all the swarming vermin –

all the swarming vermin of 'cultured people', who batten upon the sweat of every hero! –

19

I establish circles around me, and sacred boundaries; ever fewer climb with me up ever higher mountains; I build a mountain range out of ever more sacred mountains. –

But wherever you may climb with me, oh my brothers, see to it that no *parasite* climbs with you!

Parasite: it is a worm, slithering, supple, that is out to grow fat on your sick, sore crannies.

And *this* is its art: to make out the weary places in climbing souls; it makes its revolting nest in your grief and discouragement, in your tender modesty.

Where the strong man is weak, where the noble man is all too gentle – that is where it makes its revolting next; the parasite dwells where the great man has his little crannies of soreness.

Which is the highest type of all existence and which the lowest? The parasite is the lowest type; but the highest type is he who nourishes the most parasites.

For the soul that has the longest ladder and can reach down furthest – how should the most parasites not sit upon it? –

the most capacious soul, which can run and stray and roam the furthest within itself; the most necessary soul, which plunges into chance out of sheer pleasure; –

the existing soul, which dives into becoming; the possessing soul, which *wants* to be part of willing and demanding; –

the soul that flees itself, that catches itself up by the widest of circular routes; the wisest soul, to which foolishness speaks most sweetly; –

the soul that loves itself the most, in which all things have their currents and counter-currents and ebbing and flowing: – oh how should *the highest soul* not have the worst parasites?

20

Oh my brothers, am I then cruel? But I say: whatever falls should be given a push, too!

Everything of today – it is falling, it is decaying; who would want to preserve it? But I – I *want* to give it a push, too!

Do you know the relish of rolling stones into precipitous depths? – These people of today; just see how they roll into my depths!

I am a prologue to better players, oh my brothers! An example! *Follow* my example!

And anyone you do not teach to fly, teach him – *to fall faster*!

21

I love the brave; but it is not enough to be a warrior – one must also know *whom* to fight!

And often there is more bravery in restraining oneself and passing by; in order to save oneself for a worthier enemy!

You shall have only enemies who are to be hated, but not enemies you hold in contempt; you must be proud of your enemy; I have already taught you this once before.

You should save yourselves, oh my friends, for the worthier enemy; that means you must pass a great many by, –

especially the great numbers of rabble who make a noise in your ears about the people, and peoples.

Keep your eye clear of their pro and contra! There is a good deal of right there, a good deal of wrong; anyone who looks on will grow angry.

Taking a look, striking a blow – in this case, they are the same thing; that is why you should go off into the forests and let your swords sleep!

Go *your* ways! And let the people and the peoples go theirs! – dark ways, it is true, along which not one single glimmer of hope still shines!

Let the shopkeeper rule, where all that still glisters – is shop-keeper's gold! This is no longer the age of kings; those who now call themselves the people do not deserve kings.

Just see how these peoples themselves now do as the shopkeep-ers do: they glean the smallest of advantages from any rubbish that has been swept up!

They lie in wait for each other; they wait till they can do each other out of something – this they call 'being a good neighbour'. Oh blessèd, far-off time when a people will have said to itself: 'I mean to be the *master* over the peoples!'

For, my brothers, the best should rule, and the best *means* to rule! And wherever something different is taught, there – the best is *lacking*.

22

If *they* – had bread for nothing, woe! What would *they* cry out for! Their sustenance – that is their proper entertainment; and they shall have a hard time of it!

They are predators. In their 'work' – there is still depredation; in their 'earning' – there is still deception! For that reason they shall have a hard time of it!

They should therefore become better predators, subtler, can-nier, *more like human beings*; for humankind is the best predator.

Humankind has already robbed all the animals of their virtues; that is why it has been hardest, among all the animals, for humans.

Only the birds are still above them. And if humanity should even learn to fly – woe! to what height would their rapacity fly!

23

This is how I should have man and woman: the one fit for warfare, the other fit for bearing children, but both of them fit for dancing with their heads and legs.

And may that day be considered lost on which we did not dance even once! And may every truth be declared false that has not brought us any laughter!

24

Your marriages: see to it that they are not badly *contracted*! You contracted too speedily; so what follows is – *the breaking of marriage.*

And yet the breaking of marriage is better than the bending or lying of marriage! – A woman told me: 'Granted, I broke up my marriage, but first the marriage broke – me!'

I have always found the badly matched to be the most vengeful: they make the whole world pay for their no longer being single.

For this reason I want honest people to say to each other: 'We love each other: let us *see to it* that we continue to love! Or shall our promise be an error?

– 'Give us a little time and a little marriage, so that we see whether we are capable of a great marriage! It is a big thing, always to be in a couple!'

That is my counsel to all honest people; and what would my love for the superhuman amount to, and for all that is to come, if I were to counsel and speak in any other way!

To propagate yourselves not only onwards but *upwards* – to that end, oh my brothers, may the garden of marriage assist you!

25

See − he who has acquired wisdom by studying the ancient well-springs will in due course seek out the sources of the future, and new wellsprings. −

Oh my brothers, it will not be long before *new peoples* will arise, and new springs will rush down into new depths.

For the earthquake − it blocks up many wells, and people die of thirst; but it also brings to light inner strengths and secrets.

The earthquake reveals new springs. In the earthquake of ancient peoples, new springs break forth.

And if anyone should then cry out: 'See here, a well for many who are thirsty, one single heart for many who are longing, one single will for many instruments' − a *people* will gather around him, that is to say: many who are trying something new.

Who can command, who must obey − *that is what is being tested anew*! Ah, how much lengthy questing and guessing and failing and learning and renewed testing it takes!

Human society: it is an experiment. That is my teaching. − A lengthy quest − but what society seeks is the one who gives the orders! −

An experiment, oh my brothers! And *not* a contract! Shatter, shatter for me any such words that come from the soft-hearted and the half-and-halfers!

26

Oh my brothers! In whom does the greatest danger lie for the whole future of humanity! Is it not in the good and the just? −

− in those who say and feel in their hearts: 'We already know what is good and just, and we possess it, too; woe to those who are still searching!' −

And whatever harm the wicked may do − the harm done by the good is the most damaging harm!

And whatever harm those who vilify the world may do − the harm done by the good is the most damaging harm!

Oh my brothers, there was one who once looked into the hearts of the good and the just, and declared: 'These are the Pharisees.' But no one understood what he meant.

The good and the just themselves were prevented from understanding him; their spirit is held captive by their clear conscience. The stupidity of the good is inexhaustibly resourceful.

But this is the truth: the good *must* be Pharisees – they have no choice!

The good *must* crucify the one who devises his own virtue! That *is* the truth!

But the second man to discover their country, the country, heart and soil of the good and the just, was the one who asked: 'Whom do they hate the most?'

Most of all they hate the *creator*: the one who breaks the tablets and the old values, the breaker – they call him a law-breaker.

For the good – they *cannot* create; they are always the beginning of the end; –

they crucify the one who writes new values on new tablets, they sacrifice the future *to themselves* – they crucify the whole future of humanity!

The good – have always been the beginning of the end. –

27

Oh my brothers, have you also understood this teaching? And what I once said about the 'last human'? –

In whom does the greatest danger lie for the whole future of humanity? Is it not in the good and the just?

Shatter the good and the just, shatter them for me! – Oh my brothers, have you also understood this teaching?

28

You flee from me? You are frightened? You tremble at this teaching?

Oh my brothers, when I called upon you to shatter the good and the tablets of the good; it was only then that I embarked humankind on their high seas.

And only now does the great terror, the great looking-all-around, the great sickness, the great revulsion, the great sea-sickness come upon them.

The coastlines and safe havens taught to you by the good were false; you were born and kept secure in the lies of the good. Everything has been falsified and twisted by the good, down to the very bottom.

But he who discovered the country of 'humankind' discovered another country too: 'the future of humanity'. Now you shall be sea-farers, brave, patient seafarers!

I would have you walk upright, oh my brothers; learn in good time to walk upright! The ocean is stormy; many are out to use you as a help to stand up again.

The ocean is stormy; all things are in the ocean. Very well! Onwards, you old seaman's-hearts!

What price the fatherland! *There* is where our helm will take us, where our *children's country* is! Out over there, more stormy than the ocean, is where our great longing goes storming! –

29

'Why so hard?' the kitchen coal once said to the diamond; 'after all, are we not close relations?'

Why so soft? Oh my brothers, that is *my* question to you; after all, are you not – my brothers?

Why so soft, so softening and yielding? Why is there so much denial and refusal in your hearts? So little fate in your gaze?

And if you refuse to be fates, to be unrelenting; how can you be – victorious with me?

And if your hardness refuses to flash and cut and slash; how can you one day – create with me?

For creators are hard. And it must seem a blessèd state to you, to press your hand upon millennia as upon wax, –

a blessèd state, to write upon the will of millennia as upon bronze – harder than bronze, nobler than bronze. Only the noblest is absolutely hard.

This new tablet, oh my brothers, I place above you: *become hard!* –

30

Oh my will! You turning-point of all need, *my* necessity! Preserve me from all petty victories!

Oh my soul's destiny, which I call fate! You-in-me! Over-me! Preserve and save me for one single great fate!

And your last greatness, my will, save for your last – that you may be unrelenting *in* your victory! Ah, who has not been defeated by his own victory!

Ah, whose eye has not dimmed in this drunken twilight! Ah, whose foot has not stumbled and in victory forgotten – how to stand!

– That I may one day be ready and ripe in the great noon: ready and ripe like glowing bronze, like a cloud pregnant with lightning, and like a swelling udder of milk;

– ready for myself and my most hidden will: a bow ardent for its arrow, an arrow ardent for its star;

– a star ready and ripe in its noon, glowing, penetrated, blessèd before the annihilating arrows of the sun;

– a sun itself and an unrelenting sun-will, ready for annihilation in victory!

Oh will, turning-point of all need, *my* necessity! Save me for one single great victory! –

Thus spake Zarathustra.

The Convalescent

1

One morning, not long after his return to the cave, Zarathustra sprang up from his bed like a madman, cried out in a terrible voice, and behaved as if there were someone else still lying on the bed, who would not get up from it; and the sound of Zarathustra's voice was such that his own animals came to him, startled, and all the other animals fled the caves and refuges near to Zarathustra's cave – flying, fluttering, creeping, jumping, according to the kind of feet or wings they had been given. But Zarathustra spoke these words:

Up, abysmal thought, up from my depths! I am your cock and your dawn, you sleepy worm: up! up! My voice will crow you awake, see if it doesn't!

Loosen the fetters on your ears; listen! For I want to hear you! Up! Up! There is enough thunder here to make even graves listen!

And wipe the sleep from your eyes, and all the stupidity and blindness! Hear me with your eyes, too: my voice is a medicine even for those born blind.

And once you are awake, I shall have you stay awake forever. It is not *my* way to waken great-grandmothers from their sleep in order to bid them – sleep on!

Are you moving, stretching, croaking? Up! Up! I would not have you croak – but speak! Zarathustra, the Godless, is calling you!

I, Zarathustra, the advocate of life, the advocate of suffering, the advocate of the circle – I am calling you, my most abysmal thought!

Hail unto me! You are coming – I hear you! My abyss *is speaking*, I have upturned my bottom-most depth to the light!

Hail unto me! Come! Give me your hand – ha! Don't! Ha ha! – Revulsion, revulsion, revulsion – – – woe is me!

2

Barely had Zarathustra uttered these words, however, but he collapsed like a dead man and for a long time remained like a dead man. When he again came to himself, he was pale, though, and trembled, and remained lying down, and for a long time refused anything to eat or drink. He continued in this condition for seven days; his animals, however, left him neither by day nor by night, except when the eagle flew out to fetch food. And whatever it collected and carried off, it laid on Zarathustra's bed; so that Zarathustra at length lay beneath yellow and red berries, grapes, rose-apples, fragrant herbs and pine cones. But at his feet two lambs lay outstretched which the eagle had stolen, with some difficulty, from their shepherds.

At last, after seven days, Zarathustra sat up in his bed, took a rose-apple in his hand, smelt it, and found its fragrance pleasing. At this, his animals believed the time had come to talk to him.

'Oh Zarathustra,' they said, 'you have now been lying in that state for seven days already, with heavy eyes; will you not get to your feet again at last?

'Step out of your cave; the world awaits you like a garden. The playful breeze is laden with heavy fragrances that wish to come to you; and all the streams would like to run after you.

'All things long for you, but you have remained alone for seven days – step out of your cave! All things wish to be your physicians!

'Maybe a new understanding has come to you, sour and weighing heavy? Like leavened dough you lay; your soul rose and swelled over the brim.' –

'Oh my animals,' answered Zarathustra, 'go on talking like this, and let me listen! Hearing you talk is so refreshing to me; where there is talk, the world indeed lies before me like a garden.

'How sweet it is that there are words and sounds; are words and sounds not rainbows and ostensible bridges between things separated forever?

'To every soul belongs a world apart; for every soul, every other soul is an afterworld.

'Between the most alike, semblance tells the most beautiful lies; for the slightest of gaps is the hardest to bridge.

'For me – how could there be an outside-me? There is no outside! But any sounds cause us to forget that; how sweet it is that we forget!

'Are things not given names and sounds, that humankind might take delight in them? Speech is a fine tomfoolery: it enables humanity to dance across everything.

'How sweet is all talking, and all the lies of sounds! With sounds, our love dances on many-coloured rainbows.'

– 'Oh Zarathustra,' the animals responded, 'for such who think as we do, all things are themselves dancing: they approach, and reach out their hands, and laugh and turn quickly away – and return.

'Everything goes, everything returns; the wheel of being rolls eternal. Everything dies, everything blossoms afresh; the year of being runs eternal.

'Everything breaks, everything is mended; the selfsame house of being is forever being built. Everything departs, everything offers greetings once again; the ring of being is forever true to itself.

'At every moment, being begins; the ball of there rolls around every here. The centre is everywhere. The path of eternity is crooked.' –

'Oh you jokers and barrel-organs!' answered Zarathustra, and smiled again: 'how well you know what had to be accomplished in seven days; –

'and how that monster slithered into my throat and was choking me! But I bit off its head and spat it out.

'And you – you have already made a hurdy-gurdy song of it? But here I lie, still weary from the biting and spitting out, still sick with my own deliverance.

'*And you looked on at it all*? Oh my animals, are even you cruel? Did you want to observe my great pain, as humans do? For man is the cruellest animal.

'Hitherto he has felt most satisfied by tragedies, bullfights and crucifixions; and when he invented hell for himself, see: that was his heaven on earth.

'Whenever the great man cries out, instantly the little man comes running, his tongue hanging out with sheer relish. He, though, calls it his "compassion".

'The little man, especially the poet – how eagerly he accuses life in words! Just listen – but be sure to hear the relish in all the accusing!

'These accusers of life are eclipsed by life with a wink. "You love me?" says the hussy – "just wait a while, I don't have any time for you yet."

'The human is the cruellest of animals towards itself; and in all who call themselves "sinners" and "bearers of the cross" and "penitents", be sure to hear the relish in that lamenting and accusing!

'And do I myself, in saying this, mean to be humanity's accuser? Ah, my animals, if I have learnt one thing it is that the worst wickedness in humanity is necessary for its best –

'that all the worst wickedness is humanity's best strength, and the hardest stone for the highest creator; and that man must become better *and* more wicked –

'it was not to that stake that I was tied – to my knowledge that humankind is wicked; no, I cried out as no one has ever cried before:

"Ah, that his worst wickedness is so very paltry! Ah, that his best is so very paltry!"

'An immense aversion to humankind – *that* was what choked me and slithered into my throat; and what the prophet prophesied: "It is all one, nothing is worthwhile, knowledge chokes."

'A long twilight went limping ahead of me, a sorrowfulness weary unto death and intoxicated with death, which spoke with a yawning mouth.

'"Eternally he keeps returning, the human you are weary of, the little man" – thus my sorrowfulness yawned, and dragged its feet, and could not fall asleep.

'Humankind's earth became a cave to me, its chest sank in, everything living became human decay and bones and the rotting past to me.

'My sighing sat upon all of the graves of humanity, and was unable to stand up again; my sighs and questions croaked and choked and gnawed and lamented by day and night:

'"Ah, humankind returns eternally! The little man returns eternally!"

'I had once seen both of them naked, the greatest of humans and the littlest: all too similar to each other, even the greatest all too human!

'The greatest all too little! – that was what left me weary of humanity! And even the littlest returning eternally! – that was what left me weary of all existence!

'Ah, revulsion, revulsion, revulsion!' – Thus spake Zarathustra, and he sighed and shuddered; for he remembered his sickness. At this, however, his animals would not allow him to go on talking.

'Do not say any more, convalescent!' – thus his animals made reply to him – 'but go out where the world awaits you like a garden.

'Go out to the roses and bees and flocks of doves! In particular, go to the songbirds, to learn from them *how to sing*!

'For singing is for convalescents; let the healthy talk. And even if the healthy man should want songs as well, he wants other songs than the convalescent.'

– 'Oh you jokers and barrel-organs, do be quiet!' answered Zarathustra, and he smiled at his animals. 'How well you know what consolation I devised for myself in seven days!

'That I might have to sing once again – *that* was a consolation I devised for myself, and *this* convalescence. Do you propose to make a hurdy-gurdy song out of that, too?'

'Do not say any more,' his animals replied once more; 'rather, convalescent, make yourself a lyre first, a new lyre!

'For just see, oh Zarathustra: your new songs require new lyres.

'Sing and foam over, oh Zarathustra. Heal your soul with new songs, that you may bear your great fate, that has never yet been the fate of any human being!

'For your animals well know, oh Zarathustra, who you are and who you must become: see, *you are the teacher of eternal return* – that is now *your* fate!

'That you must be the first to hand down this teaching – how should this great fate not be your greatest danger and sickness as well!

'See, we know what you teach: that all things eternally return, ourselves together with them, and that we have already been here an infinite number of times, and all things with us.

'You teach that there is a great year of becoming, an immensity of a great year, which, like a sand-glass, must newly turn over again and again, that it may run down and run out again and again; –

'so that all of these years are identical to each other, in the greatest and in the smallest respects, – so that we ourselves are identical to ourselves in every great year, in the greatest and in the smallest respects.

'And if you were now to die, Zarathustra: see, we know too what you would say to yourself – but your animals beg you not to die yet!

'You would say – without trembling, but breathing again for sheer bliss, for you would have been unburdened of a great heaviness and clamminess, you most patient of men! –

'"Now I die and fade away," you would say, "and in no time at all I shall be nothing. Souls are as mortal as bodies.

'"But the tangle of causes in which I am caught will return – it will create me again! I myself am one of the causes of eternal return.

'"I shall return, with this sun, with this earth, with this eagle, with this serpent – not to a new life or a better life or a similar life;

'"– I shall return eternally to this identical, selfsame life, in the greatest and in the smallest respects, in order to teach once again the eternal return of all things, –

'"– in order to teach once again the doctrine of the great noon of the earth and of humankind, in order to proclaim the superhuman to humankind once again.

'"I have spoken, and now I am broken by what I have spoken: that is the will of my eternal destiny – as a prophet I perish!

'"The hour has now come when he who is going under shall bless himself. So ends Zarathustra's downfall."' – –

When the animals had spoken these words, they fell silent and waited for Zarathustra to say something to them; but Zarathustra did not hear that they were silent. Rather, he lay still, with his eyes closed as if asleep, although he was not sleeping; for he was conversing with his soul at that moment. The serpent and the eagle, however, finding him silent in this fashion, respected the great stillness about him, and considerately withdrew.

Of the Great Longing

Oh my soul, I taught you to say 'today' and 'once' and 'formerly', and to dance your round-dance over every here and there and yonder.

Oh my soul, I delivered you from every nook and cranny, I brushed the dust, spiders and twilight off you.

Oh my soul, I washed you free of petty shame and the virtue of nooks and crannies, and persuaded you to stand naked before the eyes of the sun.

With the storm that is called 'spirit' I blew across your heaving ocean; I blew away all the clouds, I strangled even the strangler called 'sin'.

Oh my soul, I gave you the right to say 'no' like the storm, and to say 'yes' as the clear sky says yes; as still as light you now stand and go through storms of negation.

Oh my soul, I gave you back freedom over what is created and uncreated; and who knows as you know the delight of what is to be?

Oh my soul, I taught you contempt that comes not as a dish for worms – the great, the loving contempt which is most loving where it is most contemptuous.

Oh my soul, I taught you to persuade in such a way that you persuaded the foundation reasons themselves unto you – like the sun that even persuades the ocean to rise unto its height.

Oh my soul, I took from you all obeying, knee-bending and saying of 'master'; I myself gave you the names 'turning-point of all need', and 'fate'.

Oh my soul, I gave you new names and many-coloured playthings, I called you 'fate' and 'girth of girths' and 'umbilical cord of time' and 'azure bell'.

Oh my soul, I gave your soil all manner of wisdom to drink, all of the new wines and also all of the immemorially ancient strong wines of wisdom.

Oh my soul, I poured every sun and every night and every silence and every longing upon you; – and you grew up before me like a vine.

Oh my soul, abundant and heavy you stand there now, a vine with swelling udders and clustering brown-gold wine-grapes; –

– thronged and squeezed by your good fortune, expectant because of the sheer superfluity and abashed by your own expectancy.

Oh my soul, nowhere is there now a soul more loving, and more embracing, and greater of compass! Wherever might future and past be closer together than in you?

Oh my soul, I gave you everything, and all my hands have been emptied through you: – and now! Now, smiling and full of melancholy, you say to me: 'Which of us should be thankful? –

– 'is it not for the giver to be thankful that the receiver has taken? Is giving not a natural need? Is taking not – showing mercy?'

Oh my soul, I understand the smiling of your melancholy; your very abundance is now stretching out its longing hands!

Your copiousness gazes out across surging seas and searches and waits; the longing of superfluity gazes out of the smiling heaven of your eyes!

And truly, oh my soul! Who could see your smile and not dissolve into tears? The very angels dissolve into tears at the overkindness of your smile.

It is your kindness and over-kindness that declines to lament or to weep; and yet, oh my soul, your smile longs for tears, and your trembling mouth for sobs.

'Is not all manner of weeping a lament? And all manner of lamenting an accusation?' This is what you say to yourself; and that, oh my soul, is why you would rather smile than pour out your sorrows,

– pour out in a torrent of tears all your sorrows at your copiousness and at the urge the vine has for the vintner and the vintner's knife!

But if you will not weep, nor weep away your purple melancholy, you will have to sing, oh my soul! – See, I smile myself as I foretell this to you:

– to sing with a rushing song, till all the oceans fall silent in order to listen to your longing,

– till over the silent longing oceans the barque floats, the golden miracle about whose gold all good and bad and wondrous things are leaping;

– and many animals great and small as well, and every thing that has light, wondrous feet on which it can run along violet-blue paths,

– onwards to the golden miracle, the freely willed barque, and to its master; he, though, is the vintner, who waits with his diamond vintner's knife,

– the great one who will cut you loose, oh my soul, the nameless one – for whom it will remain for the songs of the future to find names! And truly, your breath is already fragrant with songs of the future,

– already you are glowing and dreaming, already you are drinking thirstily from all the deep, resounding wells of consolation, already your melancholy is resting in the bliss of future songs! – –

Oh my soul, now I have given you everything and even the last of me, and all my hands have been emptied through you: – *such that I bade you sing*, see, that was the last I had to give!

Such that I bade you sing, speak now, speak: *which* of us should now – be thankful? – Even better still: sing to me, sing, oh my soul! And let me give thanks! –

Thus spake Zarathustra.

The Second Dance Song

1

Lately I gazed into your eyes, oh Life; I saw gold glinting in your night-eyes, – my heart stood still with the delight of it:

I saw a golden barque glinting on the waters of night, a golden rocking barque, sinking, drinking, waving anew!

You cast a glance at my feet, which were twitching to dance: a rocking glance, laughing, inquiring, melting;

Just twice you clacked the castanets in your dainty hands – and already my feet were rocking with the urge to dance. –

My heels reared, my toes listened, striving to understand you; the dancer, after all, has his ears – in his toes!

I leapt to you – you fled away from my leap; and the tongues of your fleeing, flying hair flickered towards me!

I leapt back from you and your serpents; and there you stood, half turned, your eyes full of desire.

With your crooked glances – you teach me crooked ways. And by taking crooked ways my feet learn – guile!

I fear you near, I love you far; when you flee me, you lure me onwards, when you seek me, I grind to a halt; – I suffer, but what would I not suffer gladly for you! –

whose coldness inflames, whose hatred seduces, whose flight binds, whose mockery – touches;

who would not hate you, great one who binds, entwines, seduces, seeks and finds! Who would not love you, you innocent, impatient, swift-as-the-wind, child-eyed sinner!

Where are you leading me now, you unbridled bride of virtue? And are you fleeing me again, you sweet little wild one, you ingrate!

I come dancing after you, I follow even where the spoor is faint. Where are you? Give me your hand! Or just a finger!

There are caves and thickets here; we shall lose our way! – Stop! Stay still! Do you not see the owls and bats flitting about?

You owl! You bat! Are you out to hoodwink me? Where are we? You learnt this howling and yapping from the dogs.

Sweetly you bare your little white teeth at me. Your wicked eyes leap out at me from under your curly little mane.

It is a dance over rough country; I am the huntsman, – will you be my hound or my chamois?

Now, heel! And quickly away, you wicked springer! Up, now! And over! – Woe! In trying to jump I have myself fallen down.

Oh see me lying, overweening spirits, begging for mercy! Dearly I should like to take – gentler paths with you! –

– the paths of love amid the stillness of colourful bushes! Or along the lakeside over there, where goldfish swim and dance!

You are tired now? There are sheep over there, and the red of sunset; is it not a fine thing, to sleep when the shepherd is playing his pipes?

You are so dreadfully tired? I shall carry you, just let your arms hang down! And if you are thirsty – I do have something, but your mouth will not drink it! –

– Oh this accursèd, nimble, supple snake and slippery witch! Where have you gone? But on my face I feel two spots and red blotches, from your hand!

I am truly tired of being your shepherd, forever sheepish! You witch, if I have sung for you until now, now *you* shall – cry out for me!

To the rhythm of my whip you shall dance and cry out! I did not forget my whip, did I? – No! –

2

Then Life made this reply to me, holding her dainty ears closed as she did so:

'Oh Zarathustra! Do not crack your whip so fearfully! After all, you know that noise murders thoughts – and I am just having such delicate thoughts.

'Both of us are regular ne'er-do-wells and ne'er-do-ills. Beyond good and evil we have found our island and our green meadow – just the two of us! And because that is how it is, we must be good to each other!

'And even if we do not love one another from the very foundations – must people be at loggerheads if they do not love one another from the very foundations?

'And you know that I am well disposed to you, often too well; and the reason is that I am jealous of your wisdom. Ah, that crazy old fool, wisdom!

'If your wisdom were one day to desert you, ah! my love would quickly desert you as well.' –

At this point, Life took a thoughtful look back and around her, and said softly: 'Oh Zarathustra, you are not loyal enough to me.

'You do not love me remotely as much as you say; I know you are thinking that you will soon want to leave me.

'There is an old, heavy, deep-sounding bell, the sound of which carries as high up as your cave at night; –

– 'whenever you hear that bell toll the hour of midnight, then between the first and the twelfth strokes you are thinking it –

– 'you are thinking it, oh Zarathustra, I know it, you are thinking that you want to leave me soon!' –

'Yes,' I answered hesitantly, 'but you also know' – and I said something in her ear, right through her tangled, blonde, witless locks.

'You *know* that, oh Zarathustra? No one knows that.' – –

And we gazed at each other and looked at the green meadow, on which the cool evening was just settling, and wept together. – At that time, however, Life was dearer to me than all my wisdom had ever been. –

Thus spake Zarathustra.

3

One!
Oh man! Beware!
Two!
What does deep midnight's voice declare?
Three!
'I wake from sleep,'
Four!
'Wake from a dreaming deep and fair:' –
Five!
'The world is deep,'
Six!
'Deeper than day was yet aware.'
Seven!
'Deep is its woe,' –
Eight!
'Desire – deeper than agony;'
Nine!
'Woe says: Die! Go!'
Ten!
'Desire, though, craves eternity' –
Eleven!
– 'craves deepest deep eternity!'
Twelve!

The Seven Seals
(or: The Yes and Amen Song)

1

If I am a soothsayer, and full of that prophetic spirit that moves along the high ridge between two oceans –

moves as a heavy cloud between past and future, – a foe to the sultry lowlands and to all that is weary and can neither die nor live –

ready for lightning in its dark bosom, and for redeeming rays of light; pregnant with lighting flashes that say yes! laugh yes! to prophetic bolts of lightning –

– but blessèd is he who is pregnant in this way! And truly, he who would one day ignite the light of the future must first hang long upon the mountains, as bad weather!

Oh how should I not lust after eternity, and for the wedding ring of rings – the ring of return!

Never yet have I found the woman by whom I wanted children, unless it be this woman whom I love; for I love you, oh Eternity!

For I love you, oh Eternity!

2

If ever my wrath broke open graves, moved boundary stones, and rolled ancient tablets, shattered, into precipitous chasms;

if ever my scorn blew mouldered words away, and I came upon cross-spiders like a broom, and upon old musty burial chambers as a wind sweeping all before it;

if ever I sat rejoicing where the ancient gods lie buried, blessing the world, loving the world, beside the monuments to those who in olden days vilified the world;

for I love even churches and the tombs of gods, as long as heaven is looking down with a clear eye through their smashed roofs; I like to sit, like grass and red poppies, on the rubble of churches:

Oh how should I not lust after Eternity, and for the wedding ring of rings – the ring of return!

Never yet have I found the woman by whom I wanted children, unless it be this woman whom I love; for I love you, oh Eternity!

For I love you, oh Eternity!

3

If ever a breath has come to me of the creative breath and celestial necessity that compels even accidents to dance the round-dances of stars;

if ever I have laughed with the laughter of the creative light-ning, which the long thunder of the deed follows, rumbling but obedient;

if ever I have played dice with the gods at the table of the gods, the earth, so that the earth quaked and broke open and snorted out torrents of fire;

– for the earth is a table of the gods, atremble with creative new words and the dice-throws of the gods:

Oh how should I not lust after Eternity, and for the wedding ring of rings – the ring of return!

Never yet have I found the woman by whom I wanted children, unless it be this woman whom I love; for I love you, oh Eternity!

For I love you, oh Eternity!

4

If ever I have drunk full draughts from that frothing, spicy mixing-jug in which all things are well mixed;

if ever my hand moulded the remotest together with the closest and fire together with spirit and desire together with suffering and the worst together with the kindest;

if I myself am a grain of that redeeming salt which makes all things in the mixing-jug mix well;

for there is a salt that joins good with evil; and even the worst evil is worth using to add spice, and for the last frothing-over:

Oh how should I not lust after Eternity, and for the wedding ring of rings – the ring of return!

Never yet have I found the woman by whom I wanted children, unless it be this woman whom I love; for I love you, oh Eternity!

For I love you, oh Eternity!

5

If I am attached to the sea and all that is marine in nature, and most attached when it angrily contradicts me;

if that questing desire is in me, that sets its sails for the undiscovered, and if a seafarer's pleasure is in my own pleasure;

if ever I shouted in my rejoicing: 'The coast has been lost to view – now the last chain has fallen from me –

'boundlessness surges all about me, far away space and time glitter, very well! onwards! old heart!' –

Oh how should I not lust after Eternity, and for the wedding ring of rings – the ring of return!

Never yet have I found the woman by whom I wanted children, unless it be this woman whom I love; for I love you, oh Eternity!

For I love you, oh Eternity!

6

If my virtue is a dancer's virtue, and I have often jumped with both feet in golden-emerald rapture;

if my wickedness is a laughing wickedness, at home beneath rose bowers and hedges of lilies;

– for in laughter all evil is present, but it is sanctified and absolved by its own blessèdness; –

and if this is my alpha and omega: that all heavy things shall become light, all bodies shall be dancers, all spirits shall be birds; and truly that is my alpha and omega! –

Oh how should I not lust after Eternity, and for the wedding ring of rings – the ring of return!

Never yet have I found the woman by whom I wanted children, unless it be this woman whom I love; for I love you, oh Eternity!

For I love you, oh Eternity!

7

If ever I outstretched silent heavens above me, and flew with my own wings into my own heavens;

if I have swum in deep distances of light, playing, and the wisdom of birds entered into my freedom; –

– but the wisdom of birds speaks like this: 'See, there is no above, no below! Fling yourself about, onwards, back, you who are light! Sing! do not speak any longer!

– 'are not all words made for those who are heavy? Are not all words lies to those who are light? Sing! do not speak any longer!' –

Oh how should I not lust after Eternity, and for the wedding ring of rings – the ring of return!

Never yet have I found the woman by whom I wanted children, unless it be this woman whom I love; for I love you, oh Eternity!

For I love you, oh Eternity!

PART FOUR

Ah, where in the world have greater follies been done than by the compassionate? And what in the world has caused more suffering than the follies of the compassionate?

Woe to all lovers who do not still command a height that is above their compassion!

Once the devil said to me: 'Even God has his hell: it is his love of humanity.'

And recently I heard him say this: 'God is dead; God has died of his pity for humanity.'

Zarathustra, 'Of the Compassionate'

The Honey Sacrifice

− And once again months and years passed over Zarathustra's soul, and he paid no heed; his hair, however, turned white. One day, when he was sitting on a stone outside his cave and gazing in silence into the distance − the view there is of the ocean, though, and twisting precipitous depths − his animals gathered contemplatively around him, and at length stood confronting him.

'Oh Zarathustra,' they said, 'are you perhaps on the lookout for your happiness?' − 'Of what consequence is happiness!' he answered. 'It is a long time since I aspired to happiness. My aspiration is all for my work.' − 'Oh Zarathustra,' the animals then said, 'you say that as one who has more than enough of what is good. Are you not lying in a sky-blue lake of good fortune?' − 'You jokers,' answered Zarathustra, smiling, 'how well you chose that image! But you know too that my happiness is heavy and not like a flowing wave of water: it pressures me, and will not leave me, and behaves like molten pitch.' −

At this, the animals walked contemplatively around him once again, and then stood confronting him once more. 'Oh Zarathustra,' they said, 'is *that* why you are growing more and more sallow and dark, despite the white and flaxen appearance of your hair? Just see, you are sitting in your pitch!' − 'What's that you are saying, my animals,' said Zarathustra, laughing: 'truly, I was speaking ill when I spoke of pitch. What is happening to me is what happens to every fruit that ripens. It is the *honey* in my veins that makes my blood thicker, and my soul more tranquil, too.' − 'That must be it, oh Zarathustra,' answered the animals, and thronged up to him; 'but would you not like to climb a high mountain today? The air is clear, and today you can see more of the world than ever.' − 'Yes, my animals,' he answered, 'you give splendid advice, after my own heart; today I shall climb a high mountain! But be sure that I have honey to hand up there, yellow, white, fine, icy-fresh golden honey from the comb. For know this: I propose to offer the honey sacrifice up there.' −

But when Zarathustra was at the mountaintop he sent the animals home that had accompanied him, and now found himself alone; – and he laughed whole-heartedly, looked about him, and spoke thus:

Speaking of offerings and honey sacrifice was no more than a stratagem of speech, and, truly, a useful foolishness! Up here I can speak more freely than before the caves and domestic animals of hermits.

Sacrifice, indeed! I squander what is given to me, – a squanderer with a thousand hands, me! How should I dare call that – a sacrifice!

And when I craved honey, I was merely craving bait and sweet syrup and gum, which even growling bears and wondrous, sullen, evil birds have an appetite for;

– the finest bait, such as serves the needs of hunters and fishermen. For, though the world is like a dark forest of animals and a pleasure garden for all wild hunters, nonetheless I think it far more, and preferably, a teeming and unfathomable ocean,

– an ocean full of many-coloured fish and crabs, such as even gods might hunger after, such as would make them fishermen and casters of nets; that is how rich the world is in wondrous things, great and small!

Especially the world of humankind, the ocean of humankind; – *there* I shall now cast my golden fishing-line and say: Open, abyss of humanity!

Open, and throw me your fish and glistening crabs! Today, with my finest bait, I shall lure the most wondrous of human fish!

I shall cast my happiness itself far and wide, between sunrise, noon and sunset, to see whether many human fish are not taught by my happiness to tug and twitch.

Until they, biting on my sharp, hidden hooks, have to come up to *my* height, the most colourful groundlings of the depths to the most wicked of all fishers of men.

For *that* is who I am, from the very foundations and from the very beginning, drawing, drawing hitherwards me, drawing upwards, raising up, a drawer, raiser and taskmaster, who not for nothing once told himself: 'Become the one you are!'

So now humankind may come *up* to me in this way; for I am still waiting for signs that it is time for me to go down; I myself am not yet going down, as I must, among humankind.

Therefore I wait here, cunning and mocking on the high mountains, not impatient, not patient, but rather as one who has lost even the patience he had acquired – because he no longer 'endureth'.

For my fate is giving me time: has it forgotten me? Or is it sitting in the shadows behind a great rock, catching flies?

And truly, I am grateful to my eternal fate for not harrying and pressuring me and leaving me time for jests and wicked mischief; today, for instance, I have climbed this high mountain to go fishing.

Has anyone ever caught fish on a high mountain? And even if what I am intending and doing up here is foolishness, better that, than that I should grow solemn from waiting down there, and green and sallow –

– grow, from waiting, to be a puffed-up snorter of wrath, a holy storm of howling from the mountains, an impatient man yelling down to the valleys: 'Listen to me, or I shall lash you with the scourge of God!'

Not that I should bear wrathful people of that sort any ill-will on that account; they serve well enough for me to laugh at! They must really be impatient, these great booming drums that have to get a word in, today or never!

I, though, and my fate – we do not speak to today, nor do we speak to never; we do have patience and time, and time again, for our speech. For one day it must come, and it may not pass by.

What must come one day, and may not pass by? Our great hazar, that is to say: our great far-off empire of humanity, the thousand-year empire of Zarathustra.

How far off may that 'far-off' be? What concern is that of mine? But to my mind it is no less a certainty for that – I stand securely with both feet on this foundation,

– on an everlasting foundation, on hard, primordial rock, on this highest, hardest, primordial range of mountains to which all the winds come as to a weathershed, asking: where? and: whence? and: whither?

Laugh here, laugh my bright and wholesome wickedness! Throw it down from the high mountains, your glittering, mocking laughter! Take your glittering as a bait to lure the fairest human fish!

And whatever belongs to *me* in all the oceans, my in-and-for-my-self in all things – fish *that* out for me, bring *that* up to me here; that is what I am waiting for, the most wicked of all fishermen.

Out there, out there, my fishing-line! In there, down there, bait of my happiness! Drip down your sweetest dew, honey of my heart! Bite, my fish-hook, into the belly of all black doomfulness!

Far and wide, far and wide, my eye! Oh how many oceans all around me, what dawning human futures! And above me – what rosy tranquillity! What cloudless silence!

The Cry of Distress

On the following day, Zarathustra was sitting once again on his stone outside the cave while the animals were out and about in the world, to find fresh food to bring home – including fresh honey, for Zarathustra had used up or wasted the old honey, to the very last. But as he was sitting there with a stick in his hand, tracing the shadow of his form on the ground, thinking – and, truly, not about himself and his shadow! – he was suddenly alarmed and taken aback to see, beside his own shadow, another shadow. And as he was quickly looking about him and standing up, see: beside him stood the prophet, the same to whom he had once given food and drink at his table, the proclaimer of the great weariness, who taught: 'It is all one, nothing is worthwhile, the world is without meaning, knowledge chokes.' But his countenance had undergone a transformation in the meantime; and when Zarathustra gazed into his eyes, his heart was alarmed anew: so many evil tidings and ashen flashes of lightning were passing across that face.

The prophet, who had perceived what was occurring in Zara-thustra's soul, wiped his face with his hand as if he meant to wipe it away; Zarathustra did the same. And when both of them had silently composed and fortified themselves in this way, they shook hands as a sign that they wished to recognize each other once again.

'Welcome,' said Zarathustra, 'prophet of the great weariness. Not for nothing shall you once have been a guest at my table. Eat and drink with me today, too, and forgive a contented old man if he sits down at table with you!' – 'A contented old man?' answered the prophet, shaking his head; 'but whoever you are or wish to be, oh Zarathustra, your time being it up here is all but done – your barque will presently not be sitting high and dry any longer!' – 'Am I sitting high and dry?' asked Zarathustra, laughing. – 'The waves around your mountain are rising higher and higher,' answered the prophet, 'waves of great distress and sorrow. Soon they will lift your barque as well and carry you away.' – Zarathustra, astonished, was silent in response. – 'Do you still hear nothing?' went on the prophet, 'no rushing and roaring sounds rising from the depths?' Zarathustra again remained silent and listened; and he heard a long, long cry, which the abysses threw one to another and passed on, since none wanted to keep it, so evil was the sound.

'You woeful proclaimer,' said Zarathustra at length, 'that is a cry of distress, and a human cry, in all likelihood from a black sea. But what concern is human distress of mine? My ultimate sin, reserved unto me – perhaps you know what it is called?'

– 'Compassion!' answered the prophet from an overflowing heart, and raised both hands high, 'Oh Zarathustra, I come to seduce you to your ultimate sin!' –

And barely had these words been uttered but the cry rang out once more, longer and more fearful than before, and much closer too. 'Do you hear? Do you hear, oh Zarathustra?' cried the prophet. 'That cry is for you. It is calling you: come, come, come, it is time, it is high time!' –

Zarathustra, confused and shaken, was silent at this; at length he asked, like a man hesitating within himself: 'And who is it that is calling me?'

'But you well know who it is,' answered the prophet brusquely. 'Why are you hiding? It is *the higher human* that cries out for you!'

'The higher human?' cried out Zarathustra, horror-struck: 'what does *he* want? What does *he* want? The higher human! What does he want here?' – and his skin broke out in sweat.

The prophet, however, made no response to Zarathustra's fears, but listened and listened to the depths. But when there had been silence there for a long time, he turned his gaze back and saw Zarathustra standing trembling.

'Oh Zarathustra,' he began in a voice of sadness, 'you are not standing there like a man made giddy with happiness; you shall have to dance if you are not to fall over!

'But even if you were to dance before me, and perform all your sideways leaps, no one could tell me: "See, this is the last happy man dancing here!"

'If anyone were to come up to these heights in search of *that* man, it would be in vain: he would find caves, certainly, and more caves, and hiding places for those in hiding, but not mineshafts of happiness and treasure chambers and new gold-seams of happiness.

'Happiness – how could happiness be found among recluses and hermits of this kind! Must I still seek ultimate happiness on fortunate isles, far away in the forgotten oceans?

'But it is all one, nothing is worthwhile, it is no use seeking, nor are there any fortunate isles any longer!' – –

Thus sighed the prophet; on his last sigh, however, Zarathustra brightened and regained his assurance, like one emerging from a deep gorge into the light. 'No! No! Thrice no!' he exclaimed in powerful tones, and he stroked his beard. 'On *that* point I know better! There are still fortunate isles! On *that* be quiet, you doomful windbag!

'Stop splashing on about these things, you morning rain-cloud!

Am I not standing here wet with your dismalness, and soaked like a dog?

'Now I shall give myself a shake and run away from you, to dry off again; there is no occasion to be surprised at that! Do you find me discourteous? But this is *my* court.

'But as for your higher man: very well! I shall look for him right away, in those forests over there; *that* was where his cry came from. Perhaps some wicked beast is setting upon him.

'He is in *my* realm; I shall not have him come to any harm here! And truly, there are many wicked beasts in my parts.' –

With these words Zarathustra turned to go. But the prophet rejoined: 'Oh Zarathustra, you are a rogue!

'I am well aware that you want to be rid of me! You would rather run off into the forests and hunt wicked beasts.

'But how will that help you? After all, once evening comes you will have me once again; I shall sit there in your own cave, patient and heavy as a log – and wait for you!'

'So be it!' Zarathustra shouted back as he departed, 'and whatever is mine in my cave is yours as well, my guest!

'But if you should still find honey there – go ahead, lick it up, you growling bear, and sweeten your soul! Let us both be in good spirits in the evening,

– 'in good spirits and glad that this day has ended! And you yourself shall be my dancing bear, dancing to my songs.

'You do not believe it? You shake your head? Very well! On you go, old bear! But I too – am a prophet!'

Thus spake Zarathustra.

Conversation with the Kings

1

Zarathustra had not been on his way through his mountains and forests for even an hour when all at once he saw a strange procession. On the very same path he intended to go down by, two kings were approaching, adorned with crowns and purple sashes and as colourful as flamingos; they were driving a laden ass before them. 'What are these kings doing in my realm?' Zarathustra said in astonishment to his heart; and quickly he hid behind a bush. But when the kings had approached as far as where he stood, he said half aloud, like a man talking to himself: 'Strange! Strange! This is perplexing! I see two kings – but only one ass!'

At this the two kings stopped, smiled, looked across to where the voice had come from, and then gazed into each other's faces. 'Our own people doubtless think such things as well,' said the king on the right, 'but they do not say them out loud.'

But the king on the left shrugged his shoulders and answered: 'It is probably a goatherd. Or a hermit who has lived too long among the rocks and trees. The fact is that being out of polite society ruins one's manners.'

'Manners?' returned the other king, tetchily and bitterly. 'What is it that we are avoiding, then? Is it not "manners"? Is it not "polite society"?

'It is better, truly, to live among hermits and goatherds than with our gilded, false, painted rabble – even if it calls itself "polite society",

– 'even if it calls itself "nobility". But there everything is false and rotten, starting with the blood, thanks to woeful diseases of old, and even more woeful quacks.

'To my mind, the finest and dearest of men in these times remains a healthy peasant, coarse, cunning, obstinate, with stamina; that is the noblest of breeds nowadays.

'The peasant is the finest of men in these times; and the peasant breed should be master! But this is the kingdom of the rabble – I shall not be taken in any longer. A rabble, though, is a hotchpotch.

'Rabble-hotchpotch: everything in it is mixed up with everything else, saint and scoundrel and Junker and Jew and every kind of beast from Noah's Ark.

'Manners! All things are false and rotten with us. No one knows how to show reverence any more: *that* is what we are running away from. They are sickly-sweet importunate curs, they gild palm leaves.

'This is the revulsion that is choking me: that we kings have ourselves become false, draped and disguised in the old yellowed pomp of our grandfathers, showpieces for the stupidest and the craftiest and whoever is striking power deals in these times!

'We *are not* the first among men – and yet must affect to be; at last we have grown tired and disgusted with this deception.

'We have been avoiding the riff-raff, all these loudmouths and scribbling blowflies, the stench of shopkeepers, the antics of ambition, the foul breath; pooh, to live among the riff-raff,

– 'pooh, to affect to be the first among riff-raff! Ah, revulsion! Revulsion! Revulsion! What do we kings matter any more!' –

'Your old malady is besetting you,' said the king on the left at this point'; 'revulsion is besetting you, my poor brother. But you well know that someone is listening to us.'

Immediately Zarathustra, who had opened wide his ears and eyes at these speeches, stood up from his hiding place, stepped towards the kings, and began:

'He who is listening to you, he who gladly listens to you, oh kings, is called Zarathustra.

'I am Zarathustra, who once said: "What do kings matter any longer?" Forgive me, but I was pleased to hear you say to each other: "What do we kings matter any more!"

'This, however, is *my* realm and my dominion; whatever are you looking for in my realm? But perhaps on your way you have *found* what *I* am looking for: that is, the higher man.'

When the kings heard this, they beat their breasts and said as one: 'We have been recognized!

'With the sword of these words you have cut through the deepest darkness of our hearts. You have identified our distress; for see! we are on our way to find the higher man –

'– the man who is higher than we; although we are kings. It is to

231

him that we are leading this ass. For the highest man shall also be the highest master on earth.

'There is no harder misfortune in all human fate than when the powerful on earth are not also the first among men. When that happens, all things are false and askew and monstrous.

'And when they are the last among men, and more beast than human, then the rabble's stock keeps on rising, until at last the rabble-virtue declares: "See, I alone am virtue!"' –

'What did I just hear?' answered Zarathustra; 'what wisdom in kings! I am delighted, and, truly, I already feel an urge to write a poem about it; –

'– though it may well not be a poem fit for Everyman's ears. I have long since abandoned any consideration I had learnt for long ears. Very well! On we go!'

(But at this point the ass got a word in too; what he said, clearly and maliciously, was: Yee-hah.)

'Way back in time, in AD one, I think,
The sybil said these words, drunk without drink:
"Woe, all is woe!
Decay! Decay! The world's never sunk so low!
Rome has become a whore, and a brothel too,
Rome's Caesar is a beast, and God – a Jew!"'

2

The kings took great pleasure in these lines of Zarathustra's. The king on the right said: 'Oh Zarathustra, how well we did to set forth to see you!

'Your enemies, you see, showed us your image in their mirror; you gazed out with a devil's grimace, laughing scornfully, so that we were afraid of you.

'But that made no difference! Time and again you stung our ears and hearts with your sayings. At length we said: what does it matter how he looks!

'We must *hear* him, the one whose teaching is: "You should love peace as a means to new wars, and a short peace more than a long one."

'No one has ever uttered such warlike words: "What is good? To be brave is good. It is the good war that hallows any cause."

'Oh Zarathustra, the blood of our fathers stirred in our bodies at such words; it was like the springtime speaking to old wine-casks.

'Our fathers were fond of life when swords were entwined like red-flecked serpents; the sun of any peace seemed to them bland and feeble, but a long peace left them ashamed.

'How they sighed, our fathers, when they saw shiny, parched swords on the wall! Like them they thirsted for war. For a sword wants to drink blood, and sparkles with desire.' – –

While the kings were eagerly talking and chattering about the happiness of their fathers in this fashion, Zarathustra was overcome by no small urge to ridicule their enthusiasm; for the kings he saw before him were visibly of a most peaceable nature, with aged and refined faces. But he controlled himself. 'Very well!' he said: 'that is the way, and over there is Zarathustra's cave; and this day shall have a long evening! But now a cry of distress is calling me hastily away from you.

'It will honour my cave, if kings wish to sit and wait in it; but the truth is that you will have to wait a long time!

'Well – what of it? Where does one better learn how to wait nowadays than at courts? And the entirety of the virtue that has remained to kings – is it not known today as *being able* to wait?'

Thus spake Zarathustra.

The Leech

And Zarathustra went on thoughtfully, further and deeper, through forests and past marshy grounds; but, as happens to anyone who ponders difficult matters, he unintentionally stepped on a man as he walked. And see, all at once a cry of pain and a couple of curses and twenty dreadful profanities sprayed into his face; startled, he raised his stick and struck the man he had stepped on, too. Right away, however, he regained his presence of mind; and his heart laughed at the foolishness he had just perpetrated.

'Forgive me,' he said to the man he had stepped on, who had stood up in a fury and then sat down again; 'forgive me and, above all, listen to a parable first.

'Just as a wanderer dreaming of faraway things unintentionally stumbles over a dog sleeping on a lonely road, a dog lying in the sun;

'– just as both of them start up, and confront each other like mortal enemies, each of the two scared to death; so too it happened with us.

'And yet! And yet – had things gone just a little differently, they would have hugged each other, that dog and that solitary! After all, they are both – solitaries!'

– 'Whoever you may be,' said the man who had been stepped on, still in a fury, 'you are hurting me not only with your foot but with your parable too!

'Look, am I a dog?' – And the man who was sitting rose and drew his bare arm out of the swamp. For he had been reclining on the ground at first, concealed and imperceptible, like a man stalking game in marshland.

'But what are you doing!' cried Zarathustra in alarm, for he saw a good deal of blood running down the bare arm, – 'what has happened to you? Has some fearful beast bitten you, you poor wretch?'

The bleeding man laughed, still angry. 'That's none of your business!' he said, and made as if to go. 'I am at home here, and in my own realm. Whoever it may be that asks me questions, I'm hardly going to answer a halfwit!'

'You are mistaken,' said Zarathustra compassionately, and held the man fast; 'you are mistaken. This is not your realm but mine, and I shall not have anyone come to harm in it.

'Still, call me what you will – I am the one I must be. The name I give myself is Zarathustra.

'Very well! Up over there is the path to Zarathustra's cave; it is not far, – would you not like to tend your wounds in my home?

'You poor wretch, this life has dealt harshly with you: first a beast bit you, then a man stepped on you!' – –

But when the man who had been stepped on heard the name of Zarathustra, he was transformed. 'Whatever is happening to me!' he exclaimed; 'if there is *anyone* who still matters to me in this life, it is that one man, Zarathustra, and that one animal that lives on blood, the leech!

'It was on account of the leech that I was lying here beside the swamp like a fisherman, and my outstretched arm had already been bitten ten times when a fairer leech bit me for my blood, Zarathustra himself!

'Oh happiness! Oh miracle! Praised be this day that lured me into this swamp! Praised be the best, liveliest cupping-glass alive today, praised be the great leech of the conscience, Zarathustra!' –

So spoke the man who had been stepped on; and Zarathustra was pleased by his words and their refined, respectful manner. 'Who are you?' he asked, and offered him his hand; 'there is still a lot between us to be cleared up and placed in a happier light; but I sense that already a clear, bright day is breaking.'

'I am *the conscientious man of the spirit*,' answered the other, 'and hardly anyone is stricter, more severe and more rigorous in matters of the spirit than I, except for the one from whom I learnt, Zarathustra himself.

'Better to know nothing than to half-know a great many things! Better to be a fool on one's own mettle than a wise man as others conceive it! I – get to the very foundation of things:

– 'what does it matter if it be great or small? If it be called swamp or heaven? A hand's-breadth of ground is enough for me; as long as it really is a true foundation!

– 'a hand's-breadth of ground; one can stand on that. In the right science of knowledge there is no such thing as great or small.'

'So perhaps you are an expert on the leech?' asked Zarathustra. 'And you inquire into the bottommost foundation of the leech, conscientious as you are?'

'Oh Zarathustra,' answered the man who had been stepped on, 'that would be an immense task; how should I dare undertake it!

'But what I am a master and connoisseur of is the leech's *brain*; – that is *my* world!

'And it is indeed a world! But forgive me if my pride speaks at this point, for on these matters I have no equal. That is why I said "I am at home here".

'How long have I been investigating this one thing, the brain of the leech, in order that the slippery truth might not slip away from me any longer! This is *my* realm!

– 'for this, I have thrown away everything else; for this, everything else has become a matter of indifference to me; and right beside my knowledge is my black ignorance.

'The conscience of my spirit requires me to know one thing and otherwise be ignorant of everything; I am revolted by any half-measures of the spirit, by all things misty, drifting, blathering.

'Where my honesty ceases, I am blind, and want to be blind. Where I want to know, however, I also want to be honest, that is to say: tough, rigorous, precise, harsh, unrelenting.

'The fact that *you*, oh Zarathustra, once declared: "The spirit is the life that cuts into its own life" – that led and seduced me to your teaching. And truly, I have increased my own knowledge with my own blood!'

'As the evidence tells me,' interjected Zarathustra; for the blood was still running down the bare arm of the conscientious man. For ten leeches had bitten a hold on it.

'Oh you wondrous fellow, how much this evidence tells me – that is, how much you yourself tell me! And it might not be proper to pour all of it into your exacting ears!

'Very well! Let us part here! But I should be glad to find you again. Up over there is the path to my cave; there you shall be a dear guest of mine tonight!

'And Zarathustra would also like to atone to your body for stepping on it; I shall think about that. But now a cry of distress is calling me hastily away from you.'

Thus spake Zarathustra.

The Sorcerer

1

But when Zarathustra walked around an outcrop of rock he saw, not far below him on the same path, a person who was twitching his limbs about like a man in a fit of rage, finally falling to the ground 0n his belly. 'Stop!' Zarathustra said to his heart at this – 'that man over there must surely be the higher man. That dreadful cry of distress came from him. I shall see if I can give any help.' But when he ran to the place where the man lay on the ground he found a trembling old man with staring eyes; and, no matter how hard Zarathustra tried to help him up and set him on his legs again, it was in vain. The unfortunate man did not appear to notice that there was someone with him, either; instead, he kept looking about him, making moving gestures, like one forsaken by all the world and grown lonely. At length, however, after a great deal of trembling, twitching and jack-knifing, he began to wail in this fashion:

> Who warms me still, who loves me still?
> Give me your hot hands!
> Give me coal-warmers for the heart!
> Outstretched, shuddering,
> Like a man half dead whose feet are being warmed –
> Shaken, ah! by unknown fevers,
> Trembling at sharp, icy arrows of frost,
> Hunted by you, thought!

Unnameable! Shrouded! Terrible!
You hunter behind the clouds!
Struck down by your lightning-bolt,
You, scornful eye, gazing at me from darkness:
– that is how I lie,
Contorting, twisting myself, tormented
By every everlasting torture,
Hit
By you, cruel hunter,
You unknown – God!

Strike deeper!
Strike one more time!
Sting, shatter this heart!
What is the meaning of this torture
With tooth-blunt arrows?
Why are you gazing once again,
Not tired of human misery,
With *Schadenfroh* eyes of divine lightning?
You do not want to kill,
Only to torture, torture?
Why – torture *me*,
You *Schadenfroh* unknown God?

Aha! Are you stealing up?
At such a midnight hour
What do you want? Speak!
You oppress me, press me –
Ha! Far too close already!
Get away! Away!
You hear me breathing,
You listen to my heart,
Jealous one –
But jealous of what?
Get away! Away! Why the ladder?

Do you want to come in,
Into my heart,
Climb in, into my inmost
Secret thoughts?
Shameless one! Unknown – thief!
What are you after by stealing,
What are you after by listening,
What are you after by torturing,
You torturer!
You – hangman god!
Or shall I, like a dog,
Roll about before you?
All devotion, beside myself with rapture,
Wagging love of – you!

In vain! Sting on,
Most cruel of thorns! No,
Not a dog – I am merely your game,
Most cruel of hunters!
The proudest of your captives,
Your robber behind the clouds!
Speak at last –
What do you want, highwayman, from *me*?
You, shrouded in lightning! You, unknown one! Speak,
What do you *want*, unknown god? – –

What? A ransom?
How much ransom do you want?
Demand a lot – so says my pride.
Do not say much – so says my other pride!
Aha!

You want – me? Me?
All of me?

Aha!

And you torture me, fool that you are,
You torture my pride?
Give me *love* – who warms me still?
Who loves me still? – give me your hot hands,
Give me coal-warmers for the heart,
Give me, the loneliest of all,
Who has been taught by ice,
Ah! sevenfold ice, to long
For enemies, for enemies themselves,
Give, yes, yield up to me,
Most cruel enemy –
Yourself! – –

Gone!
He himself has fled,
My last and only companion,
My great enemy,
My unknown,
My hangman-god! –

– No! Come back,
With all your tortures!
Oh do come back
To the last of all the solitaries!
All the streams of my tears
Run their courses to you!

And the last flame of my heart –
It flares up to *you*!
Oh do come back,
My unknown god! My pain! My final – happiness!

2

At this point, however, Zarathustra could no longer restrain himself, took his stick, and set about belabouring the wailing man as hard as he could. 'Desist!' he shouted at him, laughing wrathfully, 'desist, you play-actor! You faker! You liar from the very foundations! I know you for what you are!

'I'll warm your legs for you, see if I don't, you wicked sorcerer. I well know how to make things hot for the likes of you!'

– 'Leave off,' said the old man, and jumped up from the ground; 'don't hit me any more, oh Zarathustra! I was only having fun!

'Things like that are part of my art; I was out to test you when I gave you that sample! And truly, you saw through me well!

'But you too – have given me no small sample of yourself: you are *hard*, oh wise Zarathustra! You hit hard with your "truths", your cudgel forces out of me – *this* truth!'

– 'Do not flatter,' answered Zarathustra, still worked up and frowning darkly, 'you play-actor from the very foundations! You are false; how can you speak – of truth!

'You peacock of peacocks, you ocean of vanity, *what* were you acting out before me, you wicked sorcerer – *who* was I supposed to believe in when you were wailing in such a fashion?'

'The *penitent of the spirit*,' said the old man; 'I was playing – *him*. You yourself once coined the expression –

– 'the poet and sorcerer who eventually turns his spirit against himself, the man transformed who is frozen to death by his own evil knowledge and conscience.

'And do simply admit it: it did take a long time for you to see through my art and lying, oh Zarathustra! *You believed* in my distress when you held my head in both your hands, –

– 'I heard you wailing: "He has not been loved too little, loved too little!" My malice rejoiced within me at having deceived you so far.'

'You may have deceived more sophisticated men than me,' said Zarathustra harshly. 'I am not on my guard against deceivers, I *must* be without caution: that is how my fate would have it.

241

'But you – *must* deceive; that much I know of you. You must forever be ambiguous, to a twofold, threefold, fourfold, fivefold degree! Even what you have just confessed was not remotely true or false enough, to my mind!

'You evil faker, how could you do anything else! If you presented yourself naked to your doctor, you would still paint over your illness with make-up.

'In the same way you painted over your lie just now, when you said: "I was *only* having fun!" There was *seriousness* in that, too – you *are* something of a penitent of the spirit!

'I divine you well: you have become the one who enchants the multitude, but you have no lie or cunning left to use on yourself – you are disenchanted with yourself!

'You have reaped revulsion as your sole truth. Not one of your words is genuine any more, but your mouth is; that is, the revulsion that clings to your mouth.' – –

– 'But who are you!' the old sorcerer exclaimed at this point, in a defiant voice; 'who dares to speak to *me* in this way, the greatest man alive today?' – and a green flash of lightning shot from his eye at Zarathustra. But right away he changed, and said sadly:

'Oh Zarathustra, I am weary of it, I am revolted by my arts, I am not *great*, why do I put on a pretence! But, as you well know – I did seek greatness!

'I wanted to play a great man's part, and I convinced many people; but that lie went beyond my strength. That is what is now breaking me.

'Oh Zarathustra, everything about me is a lie; but that I am breaking apart – this is *genuine*!' –

'It honours you,' declared Zarathustra sombrely, gazing down and aside, 'it honours you that you sought greatness, but it betrays you too. You are not great.

'You wicked old sorcerer, *this* is the best and most honest quality that I honour in you: that you have wearied of yourself, and have acknowledged it: "I am not great."

'In *that* I honour you as a penitent of the spirit; and, even if only for a fleeting breath, for that one moment you were – genuine.

'But tell me, what are you doing here in *my* forests and crags? And when you laid yourself in my path, what test were you putting me to? –

– 'what were you tempting *me* to?' –

Thus spake Zarathustra, and his eyes glittered. The old sorcerer was silent for a while, then said: 'Did I tempt you? I only – seek.

'Oh Zarathustra, I am looking for someone who is genuine, upright, simple, straightforward, a man of complete honesty, a repository of wisdom, a saint of understanding, a great human being!

'Do you not know, oh Zarathustra? I am looking for Zarathustra.'

– And at this point a long silence ensued between the two; Zarathustra, however, became deeply immersed within himself, and closed his eyes. But then, returning to his interlocutor, he seized hold of the sorcerer's hand and, replete with courtesy and guile, announced:

'Very well! Up over there is the path to Zarathustra's cave. There you may seek whomever it may be you wish to find.

'And ask my animals for advice, my eagle and my serpent; they shall help you seek. But my cave is big.

'Granted, I myself – I have never yet beheld a great man. The most refined of people today have an eye that is too coarse for what is great. It is the empire of the rabble.

'I have come across many a one who stretched and puffed himself up, and the people exclaimed: "Look, a great man!" But what good are all the bellows? In the end, the wind puffs out again.

'A frog that has been blowing itself up for too long will burst in the end: the wind puffs out. To prick the belly of an inflated windbag is excellent sport, to my mind. Hear what I say, lads!

'The present day belongs to the rabble; which of them still *knows* what is great, what small! Who could engage in a fortunate quest for greatness today? Only a fool; the fool would be fortunate.

'You seek great men, you wondrous fool? Who *taught* you to?

Is this the time to do it? Oh you wicked seeker, why – do you tempt me?' – –

Thus spake Zarathustra, consoled in his heart, and continued, laughing, on his way.

Retired from Service

Not long after Zarathustra had parted from the sorcerer, however, he once again saw someone sitting by the path he was walking along: a tall, dark man with a gaunt, pale face. *This* man properly put him out of sorts. 'Woe,' he said to his heart, 'there sits affliction, disguised, looking to my mind a priestly sort; what are people like *that* doing in my realm?

'What! Barely have I got away from that sorcerer but another master of the black arts must needs cross my path, –

– 'some wizard who practises the laying-on of hands, some dark miracle-worker by the grace of God, some anointed vilifier of the world – the devil take him!

'But the devil is never in the place that would properly be his; he always comes too late, this cursèd dwarf and clubfoot!'

In this manner Zarathustra cursed impatiently in his heart, and wondered how he might slip past the dark man, gaze averted. But see, it turned out differently; for the seated man had already noticed him at the same moment, and, not unlike a man whom unexpected good fortune has befallen, he leapt to his feet and made for Zarathustra.

'Whoever you are, wanderer,' he said, 'help one who has lost his way, a seeker, an old man who may easily come to harm here!

'This world here is unfamiliar to me, and remote, and I have heard wild animals howling; and he who could have given me protection is himself no more.

'I was looking for the last pious person, a saint and hermit, who was the only one, in his forest, who had not yet heard what the whole world now knows.'

'*What* does the whole world now know?' asked Zarathustra. 'Might it be this – that the old god in whom the whole world used to believe is no longer alive?'

'You have said it,' answered the old man, downcast. 'And I served that old god until his final hour.

'Now, however, I am retired from service, without a master, and nonetheless not free, nor cheerful any more for even a single hour, except in my memories.

'That is why I climbed into these mountains, that I might at last celebrate a festival once again, as becomes an old pope and church father; for, you see, I am the last pope! – a festival of pious memories and divine services.

'Now, however, he himself is dead, the most pious of men, that saint in the forest who continuously praised his god with singing and droning.

'When I found his cabin I no longer found the man himself – but I did find two wolves in it, howling over his death – for all the animals loved him. At that I ran away.

'So did I come to these forests and mountains to no purpose? My heart resolved at this that I should seek out another, the most pious of all those who do not believe in God – that I should seek out Zarathustra!'

So said the old man, and took a sharp look at the man standing before him; Zarathustra, however, took hold of the old pope's hand and for a long time contemplated it with admiration.

'Just see, venerable man,' he then said, 'what a beautiful, long hand! It is the hand of one who has always given out blessings. But now it is holding fast the one you are seeking, me, Zarathustra.

'It is I, the godless Zarathustra, he who says: "Who is more god-less than I, that I may enjoy his instruction?"' –

Thus spake Zarathustra, and his gaze penetrated the thoughts and second thoughts of the old pope. At last the latter began:

'He who loved and possessed him the most has now also lost him the most;

− 'see, I myself am surely the more godless of us two now? But who could take pleasure in that!' −

'You served him to the last,' asked Zarathustra thoughtfully, after a profound silence; 'do you know *how* he died? Is what people say true, that he choked on compassion,

− 'that he saw the human hanging on the cross and could not bear it, that love of humankind became his hell and, in the end, the death of him?' − −

But the old pope made no reply, instead looking warily away and aside with a pained and sombre expression.

'Let him be gone,' said Zarathustra after long reflection, continuing to look the old man straight in the eye.

'Let him be gone. He has passed on. And, while it honours you that you speak only well of this deceased, you know as well as I do *who* he was; and that he moved in mysterious ways.'

'Between ourselves,' said the old pope, brightening − 'where only our three eyes may see' (for he was blind in one eye) − 'in matters concerning God I am more enlightened than Zarathustra himself − and have every right to be so.

'My love served him long years, my will attended upon his will entire. A good servant knows everything, though, including things that his master conceals from himself.

'He was a hidden god, full of secrecy. Truly, he even used stealth and subterfuge in order to come by a son. At the door into belief in him stands adultery.

'Whoever praises him as a god of love has too low an opinion of love itself. Did not this god want to be a judge as well? But the lover loves beyond reward and punishment.

'When he was young, this Oriental god, he was hard and vengeful and built himself a hell, to the delight of his favourites.

'At length, however, he grew old and soft and mellow and compassionate, more like a grandfather than a father, but most of all like an unsteady old grandmother.

'There he sat, shrivelled up, in his inglenook, grieving over his weak legs, weary of the world, weary of will, and one day he choked on his own all-too-great compassion.' – –

'Old pope,' put in Zarathustra at this point, 'did you see *that* with your own eyes? No doubt it could have been like that: like that, *and* differently. Invariably, when gods die, they die many kinds of death.

'But very well! One way or another, one way and another – he is gone! He was not to the taste of my own ears and eyes. I shall say nothing worse of him.

'I love everything that is clear-eyed and speaks honestly. But he – you know it well, old priest, there was something of your own manner about him, the manner that priests have – he was ambiguous.

'He was unclear as well. How he raged at us, that wrathful snorter, because we were not good at understanding him. But why did he not speak more clearly?

'And if our ears were at fault, why did he give us ears that heard him poorly? If there was mud in our ears, very well! – who put it there?

'He was a potter who had not fully learnt his skills – too much of what he attempted went wrong! But to take revenge on his pots and creations for having turned out badly – that was a sin against *good taste.*

'Even in piety there is good taste; at last it declared, "Away with a god of *this* sort! Better to have no god, better to shape one's fate by one's own mettle, better to be a fool, better to be God oneself!"'

– 'What do I hear!' the old pope said at this point, pricking up his ears; 'oh Zarathustra, you are more pious than you suppose, with this lack of faith! It was some god within you that converted you to your godlessness.

'Is it not your very piety that no longer permits you to believe in a god? And your overwhelming honesty will yet transport you beyond good and evil, too!

'Just see: what has been kept for you? You have eyes and hands and a mouth, which for all eternity have been destined for blessing. One does not bless with the hand alone.

'Although you would be the most godless of all, I scent about you a secret, sacred, pleasing fragrance, born of long blessings; it fills me with happiness and trepidation.

'Let me be your guest, oh Zarathustra, for a single night! Nowhere on earth shall I now feel better than with you!'

'Amen! So be it!' declared Zarathustra, in great astonishment. 'Up over there is the path, there lies Zarathustra's cave.

'Indeed, I should gladly accompany you there myself, venerable man, for I love all pious men. But now a cry of distress is calling me hastily away from you.

'I shall not have anyone come to any harm in my realm; my cave is a goodly haven. And best of all I should like to set every mournful person on firm land and firm legs again.

'But who could lift *your* heavy spirits from your shoulders? I am too weak for that. Truly, we might be waiting a long time until someone awakened your god for you once more.

'For that old god is no longer alive: he is quite dead.' –

Thus spake Zarathustra.

The Ugliest Man

– And once again Zarathustra's feet took their way among mountains and forests, and his eyes searched and searched, but the one they wanted to see, who suffered greatly and cried out in distress, was nowhere to be seen. All along the way, though, he was jubilant at heart, and thankful. 'What good things', he said, 'this day has given to me, to compensate for beginning badly! What strange people I have found to talk to!

'Now I shall chew their words for a long time, as I would good grain; my teeth shall grind and crush them till they flow into my soul like milk!' – –

But when the path once again led around an outcrop of rock, the landscape was suddenly transformed, and Zarathustra entered a realm of death. Here, black and red crags sheered up starkly; no grass, no tree, no birdsong. It was a valley that every animal avoided, including beasts of prey, with the one exception of a species of ugly, thick, green snakes that went there to die when they grew old. For that reason, the shepherds called that valley: Snakes' Death.

For his part, Zarathustra was immersed in dark recollections, for he had the sense of having stood in that valley once before. And many weighty matters burdened his mind, so that he proceeded slowly, and ever more slowly, and finally stood still. But when he opened his eyes he saw something sitting by the wayside, human in form and yet scarcely like a human being, something inexpressible. And at a stroke Zarathustra was beset by immense shame for having beheld such a thing with his own eyes; blushing right up to his white hair, he averted his gaze and put his foot forward to leave the dreadful place. But at that moment the dead wasteland made a sound: up from the ground came a gurgling, gargling noise like water in blocked-up pipes at night; and at length it resolved itself into a human voice and human utterance, to this effect:

'Zarathustra! Zarathustra! Guess my riddle! Speak, speak! What is *revenge on the witness*?

'I am luring you back! The ice is slippery here! Take care, take care that your pride does not break its legs here!

'You suppose yourself wise, proud Zarathustra! So guess the riddle, you tough nutcracker, – the riddle that is me! Speak out – who am *I*!'

– But when Zarathustra had heard these words, what do you imagine went on in his soul? *He was overcome by compassion*; and all at once he collapsed, like an oak tree that has long withstood numerous woodcutters, – heavily, suddenly, to the alarm even of those who intended to fell it. But promptly he got up again from the ground, and his countenance hardened.

'I know you well,' he declared in tones of brass: '*you are the murderer of God*! Let me go.

'You could not *endure* the one who saw *you* – who saw you

unceasingly, through and through, you ugliest of men! You took revenge on the witness!'

Thus spake Zarathustra, and he made as if to go; but the inexpressible one clutched at the hem of his robe and began once again to gurgle and to grope for words. 'Stay!' he said at last –

– 'stay! Do not pass by! I have guessed what axe it was that felled you; hail unto you, oh Zarathustra, that you are standing again!

'You have divined, I am well aware, how the man feels who killed him – the murderer of God. Stay! Sit down beside me – it is not pointless.

'To whom did I mean to go if not to you? Stay, sit down! But do not look at me! In that way, honour – my ugliness!

'They persecute me; now *you* are my last refuge. *Not* with their hatred, *not* with their henchmen: – oh, I should scoff at such persecution, I should be proud and merry!

'Has not all success until now been with those who have been well persecuted? And those who persecute well easily learn to follow; – after all, they are already coming on behind! But it is their *pity* –

– 'it is their pity I am fleeing from and seeking refuge with you. Oh Zarathustra, protect me, you my last refuge, the only one who guessed at me;

– 'you divined how the man feels who has killed *him*. Stay! And if you will go, impatient man, do not take the path I came by. *That* way is bad.

'Are you angry with me because I have babbled in my incoherent way for too long? Because I am even offering you advice? But know: it is I, the ugliest man,

– 'who also has the biggest, heaviest feet. Wherever *I* have walked, the way is bad. I trample every path into death and shame.

'But that you passed me by in silence; that you blushed, as I well saw: by these things I knew you to be Zarathustra.

'Anyone else would have thrown me his alms, his pity, in a look and a word. But for that – I am not enough of a beggar, as you guessed –

– 'for that I am too rich, rich in what is great, in what is awful, in what is ugliest, in what is most inexpressible! Your shame, oh Zarathustra, *honoured* me!

'With difficulty I extricated myself from the crowd of the compassionate – wanting to find the only one who today teaches: "Compassion is intrusive" – you, oh Zarathustra!

– 'whether it be the compassion of a god or of humankind, compassion runs counter to modesty. And not wanting to help can be more distinguished than that virtue that comes bounding up.

'*That*, however, is what is seen as the very definition of virtue among the little people today: compassion. They are not in awe of great misfortune, or great ugliness, or great failure.

'I look beyond all of them as a dog looks over the backs of teeming flocks of sheep. They are grey little people, well disposed in will and wool alike.

'As a heron gazes contemptuously across shallow pools, with its head held back, so I gaze across the teeming mass of grey little waves and wills and souls.

'For too long they have been agreed with, these little people; and *so*, in the end, they have been given power, too – and now they teach: "Only what little people declare to be good is good."

'And "truth" nowadays is what the preacher has said who himself came from their midst, that wondrous saint and advocate of the little people who has attested of himself: "I – am the truth."

'This immodest man has long been making the little people's cock's-comb bristle up – he, who taught no small error when he taught: "I – am the truth."

'Was ever a more polite response made to an immodest man? – You however, oh Zarathustra, passed him by and said: "No! No! Thrice no!"

'You warned against his error, you were the first to warn against compassion – not everyone, not no one, but yourself and those of your own kind.

'You are shamed by the shame of the great sufferers; and truly, when you say: "a heavy cloud will come from compassion, beware, humanity!"

– 'when you teach "all creators are hard, all great love is superior to compassion"; oh Zarathustra, how well versed you strike me as being in weather signs!

'You yourself, however – warn yourself against *your own* compassion, too! For many are on the way to you, many who are suffering, doubting, despairing, drowning, freezing –

'I warn you against myself, too. You have guessed my best, worst riddle: myself, and what I have done. I know the axe that fells you.

'But he – *had* to die: he saw with eyes that saw everything, – he saw the depths and bottommost foundations of humanity, all its hidden-away disgrace and ugliness.

'His compassion knew no shame: he crept into my dirtiest corners. Most prying, over-intrusive, over-compassionate, he had to die.

'He always saw *me*: I wanted to be revenged on a witness of that kind – or not live myself.

'The god who saw everything, *even the human*: that god had to die! Man could not *endure* that such a witness live.'

So spoke the ugliest man. Zarathustra, however, stood up and prepared to leave; for he was chilled to his very bowels.

'You inexpressible creature,' he said, 'you have warned me against your path. By way of thanks for that, I commend mine to you. See, up there lies Zarathustra's cave.

'My cave is big and deep and has many a nook – the most hidden of men will find a place of concealment there. And close by there are a hundred crannies and back-ways for creatures that creep, flap and jump.

'You outcast, cast out by yourself, do you not want to live among humankind and human compassion? Very well, then do as I do! That way you will learn from me, too. One learns only by doing!

'And first of all, and above all, talk to my animals! The proudest of animals and the most resourceful of animals – they may well be the right ones to advise us both!' – –

Thus spake Zarathustra, and he went on his way, more thoughtfully and even more slowly than before; for he was asking a good many questions of himself, and was hard put to know the answers.

'What a poor thing humankind really is!' he thought within his heart – 'how ugly, how gargling, how full of harboured shame!

'They tell me humanity loves itself; ah, how great must that self-love be! How much contempt it has for itself!

'This creature, too, loved himself as much as he held himself in contempt, – he is a great lover, to my mind, and great in his contempt.

'I have found no other who has held himself in more profound contempt; *that* too is height. Woe, was *he* perhaps the higher human – the one whose cry I heard?

'I love those who are great in contempt. But the human is something that must be overcome.' – –

The Voluntary Beggar

When Zarathustra had left the ugliest man, he felt cold and lonely; for a great deal of coldness and loneliness was coursing through his senses, so much so that his very limbs were growing colder from it. But as he climbed higher and higher, now up, now down, now past green pastures, now over wild, stony places too, where some impatient stream would doubtless have made its bed at one time – he presently felt warmer and more warm-hearted again.

'Whatever has happened to me?' he wondered. 'Something warm and living is revitalizing me. It must be nearby.'

When he looked about, however, and tried to make out who was lending him solace in his solitude, see: it was cattle, standing together on a rise; their closeness and their odour had warmed his heart. But these cows appeared to be listening, rapt, to someone who was speaking, and they took no notice of the walker approaching. Once Zarathustra had reached them, though, he could distinctly hear a human voice speaking from the midst of the cows; and plainly they had all turned their heads towards the speaker.

Zarathustra bounded up to them with a will, and drove the animals apart, fearing that someone had been hurt there, which the sympathy of the cattle could hardly help. But in this he was mistaken; for it turned out, see, that a man was sitting on the ground, apparently urging the animals not to be afraid of him – a peaceable man, a mountain preacher, from whose eyes goodness itself preached. 'What are you looking for here?' exclaimed Zarathustra, taken aback.

'What am I looking for?' answered the man: 'the same thing that you are looking for, you who disturb the peace! That is to say, happiness on earth.

'To that end, though, I wish to learn from these cows. For, you see, I have been talking to them half the morning already, and they were just on the point of telling me what they know. Why do you disturb them?

'Except we be converted and become as the cattle, we shall not enter into the kingdom of heaven. For there is one thing we should learn from them: rumination.

'And truly, if a man should gain the whole world and not learn this one thing, rumination, what would it profit him! He would not be rid of his affliction –

'his great affliction; which in these times, however, is known as *revulsion*. Who in these times does not have his heart, mouth and eyes full of revulsion? You too! You too! But just look at these cows!' –

So said the mountain preacher, and then turned his gaze to Zarathustra – for it had rested lovingly on the cows till this moment; but at that point he was transformed. 'Who is this I am talking to?' he cried out in alarm, and he sprang up from the ground.

'This is the man without revulsion, this is Zarathustra himself who has overcome the great revulsion, this is the eye, this is the mouth, this is the heart of Zarathustra himself.'

And, while he was speaking these words, he kissed the hands of the one he was addressing, his eyes brimming over, and behaved in every way like one to whom a costly gift and jewel has unexpectedly fallen from heaven. The cows, for their part, looked on at all of this in perplexity.

'Do not speak of me, you wondrous man, you gentle-spirited man!' said Zarathustra, fighting his own tenderness. 'First tell me about yourself! Are you not the man who once discarded his great wealth and voluntarily became a beggar, −

− 'who was ashamed of his wealth and of the rich, and fled to the poorest of the poor, to give them his abundance and his heart? But they received him not.'

'But they received me not,' said the voluntary beggar, 'as you know. So in the end I went to the animals, and to these cows.'

'And in that way you learnt,' Zarathustra interrupted the speaker, 'that it is harder to give well than to take well, and that to make a gift well is an art, and the final, subtlest master art of goodness.'

'Particularly nowadays,' answered the voluntary beggar 'today, that is, when all that is lowly has become rebellious and wary and in its own way haughty; that is, in the manner of the rabble.

'For the hour has come, as you know, for the great, evil, long-lasting, gradual uprising of the rabble and slaves; it grows and grows!

'Now, all manner of beneficence and small donation outrages the rabble; and the super-rich had better be on their guard!

'Anyone who dribbles nowadays, like a fat-bellied bottle from a too-narrow neck: − today, people will gladly break the necks of bottles like that.

'Lascivious greed, bilious envy, sour vengefulness, the pride of the rabble: all of this I can see at a glance. It is no longer true that the poor are blessèd. The kingdom of heaven, though, is found among cattle.'

'And why is it not among the rich?' demanded Zarathustra, testing him, all the while warding off the cows, which were snuffling familiarly at the man of peace.

'Why are you testing me?' replied the latter. 'You yourself

know it even better than I. What was it that drove me to the poorest of the poor, oh Zarathustra? Was it not revulsion at the richest among us?

– 'revulsion at those in penal servitude to riches, gleaning their advantage from any rubbish, with their cold eyes and lewd thoughts, revulsion at this rabble that stinks to heaven,

– 'revulsion at this gilded, faked rabble whose fathers were pickpockets or carrion birds or rag-and-bone men, with womenfolk compliant, lascivious, oblivious; – for all of them are not far from being whores –

'rabble above, rabble below! What do "poor" and "rich" still signify today? I put the distinction from my mind – then I fled, further, ever further, till I came to these cows.'

So said the man of peace, and he snuffled too, and perspired as he spoke, leaving the cows once again in perplexity. Zarathustra, however, steadily gazed into his face with a smile as he was speaking so harshly, and silently shook his head.

'You are doing yourself an injury, mountain preacher, in using words of such harshness. Your mouth was not made for such harshness, neither were your eyes.

'Nor your stomach, either, to my way of thinking: *it* finds all such fulmination and detestation and vituperation horrid. Your stomach requires milder things: you are no butcher.

'Far more, you strike me as a man of plants and roots. Perhaps you grind corn. But you are surely averse to the pleasures of the flesh, and love honey.'

'You have divined me well,' answered the voluntary beggar, his heart eased. 'I do love honey, I also grind corn, for I was seeking whatever is sweet-tasting and promotes good breath;

'also, whatever takes a long time, a day's work and a mouth's work for gentle-spirited idlers and sluggards.

'These cows have indeed taken this the furthest: they have come up with rumination and lying in the sun. What is more, they abstain from all weighty thoughts that puff up the heart.'

– 'Very well!' said Zarathustra: 'you ought to see *my* animals, too, my eagle and my serpent, – their like is not to be found on earth today.

'See, up over there is the path to my cave; be my guest for this night. And talk with my animals about the happiness of animals, –

– 'until I return home myself. But now a cry of distress is calling me hastily away from you. You will also find fresh honey in my cave, icy-fresh golden honey from the comb: eat of it!

'But now bid farewell to your cows, right away, you wondrous man, you gentle-spirited man! – even though it may be hard for you, since they are your warmest friends and instructors!' –

– 'Except for one, whom I hold even more dearly,' answered the voluntary beggar. 'You yourself are good, and even better than a cow, oh Zarathustra!'

'Away, away with you! you dreadful flatterer!' yelled Zarathustra maliciously – 'Why are you corrupting me with such praise, and the honey of flattery?

'Away, away from me!' he yelled once again, and swung his stick at the tender beggar; but the latter speedily ran away.

The Shadow

But scarcely had the voluntary beggar run away, and Zarathustra was alone again, but he heard a new voice behind him, calling: 'Stop! Zarathustra! Wait for me! It's me, oh Zarathustra, me, your shadow!' Zarathustra did not wait, however, for he felt suddenly out of humour on account of all the hustle and bustle in his mountains. 'What has become of my solitude?' he said.

'Truly, it is becoming too much for me; these mountains are crowded, my realm is no longer of *this* world, I need new mountains.

'My shadow is calling me? What does my shadow matter! Let it run after me! I – shall run away from it.' –

Thus spake Zarathustra to his heart, and he ran off. But the one who was behind him followed; so that presently there were three of them running, one behind the other, the voluntary beggar in front, then Zarathustra, and, third and last, his shadow. They had not been running like this for long when Zarathustra realized that he was being foolish, and at one go shook off all his ill-humour and antipathy.

'Why,' he pronounced, 'have not the most laughable of things occurred among us old hermits and saints from time immemorial?

'Truly, my folly has grown high in the mountains! Now I hear six old-fool legs rattling along one behind the other!

'But may Zarathustra really be afraid of a shadow? In any case, it strikes me that it has longer legs than I.'

Thus spake Zarathustra, laughing with his eyes and his bowels, and he stopped and turned round quickly – and see, in so doing he almost knocked his follower and shadow to the ground, so hard on his heels was the latter already following him, and so weak was he, too. For when he assessed him with his eyes, he was frightened as if by the sudden appearance of a ghost, so thin, dark, hollow and worn-out did this pursuer look.

'Who are you?' asked Zarathustra vehemently, 'what are you doing here? And why do you call yourself my shadow? I do not like you.'

'Forgive me,' answered the shadow, 'for my being it; and if you do not like me, very well, oh Zarathustra! for that, I praise you and your good taste.

'I am a wanderer, who has already come a long way at your heels, forever moving on, but without a destination, and without a home, too; so that, truly, I am well-nigh the eternal Wandering Jew, except that I am not eternal, nor am I a Jew.

'What? Must I be on my way forever? Whirled by every wind, with no settled place, driven on! Oh earth, you have become too round for me!

'I have already sat on every surface, like weary dust I have fallen asleep on mirrors and window-panes. Everything takes from me, nothing gives, I am growing thin, – I am almost like a shadow.

'But to you, oh Zarathustra, I flew, and you I followed for the longest time; and, even though I hid from you, I was still your best shadow: wherever you sat, I sat too.

'With you I roamed the remotest, coldest worlds, like a ghost walking the winter rooftops and snow of its own free will.

'With you I strove towards all that was forbidden, worst, furthest away; and if anything about me is a virtue, it is that I had no fear of any prohibition.

'With you I shattered whatever my heart had ever revered, I toppled every boundary stone and statue, I pursued the most dangerous of desires, – truly, at some time I went beyond every crime.

'With you I have discarded the belief I had learnt in words and values and great names. When the devil sheds his skin, does his name not fall away as well? – for that too is a skin. Perhaps the devil himself is – a skin.

'"Nothing is true, everything is permitted": that is what I told myself. I plunged into the coldest of waters, with head and heart. Ah, how often I stood naked for that reason, like a red crab!

'Ah, where have all my goodness and shame and belief in those who are good gone! Ah, where is that mendacious innocence that I once possessed, the innocence of the good and their noble lies!

'Truly, too often I followed hard on the heels of the truth; then it kicked me in the head. Sometimes I supposed I was lying, and see! it was only then that I hit – the truth.

'Too much has become clear to me; now it no longer matters to me. Nothing that I love is alive any more – how should I still love myself?

'"To live as I please, or not to live at all": that is how I wish it to be, that is what the holiest of men wants too. But, woe! how is it that *I* still have – desire?

'Do *I* still have – a goal? A port to which *my* sail is headed?

'A fair wind? Ah, only the one who knows *where* he is heading knows too which wind is a fair wind, a wind that will bear him onwards.

'What else was left for me? A heart weary and insolent; a restless will; flapping wings; a broken backbone.

'This seeking for *my* home: oh Zarathustra, do you know that this seeking has been *my* affliction, it is eating me up.

'Where is – *my* home? I am asking and seeking for it and have searched for it but I have not found it. Oh eternal everywhere, oh eternal nowhere, oh eternal – in vain!'

So said the shadow, and Zarathustra's face grew longer at its words. 'You are my shadow!' he said at last, sadly.

'Your danger is no small one, you free spirit and wanderer! You have had a bad day; see to it that the evening is not even worse!

'Those such as yourself, who have no settled place, end by supposing even a prison blessèd. Have you ever seen criminals sleeping in prison? They sleep peacefully, they enjoy their new security.

'Beware, lest in the end some narrow belief, some tough, rigorous delusion, take a hold on you! For you will henceforth be seduced and tempted by anything that is narrow and firm.

'You have lost your goal; woe, how will you laugh off and cope with that loss? In losing it – you have also lost your way!

'You poor rover, dreamer, weary butterfly! Do you want a place to rest and call home this evening? Then go up to my cave!

'Up over there is the path to my cave. And now I shall quickly run away from you again. Already it is as though a shadow lay upon me.

'I shall run alone, so that it grows bright about me once more. For that, I must needs stay sturdily on my feet for a long time. But this evening at my home we shall – dance!' – –

Thus spake Zarathustra.

At Noon

– And Zarathustra ran and ran and found no one else and was alone and found himself time and again and enjoyed and drank in his solitude and thought of good things, – for hours on end. Around noon, however, when the sun was right over Zarathustra's head, he passed an old, crooked and gnarled tree that had been wholly embraced by the rich love of a vine and was hidden from itself; an abundance of yellow grapes hung down to the wanderer. Seeing this, he felt a desire to satisfy a slight thirst and pluck a grape; but, as he was already reaching out his arm to do so, a greater desire to do something else came upon him: that is, to lie down by the tree at the hour of high noon and sleep.

This Zarathustra did; and as soon as he was lying on the ground, in the tranquillity and intimacy of the many-coloured grass, he forgot his slight thirst and fell asleep. For, as Zarathustra's saying goes: one thing is more necessary than another. His eyes, though, remained open; – they did not tire of beholding and celebrating the tree and the love of the vine. As he fell asleep, however, Zarathustra spake thus to his heart:

Soft! Soft! Has not the world just become perfect? What is happening to me?

As a delicate breeze, unseen, dances upon the smooth surface of the sea, light, light as a feather, so – sleep dances upon me.

It does not close my eyes, it leaves my soul awake. It is light, truly! light as a feather.

It persuades me, I know not how? – it caresses me in my innermost places with a flattering hand, it compels me. Yes, it compels me, so that my soul stretches out; –

– how it grows long and weary, my wondrous soul! Did the evening of a seventh day come upon it just now at noon? Has it already been strolling blissfully among good and ripe things for too long?

It stretches out, long, long, – longer! It lies still, my wondrous soul. It has tasted too many good things already; this golden sorrowfulness weighs upon it; it pulls a face.

– Like a ship that has entered its most tranquil bay; – now it leans against the earth, tired after its long voyages and the hazardous oceans. Is the earth not more faithful?

When such a ship docks against the land, nestling against it – it is sufficient if a spider spins a thread to it from the land. No stronger ropes are required.

Like a weary ship such as this, in the most tranquil of bays – I too now come to rest close to the earth, faithful, trusting, waiting, bound to it by the finest of threads.

Oh happiness! Oh happiness! Do you propose to sing, oh my soul? You are lying in the grass. But this is the intimate, solemn hour when no shepherd plays his flute.

Be wary! The heat of noon sleeps upon the fields. Do not sing! Quiet! The world is perfect.

Do not sing, you bird of grass, oh my soul! Do not so much as whisper! Just see – quiet! Old noon is asleep, he is moving his mouth: is he not drinking a drop of happiness –

– an old brown drop of golden happiness, golden wine? It sweeps across him, his happiness laughs. This – is how a god laughs. Quiet! –

'How little it takes, happily, to achieve happiness!' So I once said, and supposed myself clever. But it was blasphemy: I have learnt *that* now. Clever fools speak better.

'It is precisely the littlest thing, the softest, lightest, the rustle of a lizard, a breath, a swish, the twinkling of an eye – it is *little* that defines the *best* happiness. Quiet!

'What has happened to me? Listen! Did time fly away? Am I not falling? Did I not fall – listen! – into the well of eternity?

– 'What is happening to me? Quiet! I am being stabbed – woe! – in the heart! In the heart! Oh break, break, heart, after such happiness, after such a stab!

– 'What? Has not the world just become perfect? Round and ripe? Oh that golden, round circle – where is it flying to? Let me run after it! Whoosh!

'Quiet' – – (and at this point Zarathustra stretched, and sensed that he was sleeping).

'Up!' he said to himself, 'you sleeper! You noontide sleeper!

Very well, on with you, old legs! It is time, more than time, and a good part of the way is still ahead of you –

'Now you have slept as long as you needed. How long was it? Half an eternity! Very well, on with you, my old heart! How long, after such a sleep, do you need to wake?'

(But at this he fell asleep once more, and his soul spoke out against him, and resisted, and lay down again.) – 'Let me be! Quiet! Has not the world just become perfect? Oh that golden, round ball!' –

'Get up,' said Zarathustra, 'you little thief, you lazybones! What? Still stretching, yawning, sighing, falling into deep wells?

'Whoever are you? Oh my soul!' (and here he started, because a ray of sunlight fell from the heavens upon his face).

'Oh sky above me,' he said, sighing and sitting up straight, 'are you watching me? Are you listening to my wondrous soul?

'When will you drink this drop of dew that has fallen on all earthly things – when will you drink this wondrous soul –

– 'when, wellspring of eternity! serene and terrible abyss of noon! When will you drink my soul back into yourself?'

Thus spake Zarathustra, and he got up from his resting-place by the tree as though from a strange intoxication; and see, the sun was still right above his head. One might rightly infer from that, though, that Zarathustra had not been sleeping for long.

The Greeting

It was not until the late afternoon that Zarathustra, after long searching and roaming about in vain, returned home to his cave. When he was facing it, however, and not twenty paces away, something happened that he was now least of all expecting: once again he heard the great *cry of distress*. And, astonishingly! this time it came from his own cave. It was, however, a strange, long-drawn-out cry of varying character, and Zarathustra distinctly made out that it was compounded of numerous voices; even if, when heard from a distance, it might well sound like a cry from a single mouth.

At this, Zarathustra bounded towards his cave, and see! what a scene awaited him following that theatre of voices! For there they all sat together, whom he had passed during the day: the king on the right and the king on the left, the old sorcerer, the pope, the voluntary beggar, the shadow, the conscientious man of the spirit, the sorrowful prophet and the ass; the ugliest man, however, had placed a crown on his own head and wound two purple sashes around himself – for he loved to dress up and pretend to be beautiful, as all ugly people do. In the midst of this sorry gathering, though, stood Zarathustra's eagle, bristling and agitated, for it was expected to give answers to too many things for which its pride had no answer; the subtle serpent, for its part, hung about its neck.

Zarathustra gazed upon all of this in great amazement; then he examined each one of his guests with affable curiosity, read what was in their souls, and marvelled once again. By now those gathered there had risen from their seats and were waiting reverentially for Zarathustra to speak. Zarathustra, however, spake thus:

'You despairers! You wondrous ones! Was it *your* cry of distress I heard, then? And now I also know where to look for the one I sought in vain today: *the higher man* –

– 'he is sitting in my own cave, the higher man! But why am I surprised? Did I myself not lure him to me with honey offerings and the cunning calling-notes of my happiness?

'It seems to me, though, that you are poor company for each other – do you not trouble each other's hearts, you who cry in distress, when you sit here together? First, someone else will have to come,

– 'one who makes you laugh again, a kindly, jolly clown of a chap, a dancer and a breath of fresh air and a scamp, some old fool; – what do you think?

'Do forgive me, you despairers, for uttering such petty words before you, unworthy in truth of such guests! But you do not guess *what* makes my heart wilful: –

− 'it is you yourselves, and the sight of you, if you will forgive me! For anyone grows in courage to see the despairing. To encourage someone who is despairing − everyone imagines himself strong enough to do that.

'You have given that strength to myself − a fine gift, my noble guests! A worthy gift for guests to give! Very well, then do not be angry if I now offer you something of mine.

'This is my realm and my domain; but what is mine shall be yours for this evening and the night. My animals shall serve you; may my cave be your place of rest!

'In my house and home, none shall despair. On my territory, I shall protect everyone from wild animals that beset him. And that is the first thing I offer you: safety!

'But the second is: my little finger. And once you have that, just take the whole of the hand as well, go ahead! and the heart into the bargain! Welcome here as my guests, welcome, friends!'

Thus spake Zarathustra, and he laughed out of love and malice. Following this greeting, his guests bowed once more and remained reverentially silent; the king on the right, however, answered him on their behalf.

'By the manner in which you have offered us your hand and your greeting, oh Zarathustra, we recognize you as Zarathustra. You have humbled yourself before us; you have almost pained our reverence; −

− 'but who would have been able to humble himself with such pride, in your manner? *That* is restorative to us, a balm to our eyes and hearts.

'Simply to see all of this we would gladly climb mountains higher than this mountain. After all, we came here eager to see, we wanted to see whatever makes dim eyes bright.

'And see, already all of our cries of distress are at an end. Already our senses and hearts are open and delighted. It will not take much for our courage to grow wilful.

'Nothing more cheering grows on earth, oh Zarathustra, than

a lofty, strong will; it is the fairest growth of the earth. An entire landscape gains its freshness from one such tree.

'To the pine tree I compare anyone who grows up like you, oh Zarathustra: tall, silent, hard, solitary, of the best and supplest wood, majestic –

– 'in the end, however, reaching out powerful green branches for its dominion, putting robust questions to the winds and storms and whatever else inhabits the high places,

– 'giving more robust answers, a commander, a victor: oh who would not climb high mountains in order to see such trees?

'Even the sombre and the wayward are refreshed at your tree, oh Zarathustra. At the sight of you, those who have no settled place become secure, and their hearts are healed.

'And truly, many hearts gaze towards your mountain and tree in these times; a great longing is abroad, and there are those who have come to ask: who is Zarathustra?

'And anyone into whose ear you have ever dripped your song and your honey, all the hidden ones, the hermits, in their ones and twos, they all suddenly said to their hearts:

'"Is Zarathustra still alive? There is no point in living any more, it is all one, all is vain: or – we must live with Zarathustra!

'"Why does he not come, who has been proclaiming himself for so long?" many ask; "has solitude gobbled him up? Or shall we go to him?"

'Now solitude itself becomes rotten, and crumbles like a tomb falling apart that can no longer hold its dead. Everywhere one sees the resurrected.

'Now the waves rise and rise about your mountain, oh Zarathustra. And however high your summit may be, many must go up to you; your barque will not be left high and dry for much longer.

'And if we despairers have now come into your cave and have already ceased to despair, it is merely a token, a sign that better men are on their way to you, –

– 'for it is on its way to you, itself, the last remnant of God among humanity, that is to say: all humankind with a great longing, a great revulsion, a great weariness,

– 'all who do not wish to live unless they learn to *hope* again – unless they learn from you, oh Zarathustra, the great hope!'

So spoke the king on the right, and he took Zarathustra's hand in order to kiss it; but Zarathustra warded off his veneration and took a step back, startled, silently and abruptly, as if fleeing into far-away distances. After a short while, though, he was once again with his guests, gazed at them with bright and scrutinizing eyes, and said:

'My guests, you higher men, I shall speak plainly and in plain German to you. It was not for *you* that I was waiting here in these mountains.'

('Plainly and in plain German? God have mercy!' the king on the left said at this point, aside; 'one can tell that he is unfamiliar with the good Germans, this wise man from the Orient!

'But he means "coarsely and in coarse German" – very well! Nowadays that shows not the worst of taste!')

'Truly, you may all be higher men,' Zarathustra went on; 'but for me – you are not high and strong enough.

'For me, that is to say: for the inexorable force within me that is silent but will not always be silent. And if you belong to me, it is not as my right arm belongs to me.

'Whoever stands on sickly and delicate legs, as you do, wants more than anything else, whether he knows it or conceals it from himself: to be *spared*.

'My arms and my legs, however, I do not spare. I do not spare *my warriors*; how could you then be fit for *my* war?

'With you, I should still spoil very victory. And there are those among you who would fall down simply at the sound of my loud drums.

'You are not sufficiently comely or well born for me, either. I require pure, smooth mirrors for my teachings; on your surface, my very reflection is distorted.

'Your shoulders are burdened with many a load, many a memory; there are evil dwarves squatting in your nooks. There is also a rabble hidden away in you.

'And even though you may be of a high and higher order, there is much about you that is crooked and malformed. There is not a smith in the world who could hammer you straight and into shape for me.

'You are only bridges; may men higher than you cross over by stepping upon you! You have the significance of steps; so do not be annoyed at the one who climbs over you up to *his* height!

'From your seed, a genuine son and perfect heir may one day grow for me; but that is far away. It is not you yourselves to whom my legacy and name belong.

'It is not for you that I am waiting here in these mountains, it is not with you that I may make the descent for the last time. You came to me merely as signs that higher ones are already on their way to me, –

– '*not* those of the great longing, the great revulsion, the great weariness, and what you called the last remnant of God.

– 'No! No! Thrice no! It is for *others* that I am waiting here in these mountains, and I shall not stir my foot from here without them,

– 'for higher, stronger, more victorious, more good-tempered ones, such as are built four-square in body and soul; it is *laughing lions* that must come!

'Oh my guests, you wondrous ones, have you not heard anything yet of my children? And that they are on their way to me?

'Speak to me of my gardens, of my Fortunate Isles, of my beautiful new kind, – why do you not speak to me of these things?

'This gift of the guests I request of your love: that you speak to me of my children. To that end I am rich, to that end I became poor; what did I not give,

'what would I not give, to have one thing: *these* children, *this* living planting, *these* trees of life of my will and of my highest hope!'

Thus spake Zarathustra, and abruptly broke off his discourse; for he was overcome with longing, and his heart was so moved that he closed his eyes and mouth. And all his guests were silent as well, and stood motionless and disconcerted; except that the old prophet made signs with his hands and movements.

The Last Supper

It was at this point that the prophet interrupted the greetings of Zarathustra and his guests; he pushed to the fore like one with no time to lose, seized hold of Zarathustra's hand, and exclaimed: 'But Zarathustra!

'One thing is more necessary than another, as you yourself say; very well, one thing is now more necessary to *me* than everything else.

'One word at the proper moment: did you not invite me to a *meal*? And there are many here who have come a long way. You do not mean to feed us nothing but speeches?

'And anyway, to my mind you have all been thinking too much about freezing, drowning, suffocating, and other physical emergencies; but none of you has given a thought to *my* emergency, that is: starvation' –

(So said the prophet; when Zarathustra's animals heard the words, however, they ran away in alarm. For they could see that everything they had brought home during the day would not be enough to fill this one prophet.)

'And dying of thirst,' added the prophet. 'And although I hear water here, splashing forth plentifully and inexhaustibly, like speeches of wisdom, I – want *wine*!

'Not everyone is a born water-drinker like Zarathustra. What's more, water is no good for weary, sagging men; wine is the proper thing for *us*, – only *wine* can restore us in an instant, and give us our health spontaneously!'

At this, when the prophet requested wine, the king on the left, the silent one, also chanced to say his piece. 'As for wine,' he announced, '*we* have taken care of that, I together with my brother, the king on the right; we have wine enough – an entire ass's load of it. So all that is lacking is bread.'

'Bread?' responded Zarathustra, and he laughed. 'Bread is the one thing that hermits do not have. But man does not live by bread alone, but also by the flesh of good lambs, of which I have two.

– 'Let *them* be slaughtered right away, and prepared spicily, with sage; that is how I like it. Neither is there any lack of roots and fruits, good enough even for gourmets and epicures; nor of nuts or other riddles to crack.

'Soon, then, we shall be making a fine supper together. But anyone who wants to eat will have to lend a hand too, even the kings. At Zarathustra's, you see, even a king may be a cook.'

This proposal very much appealed to all of them; except that the voluntary beggar objected to meat and wine and spices.

'Just listen to this glutton, Zarathustra!' he said jokingly: 'does one go into caves and up into the mountains for meals of this kind?

'Certainly, I now understand what he once taught us: "Praised be a moderate poverty!" – and why he wants to abolish beggars.'

'Be of good cheer,' Zarathustra answered him, 'as I am. Abide by your customary ways, you excellent fellow. Grind your corn, drink your water, praise your cooking; as long as it makes you happy!

'I am a law unto my own kind only, I am not a law for all. Those who are with me, though, must be strong in their bones and light on their feet, –

– 'merry at wars and at festivals, neither melancholics nor dreamers, as ready for the toughest tasks as for the feasts, healthy and hale.

'The best are of my kind and are mine; and what we are not given, we take: – the best food, the clearest sky, the strongest thoughts, the most beautiful women!' –

Thus spake Zarathustra; but the king on the right rejoined: 'Curious! Were ever such clever things heard from the mouth of a wise man?

'And truly, it is the most curious thing about a wise man, if he is clever on top of everything, and no ass.'

So said the king on the right, and he marvelled; but the ass replied to his speech with a mischievous 'Yee-hah'. Yet this was the beginning of that long meal which is known to the history books as 'The Last Supper'. And at that meal the talk was of nothing other than *the higher man.*

Of the Higher Man

1

When I went among humankind for the first time, I committed the folly of hermits, the great folly: I set up in the marketplace.

And when I spoke to everyone, I was speaking to no one. In the evening, however, tightrope-walkers and corpses were my companions; and I myself well-nigh a corpse.

On the new morrow, though, a new truth came to me: I learnt to say, 'What are the marketplace and the rabble and the din of the rabble and the rabble's long ears to me!'

You higher men, learn this from me: in the marketplace nobody believes in higher men. And if you want to speak there, go ahead! But the rabble will blink and say, 'We are all equal.'

'You higher men,' – thus the rabble, blinking – 'there are no higher men. We are all equal. Humans are humans. Before God – we are all equal!'

Before God! – But now that god has died. Before the rabble, though, we do not want to be equal. You higher men, get out of the marketplace!

2

Before God! – But now that god has died! You higher men, that god was the greatest danger to you.

Only since he has lain in his grave have you been resurrected. Only now is the great noon approaching, only now will the higher man become – the master!

Have you understood what I have said, oh my brothers? You are alarmed; are your hearts reeling? Is the abyss yawning for you? Is the hound of hell barking at you here?

Very well! Onwards, you higher men! Only now is the mountain of humanity's future in labour. God has died; now *we* want – the superhuman to live.

3

Nowadays the most reflective are asking: 'How shall humanity survive?' Zarathustra, however, is the first and only one to ask: 'How shall humanity be *overcome*?'

I have the superhuman at heart, *that* is my first and only concern, – and *not* the human; not the closest, not the poorest, not the most suffering, not the best –

Oh my brothers, what I can love in the human is that it is both a crossing-over and a going-down. And in you too there is much that makes me love and hope.

The fact that you feel contempt, you higher men, gives me hope. For those who are great in contempt are the great venerators.

The fact that you feel despair is greatly to be honoured. For you did not learn how to submit. You did not learn the petty stratagems of resourcefulness.

For today the little people are the masters: they all preach submissiveness and acquiescence and resourcefulness and diligence and consideration and the long *and so on* of the petty virtues.

Whatever is womanish, whatever has a servant's way, and especially the hotchpotch of the rabble: that is what now aims to be master over all humanity's fate – oh revulsion! revulsion! revulsion!

That keeps on asking and asking and does not tire of it: 'How shall humanity survive, best, longest, most pleasantly?' And that – makes them the masters of today.

Overcome these masters of today for me, oh my brothers, – these little people; *they* are the greatest danger to the superhuman!

Overcome for me, you higher men, the petty virtues, the petty stratagems of resourcefulness, the grain-of-sand considerations, the ant-like scrabbling in a heap, the pitiable comfort, the 'happiness of the greatest number' – !

And despair rather than submit. And, truly, I love you because you do not know how to live in these times, you higher men! In that way *you* live – best of all!

4

Do you have courage, oh my brothers? Are you hearty? *Not* courage before witnesses, but the courage of the hermit or the eagle, which is not observed even by any god.

Cold souls, mules, blind people, drunkards do not count as hearty with me. He who has a heart is the one who knows fear but *masters* fear, who sees the abyss but sees it with *pride* –

who sees the abyss but sees it with the eyes an eagle, *grasps* it with the talons of an eagle; he has courage. – –

5

'Man is evil' – so all the wisest of men have declared, to console me. Ah, if only that is still true today! For evil is the best strength of humanity.

'Humanity must become better and more evil' – that is *my* teaching. The greatest evil is essential to the best in the superhuman.

It may have been good for that preacher of the little people to suffer and bear the sin of humankind. I, however, delight in great sin as my great *consolation*. –

Such things are not said for long ears, though. Nor does every word have a place in every mouth. These are subtle, remote matters, not to be grasped at with sheep's hooves!

6

You higher men, do you suppose I am here to set to rights whatever you have done badly?

Or that I want to go on making more comfortable beds for you who suffer? Or showing new and easier pathways to you who have no settled place, you who have wandered or climbed the wrong way?

No! No! Thrice no! Ever more and ever better of your sort shall perish, – for life shall be ever tougher and harder for you. Only in this way,

– only in this way will humankind grow up to *that* height where lightning will strike and shatter it: high enough for lightning!

My thoughts and my longing go to whatever is few, and long-enduring, and far-off; how could your petty, numerous, brief misery be of any concern to me!

You are not yet suffering enough, to my mind! For you are suffering on your own account, not yet *on account of the human*. You would be lying if you said anything else! None of you suffers what I have suffered. – –

7

It is not enough for me that lightning no longer does any harm. I do not want to conduct it away; I want it to learn – to work for *me*. – My wisdom has long been gathering like a cloud; it is growing stiller and darker. This is the way of all wisdom that will *one day* deliver lightning bolts. –

For these people of the present day I do not wish to be *light*, to be called light. *These* – I wish to blind; lightning of my wisdom, put out their eyes!

8

Do not aim for anything that is beyond your capacity; there is a woeful falseness in those who aim beyond their capacity.

Particularly when they aim for great things! For they awaken mistrust of great things, these subtle counterfeiters and actors; –

– until in the end they are false before themselves, squint-eyed, whitewashed worm-ridden rot, cloaked in powerful words, in virtuous display, in dazzling false works.

Be on your guard, you higher men! For there is nothing in the present day that I count more precious and more uncommon than honesty.

Does this present day not belong to the rabble? The rabble, however, does not know what is great, what is small, what is straight and honest; it is innocently crooked, it invariably lies.

9

Be possessed of a sound mistrust, you higher men, you who are hearty and open-hearted! And keep your reasons secret! For this present day belongs to the rabble.

Who could overthrow with reasons anything that the rabble has once learnt to believe without reason?

And in the marketplace one is convincing through gestures. But reasons rouse the rabble's mistrust.

And if the truth has been victorious for once, ask yourselves with a sound mistrust: 'What powerful error was fighting on its side?'

Beware of the scholars as well! They hate you; for they are barren! They have cold, dried-up eyes; before their gaze, every bird is plucked bare of feathers.

Such people brag that they do not lie; but an inability to lie is not by a long way the same as a love of truth. Be on your guard!

Freedom from fever is not by a long way the same as understanding! I have no faith in frozen spirits. Those who cannot lie do not know what truth is.

10

If you want to ascend high up, use your own legs! Do not have yourselves *carried* up, do not sit on the backs and heads of strangers!

But you mounted a horse? Now you are riding briskly up towards your goal? Go right ahead, my friend! But your lame foot is on the horse with you!

When you are at your goal, when you jump down from your horse: it will be there, at your *height*, you higher man – that you will stumble!

11

You creators, you higher men! One is pregnant only with one's own child.

Do not let anyone dictate to you or talk you into anything! After all, who is *your* neighbour? And even if you are acting 'for your neighbour' – you are still not creating for him!

Unlearn that 'for', you creators; it is your very virtue that requires you to do nothing 'for' or 'so that' or 'because'. You should seal up your ears against these false little words.

That 'for your neighbour' is a virtue only among the little people; their talk is of 'birds of a feather' and 'one good turn'; – they have neither the right nor the strength for *your* selfishness!

Your selfishness, creators, contains the caution and the providence of the pregnant! What no one has yet set eyes on, the fruit; that is guarded and protected and nourished by the whole of your love.

Where the whole of your love is, with your child, the whole of your virtue is as well! Your work, your will, is *your* 'neighbour'; let no one persuade you of false values!

12

You creators, you higher men! Anyone who has to give birth is sick; but anyone who has given birth is unclean.

Ask women: one does not give birth for fun. Pain makes hens and poets cackle.

You creators, there is a good deal about you that is unclean. That is because you had to be mothers.

A new child: oh how much new dirt has also come into the world! Make way there! And anyone who has given birth should wash his soul clean!

13

Do not be virtuous beyond your powers! And demand nothing of yourselves that goes against probability!

Walk in the footsteps made by the virtue of your fathers! How could you climb high if the will of your fathers did not climb with you?

But whoever wishes to be the first should watch out that he does not become the last! And where the vices of your fathers are found, do not affect to be saints!

He whose forefathers loved women and strong wine and roast boar; what price he require chastity of himself?

It would be foolishness! To my mind it would truly be a great deal if such a man were husband to one or two or three women.

And if he founded monasteries, and inscribed over the door: 'The way to all that is holy', – I should still say: Pointless! It is yet more foolishness!

And if he founded a house of correction and a sanctuary for himself, good for him! But I do not believe in it.

What grows in solitude is what a man takes into it, including the beast within himself. This being the case, many should be advised against solitude.

Has there ever been anything filthier on earth than the desert saints? Not only the devil kept *close to them* – but the swine too.

14

Wary, shamed, awkward, like a tiger that has failed in a leap: that, you higher men, is how I have often seen you slink away. You failed in a *throw*.

But what of it, you dice-throwers! You have not learnt to play and mock as one ought to play and mock! Are we not always sitting at a big table for mockery and playing?

And if you have failed in something great, does that make you yourselves – failures? And if you yourselves are failures, does that

277

make humanity – a failure? If humanity is a failure, however, very well! onwards!

15

The higher its kind, the more infrequently a thing succeeds. You higher men here, are you not all – failures?

Be of good courage, what does it matter? How much remains possible! Learn to laugh at yourselves as one ought to laugh!

No wonder that you failed and half succeeded, you who are half broken! Is it not pressing and thrusting within you – humanity's *future*?

All that is furthest, deepest, highest like the stars, in humanity – humanity's immense strength – is not all of it frothing in your pot?

No wonder many a pot is broken! Learn to laugh at yourselves as one ought to laugh! You higher men, oh how much remains possible!

And, in truth, how much has already succeeded! How rich is this earth in small, good, perfect things, in things that have turned out well!

Surround yourselves with small, good, perfect things, you higher men! Their golden ripeness heals the heart. Whatever is perfect teaches one to hope.

16

What has hitherto been the greatest sin here on earth? Was it not the words of him who said: 'Woe unto those who laugh here!'

Did he himself find nothing to laugh about on earth? In that case, he was not looking well. A child will still find something to laugh about here.

He – did not love enough; otherwise he would also have loved us, who laugh! But he detested and scorned us. He promised us wailing and gnashing of teeth.

Must one be quick to curse, where one does not love? That –
strikes me as bad taste. But that was what he did, this unconditional
man. He came from the rabble.

And he himself simply did not love enough; otherwise he would
not have been so angry at not being loved. Great love never *wants*
love; – it wants more than that.

Give a wide berth to all such unconditional men! They are of a
poor, sickly sort, a rabble sort; they look upon this life malevolently,
they have the evil eye for this earth.

Give a wide berth to all such unconditional men! They have
heavy feet and stuffy hearts; – they do not know how to dance. How
could the earth be light for such people!

17

All good things approach their goals obliquely. Like cats they arch
their backs, they purr inwardly at their imminent good fortune, – all
good things laugh.

The stride indicates whether a man his walking *his own* path:
just see me stepping out! But he who is nearing his goal dances.

And truly, I have not become a statue, I am not standing here
yet, rigid, a stony stump, a pillar; I love running quickly.

And though there are swamps and deep bleakness on earth, the
light of foot will run even across mud, and dance as on swept ice.

Lift up your hearts, my brothers, high! higher! And let me not
see you forgetting your legs! Lift your legs too, you splendid dancers; and, better still, stand on your heads!

18

This crown of the man who laughs, this crown of wreathed roses;
I myself have placed this crown on my head, I myself declared my
laughter holy. I found no one else in the present day who was strong
enough to do it.

Zarathustra the dancer, Zarathustra the light, who beckons with his wings, ready to fly, waving to all the birds, prepared and all set, blissfully light of instinct; –

Zarathustra the prophet, Zarathustra the laughing prophet, neither impatient nor unconditional, one who loves leaps and side-leaps; I myself have placed this crown on my head!

19

Lift up your hearts, my brothers, high! higher! And let me not see you forgetting your legs! Lift your legs too, you splendid dancers; and, better still, stand on your heads!

There are animals that are heavy of foot even in good fortune. There are those that are clumsy-footed from the start. Their efforts are strange to see, like an elephant trying to stand on its head.

But it is still better to be foolish in good fortune than foolish in misfortune, better to dance clumsily than to walk lame. So learn my wisdom from me: even the worst thing has two good obverse sides, –

– even the worst thing has good dancing legs; so learn from me, you higher men, to stand on your own well-made legs!

Cast off the trumpeting of misery and all the rabble sorrowfulness you have learnt! Oh how sad the rabble's jokers seem to me today! But this present day belongs to the rabble.

20

Be like the wind when it rushes out from its mountain caves; it means to dance to its own pipes, the oceans tremble and rise beneath its footsteps.

He who gives wings to asses and milks lionesses – praised be that excellent, unbridled spirit who comes like a storm wind to every present day and every rabble, –

– who is an enemy to all thistle-heads and nitpicker-heads and all withered leaves and weeds: praised be that wild, excellent, free storm-spirit that dances on marshes and miseries as upon meadows!

– who detests the rabble's consumptive curs and all dismal

breeds grown out of true: praised be that spirit of all free spirits, the laughing storm who blows dust in the eyes of all that festers and sees blackness!

You higher men, the worst thing about you is: none of you has learnt to dance as one ought to dance – beyond yourselves! What does it matter that you have failed!

How much remains possible! So do learn to laugh beyond yourselves! Lift up your hearts, you splendid dancers, high! higher! And let me not see you forgetting to laugh well, too!

This crown of the man who laughs, this crown of wreathed roses: I throw this crown to you, my brothers! I have declared laughter holy; you higher men, *learn* to laugh for me!

The Song of Melancholy

1

When Zarathustra delivered these discourses, he was standing near the entrance to his cave; with the last words, however, he slipped away from his guests and fled for a short time into the open.

'Oh pure scents about me,' he exclaimed, 'oh blessèd stillness about me! But where are my animals? Come here, come here, my eagle and my serpent!

'Tell me, my animals: these higher men, taken all together – do they perhaps not *smell* good? Oh pure scents about me! Only now do I know and feel how I love you, my animals.'

– And Zarathustra spake once more: 'I love you, my animals!' But when he said these words the eagle and the serpent pressed close to him and gazed up at him. The three of them stood like this in silence, and sniffed and snuffled the good air together. For the air here outside was better than with the higher men.

2

Barely had Zarathustra left his cave, however, but the old sorcerer got to his feet, cast a sly look around, and announced: 'He has gone!

'And already, you higher men – to think that I am tickling you with that term of praise and flattery, as he himself does! – already my wicked spirit of deceit and sorcery is besetting me, my melancholy devil,

– 'who is an adversary of this Zarathustra from the very foundations; forgive him for that! Now he *wishes* to perform some magic before you, this is *his* hour; I wrestle in vain with this wicked spirit.

'To all of you, whatever honours you confer upon yourselves with words, calling yourselves "the free spirits" or "the men of truth" or "the penitents of the spirit" or "the unfettered" or "the men of great longing" –

– 'to all of you, who suffer *the great revulsion* as I do, for whom the old god has died but no new god yet lies in his cradle and swaddling-clothes, – to all of you, my wicked spirit and devil of sorcery is well disposed.

'I know you, you higher men, I know him, – I also know this monster whom I love against my will, this Zarathustra; often I think that he himself is like the beautiful mask of a saint,

– 'is like some new, wondrous mummery which my wicked spirit, the melancholy devil, revels in; – often I think that I love Zarathustra for my wicked spirit's sake. –

'But already *he* is besetting and compelling me, this spirit of melancholy, this devil of the evening twilight; and, truly, you higher men, he has a desire –

– 'just open your eyes! – he has a desire to come *naked*, whether in male or female form I do not know; but he is coming, he is compelling me, woe! open up your senses!

'Day is fading, evening is coming to all things now, even to the best of things; listen now and see, you higher men, what devil, be it man or woman, this spirit of evening melancholy is!'

So said the old sorcerer, cast a sly look around, and then picked up his harp.

3

When the air's brightness is fading,
When the dew's consolation
Is settling on the earth,
Invisible, unheard as well –
For dew the comforter
Wears soft shoes like all tender comforters;
Do you recall, hot heart, do you,
How you once thirsted
For heavenly tears and dropping dew,
Scorched and weary you thirsted,
While on the yellow paths of grass
The spiteful beams of evening sun
Ran all around, amid black trees,
Dazzling beams of glowing sun, *Schadenfroh*.

'A suitor for the *truth*? You?' – so they sneered –
'No! Only a poet!
An animal, cunning, preying, slinking,
That has to lie,
That knowingly, willingly has to lie:
Lusting after prey,
Masked in motley,
A mask to itself,
A prey to itself –
That – a suitor for the truth?
No! Only a fool! Only a poet!
Only speaking motley,
Yelling motley from behind fools' masks,
Climbing about on lying word-bridges,
On many-coloured rainbows,
Between false heavens
And false earths,
Roving here, floating there, –

Only a fool! *Only* a poet!

'That – a suitor for the truth?
Not still, rigid, smooth, cold,
Become an image,
Become a pillar of a god,
Not standing in front of temples,
The guard at a god's door;
No! Opposed to those statues of truth,
More at home in any wilderness than in front of temples,
Full of the wilfulness of cats,
Leaping through every window,
Whoosh! into anything chance may bring,
Sniffing out every jungle,
Sniffing with addicted longing,
That you might run in jungle
Sinfully healthy and many-coloured and beautiful
Among parti-coloured beasts of prey,
Run with lustful chaps,
Blissfully scornful, blissfully hellish, blissfully bloodthirsty,
Preying, slinking, lying;

'Or like the eagle that stares
For long, long times into abysses,
Into *its* abysses; – –
Oh how they circle down,
Downwards and in,
Into ever deeper depths! –
Then,
Suddenly, in one straight move,
In a flight like a shot,
Pouncing on *lambs*,
Abruptly down, ravenous,
Lusting for lambs,
Grudging all lamb-souls,

Grimly grudging all that looks
Sheep-like, lamb-eyed, curly-woolled,
Grey, with lamb-and-sheep goodwill!

'So too
Like the eagle, like the panther,
Are the longings of the poet,
Are *your* longings behind a thousand masks,
You fool! You poet!

'You who have seen the human
As God and as sheep; –
To *tear* the god in the human
And so too the sheep in the human,
And *laugh* as you tear –

'*That, that* is your bliss!
The bliss of the panther and eagle!
The bliss of the poet and fool!' – –

When the air's brightness is fading,
When the sickle of the moon
Is creeping green and envious
Amid the purple reds of dusk; –
Enemy to day,
Secretly with every step
Scything at the hammocks of the roses
Till they fall,
Pale, fall nightward, down;

So I myself once fell
From my madness of truth,
From my longings of the day,
Weary of day, sick from the light, –
Fell downwards, eveningwards, shadowwards;
Burnt and thirsty
From one truth; –

285

Do you recall, hot heart, do you,
How you once thirsted? –
That I be banished
From all truth,
Only a fool!
Only a poet!

Of Science

So sang the sorcerer; and all who were assembled there were caught unawares, like birds, in the net of his sly and melancholy sensuousness. Only the conscientious man of the spirit was not taken in; without delay he took the harp from the sorcerer and cried out: 'Air! Let in some fresh air! Let Zarathustra in! You are making this cave stuffy and poisonous, you evil old sorcerer!

'You are leading us into unknown desires and wildernesses, you deceitful, subtle man. And woe if such as you make a song and dance about the *truth*!

'Woe unto all free spirits who are not on their guard against sorcerers of *such* a kind! That is the end of their freedom; your teaching and your tempting aim back into prisons, –

'you old melancholy devil, a bird-call lures from out of your lament; you are like those whose praise of chastity is a closet invitation to sensuous excesses!'

So said the man of conscience; the old sorcerer, however, looked around, relishing his victory, and for its sake swallowed down the vexation caused him by the conscientious man. 'Be quiet!' he said in temperate tones, 'good songs need a good space to resound in – after good songs one should keep a long silence.

'That is what all of these here are doing, the higher men. But you, I take it, have understood little of my song? There is not much of the spirit of magic in you.'

'You praise me', rejoined the conscientious man, 'in distinguishing me from yourself. Very good! But you others, what do I see? You are all still sitting there with eyes of lust; –

'You free souls, what has become of your freedom! To my mind you are well-nigh like men who have spent a long time watching bad girls dancing in the nude; your souls are dancing too!

'In you, you higher men, there must be more of what the sorcerer called his wicked spirit of deceit and sorcery – we must be different, presumably.

'And in truth we talked and thought enough together, before Zarathustra returned home to his cave, for me not to know it: we *are* different.

'We are *looking for* different things, you and I, even up here. For my part, I am looking for *more security*; that is why I came to Zarathustra. He, after all, is still the sturdiest tower and will –

– 'in these days when everything is teetering , when all the earth is quaking. But you, when I see the expressions in your eyes, I almost have the feeling that you are after more *insecurity*,

'more horror, more danger, more earthquakes. I almost have the feeling – forgive me my presumption, you higher men – that you are lusting,

– 'lusting for the most dreadful and dangerous of lives, such as frightens *me* the most: for the life of wild animals, for forests, caves, steep mountains, and twisty gorges.

'And it is not those who guide you *out of* danger whom you like best, but those who lead you away from all the paths, the tempters. But even if a lust such as this is *really* present in you, I nonetheless consider it *impossible.*

'Fear – that is, humankind's hereditary and fundamental sensation; in fear lies the explanation of all things, whether original sin or original virtue. Out of fear arose *my own* virtue, too: knowledge.

'Fear of wild animals – this has been bred into humankind for the longest time, and includes the animal man hides within himself and fears; – Zarathustra calls it "the inner beast".

'Age-old fear of this kind, ultimately grown subtle, spiritual, intellectual – it seems to me that that is what is nowadays known as: knowledge.'

So said the conscientious man; but Zarathustra, who had just returned to his cave and, hearing this last speech, had guessed at what was meant, threw a handful of roses to the conscientious man and laughed at his 'truths'. 'What's this?' he exclaimed. 'What did I just hear? Truly, it occurs to me that you are a fool, or else I am myself; and I shall turn your "truth" upside-down without more ado.

'*Fear*, you see – is the exception for us. Courage, though, and adventure, and relish of the uncertain, of what no one has dared, – *courage* seems to me the whole prehistory of humanity.

'Man has envied the wildest, most courageous animals all their virtues, and has robbed them of them; only by doing so did he become – man.

'*That* courage, ultimately grown subtle, spiritual, intellectual, that human courage with eagle wings and the cunning of the serpent: that, it seems to me, is what is nowadays known as' –

'*Zarathustra!*' all of those sitting together cried as if from a single mouth, and they all burst into loud laughter; it rose from them like a heavy cloud, though. The sorcerer laughed too, and said cannily: 'Very good! It has gone, my wicked spirit!

'And did I not warn you against him myself, when I said he was a fraud, a liar and a deceiving spirit?

'What's more, especially when he shows himself naked. But what can *I* do about his mischievous ways? Did *I* create him and the world?

'Very well! Let us be good again and of good cheer. And even if Zarathustra casts bad-tempered glances – just look at him! he is cross with me; –

– 'before night falls he will learn afresh to love and praise me, he cannot live long without committing such follies.

'*He* – loves his enemies; he has the best understanding of that art of any I have seen. But he takes revenge for it – on his friends!'

So said the old sorcerer, and the higher men applauded him;

so that Zarathustra went about, mischievously and lovingly shaking his friends' hands, – as if he were one who had to make amends and apologize to them all for something. But when in doing so he came to the entrance to his cave, the desire for the fresh air outside and for his animals came upon him once more, – and he made to slip outside.

Among the Daughters of the Desert

1

'Do not go!' said the wanderer who called himself Zarathustra's shadow, 'stay with us, or the old dismal despondency may beset us once again.

'The old sorcerer has already served up his worst for us, and just see: the devout old pope over there has tears in his eyes and has put out once again on to the sea of melancholy.

'Well may these kings still be putting a good face on things before us; for that is something *they* have today learnt best of all of us! If they had no witnesses, though, I wager that the woeful charade would start anew even with them –

– 'the woeful charade of scudding clouds, of damp depression, of overcast skies, of stolen suns, of howling autumn winds,

– 'the woeful charade of our howls and cries of distress; stay with us, oh Zarathustra! There is a great deal of hidden misery here that wants to speak, a great deal of evening, of cloud, of stuffy air!

'You nourished us with the strong fare of men, and powerful dicta; do not allow us to be beset once again, for dessert, by soft, effeminate spirits!

'You alone make the air about you bracing and clear! Have I ever found such fresh air on earth as with you in your cave?

'For I have seen many lands, my nose has learnt to assess and appraise air of many kinds; but with you my nostrils are savouring their greatest pleasure!

'Except, – except – oh, forgive me an old memory! Forgive me an old after-dinner song that I once composed among the daughters of the desert –

– 'for the air in their parts was fresh, bright, Oriental air; there I was furthest from cloudy, damp, melancholy old Europe!

'At that time I loved Oriental girls of that kind, and another blue kingdom of heaven over which hang neither clouds nor thoughts.

'You would not believe how daintily they say there when they were not dancing, immersed, but not in thoughts, like little secrets, like beribboned riddles, like dessert nuts –

'many-coloured and enigmatic, indeed! but without clouds riddles that can be guessed; it was for the sake of such girls that I thought up, at that time, an after-dinner psalm.'

So said the wanderer and shadow; and before anyone made reply he had seized the old sorcerer's harp, crossed his legs, and was gazing calmly and sagely about him; – with his nostrils, however, he drew the air in slowly and inquiringly, like a man tasting the new and unfamiliar air of new countries. Then he began to sing, in a kind of roar.

2

The desert is growing; woe unto him who harbours deserts within!

> – Ha! Solemnly!
> Solemnly indeed!
> A worthy beginning!
> Solemn in an African manner!
> Worthy of a lion
> Or of a moral howling monkey –
> But nothing for you,
> You dearest of friends,
> At whose feet I,
> For the first time,
> A European beneath the palms,

Am permitted to sit. Selah.

Truly wondrous!
Here I now sit,
Close to the desert and yet
So far from the desert again,
Nor in anything laid waste;
Swallowed down, in fact,
By this smallest of oases; –
It simply opened, yawning,
Its delicate mouth,
Its most fragrant of all little mouths;
I fell right in,
Down, right through – among you,
You dearest of friends! Selah.

Hail, all hail to that whale
If he made his guest
As welcome as this! – you follow
My learned allusion?
All hail to his belly
If it was
As lovely an oasis belly
As this; which, though, I beg to doubt –
Coming from Europe as I do,
Which is more addicted to doubt
Than any little elderly wives.
May God make this better!
Amen!

Here I now sit
In this smallest of oases,
Like a date,
Brown, fully sweet, flush with gold,
Lusting for a girl's full mouth
But even more for girlish

Ice-cold, snow-white, incising
Teeth; it is for these
That the hearts of all hot dates long. Selah.

Like these same southern fruits,
All too like them,
Here I lie, with little
Winged beetles
Dancing and playing around me,
And also with even smaller,
More foolish and more spiteful
Wishes and notions,
Besieged by you,
You mute premonitory
Girl-cats,
Dudu and Suleika,
– *Ensphinxed*, to cram much feeling
Into a single word
(May God forgive me
This language sin!)
– Here I sit, sniffing the best of air,
Truly air of paradise,
Bright, light air, rayed with gold,
As good an air as ever
Fell down from the moon –
Whether by chance
Or from exuberance,
As the old poets tell.
Doubter that I am, however,
I beg to doubt it,
Coming as I do from Europe
Which is more addicted to doubt
Than any little elderly wives.
May God make this better!
Amen!

Drinking this fairest of air,
My nostrils flared like goblets,
Without a future, without memories,
Here I sit, thus,
You dearest of friends,
And watch the palm tree,
Which, like a dancing-girl,
Bends and bows and sways its hips,
– One does the same if one looks on for long!
Like a dancing-girl who, so I'd say,
Has stood too long, dangerously long,
Always, always on just one leg?
– So that she has forgotten, so I'd say,
Her other leg?
At any rate,
I sought in vain
The missing twin jewel
– That is, the other leg –
In the holy vicinity
Of her dearest, most delicate,
Flared, fluttering, flitting little skirt.
And if you'll believe me entirely,
You beautiful friends:
She has lost it!
It's gone!
Gone forever!
The other leg!
Oh what a shame about that lovely other leg!
Where – may it now be, abandoned and grieving?
The lonely leg?
Frightened, perhaps,
Facing a furious, buff, blond-maned
Monster of a lion? Or even
Chewed and gnawed to pieces already –

For pity's sake, woe! woe! gnawed to pieces! Selah.

Oh do not weep,
Tender hearts!
Do not weep, you
Date-hearts! Milk-bosoms!
You little heart-bags
Of liquorice!
Weep no more,
Pale Dudu!
Be a man, Suleika! Courage! Courage!
– Or would perhaps
Something fortifying, to fortify the heart,
Be in place here?
An unctuous saying?
A solemn exhortation? –

Ha! Up, dignity!
Dignity of virtue! Dignity of the European!
Blow, blow again,
Bellows of virtue!
Ha!
Roar once more,
Roar morally!
Roar like a moral lion
Before the daughters of the desert!
For the howling of virtue,
You dearest of girls,
Is more than anything
The ardour of Europeans, the ferocious greed of Europeans!
And here I stand
As a European,
I cannot do otherwise, so help me God!
Amen!

The desert is growing; woe unto him who harbours deserts within!

The Awakening

1

After the song of the wanderer and shadow, the cave suddenly filled with noise and laughter; and, as the assembled guests were all talking at the same time, and even the ass, encouraged by their example, no longer held his peace, a mild aversion and scorn for his visitors came upon Zarathustra, even though he rejoiced in their good cheer, which he took to be a sign of recovery. So he stole out into the open and addressed his animals.

'What has become of their distress now?' he said, already breathing better following his little attack of antipathy, – 'with me, it seems, they have forgotten all about crying in distress!

– 'though not, unfortunately, about crying.' And Zarathustra stopped his ears, for at that very moment the ass's yee-hah blended wondrously with the jubilant din of these higher men.

'They are in high spirits,' he resumed, 'and, who knows, perhaps at the expense of their host; and, though they have learnt from me to laugh, it is still not *my* laughter that they have learnt.

'But what of it! They are old people; they convalesce in their own way, they laugh in their own way; my ears have endured worse without bec0ming out of sorts.

'This day is a victory; already it is falling back, it is fleeing, *the spirit of heaviness*, my old arch-enemy! How well this day bids fair to end, that began so ill and ominously!

'And it *means to* end. Evening is already falling; the fair rider is riding in across the ocean! How he sways, the blessèd one returning, on his purple saddle!

'The gaze of the heavens is clear, too, and the world lies deep; oh all you wondrous ones who have come to me, it really is worth living with me!'

Thus spake Zarathustra. And again the racket and laughter of the higher men was heard from the cave; so he resumed.

'They are biting, my bait is working; their enemy – the spirit of heaviness – is falling back before them as well. Already they are learning to laugh at themselves; am I hearing aright?

'My man's fare, my juicy and fortifying discourse, is working; and, truly, I did not feed them with vegetables that bloat! But with warriors' fare, conquerors' fare; I awakened new desires.

'There are new hopes in their arms and legs, their hearts are stretching. They are finding new words. Soon their spirits will be breathing wilfulness.

'Fare of this sort may well not be for children, nor for maids old and young filled with longing. A different course of persuasion is used in addressing their innards; I am not their physician or teacher.

'*Revulsion* is falling back before these higher men; onwards! that is my victory. In my realm they are attaining security, all of the witless shame is fleeing, they are unburdening themselves.

'They are unburdening their hearts, good hours are returning to them, they are celebrating and ruminating, – they are becoming *grateful*.

'That I take to be the best sign: they are becoming grateful. Before long they will be thinking up festivals and putting up memorials to their pleasures of old.

'They are *convalescents*!' Thus spake Zarathustra merrily to his heart, and gazed out; his animals, for their part, thronged close to him, and honoured his happiness and his silence.

2

Suddenly, however, Zarathustra's ear was alarmed; for the cave, which had been full of noise and laughter until then, abruptly fell deathly still; – his nose, though, scented a sweet-smelling smoke and incense, as of burning pine cones.

'What is going on? What are they up to?' he wondered, and he stole up to the entrance in order to watch his guests unobserved. But, wonder of wonders! what must he needs behold with his own eyes!

'They have all grown *pious* again, they are *praying*, they are mad!' – he said, astonished beyond all measure. And indeed, all of those higher men, the two kings, the emeritus pope, the wicked sorcerer, the voluntary beggar, the wanderer and shadow, the old prophet, the conscientious man of the spirit, and the ugliest man: they were all down on their knees like children and credulous old women, worshipping the ass. And at that moment the ugliest man began to gurgle and snort, as if something inexpressible were trying to get out of him; but when he did actually manage to put it into words, see, it was a pious, strange litany in praise of the worshipped and smoke-enveloped ass. The litany went like this:

Amen! And praise and honour and wisdom and thanks and glory and strength be to our god forever and ever!

– The ass for his part responded by braying yee-hah.

He bears our burden, he has taken upon himself the form of a servant, he is patient of heart and never says 'no'; and he who loves his god chastises him.

– The ass for his part responded by braying yee-hah.

He says nothing, except for an unfailing 'yes' to the world that he created; in this way he glorifies his world. He shows his cunning in saying nothing: that way he is seldom proved wrong.

– The ass for his part responded by braying yee-hah.

He passes through the world without attracting attention. Grey is the body colour in which he wraps his virtue. If he has spirit, he conceals it; but everyone believes in his long ears.

– The ass for his part responded by braying yee-hah.

What a covert kind of wisdom it is, to have long ears and only ever say 'yes' and never 'no'! Did he not create the world in his own image, that is: as stupid as possible?

– The ass for his part responded by braying yee-hah.

You walk along straight and crooked paths; you care little what we humans consider straight or crooked. Your realm is beyond good and evil. Your innocence consists in not knowing what innocence is.

– The ass for his part responded by braying yee-hah.

See how you thrust no one away, neither beggars nor kings. You suffer the little children to come to you, and, if naughty boys tease you, you utter your simple-minded yee-hah.

– The ass for his part responded by braying yee-hah.

You love she-asses and fresh figs, you are not one to spurn a mouthful. A thistle will tickle your fancy if you happen to be hungry. In that lies the wisdom of a god.

– The ass for his part responded by braying yee-hah.

The Ass Festival

1

At this point in the litany, however, Zarathustra could contain himself no longer. He himself yelled yee-hah, even louder than the ass, and he leapt into the midst of his maddened guests.

'But what are you doing, you children of humanity?' he exclaimed, hauling the worshippers up from the ground. 'Woe, if anyone other than Zarathustra had been watching;

'Everyone's judgement would be that with your new faith you are the worst of blasphemers or the most foolish of old women!

'And you, old pope: how does worshipping an ass as a god in this way go with what you are?'

'Oh Zarathustra,' answered the pope, 'forgive me, but in questions concerning God I am more enlightened than even you. And that is quite proper.

'Better to worship God in this form than in none at all! Think about this maxim, my exalted friend: you will quickly realize that there is wisdom in such a saying.

'He who said "God is a spirit" – he took the biggest step and leap yet taken on earth towards unbelief; a declaration such as that is not easily made good on earth!

'My old heart leaps and bounds to think that there is still something on earth to worship. Oh Zarathustra, forgive the pious old heart of a pope for that!' –

– 'And you,' said Zarathustra to the wanderer and shadow, 'you describe yourself as a free spirit, and suppose yourself one? And you practise idolatry and priestly rituals of this sort?

'Truly, you are behaving even worse here than you do with your naughty brown girls, you wicked new believer!'

'Badly enough,' replied the wanderer and shadow, 'you are right; but what can I do about it! The old god is alive once again, oh Zarathustra, say what you will.

'It is all the ugliest man's fault: he woke him up again. And if he says it was he who killed him, back then: with the gods, death is always a mere prejudice.'

'And you,' said Zarathustra, 'you wicked old sorcerer, what were you doing! Who in these free times will go on believing in you, if *you* believe in this sort of godly asininity?

'What you did was a stupidity; how could you, clever as you are, do anything so stupid!'

'Oh Zarathustra,' answered the canny sorcerer, 'you are right, it was a stupidity, – and it has been hard enough to bear.'

'And even you,' said Zarathustra to the conscientious man of the spirit, 'just consider, and lay your finger against your nose! Is nothing that is happening here against your conscience? Is your spirit not too pure for this praying and the vapours of these brethren?'

'There's something in it,' answered the conscientious man, laying his finger against his nose – 'there is something in this play-acting that does my conscience good, in fact.

'I may not be able to believe in God, but one thing is certain: God seems most believable to me in this form.

'God is supposed to be eternal, according to the testimony of the most pious; anyone who has that much time will take his time. As slowly and as stupidly as possible: *that* is how someone like that can get well ahead.

'And anyone who has too much spirit might easily become

infatuated with stupidity and foolishness. Just think of yourself, oh Zarathustra!

'Yes indeed, you yourself! – even you could become an ass through superfluity and wisdom.

'Does not a perfectly wise man like to walk along the most crooked of paths? Appearances teach this, oh Zarathustra, – *your* appearance!'

'And, last, you yourself,' said Zarathustra, and he turned to the ugliest man, who was still lying on the ground with his arm raised up to the ass (he was giving it wine to drink). 'Speak, you inexpressible one; what have you been doing!

'You strike me as transformed, your eyes are glowing, the mantle of the sublime cloaks your ugliness; *what* have you done?

'Is what they say true: that you woke him up again? And what for? Was he not killed and done away with for good reason?

'You yourself strike me as awakened; what have you done? Why-ever did *you* reform? Why did *you* convert yourself? Speak out, you inexpressible one!'

'Oh Zarathustra,' answered the ugliest man, 'you are a rogue.

'Whether *he* is still alive, or alive again, or properly dead, – which of us two knows that best? I'm asking you.

'One thing I do know, however, – it was from you yourself that I learnt it in days gone by, oh Zarathustra: he who would kill most thoroughly, *laughs*.

'"It is not by anger but by laughter that one kills" – so you once said. Oh Zarathustra, covert one, destroyer without anger, danger-ous saint, – you are a rogue!'

2

But then Zarathustra, taken aback by so many roguish answers of this sort, bounded back to the door of his cave and, turning to all of his guests, shouted in a powerful voice:

'Oh you jesters and clowns, the lot of you! Why are you dissem-bling and hiding from me?

'How the heart of every one of you trembled with pleasure and mischief at having finally become as the little children once again, that is to say: pious, –

– 'at having finally done as children do once again, that is to say: you prayed, folded your hands, and said "Dear Lord"!

'But now leave *this* nursery to me, my own cave, where childishness of any kind is at home today. Cool off your heated childish cockiness and heartfelt clamour outside!

'Granted, except you become as little children, you shall not enter into *that* kingdom of heaven.' (And Zarathustra gestured upwards with his hands.)

'But then, we do not want to enter the kingdom of heaven: we have become men, – *so we want the kingdom of earth.*'

3

And Zarathustra once more began to speak. 'Oh my new friends,' he said, – 'you wondrous ones, you higher men, how pleased I am with you now, –

– 'since you have grown merry again! Truly, you have all blossomed; it seems to me that blooms such as yourselves call for *new festivals*,

– 'a little sturdy nonsense, some divine service and ass festival, some merry old Zarathustra-fool, a stiff breeze to blow your souls clear.

'Do not forget this night and this ass festival, you higher men! *That* you devised here at my home, and I take it as a good sign – only convalescents come up with such things!

'And if you celebrate it again, this ass festival, do it for love of yourselves, and do it for love of me, too! And in remembrance of *me*!'

Thus spake Zarathustra.

The Drunken Song

1

In the meantime, however, they had all gone outside, one after another, into the open and the cool, contemplative night; but Zarathustra himself led the ugliest of men by the hand, to show him his world of night, and the great round moon, and the silver waterfalls near his cave. At length they stood there in silence together, a gathering of old people, but with consoled and valiant hearts, and amazed in themselves that they felt so well on earth; but the inwardness of night drew closer and closer to their hearts. And once again Zarathustra reflected: 'Oh how well I am pleased by them now, these higher men!' – but he did not say it aloud, for he honoured their happiness and their silence. –

It was then, though, that the most astonishing thing on that astonishing, long day happened: the ugliest man began to gurgle and snort one more time, for the last time, and when he managed to put it into words, see, a question leapt round and pure from his mouth, a good, deep, clear question that moved the hearts of all who were listening to him.

'My dear friends all,' said the ugliest man, 'what are your feelings on this? For myself, *I* am content for the very first time to have lived my whole life – for the sake of this day.

'And attesting that much is not enough for me. It is well worth living on earth; one day, one festival with Zarathustra has taught me to love the earth.

'"Was *that* – life?" I shall say to death. 'Very well! One more time!'

'My friends, what are your feelings on this? Will you not, like me, say to death: "Was *that* – life? For Zarathustra's sake, very well! One more time!"' – –

So said the ugliest man; but it was not long before midnight. And what do you suppose happened next? As soon as the higher men heard his question, they suddenly became aware of their transformation and convalescence, and of who it was that had given them these; and they bounded up to Zarathustra, thanking, venerating, caressing, kissing his hands, each according to his own manner; so that some were laughing, some crying. The old prophet, however, danced with pleasure; and even if he was full of sweet wine just then, as some who tell the tale maintain, he was definitely even fuller of sweet life and had renounced all weariness. There are even those who tell that the ass danced on that occasion: not for nothing had the ugliest man given him wine to drink earlier. This may have been so, or it may have been different; and if in truth the ass did not dance that evening, greater and stranger marvels than the dancing of an ass did occur at that time. In short, as Zarathustra's saying has it: 'What does it matter!'

2

When this business with the ugliest man happened, Zarathustra for his part stood there like a man who was drunk: his gaze grew dim, his tongue babbled, his legs were unsteady. And who could hazard what thoughts were passing across Zarathustra's soul at that moment? But his spirit appeared to fall back, and flee ahead, and was away in the distance and, as it were, 'moving along the high ride between two oceans', as it is written,

– 'moving as a heavy cloud between past and future'. Gradually, however, while the higher men held him in their arms, he partly came round, and warded off with his hands the revering and anxious throng; yet he did not speak. All at once, however, he quickly turned his head, for he seemed to hear something; and, placing a finger to his lips, he said: *'Come!'*

And at once it grew still and mysterious all around; from far below, though, the toll of a bell could gradually be heard. Zarathustra listened to it, as did the higher men; but then he placed his finger to his lips a second time and said once more: *'Come! Come! Midnight is nigh!'* – and his voice was altered. Yet still he did not move from the spot; and it grew even more still and mysterious, and all were listening, including the ass and Zarathustra's animals of honour, the eagle and the serpent, and so too Zarathustra's cave and the great, cool moon and the night itself. Zarathustra, however, held his hand to his lips for the third time and said:

'Come! Come! Come! Let us walk now! The hour has come; let us walk into the night!'

3

You higher men, midnight is night; I want to say something in your ears, as that old bell is saying it in mine, –

– as secretly, as terribly, as heartily, as that midnight bell is saying it to me, which has experienced more than any one human;

– which told the strokes of your forefathers' heartfelt pains – ah! ah! how it sighs! how it laughs in its dream! the ancient, deep, deep midnight!

Quiet! Quiet! Things can be heard which may never make a sound by day; but now, in the cool air, when all the clamour of your hearts has fallen silent too, –

– now it speaks, now it is heard, now it steals into souls at night that are too wide awake; ah! ah! how it sighs! how it laughs in its dream!

– do you not hear it, secretly, terribly, heartily speaking to you, the ancient, deep, deep midnight? *Oh man, beware!*

4

Woe is me! Where has the time gone? Did I not sink into deep wells? The world is sleeping –

Ah! Ah! The dog is howling, the moon is shining. I should rather die, die, than tell you what my midnight heart is thinking now.

Now I have died. It is finished. Spider, why are you spinning around me? Are you after blood? Ah! Ah! the dew is falling, the hour is approaching –

– the hour when I am frosty and freezing, which demands and

demands and demands: 'Who has heart enough for it?

– 'who shall be master of the earth? Who will say: *this* is how you shall run, you great and little rivers!'

– the hour is approaching; oh man, oh higher man, beware! this message is for discerning ears, for your ears – *what does deep midnight's voice declare?*

5

I am borne away, my soul is dancing. The day's work! The day's work! Who shall be master of the earth?

The moon is cool, the wind is silent. Ah! Ah! Have you flown high enough yet? You were dancing; but a leg is not a wing.

You good dancers, now all the pleasure is over, the wine is down to the lees, all the goblets are cracked, the graves groan.

You have not flown high enough; now the graves groan: 'Redeem the dead! Why is the night so long? Is the moon not making us drunk?'

You higher men, redeem the graves, awaken the corpses! Ah, why is the worm still digging away? The hour is approaching, approaching, –

the bell booms, the heart creaks on, the woodworm, the heart's-worm, still digs away. Ah! Ah! *The world is deep!*

6

Sweet lyre! Sweet lyre! I love your sound, your drunken, doomful sound! – from how long ago, how far away, does your sound reach me, from far off, from the pools of love!

Old bell, sweet lyre! All manner of pain has torn your heart, the pain of the father, the pain of the fathers, the pain of the forefathers, your utterance grew ripe, –

– ripe like a golden autumn, and afternoons, ripe like my hermit heart – now you say: the world itself has ripened, the grape is turning brown,

– now it wants to die, to die of happiness. You higher men, do you not smell it? An intimate odour is welling up,

– a fragrance and odour of eternity, a rosy, blessèd, brown, golden wine scent of ancient happiness,

– of drunken midnight death-knell happiness, which sings: *The world is deep, deeper than day was yet aware!*

7

Leave me alone! Leave me alone! I am too pure for you. Do not touch me! Has my world not just achieved perfection?

My skin is too pure for your hands. Leave me alone, you stupid, foolish, dull day! Is not midnight brighter?

The purest shall be masters of the earth, the most unrecognized, the strongest, the midnight souls, who are brighter and deeper than any day.

Oh day, are you groping for me? Are you feeling for my happiness? Do I appear wealthy, lonely, a hoard of treasure, a chamber of gold?

Oh world, do you want *me*? Do I appear worldly? Do I appear spiritual? Do I appear divine? But, day and world, you are too clumsy, –

– you have wilier hands, you are reaching out for deeper happiness, for deeper unhappiness, you are reaching for some god or other, you are not reaching for me;

My unhappiness, my happiness is deep, you wondrous day, but nonetheless I am no god, no divine hell; *deep is its woe.*

8

God's woe is deeper, you wondrous world! Reach for God's woe, not for me! What am I! A drunken, sweet lyre, –

– a midnight lyre, a knell of foreboding that no one understands but which *must* speak out, before the deaf, you higher men! For you do not understand me!

Gone! Gone! Oh youth! Oh noon! Oh afternoon! Now evening and night and midnight have come, – the dog is howling, the wind;

– is the wind not a dog? It whines, it yaps, it howls. Ah! Ah! how it sighs! how it laughs, how it rattles and wheezes, – midnight!

How she speaks in sober tones, this drunken poetess! Has she overdone the drunkenness? Is she now too awake? Is she regurgitating?

Old, deep midnight is regurgitating her woe in her dream, and still more her desire. Desire, after all, though woe be deep; *Desire is deeper than agony.*

9

You grape-vine! Why do you glorify me? After all, I have cut you! I am cruel, you are bleeding; – what designs does your glorification have upon my drunken cruelty?

'Whatever has achieved perfection, everything that is ripe – desires to die!' So say you. Blessèd, blessèd be the vintner's pruning-knife! But everything unripe wants to live; woe!

Woe says: 'Die! Go, woe!' But everything that suffers wants to live, that it may ripen and be merry and full of longing,

– longing for what is further away, higher, brighter. 'I crave heirs,' says everything that suffers, 'I crave children, I do not crave *myself*,' –

But desire does not crave heirs, does not crave children, – desire craves itself, craves eternity, craves return, craves everything eternally the same.

Woe says: 'Break, bleed, heart! Walk, leg! Wing, fly! Onwards! Upwards! Pain!' Very well! On and up! Oh my old heart; *Woe says: Die! Go!*

10

How does it seem to you, higher men? Am I a prophet? A dreamer? A drunk? An interpreter of dreams? A midnight bell?

A drop of dew? The haze and fragrance of eternity? Do you not hear it? Do you not scent it? My world has just achieved perfection, midnight is also noon, –

pain is also a desire, a curse is also a blessing, night is also a sun, – be off with you, or else you shall learn: a wise man is also a fool.

Did you ever say 'yes' to a single desire? If you did, oh my friends, you also said 'yes' to *all* woe. All things are interlinked, intertwined, in love, –

– if ever you wanted to have one moment a second time, if ever you said: 'I like you, happiness! Quickly, now! That moment!' you were wanting *everything* back!

– everything all over again, everything forever and ever, everything interlinked, intertwined, in love, oh you so *loved* the world, –

you eternal ones, you love it eternally and for all time; and even to woe you say: Go, but return! *For desire craves eternity!*

11

All desire craves eternity for all things, craves honey, craves the lees, craves drunken midnight, craves graves, craves the consolation of tears at the graveside, craves the gilded sunset –

what does desire not crave! It is thirstier, heartier, hungrier, more terrible, more intimate than any woe, it craves *itself*, it bites into *itself*, the will of the ring struggles within it, –

– it craves loves, it craves hatred, it is opulently wealthy, it gives, throws away, begs someone to take it, thanks the taker, and would dearly like to be hated, –

– desire is so wealthy that it thirsts for woe, for hell, for hatred, for disgrace, for the cripple, for *world*, – this world, after all, oh you know it well!

You higher men, it is you that it craves, boundless and blessèd desire, – your woe that it craves, you wayward ones. All everlasting desire longs for what is wayward.

For all desire craves itself, for that reason craves heartache too! Oh happiness, oh pain! Oh break, heart! You higher men, learn this: desire craves eternity,

– desire craves eternity for *all* things, *craves deepest deep eternity*!

12

Have you learnt my song now? Have you made out what it means? Very well! On and up! You higher men, sing me my roundelay now! Now sing me the song called 'Once again' yourselves, the meaning of which is 'for all eternity' – sing, you higher men, Zarathustra's roundelay!

> *Oh man! Beware!*
> *What does deep midnight's voice declare?*
>   *'I wake from sleep,'*
>   *'Wake from a dreaming deep and fair:' –*
>   *'The world is deep,'*
>   *'Deeper than day was yet aware.'*
>   *'Deep is its woe,' –*
>   *'Desire – deeper than agony:'*
>   *'Woe says: Die! Go!'*
>   *'Desire, though, craves eternity' –*
>   *– 'craves deepest deep eternity!'*

The Sign

On the morning after that night, however, Zarathustra sprang up from his bed, girded his loins, and emerged from his cave, glowing and strong, like a morning sun coming out from dark mountains.

'Great star,' he said, as he had said once before, 'you deep eye of happiness, what would all your happiness be without *those* to whom you bring light?

'And if they stayed in their rooms while you were already awake, coming and giving and handing out: how your proud modesty would be wrathful at that!

'Very well! they are still asleep, these higher men, while *I* am awake; *these* are not the proper companions for me! It is not for them that I am waiting here in my mountains.

'I wish to go to my work, to my day; but they do not understand what the signs of my morning are; my footfall – they do not take as a call to wake.

'They are still asleep in my cave, their dreams are still drinking my drunken songs. The ear that attends to *me*, – the *obedient* ear, is lacking them.'

– Zarathustra had said this to his heart when the sun was rising; and he gazed inquiringly on high, for he heard the sharp call of his eagle above him. 'Very well!' he called up, 'that is how I like it, and that is fitting. My animals are awake because I am awake.

'My eagle is awake and, like me, honours the sun. With the talons of an eagle it reaches for the new light. You are my proper animals; I love you.

'But still I do not have the proper humans!' –

Thus spake Zarathustra; but at that moment he suddenly felt as if countless birds were flocking and flapping about him, – the beating of so many wings, though, and the thronging about his head were so great that he closed his eyes. And in truth it was as if a cloud had fallen upon him, a cloud of arrows pouring down on a new enemy. But see, here it was a cloud of love, on a new friend.

'What is happening to me?' thought Zarathustra in his astonished heart, and he sat down slowly on the large rock by the exit of his cave. But see, as he was waving his hands about and above and below him, warding off the gentle birds, something even stranger happened to him: for his hands unwittingly brushed a thick, warm mane of hair; at the same time, moreover, a roar sounded before him, – the gentle, drawn-out roar of a lion.

'*The sign has come*,' said Zarathustra, and his heart was transformed. And in truth, as it grew light before him, a buff, powerful animal was lying at his feet, nestling its head against his knees. It loved him and did not want to leave him, like a dog that has found its old master again. The doves for their part were no less assiduous in their love than the lion; and every time a dove flitted across the lion's nose, the lion shook its head in perplexity and laughed.

In response to all of this, Zarathustra merely said: '*My children are near, my children,*' – then he fell completely silent. His heart, though, had been eased, and the tears ran from his eyes and fell upon his hands. And he paid no heed to anything any more, and sat there motionless, no longer brushing away the animals. The doves flew to and fro and settled on his shoulders and stroked his white hair and did not weary of tenderness and rejoicing. The strong lion, for its part, ceaselessly licked the tears that fell upon Zarathustra's hands, roaring and growling shyly as it did so. This was the way of these animals. –

All of this occupied a long time, or a short time: for, rightly speaking, there is *no* time on earth for things of this kind. – Meanwhile, however, the higher men in Zarathustra's cave had awoken and were lining up for a procession, to go to Zarathustra and give him their morning greeting; for they had realized on waking that he was already no longer among them. When they reached the door of the cave, though, and the sound of their paces went before them, the lion started violently, abruptly turning away from Zarathustra, and bounded towards the cave, roaring wildly; when they heard it roaring, the higher men, for their part, all yelled as if from a single mouth and fled back, and in an instant they had disappeared.

Zarathustra himself, however, numbed and disoriented, got up from his seat, looked around, stood there in amazement, inquired of his heart, reflected, and was alone. 'What was it I heard?' he said at length, slowly; 'what was it that just happened to me?'

And right away his memory returned, and at a glance he took in everything that had taken place between yesterday and today. 'Here is the rock,' he said, stroking his beard, '*this* is the one I sat on yesterday morning; and this is where the prophet came up to me, and here I first heard the cry I have just heard, the great cry of distress.

'Oh you higher men, it was of *your* distress that the old prophet gave me his prophecies yesterday morning, –

– 'it was to your distress that he meant to tempt and seduce me: oh Zarathustra, he said to me, I come to tempt you to your final sin.

'To my final sin?' exclaimed Zarathustra, and he laughed wrathfully at his own words. '*What* has been saved up for me as my final sin?'

And one more time Zarathustra became immersed in himself, and he sat down again on the large rock and pondered. Suddenly he leapt to his feet, –

'*Compassion! Compassion with the higher man!*' he cried out, and his countenance was transformed and became brazen. 'Very well! *That* – has had its time!

'My suffering and my compassion – of what account are they? Am I striving for *happiness*? I am striving for my *work*!

'Very well! The lion has come, my children are near, Zarathustra has grown ripe, my hour has come: –

'This is *my* morning, *my* day is dawning: *come now, come, you great noon!*' – –

Thus spake Zarathustra, and he left his cave, glowing and strong, like a morning sun coming out from dark mountains.

Other titles from Notting Hill Editions*

The Mystery of Being Human: God, Freedom and the NHS
Raymond Tallis

For forty years, Raymond Tallis was an NHS consultant. In this brilliant
collection, Tallis brings his signature intelligence and razor wit to the
questions that define us as human: Do we have free will? Can humanity
flourish without religion? Will science explain everything? And can the
NHS – an institution that relies on compassion over profit – survive?

Humiliation
Wayne Koestenbaum

With a disarming blend of personal reflection and cultural commentary,
American artist and cultural critic Wayne Koestenbaum walks us – at times
cajoles us – through a spectrum of mortifications, in history, current events,
literature, art, music, film, and in his own life.

My Prizes: An Accounting
Thomas Bernhard

Written in 1980, *My Prizes: An Accounting* is a caustic account of Bernhard's
experience of receiving nine major awards. What for most writers is a
moderately nerve-wracking experience, followed by the euphoria (and
relief) at having won, Bernhard's hatred of everything to do with literary
prizes is laid bare in this mordant, yet viciously funny, memoir by one of
Europe's most famous literary *enfants terribles*.

Thoughts of Sorts
Georges Perec
Translated by David Bellos and Introduced by Margaret Drabble

Celebrated as the man who wrote an entire novel without using the
letter 'e', and another in the form of a vast jigsaw puzzle, Georges Perec
found humour – and pathos – in the human need for arrangement and
classification. The essays in *Thoughts of Sorts* explore the ruses by which we
find a place in the world. Is thinking a kind of sorting? Is sorting a kind
of thought?

Essays on the Self
Virginia Woolf
Introduced by Joanna Kavenna

Written between 1919, when Woolf was thirty-seven, and 1940, when she was fifty-eight, this extraordinary selection of essays includes discussions about the rights of women, the revolutions of modernity, the past, present and future of the novel and the inequalities and agonies of war. It covers a period in Woolf's life when her opinions and her circumstances changed. She was not a fixed entity, reiterating a rigid and immaculate position each time she picked up her pen, but at the heart of each essay is a singular preoccupation to do with the nature of the finite self: 'Who am I?' and, of course, 'Who is everybody else?'

What Time Is It?
John Berger & Selçuk Demirel
Introduced and Edited by Maria Nadotti

Visionary thinker John Berger and Turkish artist Selçuk Demirel come together for the last time to create this precious little volume, a playful meditation on the illusory nature of time. Our perception of time assumes a uniform and ceaseless passing of hours, but Berger suggests that time is turbulent: expanding and contracting according to the intensity of the lived moment. In this beautiful essay in pictures, Berger posits the idea that by experiencing the extraordinary, we can defy time itself.

The Foreigner: Two Essays on Exile
Richard Sennett

Richard Sennett, one of the most distinguished social thinkers in the world, has spent an intellectual lifetime exploring how humans live in cities. In this pair of essays he visits two of the world's greatest cities at crucial moments in their history to meditate on the condition of exile in both geographical and psychic space: the Jewish ghetto of Renaissance Venice, where state-imposed outsiderdom was translated into a rich community identity; and nineteenth-century Paris, a magnet for political exiles.

*All titles are available in the UK, and some titles are available in the rest of the world. For more information please visit www.nottinghilleditions.com.

A selection of our titles is distributed in the US and Canada by New York Review Books. For more information on available titles please visit www.nyrb.com